Cupid's Pursuit

by

Patrick Shanahan

An Authors OnLine Book

Text Copyright © Patrick Shanahan 2011

Cover design by Richard Taylor, BT Graphics © Patrick Shanahan

All rights reserved. No part of this publication may be reproduced, stored in a retrieval system, or transmitted in any form or by any means, electronic, mechanical, photocopy, recording or otherwise, without prior written permission of the copyright owner. Nor can it be circulated in any form of binding or cover other than that in which it is published and without similar condition including this condition being imposed on a subsequent purchaser.

Patrick Shanahan has asserted his right under the Copyright, Designs and Patents Act 1988 to be identified as the author of this work.

This is a work of fiction. Names and characters are the product of the author's imagination and any resemblance to actual persons living or dead is entirely coincidental.

British Library Cataloguing Publication Data.
A catalogue record for this book is available from the British Library

ISBN 978-0-7552-1392-4

Authors OnLine Ltd
19 The Cinques
Gamlingay, Sandy
Bedfordshire SG19 3NU
England

This book is also available in e-book format, details of which are available at www.authorsonline.co.uk

Acknowledgements

I am indebted to the following people without whose various inputs this book would not have seen the light of day.

Thank you then, to Rosemary Shrubb and Beryl Godwin for their encouragement to actually start writing in the first place; to Steve Skarratt for his speedy and informed comment and his guidance in helping correct factual error; to Charles Barker for his bravery in providing precise and practical feedback despite being an old friend; to Kevin Fisher for his on-going, selfless efforts at promoting my manuscript even before I had finished writing it, and to Richard Taylor of BT Graphics for his cover design.

A special thanks to my lovely daughter Rachael, who could have said all the right things, but gave me insightful and sensible criticism, especially on the characters.

Finally, a big thank you to my partner Penny, for her patience (night after night while I sat hidden away in my study bashing at a keyboard), for her critical opinion and for her continued encouragement to write.

Patrick Shanahan
September 2011

Author's Note

This work contains a number of colloquial references and the use of slang words. For the better understanding of the reader who may not be familiar with the terms, a glossary is included at the end of the book.

1

It was probably the final straw, the one that breaks the proverbial camel's back, an inconsequential addition to the burden I was already carrying mentally. Whatever way I describe it in hindsight, I was unaware at that point of the chain of events a simple night out would cause to unfold.

It happened like this.

I had arranged to meet with Cecil for a late Friday afternoon drink after work, a frequent occurrence that I knew would inevitably lead to a long night out on the town. I knew the pattern by now. A trawl through a variety of bars, never stopping for more than two drinks at most and, predictably, a late night club where my memory would fail completely and I would recall very little of the evening the following day. However, as I stood at the bar that afternoon full of optimism that tonight would be different, none of those thoughts occupied my mind. The usual whimsical notion that tonight would indeed be different was all that interested me. I would enjoy a convivial night out, meet the lady of my dreams and live happily ever after.

Cecil had taken himself off to the gents and I stood, wallet in hand, about to order our second beer, hoping to be noticed by the besieged bar staff who had clearly not expected such an influx of people at four thirty in the afternoon. To my right a short blonde girl stood with her hand outstretched, as if its extension amongst the sea of other similarly stretched limbs would make her more visible. As yet another eager punter joined the throng, I was jostled to one side and bumped against her.

'I'm sorry,' I said, embarrassed that she might have thought I had shoved her to gain some advantage in the queue.

She hadn't.

'Don't vorry,' she said, a smile lighting her face,' it very busy for change in here, you think?'

I detected the heavy accent.

'Yes, it is,' I replied, 'must be that everybody has decided to finish early today. Have you been waiting long?'

'I vait ages. I think they don't notice me because I am small,' she said looking up at me.

I saw my chance to be the gentleman.

'Well, if I get served before you I will tell them that you're next. What's your name? I am Matthew.'

'Aleska. Pleased to meet you Matthew. You a kind man. You have nice eyes.'

Her comment hit home. My ego felt the rush of excitement. I had intended just to be polite but I was charmed by her smiling good looks and aware that circumstances had contrived to push us together, literally. Perhaps it was fate. Suddenly I didn't mind the wait at the bar.

'That's nice of you,' I said, not sure of how I should proceed but certain that I wanted to.

Aleska filled the gap. 'Vot do you do for verk?'

'Sorry? For verk?' I said, my mind now on her and not on the question.

'Yes, for verk?'

'You mean work?'

'Yes. Is what I say. For verk?'

I was just about to reply when I felt the hand on my shoulder and heard the question.

'Can I help you mate?'

The voice was broad cockney 'sarf Lunden' and extremely deep.

I spun round. It didn't help that the guy was wearing a shirt of a similar red colour to the bar staff and almost identical black jeans. The only noticeable difference between his outfit and those of the employees was the fact that his shirt appeared several sizes bigger as he was at least six feet seven inches tall. My immediate thought was that, although this might be taking the personal service concept a little far, it was nice that he had picked me out amongst the crowd.

'Cheers, could I get two pints of Staropramen please.' I pointed to Aleska. 'Oh, and, just to say, this lady is next.'

'You taking the fucking piss, mate? Next for what?'

Surprising responses often give rise to random thought patterns and it occurred to me fleetingly that this gentleman's customer service skills could do with some honing. However, as the words 'fucking piss' reverberated through my brain, it started to dawn on me that perhaps I had misjudged the situation. The look of menace radiating from his eyes beneath the shaven headed frown, coupled with the tight grip he had now taken on my jacket, confirmed my misjudgement.

'Next...err...next for a drink. I mean, I was going to make sure she got a drink. I was –'

'A drink! You were gonna buy my bird a drink were you mate. Get her pissed, eh. That your game is it. I ought to fucking –'

'Villy! Stop it,' Aleska intervened.

It was a good job she did intervene as I suddenly experienced a total inability to form a sentence mainly due to the fact that I was still comprehending the 'my bird' remark. How was I supposed to know that this petite little blonde was with anyone, let alone the hulk that now had me in a vice like grip so that my toes were just about in contact with the floor? I mean, why wasn't she wearing an "I am with Villy t-shirt?" That would have helped my understanding of her situation.

My thought processes were brought back to reality by the sound of Cecil's voice.

'Put him down, geezer. What's going on?'

Villy's focus turned on Cecil, his menacing frown turning into a raised-eyebrow look of curiosity.

Cecil saw it. 'I'm his mate. What's the problem?'

Cecil was a good ten inches shorter than his adversary but he stood square on, his barrel chest and fixed stare emphasising his boldness.

'He's hitting on my bird, and nobody messes with my bird, you get me?' Villy said, pointing an accusing finger into my chest.

Cecil's gaze turned to me, looking for an answer.

'I didn't know that she was Villy's bird. I was just –'

'What's with the fucking Villy? The names Willy. Get it? William S Robinson to you, ex-marine, and your fucking worst nightmare if you go near my bird again. Courvoisier?'

'Err...no...no thanks. I don't drink it but nice of you –'

'What? What you on about? You get me? You getting it. Stay away from my bird. Courvoisier?'

'Err...yes...I courvois...courvois...err...I get what you're saying.'

I was definitely getting him. Loud and clear. What I was also getting was that once again any attempt to meet a girl, out there in the real world, who was available, normal, attractive and just plain nice was getting more and more difficult.

'So, what was all that about geezer,' Cecil asked as we sat at a table nursing the two pints we had eventually been able to get our hands on.

'A total misunderstanding Ces. The bloke got the wrong end of the stick. I wasn't really chatting his bird up at all. I was talking to her but I didn't know she was with someone.'

'Mate, you gotta find out straightaway. Know the lay of the land. Ask the question. Have you got a bloke...ask it before you get too deep into the chat up. It saves you wasting your whole night on some bird that ain't gonna shell out at the death as well as stopping you getting your head kicked in by some psycho. It's a win win question.'

'Maybe Cecil, but I am tired of it. How long have we been doing this? Years, now and I'm not getting anywhere.'

As I sat there staring into my glass and recovering from the shock of my verbal accosting I reflected on the past few years.

I hadn't been divorced long and although separated for almost four years, it had taken me a long time to adjust to single life again. In fact I had never really adjusted. The harsh reality of a failed long term relationship does not allow for a quick fix and by the time you make the mental adjustment from being part of a couple to the realities of single life, you are already thinking about your next relationship. That is exactly where I was at this point in my life. I wanted a new relationship.

I had never actually told Cecil that in so many words. I wouldn't have done. I wouldn't have been able to cope with the ridicule had I made such an admission. Cecil was a man's man and didn't have time for such frailty. Cecil didn't do wishy-washy. It wasn't that he didn't understand these things. He'd been there for me after my marriage break up. He had certainly made an effort to lift me out of my gloom and distract me with a social life that was far too hectic to be considered normal. He had taken me out on the town in true Cecil style. I was certain that we had visited every pub and club in London to date. All to no avail. Hangovers, close encounters with a variety of women and a reduced bank balance were the sum total of three years of trawling Cecil's favourite haunts. 'You gotta meet more birds mate,' was his mantra. Well the more I tried the harder it got. I think that was the trouble. Perhaps I was just trying too hard.

The early rush to the bar had abated and the late afternoon crowd scattered throughout the vast room had settled into a low murmur of chatter in the background. My thoughts turned back to the present.

'Nothing's changing, Ces, same old thing and I'm definitely getting tired of it,' I said.

Cecil stroked the stubble that adorned his face as if the whiskers that were the result of a failure to shave that morning might give him inspiration. Perhaps they had. He took a long gulp from his glass, placed it emphatically on the table and looked directly at me.

'Look mate, I've had an idea,' he said, 'why don't you try that internet dating stuff. Everyone is at it. It's a dead cert.'

Some inspiration. Cecil's idea of a dead cert and my perception of the same did not always meet in the middle. At thirty-nine years old having come to terms with the split from my wife I had finally allowed myself to think that perhaps I could build another relationship at some point in the future. Cecil's expression 'dead cert' did not fill me with confidence that he had any sort of longstanding association in mind.

'Internet dating? Blimey Ces, I don't know...it's not really me. I mean you don't know who is on these sites, do you? It could be full of bunny boilers and desperados. I'd sooner take my chances in an upmarket wine bar or even some sort of evening class. At least that way you get to see who you might fancy first.'

Cecil didn't try to hide his disdain. A sharp, intelligent man, his dark brown eyes would glisten with intent, almost defying any contradiction of his own strongly held views. I could see that he was not about to agree with me now.

'That's all well and good geezer,' he replied, 'but on the internet you get the numbers. There are loads of birds. How many are you likely to meet in some dumb arsed pottery class? Six, seven? The law of averages says that at least two of them will be married, two older than your mother and two will be total troglodytes. That, if you are lucky, leaves one, and mate, you can bet your bottom dollar she will be as dull as a wet weekend in Southend, otherwise what the fuck would she be doing in a pottery class?'

His logic was hard to argue with.

'I get your point Ces,' I said, 'but what about the wine bars? There are some good, upmarket places for the over thirties age group. All those classy thirty-something women, they love a wine bar.'

'Yeah, but I told you. We are talking numbers, mate. You spend your Friday night in some overpriced place where the beer is shit and, if you are lucky, you get talking to some snooty bird that's already geezered up, bit like that bird was earlier. You know the sort. She's bored with her bloke and is out looking for a bit of attention. Takes you for a mug spending all your cash buying drinks for her all night and then she sods off and leaves you standing there soon as the place shuts. The internet's a numbers game geezer. Take it from me. There are thousands of birds on there all signed up on dating sites looking for a bloke. And that's the point. They are looking, so it ain't so random. Get on the programme. You can't go wrong.'

I had to ask the question. 'Well if internet dating is that guaranteed Ces, why are you not on it?'

'I don't need to mate. I'm a Jedi. I got the Force. I can meet birds anytime. I'm a warrior. You're a worrier. That's the difference. The internet would work for you cos you like all that fannying about, all that hearts and flowers bollocks. I'm, shall we say, more direct and anyway I ain't got the patience to be sitting there in front of a fucking computer half the night.'

I wanted to make the blindingly obvious point that despite Cecil's perceived Jedi Warrior status he was still single with no significant other half, but he was on a roll.

'Look mate. Give it a go. A good mate of mine swears by it. You know what, he signed up on a site and within three days he was banging some bird in intensive care at one of them London hospitals.'

'Bloody hell Ces,' I said, nearly gagging on my beer, 'that's a bit sick. Was she conscious?'

'Conscious? What you on about? She was one of the nurses, you nobhead.'

The heavy emphasis on the word 'nobhead' brought my thoughts sharply back to my own situation. I lifted the beer to my lips, savoured the gassy sensation on my tongue and wondered if I was being a 'nobhead' in taking a negative view on internet dating. Cecil must have read my thoughts.

'You got nothing to lose, mate. Give it a go, six weeks or so. If it all goes tits up then you are only back to where you are now, no harm done. It's a no brainer.'

Whether it was the second pint of Staropramen or Cecil's persuasive enthusiasm that was wearing my sensible side down, I still don't know, but I found myself agreeing to sign up.

'Good man. Keep the dream alive,' was Cecil's response as he necked the remainder of his beer, 'now let's go get a pint somewhere'.

I still had over half my pint to drink. 'But I've have only had few sips out of this one Cecil,' I protested.

'Geezer, we can get a fucking pint in any pub in London. There's more life in a vicars underpants than in this place. Let's go.'

2

The following day, nursing a sore head as a result of the inevitable Cecil style night on the town, I sat down in front of my PC with a mug of strong coffee and a pack of chocolate biscuits. I Googled, *Dating Sites*.

There were hundreds. It wasn't hard to get confused by the array of options promising love and harmony with the perfect date. I was mesmerised by the choice. There were sites for millionaires (certainly not me), sites specialising in Russian women, sites that turned out to be nothing more than sex contacts, sites for sugar daddies, sites based on religious preferences, sites based on your star sign, and even a site if you wanted a female prisoner as a potential mate. Arranging a normal date seemed hard enough let alone trying to find a suitable meeting place for a liaison with a jailbird.

There was a site that offered chemistry inspired matches. Having had what I considered to be a near death experience with a Bunsen Burner and a test tube full of hydrochloric acid as a schoolboy, the imagery that chemistry conjured up in my mind wasn't helpful. There was even a site that was aimed at those who were bored with their current partner. Surely that was just being greedy. If you already have someone, bored or not, give the rest of us a chance to catch up first.

My head had now settled into a consistent, rhythmic throb, both temples pulsing in unison, reminding me that excess alcohol and concentration were not compatible. Another biscuit dunked in my mug. Sub-conscious comfort eating. I clicked the mouse. A site promised my money back if I hadn't found the perfect partner in six months. Six months? I'd want my money back after six weeks. I certainly didn't want to spend six months trawling through dating sites trying to find my match. My intention was to give internet dating a brief try and I still wasn't entirely convinced it was for me. The prospect of advertising myself on a dating site created a sensation of failure and even desperation. I felt like I was a geek hiding behind the computer; that I couldn't get out there and meet someone in the normal way; that I had lost the ability to impress someone enough in a face to face, one to one encounter, to make them like me. In short, signing up to a dating site made me feel inadequate.

I should have recognized that my confidence was low after a failed marriage, three years trying to get back out there on the dating scene and a divorce being finalised in the last few months. As I sifted through the web looking for the ideal site the inner conflict surfaced. How had I sunk to this level? Joining the herd looking for a date on the internet. What was wrong with me that I couldn't meet a normal woman in the normal way? All I wanted was my soul mate. Not too much to ask, was it? On the other hand it couldn't do any harm, surely. I was just giving it a go, seeing what it was all about. No agenda. I wasn't like everyone else – I didn't need to be doing this. Just taking advantage of modern technology. Nothing wrong with having a look I reasoned. My confused thought processes were not helped by the difficulty I was having in trying to find a site that I felt was normal. One that was all about boy meeting girl and organising an initial date.

Another biscuit made its way from the packet to my face, the thick, warm splurge of chocolate on my tongue melting and oozing to the corners of my mouth as I stared expectantly at the screen in front of me. A site for single parents popped up. Single parents wanting a date. Single parent meant kids. I had nothing against kids at all but at this stage in my life kids meant baggage and baggage was for Heathrow in my mind.

I was on the point of switching off the PC and calling it a day when Cupid caught my eye -*www.cupidspursuit.co.uk*. It was the first site that didn't have the word 'Date' plastered all over it, which at least suggested that something more permanent may occur other than a single meet. My interest aroused, I flicked the mouse around the first few pages.

How It Works – there is more to compatibility than trying to match you through a computer programme. We keep it simple. No complex compatibility tests, no complicated analysis. We let you choose. That had appeal. I didn't fancy being part of a scientific experiment.

I clicked on the *Couple's Stories* page. Scott and Karen were beaming back at me, hand in hand in a gondola in Venice. A Cupid's Pursuit success story apparently, now living happily ever after. Next came a *Relationships Tips* section with everything from where to go on a first date to how to behave when meeting the parents for the first time. I gave that one a miss. No sense in getting too far ahead of myself, but I had seen enough to feel comfortable with the site. Or perhaps I had seen enough sites to want to feel comfortable with this one. Whichever it was, Cupid had struck a chord. I was definitely pursuing Cupid, even if at times I felt Cupid was ignoring me. If I was going to do it, I had to bite the bullet and get on with it. No use over analysing the situation. The final chocolate biscuit disappeared. I decided to go for it and sign up.

Signing up makes it sound simple. It was for from that. Firstly, I needed a username. I thought that using my actual name might be a good idea but when I entered 'Matthew' the page told me that it had already been taken. I tried again, this time as '*Matthew7.*' That was taken too. So was '*Matthew77.*' Eventually it accepted '*Matthew777777.*' There can't be that many Matthews on one dating site? A bit cumbersome but at least it had my name in it. Next, a password and an email address were required. Simple enough and I was in. Accepted. Ready to go. Or so I thought.

Before I could browse any of the profiles I had to complete my own profile. Then I had to fill in a number of site-generated drop down boxes that invited me to tick the option that was most suitable. Why did it have to be so complicated? I just wanted to get on with it, the nerves clearly rising within as I contemplated what I was now committing to. I reached blindly for another biscuit, my fingers encountering only the empty packet, its insides coated with the remnants of semi-melted chocolate. Disappointed, I scrunched it, binned it and returned to the task in front of me.

The first drop down box was asking for my reasons for joining Cupid's Pursuit. Apart from the fact I thought this to be an unnecessary question since it must be blindingly apparent that anyone on a dating site was quite possibly hoping to meet a potential partner, it then limited the available responses to the following options: *Romance & Relationship, Pen Pals, Friendship, Marriage, Fun, Sex.*

Perhaps the normal reason for joining was considered too simplistic and the people who ran the site felt there was a need to narrow it down even further. Whatever their rationale, I considered that I should think carefully before answering this question. If I selected the obvious, *Romance & Relationship*, the ladies were bound to think I am just saying that to pander to their sensitivities and therefore cannot possibly be genuine. If I chose *Pen Pals* they will think I am some weird sad sack that lives at home with his mum; *Friendship*, I am a Billy No Mates nerd who has to resort to the internet to find someone to talk to; *Marriage*, I am clearly desperate since no self-respecting bloke would jump straight in with both feet and look for a wife on the net; *Fun*, I must want sex; *Sex*, I definitely want sex. I decided, therefore that this was too tricky to answer and left it blank. So much for not wanting to over analyse. As a result of leaving the option blank my profile now said, '*Reasons best known to himself,*' which had the effect of making me seem at best mysterious and at worst sinister.

I ploughed on through the drop down options.

What is your relationship status? What was the point of that? I wouldn't be here if I weren't single, would I?

Who are you looking for? Was that for private investigators?

Which best describes your body type? They didn't have the option *human*.

What's your best feature? Each of the options related to a body part. I ignored that, my mind not wanting to get too focused on the ridiculous.

What do you do for fun? Going out and getting hammered with Cecil was not one of the choices.

Current annual income? I left that blank too, suddenly wary of gold diggers.

It seemed that each question had a limited range of answers and I was beginning to feel slightly overwhelmed. I had to choose a response in each case and I wasn't convinced any of them said what I wanted to say about myself.

What is your favourite colour? An easy question at last. Blue.

Are you looking for certain body types? Were they expecting vampires to log on?

What languages should she speak? Amongst the options for that was something called Tagalog. I had never even heard of Tagalog although I found out later it was a language of the Philippines. Would I need to trawl through many Tagalog speakers in the UK? Given my limited linguistic abilities I considered that selecting English would definitely help in my quest for love. I ticked that box.

How would you describe your looks? I hesitated. The options were: *stunning, hot, attractive, average, don't look great* and *ugly.* Right, I thought, that's a minefield. How do I answer that? What's that box doing there anyway? It really isn't for me to judge. That's for others to decide. But I had to answer it and suddenly I needed reassurance. Perhaps the mirror in my hallway would give me some time to arrive at a fair assessment.

I got up, walked to my hallway and stood staring at the reflection that was looking back at me. Almost six feet tall give or take half a millimetre – or at least that's what I told myself. Six feet had more distinction than five feet eleven and a bit. Blue eyes, two of, or maybe a bit green, I wasn't certain. Light brown hair, cut short. I was certain of that. Medium build, perhaps even a tad on the athletic side, since I kept in reasonable shape. Handsome? I wasn't sure about that at all. Good looking? Possibly that would be an exaggeration. Classic looks? No, that made me sound Italian and I was three parts Irish. Presentable, for sure. I dressed well and took care of my appearance. Ok, in summary, I realised I wasn't George Clooney nor was I Robert de Niro but I wasn't Quasimodo's deformed ugly brother either.

I went and sat back down at the PC, none the wiser. I had to get past the '*How would you describe your looks?*' option to be able to complete the profile. There was only one choice then. I picked '*Ugly.*' A perfectly rational choice too, I figured. If I went in low the only way was up. It also avoided any potential ridicule that might be thrown at me if I'd chosen '*Stunning*' or '*Hot*' and my potential date disagreed with that assessment. As for '*average*', that sounded just too...average. It was non-committal and bland and I didn't want that association on my new venture.

There were now just two stages of the sign up process to go. Write a short description about myself and what I was looking for, upload a picture and I was done. The description and what I was looking for proved to be harder than

I thought. It's not the easiest of things to describe yourself when you have to think about it. It's even harder when you know this is your personal advert and you have to get it right as your success or failure would depend upon it. I wasn't at all confident about how to pitch it. Too frivolous and I won't be taken seriously. On the other hand too intense and I'd sound desperate, needy and high maintenance. Too cocky and I'd sound like a perv. Nothing too smarmy or creepy either. Nor did I want to be perceived as bland or dull or even nice. In fact I hated nice. I had to avoid coming across as nice. Nice was a killer. Nice was no sex appeal. If you are labelled nice by a woman you might as well hack your own cojones off with a knife and stick them in a jar by your bed. You won't be needing them anymore. I needed to be alluring, intriguing, novel, original, sexy, appealing, enigmatic, funny, unusual, odd or maybe even mad - anything but nice. But I also wanted to sound like a genuine guy. Part of me felt I might be a good catch for some lady. I was still in good shape, dressed smartly, and had my own house near Kingston in Surrey, a decent car and a good job. Now all I had to do was convey that to the waiting female population of a dating site. I hit the first letters of the keyboard.

Hi. My name is Matthew. This is my first time on an internet dating site so I am still learning the ropes! Ultimately I'm looking for love like everyone else but not going to rush into it as I feel you have to take your time and get it right. I don't have a stereotype in mind for my perfect woman but a kind, caring, down to earth lady with a good sense of humour and a hint of mischief would suit me just fine. I am hard working, practical and like a good time like the rest of us but I am now ready to settle down with the right person. I keep myself fit and still have all the bits and pieces in the right places! If any of this hits a spot with you get in touch and let's see what happens.

Ok, it probably wasn't alluring, intriguing, novel, original, sexy, appealing, enigmatic, funny, unusual, odd or even mad but I had done it. Written my blurb but I still wasn't convinced it was a piece of prose that would have the most eligible women clamouring for my attention. But then I was never completely sure that anything I did was the perfect output. I just had to live with the perfectionist streak in my nature. It was basic stuff, brief and to the point and it would have to do. On the other hand I had no desire to bare my soul on a public website at such an early stage. I could always change it if no one responded or I got a negative reaction.

Next I needed a picture. Searching through the files on my PC I found one that I was happy with and began the upload. It was a straightforward head and shoulders one. It had been taken in my office at work. Black jacket, white open neck shirt, the relaxed look. Keep it simple. No one wants to see you necking a pint of beer by a pool or with a couple of strippers hanging off you at a mate's stag do. The picture was accepted and I was up and running, ready to begin my foray into the world of internet dating.

3

As I sat in front of a computer that was now to be the conduit to my 'happy ever after', I reflected on how I had reached this point in my life. I had split from my wife Olivia four years earlier after almost ten years of marriage. It had been love at first sight, a whirlwind romance and marriage within the first year. The next four years were blissfully happy. The next two, a period of contentment, normality and routine. The following two our careers had been our priority to the detriment of our relationship. I had thrown all my energies into my job as a marketing manager for a Health and Fitness group. Olivia had pursued her career relentlessly, as an investment manager for a major city firm. The final year brought the devastating revelation that she was having an affair with some whizz kid City boy and was leaving me. A decade down the pan just like that.

Losing my marriage had hit me hard. I don't know who was to blame or even if any blame was needed. We had let it slip by I guess. We had both let the strangulating grip of familiarity squeeze the life out of the relationship. And we didn't see it happening until it was too late. I had tried to rescue it, when I realised I was losing her; tried really hard but it wasn't enough. You watch a movie or read a book where the star-crossed lovers break up but eventually get back together again. I had hoped that I could be in that movie in my relationship but each time I had seen Olivia during that final awful period to talk things through, I couldn't detect the slightest glimmer of hope that all would be well. She had gone too far with her city boy.

The first couple of years after the split were the hardest. I was still in love with Olivia and accepting it and moving on was not easy. I wouldn't be the first or the last I figured but it still was painful. My confidence hit rock bottom. I had no interest in women. Apart from work I stayed home for the first six months. I didn't want to socialise at all. I wanted to sit there and wallow in my own misery. Why? Well, I always reckoned it was because if I stopped wallowing, if I started trying to enjoy life, it would be tantamount to accepting that it was over with Olivia. The reality was the split was terminal. I just hadn't accepted it. It was nearly a year after the break up before I gradually began to get out and about courtesy of Cecil. He re-introduced me to the world of socialising as a single man. A tough call with someone so reluctant at first and especially with someone with the negative view of women I was carrying around. Cecil was a lifeline. I glimpsed a side of him at that time that I had not encountered before. His brash, egotistical, alpha male attitude to life covered up a sensitive, supportive side that recognised when I needed to talk and recognised too when I needed a diversion. And then the nights out started in earnest. After the break up I was ready to embrace any lifestyle that helped numb the pain of a separation and helped to repair my broken ego. Cecil's brand of humour, unhindered thinking and desire for a good time became a huge distraction from my reality during those dark days.

The day I walked into the office and we were introduced I saw something different in Cecil Delaney. The firm handshake, direct gaze and positive tone of voice ensured he stood out from the rest. He had a presence that could be sensed. You knew where you were with Cecil and you knew that when he spoke it was from the heart. Short on stature but big on personality, impetuous, impulsive and even reckless at times but solid as a rock. In an industry where people were constantly sucking up to customers and managers alike, he was his own man. Nothing sycophantic about him, he told it like it was whether it was the popular view or otherwise. Fate decreed that we would work closely together and we gelled. Gelled because we were different, a yin and yang relationship, complementary opposites that blended instinctively. Where Cecil was impulsive I was cautious; where he was outspoken I was diplomatic; to Cecil's audacity I applied prudence. I was the brakes on Cecil's Ferrari – a fast car needs to be able to take a corner at the right speed or it will never get round it. And it worked. Equally Cecil's impulsive nature dragged me out of my self-imposed rut; his audacity amused me and made me brave at a time when my confidence was shot. The crazy nights wiped out the moody, lonesome days until such time that a Cecil night out became the norm. Through that working relationship and the many nights out I got to know the character of the man. Underneath that brash exterior I discovered the vulnerable centre. At the tail end of another late night, after one Jack Daniel's too many, he had revealed that he had been close to someone once and he'd lost her. It had hit him hard but it was his own fault and he knew it. He'd tried to live the dream and keep a relationship going at the same time. It was never going to work. Living the dream Cecil style could not be compatible with any romantic relationship. He would never admit to his vulnerability and I would never expose it but we knew each other well and there was an unspoken understanding of one another's frailties.

The bond between us survived Cecil's inevitable departure from a firm where he would always create conflict with those he shouldn't just because he didn't know when to hold his tongue. I recalled that working relationship fondly and I would always be indebted to him for his understanding, compassion and friendship when my marriage had floundered. That friendship had remained unshakeable.

Now here I was, just a few months shy of forty years old, divorce papers to prove I was hopeless at relationships, sitting in front of a computer screen about to embark on a quest for love. Love that would last more than a decade this time, I hoped.

Tentatively I began my first search. I had to select an age range for prospective dates. I decided 30 to 45 would at least give me a good selection and would ensure I didn't go too far outside an acceptable range for a 39-year-old man. I hit the 'Search Now' button. My screen was immediately filled with an array of photographs and profiles all gazing expectantly back at me, or so it seemed. At that precise moment an indicator showed that there were 38,938 people on line. I was taken aback by that number of women on the site. This was going to take some sifting through and I had only joined for a month. It could take me six weeks to get through a quarter of these profiles and another six to sift out all the Tagalog speakers.

I started scrolling through the profiles. There were all sorts, all shapes and all sizes. Most of the pictures were head and shoulders shots with a few full length ones. A few of the pictures called into question the judgement of the owner. Surely they could see that some of the shots they had uploaded were not going to attract a second glance. Dodgy jumpers, no makeup, just got out of bed hair with backdrops that included sofas strewn with magazines and kids' toys, were not the images that would inspire a guy to think 'I gotta talk to her.'

Then there were the professionally taken photos - soft focus, expertly made up ladies, draped over luxurious sofas against some carefully arranged, unrealistic studio setting. All designed to hide a multitude of sins, I figured. There were also lots of pictures of women on holiday, in exotic locations, with the Taj Mahal or the Pyramids in the background. There were women riding camels or in full snorkelling gear. There was another lying in a hammock between two palm trees holding a drink with at least two umbrellas in it. Were these pictures meant to give us blokes an illusion of some sort of fantasy existence to be had if we hooked up with the ladies in question? Were they trying to portray themselves in a way that said choose me and your life would be an endless cycle of exotic holidays and hammocks?

I scrolled on through the gallery. A woman sitting on the roof of her car caught my eye. I wasn't sure what deep psychological message she was trying to get across. Why would you sit on the roof of your car unless you were either a total novice driver who still hadn't mastered the basics of getting inside it or you had dropped your keys down a drain and were awaiting rescue? And if either of these situations were the case, who would want their picture taken at that time anyway? Some had uploaded pictures of their pets. What's the point of that? I am unlikely to want to date your cat. One woman had more pictures of her dog on her profile than she did of herself. Perhaps she was not computer literate, had joined by mistake and was actually looking for Cruft's website. Another profile had a picture of an elephant. Just an elephant by itself. Maybe the lady in question had enjoyed a holiday in Africa but what was a photo of an elephant telling me? Why would it inspire me to click on her profile and attempt some interaction unless I was very weird. Another profile had the Manhattan skyline. Nobody in it. Just the Manhattan skyline. And another, a picture of a post box in the snow. What's that all about? Was a post box in the snow supposed to be conveying some subtle, subliminal message? If it was, I didn't get it. As a bloke I was just interested in face, body, tits and legs. Superficial, perhaps, but that would have been sufficient for me.

So, how was I to choose from that lot? I needn't have worried about choosing. I was soon to find out that the ladies do the choosing. If you are half way presentable, have teeth and hair, eventually someone will spot you. I had only been on the site half an hour when I made my first positive contact. I hadn't realised when I signed up that there was a live chat option on the site where members could communicate in real time. The screen lit up with text.

'*Hello. How are you?*'

A few simple words but I felt a rush of excitement. She was blonde, thirty-eight years old according to her profile headline and, if her picture was anything to go by, good looking.

'*Hello,*' I typed, '*I'm fine*'.

Well I didn't know what else to say. My first contact. I was nervous. I didn't want to screw it up. I still didn't know the protocols. Should I be serious or light hearted? How much information do I give about myself? I needn't have worried. The lady seemed to be a dab hand at leading the chat.

'*My name is Linda. What's yours?*'

Most of my input was responding to her lead but my spirits lifted as we chatted and I started to relax. It was basically text chat made all the more difficult by the fact that my typing skills were limited by my two fingered technique and, in my rush to convey my responses, a series of typos made it look like I was both dyslexic and illiterate. I was trying to be witty, entertaining and cool but at the same time wondering, what the hell I was doing on the site and did she think I was a weirdo? I must have been doing something right because after about half an hour of typing she asked me to give her a call and typed out her mobile number. Blimey, I thought, she doesn't waste much time, or was it me who was a bit slow on the uptake?

I called, we chatted. She sounded normal. I hoped that I did too and apart from the beginning of the conversation when she could be forgiven for thinking I had a severe stutter due to a combination of not knowing what to say and forgetting my own name, the conversation went well. So well in fact she asked me for a date. She asked me. I hadn't thought of it.

'We should have lunch sometime, Matthew,' she said.

'Err, well I was just going to put some toast on myself,' I replied, my nerves getting the better of me at the thought of an internet date actually happening.

'No, you and I,' she laughed, '...a date. Lunch together. Would you like that?'

'Oh...yes...of course. Yes...why not. I mean, yes that would be...err...great.'

'Tomorrow is good for me, if you are free, Matthew?'

'Tomorrow,' I blurted out, 'Ok...yes, tomorrow...that will be fine, Linda.'

'Excellent, Matthew. I will be wearing a blue dress, so you will know it's me. It's also my lucky colour.'

We made the arrangements. I put the phone down, my head spinning with a mix of excitement and apprehension. A date. It had taken under an hour to get a date. Or rather it had taken under an hour for a date to get me.

I called Cecil.

'Cecil, it's me, Matt. I got a date. From the internet. Tomorrow.'

'Nice one, geezer. Has she got any mates?'

'Mates? I didn't ask her about mates. Why would I ask about her mates?'

'You didn't ask? You doing a mumble swerve on me geezer? I set you up and you are going solo.'

'Ces, it's just a lunch. For two. That's what a date is, isn't it? You know, just me and her. You should be pleased. You recommended the internet dating thing.'

'Lunch?' I could hear the mocking tone in his voice. 'Lunch...what about a bit of the old hashmadishmalacka?'

'Hashmawhat, Ces? I have a lunch date with a lady from a dating site. It's a normal thing to do. We will just see how it goes,' I said, almost apologetically.

'I could come along mate. Or meet you both after your little romantic soiree.' Cecil was clearly taking the mickey.

'Give me a break Cecil. I am grateful you advised me to use the internet for a date. I am, really. But I am giving this a shot. See what happens. If it works out, maybe she has some mates you could meet, who knows? But I can't show up on a lunch date with a friend in tow. I will let you know how it goes.'

'Ok, geezer. Fancy a swift one? Fad's...in an hour.'

With a spring in my step I pitched up at MacFadden's at three o'clock. No sign of Cecil but that was normal. He was always running late. MacFadden's, or Fad's as it was commonly known, was a small bar on the edge of town struggling to do business. With few customers it lacked atmosphere and there was nothing about it that would appeal to passing trade. Dimly lit with old boxing videos constantly being replayed on two screens at one end of the main bar, it needed a lift before it disappeared into oblivion. It was not the decor that was a problem. That was all in a good state of repair. The place just needed some life, some fresh blood to change the ambience. I had been going there for a few years and, like the regulars, only seemed to use it as a meeting point. It was often deserted by late evening. As I walked in the owner, Carlos MacFadden, was behind the bar as usual. I pulled a stool up and slid onto it.

'Hola, Mateo. How's life with you?'

That was Carlos's usual greeting. For some reason he always used the Spanish version of my name. I had gotten used to it.

'Not bad Carlos. Just meeting Cecil for a beer. How's business?' I needn't have asked. Business was always the same. At best quiet, at its worst a wasteland.

'Picking up, picking up,' Carlos said rather optimistically.

'Well, seems a bit quiet just now,' I said. 'You should, I don't know, maybe get a few events going to attract people in.'

'Events? Like what?' Carlos asked.

'You know, promotional stuff. Theme nights. Give a few freebies out. That sort of stuff. We do it all the time in my game. Always marketing something. You'd be surprised how it pulls in the punters.'

'Maybe you could send me some stuff, Mateo. Some ideas.' Carlos seemed genuinely interested in what I was saying.

'Well, it's not quite the same business Carlos. Mine is all about getting people to join health clubs and stay as members. But I suppose there are similarities. Yours is all about getting customers in and keeping them. Look, just come up with some ideas of your own. Stuff you'd like to do and go for it. Party nights. Drinks specials, two for ones, freebies. You know the stuff. Then advertise in the local rag. Bung a few leaflets about. You never know. Can't be any worse than waiting around for business to walk in.'

'Ok, Mateo, maybe I will. Anyway, you and Cecil...you two cucarachas on the pull tonight then?'

'No, not tonight, Carlos...just having a quiet one.' I ordered a coke.

Carlos picked up a glass, clinked some ice into the base, hit a button on the juice gun and sprayed the dark cola mix over the glistening cubes.

'So, how's your love life Mateo. Any girlies?' he said placing the fizzing glass on a small white mat on the bar in front of me.

'Nothing new, I'm afraid, Carlos,' I said averting my gaze and reaching for the drink. I wasn't going to mention my Sunday lunch date at this stage, not only because there wasn't anything to report yet, but also I didn't want anyone knowing I was on a dating site.

Carlos took my downcast look as a cue to offer me advice on where I was going wrong with women and how it should be done. He was half South American and half Scottish, an interesting combination that left him with a soft Scottish brogue into which he would sprinkle the odd Spanish phrase or word.

At forty he was a year older than I was and looked like a cross between Bob Hoskins and Danny DeVito. Same rotund physique, same stature and same bald dome. Although he liked to portray himself as a ladies' man I had never known him to have a girlfriend or any long term relationship whatsoever. Yet he professed to be an expert on marriage and the art of snaring the 'senoritas.' In fairness sometimes he did speak some sense but it was hard to take advice from a guy who did not appear to have any practical experience of getting a relationship, let alone maintaining one. For my part, one of the biggest obstacles to adopting Carlos's recommended pulling technique was the fact that it was based around the art of Latin American dancing, his theory being that if you could dance South American style, the ladies would fall at your feet. I had seen Carlos cutting some shapes on the dance floor and was never sure whether he was executing some complex Latino moves or actually trying to drill himself down through the floorboards. I had also witnessed his interpretation of the tactile elements of Latin dancing and realized that if I ever tried the same approach I could very well find myself up on a charge for indecent assault. So whatever his technique I had resolved to treat his advice on both dancing and seduction with some degree of caution.

'Geezer! Sorry, I'm late mate, the whole area is gridlocked.'

I swivelled round in my seat in the direction of the familiar voice. Cecil had arrived.

'What, you drove here Ces?' I asked.

'Nah. Train mate. Hold up at Clapham Junction or something.'

Cecil always had the same excuse for being late. Gridlock. It didn't matter if he came by train or possibly even if he had flown in, it was always gridlock. I considered that he had perhaps picked up the expression from watching too much CNN news.

'Anyway, geezer, what the fuck are you doing drinking coke? Carlos, get this man a proper drink and one for me.'

Carlos obliged with two pints of Staropramen. Cecil took a deep slurp from his glass, ran his fingers through the healthy head of what he referred to as 'Irish hair' because it was so thick and abundant, and turned to face me.

'So, mate, you got yourself a date. Told you. See, you should listen to Ces.' Then leaning towards Carlos who was busily wiping spillage from the two beers off the bar top, he said, 'Hey, Carlos, the geezer's got a little mumble swerve tomorrow with some bird off the internet.'

I nearly choked on the beer I hadn't asked for. So much for keeping it quiet. Carlos looked up from the bar, his eyebrows knitted together in a frown that suggested puzzlement given our earlier conversation.

'Mateo…cucaracha. Why didn't you say? What is she like?' he asked.

I tried to explain to Carlos that contrary to what Cecil had said I didn't have a 'mumble swerve.' I was simply going out to Sunday lunch with a lady that I hadn't actually met yet so I couldn't really tell anyone what she was like. Consequently, at that stage I felt that there was no point in mentioning it. Carlos shrugged and returned to wiping his bar.

'Ok mate, as it's your last night as a single man I'm taking you out on the town.' Cecil gestured towards the door.

'No, Cecil, I am going home in a minute. I want to be fresh and rested tomorrow. No sense in me turning up looking like I've been out on the tiles all night, which is what I will look like if I go out with you.'

'Mate, are you going all lightweight on me now?' Cecil responded. 'I thought you were a warrior. It's a bird you are meeting tomorrow. For a bite to eat. It's not as if you are running the London marathon. What's the matter with you? Lunch is about one o'clock...am I right? And you're worrying about what you'll look like. We'll have a couple of cold ones and if you are that concerned you can sod off home early. You up for it?'

'If he's not, I am,' piped up Carlos from behind the bar.

'No Carlos. You got an empty bar to run. And speaking of empty bars, when you gonna get some decent looking barmaids in this place? The whole place could do with some atmosphere, geezer.'

Carlos shot a glance at me. I winked at him, to reinforce our earlier discussion. To my mind staff were never going to be an issue for Carlos until he got some serious business first. If it hadn't been for our custom MacFadden's may well have closed by now.

Cecil necked his beer, stifled a belch as he watched the remaining froth slide down the inside of his glass and turned back to me. 'You coming out or what geezer?'

Against my better judgement I agreed.

4

It took thirty minutes for the train to wind its way through a series of suburban stations and reach Waterloo. Waterloo was a Cecil haunt. Having lived there at one time he was familiar with the locality and knew all the bars. In fact there weren't many bars and clubs in London that Cecil didn't know. He never queued to get in anywhere. The bars that he visited regularly made him welcome. They knew he was good customer. Late night clubs were a different proposition, often more difficult to breach. For these Cecil had developed his own entrance strategy that would guarantee access. When confronted by burly bouncers that controlled entry he would produce the 'how are ya,' his term for the friendly handshake offered to the main man on the door. The feel of a crisp ten pound note against the palm of a hand seemed to be all that was needed to skip the queues and open a path to the bright lights of London's late nightlife.

Stepping off the train Cecil strolled purposefully across the station concourse, headed through the striking Victory Arch and straight down both levels of the bank of curved concrete steps that led to the street. Not once did he glance behind to see if I was keeping up. His destination was the Arch One Bar immediately opposite the station entrance. It had just turned five o'clock.

Situated in one of the old railway arches, Arch One was wide and spacious. At its far end a huge window formed most of the rear wall, below which stacks of brightly lit shelves were loaded with an impressive display of wines and spirits. A long bar counter, running from wall to wall across the span of the window, hosted a few early evening drinkers perched on tall stools along its width. We ordered two beers and sat down. A degree of unease came over me.

'Look Cecil, I told you I am taking it easy tonight, you know. I got that date tomorrow and want to show up looking half with it.'

'Keep your hair on, mate. A couple of cold ones. That's all. Just cos you are seeing some bird tomorrow doesn't mean to say you can't have a quiet one on a Saturday night with a mate, does it?'

'Yeah but I know your quiet ones and I am not going out big style tonight. That's not happening Cecil.'

'Mate, don't deny it. You are like me. We both got the barbarian gene. Only ever one large gin and tonic away from it going pear-shaped. Just accept it geezer.'

As far as I was concerned I didn't have the Cecil barbarian gene at all. Sure he had it in spades. But not me. My problem was that I still got caught up in Cecil's enthusiasm for raucous nights out. My intentions were always good but the end result often did not match the original intention.

'Well, whatever the reason Cecil, not tonight,' I said.

'Mate, trust me. A quiet one. You won't be going home tonight with tyre marks across your chest, ok.'

Cecil's attention span for any single bar never did last long. Before we had finished the first beer he was on his feet ready to move on. That didn't bode well.

We crossed the Waterloo Road and took a steady walk along Roupell Street, past the rows of 19th century terraced houses with their vividly painted front doors and varied flower arrangements on the window sills. As we reached the halfway point we passed the Kings Arms pub on the corner with Windmill Walk, its black painted facade contrasting against the lights burning brightly inside. There was an early evening crowd already drinking at the bar and I felt sure that Cecil's curiosity to see what was going on would make this our next stop. He kept walking. At the end of the road we turned right into Hatfields. A few hundred yards further on, we walked under the railway bridge and turned sharp left into Isabella Street. It was then I realised why we were there. A row of glass fronted bars panned out along one side to the left, stretching the length of the road, each one tucked neatly under the arches of the railway bridge. In front of each unit stood a collection of seats and benches underneath wide, canvas canopies, with tall, steel, patio heaters casting a warming red glow all around, inviting the passer-by in from the chill November air. It was a typical Cecil location. Plenty of choice.

We strolled into Jack's Bar. To the right a long wooden bar ran from one end of the room almost to the other. Several large circular lampshades, dangling just above head height over the counter, cast a warm amber glow across its polished surface. Behind the serving area a row of rectangular, gleaming mirrors softened the brickwork creating a feel of spaciousness and elegance. From the arched ceiling two huge, metal tubular air conditioning ducts hung like six legged space ships awaiting landing instructions. To the left side of the open floor space rows of soft furnishings, upholstered leather sofas and circular tables were occupied by early evening drinkers chatting animatedly under homely looking lampshades. The dark brick walls of the original railway arch, subdued lighting and wood floors gave an air of stylish cosy ambiance. Contemporary style meets retro sitting room charm. And somehow it worked.

Cecil took up a position at a corner of the bar nearest the entrance. From that vantage point you could see straight down into the depths of the main room, see who was coming in through the main door and also see out into the patio area. It was a classic Cecil tactic to seek a good position, get 'bar presence,' he liked to say.

The smell of fresh mint hung in the air as the staff busied themselves preparing the cocktail menu. We drank a couple of Budvars and Cecil started to ask questions about my proposed date. I couldn't tell him much at that particular moment. What little I knew had come from the site and my brief telephone conversation with Linda. I didn't want to encourage his curiosity and his enquiries about whether or not she had any friends so I changed the subject, pointing out that the bar was filling up and that there were one or two attractive women amongst the crowd. This had the effect of distracting Cecil from his questioning as he took in the scene. The clientele was a good mix of twenty somethings up to early forties, mostly casually dressed with one or two suits in evidence and a few of the ladies dressed to impress for a Saturday night on the town.

Two more Budvars appeared on the bar. The smooth, malty taste of the beer was making it very palatable and it slipped down too easily. Cecil had opened a tab. A bad omen. The beers were accompanied by two shots, Goldschlägers, cinnamon schnapps that had tiny flakes of real gold floating in the mix.

'Not for me Cecil. I told you, I'm taking it easy.'

'What are you geezer? A lightweight? It's a small shot. Knock it back. Don't be a pussy.'

I didn't think I was being a pussy but I was aware of the fact that a couple beside us had overheard Cecil's remark and were now looking at me expectantly. I felt that I was being viewed as a lightweight who couldn't down a simple little shot. I necked it.

'Good man. Fancy the bar next door?'

It wasn't so much a question as an indication of intent. Cecil was on the move again. I could have tried to dissuade him but I knew from experience what he was like. I followed him next door to Ev Bar.

Ev Bar occupied a similar space to Jack's as it was also part of the disused railway setting. Like Jack's, the ceiling followed the arc of the original arch but a series of curved wooden beams emphasised the curvature and gave it a polished natural look. The theme was one of wood and greenery, with tables carved from tree trunks and solid wooden seating all around. The entrance both inside and out had an array of hanging baskets and plant arrangements. A pale, solid tiled section of flooring created a light, airy feel even on a winter evening. The whole area was so close to mainstream London yet it seemed like some sort of well kept secret to the uninitiated. The crowd profile was similar to Jack's too, probably because many of them flitted between the two adjacent locations. Young, chatty, trendy, lively, full of expectation and anticipation for the remainder of the weekend.

Two more Budvars were ordered and placed on the bar in front of us. Another two Goldschlägers followed. The combination of the first beers, the shots and the brief inhalation of fresh air in the short walk between the bars had started to affect my mind-set. It had suddenly gone from caution to devil may care in a matter of minutes, a process I now had no control over. I sank the shot. It went down easily.

We were doing 'bar presence' again at a corner of the bar when Cecil began making small talk with two girls standing to his left. As he initiated a chat up he would invariably turn towards the girl, or girls in question, placing his body between them and anyone he was with at the time. I am sure he didn't do it deliberately. It was his sub-conscious way of protecting his territory, of staking his claim and giving out a signal that he was in charge. The reality was that this reflected some deep rooted insecurity in Cecil. The initial barrier he was making was to ensure he got the attention and that he would make the first impression. I knew from experience that eventually he would relax and let the space open up but not before he had had the opportunity to stake his claim to the prize. Although I was quite relaxed about it, the only drawback was that it made me look like a geek peering over his shoulder trying to get involved in the conversation. No easy feat when Ceil was in full flow. The alternative was to hang back at the bar and look like the dodgy mate with no conversation.

It was becoming noisier in Ev. The early evening hubbub was increasing in decibels to a wall of noise, a confused mix of conversation and background music. By the time Cecil relaxed his stance and introduced me, I couldn't actually make out all of what was being said. Nicola was the good looking one and clearly the object of Cecil's attention. Katie was, let's say, not immediately attractive at all. By the time I got involved I realised, from the bits I could hear, that Nicola was talking about her forthcoming wedding in the spring. No wonder Cecil had taken a step back. This was a dead end, a nonstarter. In his book we were standing with a 'bird' that was '*geezered up*' and one that he no longer had any interest in at all. His compensation for this disappointing turn of events was another Goldschläger. One each. Even I got compensated. With no end product from his chat up, it was only a matter of time before Cecil got bored. In his mind it was now time to move on, as there was sure to be some action somewhere else that he was missing out on. As usual I went along.

The cold night air hit with a freezing blast as we stepped out onto the street. I vaguely recall turning left and walking down the street until we entered The Cut and ended up at the junction with Blackfriars Road. Just down the road from Southwark Station we found the Baltic bar. I say found but it was clear Cecil knew where we were headed. The walk had now fuzzed my head completely

- or maybe it was the Budvar and Goldschlägers that were to blame. I wasn't thinking clearly so it didn't really matter where the blame lay.

The Baltic Bar was clean, fresh and pink. That was my impression anyway. It was something to do with the subtle lighting that reflected off the narrow bar entrance and the colourful array of bottles that adorned the shelves behind the bar that gave it a sort of magical pink glow. We sat on two of the round stools at the end of the bar. The restaurant to our right was busy. Two vodka based drinks appeared on the bar, courtesy of Cecil deciding what we should drink. The Baltic clearly specialised in vodka but I have no idea which of the many options on the menu he purchased. All I know was it was strong and was going straight to my head.

The Baltic was the last clear recollection I have of the evening. At some point we ended up in the bar of the Oxo Tower. I knew this because the following day I discovered I had a photograph of the spectacular London skyline on my mobile phone and another of me standing at the bar drinking red wine in the same establishment. The rest of the evening is cobbled together from a serious of faltering and disjointed memories. I have a dim recollection of eating Chinese food in Chinatown and a very hazy memory of walking through Soho looking for a taxi. The journey home is in the deepest recesses of my sub-conscious mind never to surface again. I have no memory of parting company with Cecil. Regrettably this was not unusual on a night out with him. I knew it had to stop.

5

I woke with a hangover bigger than an asteroid. My mouth felt like I had spent the evening drinking straight from the Dead Sea, such was my impossible thirst. I vaguely recalled getting back home at three o'clock in the morning and now felt very fragile. At some point, probably in the early hours, I appeared to have lost the ability to co-ordinate basic movements, and I now had to relearn the fundamental skills of motion as I struggled from my bed onto my feet. At least that is how it felt. A wave of nausea swept over me as I headed for the shower, its intensity forcing me to sit back down on the edge of the bed. I raised both hands to my head and began kneading my temples with firm fingers in an attempt to massage the sluggishness from my brain. As I did so my mobile bleeped with a text message.

'Looking forward to our lunch date. Linda x'.

The lunch date. I hadn't forgotten. It was just that my hung over disorientation had not allowed any semblance of a normal day to register in my consciousness at that point. I sent a text back expressing a similar sentiment although in reality my level of enthusiasm was now heavily watered down by my pounding head. I cursed Cecil when I should have been cursing myself for not sticking to my plan and staying at home. The couple of 'cold ones' had clearly turned into a full on party and I was now paying the price. I had to get myself together. I struggled down stairs, my left hand sliding along the handrail, for guidance. Fumbling shakily through the kitchen cupboard I found the Berocca, hoping that it would restore my body's depleted mineral levels back to some measure of equilibrium. I dropped the orange tablet into a half pint of water and watched as the liquid fizzed and sparkled until it looked like some sort of over enthusiastic urine sample. I gritted my teeth and downed it in one straight draught, hoping it would stay down. It did. Just.

Two slices of toast and a strong coffee later and what I really wanted to do was go back to bed. But it was almost 11am and no time for that. I took a long shower, shaved and got dressed. Smart casual look, jacket, jeans, pale blue shirt. Outwardly, I reckoned I was passable at best. From inside my head the view was altogether shakier. I called a taxi.

I had chosen a little restaurant that I knew well, midway between where we both lived. That seemed a fair arrangement for a first meeting. It was usually crowded with a nice buzz so that at least if we didn't hit it off, there was a bit of atmosphere for distraction.

The taxi got me there early. A decorator was putting some finishing touches in red to a wooden surround above the restaurant window, whistling happily as he worked atop his ladder. Obviously he hadn't spent the night on the tiles. Heading through the door I took a seat by the small wooden counter that served as both a waiting area and a bar.

I was nervous. I needn't have been. Linda showed up exactly on time, a whirl of smiles and pungent perfume.

'Matthew. Lovely to meet you,' she said enthusiastically.

'Oh yes, of course it is,' I replied, my head pounding as I tried to organise my senses, '…I mean, great to meet you too Linda.'

At least she looked like the picture she had on the site. In fact her picture didn't do her justice. Her blonde hair was tied back in a blue ribbon that matched the blue of her dress. Her make-up was soft and subtle and with the ponytail, the look was that of a woman considerably younger than her thirty-eight years. The tension in my neck, a mix of nerves and hangover, loosened slightly. I led the way towards the seating area where a waiter showed us to a table by the window and took a seat facing into the restaurant, a primitive instinct men have to ensure that they do not have their backs to a crowd. The place was full, a buzz from the diners already seated, many more now jostling their way through the front door towards the waiting area, eager to get a table. I was glad I had had the foresight to book the day before. The waiter handed us the menus.

'What would you like to drink Linda?' I asked.

'Oh, let's see,' she said, scanning the back of the menu, 'I fancy some white wine actually. And it is the weekend, so why not.'

I could think of several reasons why not, my pounding head being at least one of them. I didn't fancy any more alcohol at all but I didn't want to put a dampener on the moment and nor did I want to have to explain my reasons for not drinking.

'Chablis Ok?' I asked, looking around to catch the waiter's eye.

'Perfect. Oh, by the way, I've bought you a little present Matthew.' She reached across to the adjacent chair and began to fumble through her handbag.

I suddenly felt embarrassed. I hadn't bought her anything at all. Not even a box of chocolates. Was that the protocol? Are you supposed to buy gifts on a first date? I hadn't a clue.

'Oh, have you? You needn't have bought me anything,' I said lamely, hoping that, in some way telling her she needn't have bothered might excuse me being totally empty handed.

'Here. Open it,' she said, handing me a small neatly wrapped parcel.

I began to open it wondering what on earth she could have bought for me and why she would buy anything at all for a total stranger on a first date. Carefully removing the wrapping I revealed the contents. A tie.

'That's really nice of you Linda. Thank you,' I said, staring at the green piece of material in my hand.

'It's not just any old tie, it's a lucky tie. They are four leaf clovers in the pattern,' she said pointing at the garish emerald design.

Whatever it was it didn't look much like clover to me. In fact the tie was horrendous. I just hoped she wasn't going to ask me to put it on. Maybe it was because I was nervous or it might possibly have been as a result of the previous night's revelry but I could see my hands were shaking as I began to unfold it. Out of politeness, I laid it out on the table so that we could both admire it knowing that once it went in my pocket it would never see the light of day again. I ran a palm across the surface of the material smoothing it out in an effort to show some sort of approval. As I finished the appreciative stroke my hand inadvertently caught the saltcellar next to me tipping it over. The top must have been loose as it dropped onto its side on the table and rolled off the edge onto the floor. With the top gone the contents shot out across the table, spilling salt everywhere.

It was nothing to fuss over but perhaps I should have guessed Linda was superstitious, given her choice of gift. In one swift movement she picked up the saltcellar, poured a generous amount into her hand and, without a backward glance, threw it over her shoulder.

'Just for luck,' she said.

Unfortunately most of it landed in the cappuccino of the customer sitting right behind her just as he was about to raise the cup to take a sip. Not such good luck for him. His reaction was to lurch forward in a gagging motion and splurt the contaminated coffee all over his female companion who, in shock, reeled back catching the arm of a passing waiter who was carrying the soup of the day. The very bright red tomato consommé was then deposited effortlessly over a customer who was just about to take a seat at a table for two. Even I could tell it didn't look good on her white trousers and it was clear she didn't think much of the colour scheme as she started leaping about as much from the effect of hot liquid dripping onto her finely manicured toes, as from the horror of her sudden fashion statement. It's never a good idea to tap dance in hot soup and the inevitable result was that she ended up losing her balance whilst clutching frantically at the nearest lifeline she could, as she tried to stay upright. That happened to be a table cloth on which four diners had four very large plates of pasta perched until it was summarily yanked from beneath their gaze. The total shock at the sight of their food vanishing from the table was all too much for them. In what appeared to be a perfectly synchronised movement they simultaneously dived forward to try to salvage their doomed lunch. To no avail. Tablecloth, plates, food and guests all converged in a glutinous heap of pasta and soup on the previously pristine floor.

Linda seemed totally oblivious to the mayhem unfolding behind her, so engrossed was she in trying to get the salt back into the pot. With the saltcellar held against the table so that the open top was now level with the table surface, she brushed the spilt contents with the palm of her hand towards the table edge and into the container.

Leaning forward, she whispered, 'I wouldn't want them to think we were messy pups.'

I didn't know where to look. I glanced back in the direction of the hapless diners now clambering to their feet, clothes covered in the congealing mess that started out as their lunch. The lady in the white trousers was now standing in a rigid pose, a look of sheer disbelief on her face as she contemplated the mess of soup and pasta that decorated her outfit. The unfortunate waiter was apologising profusely whilst, from a kneeling position in front of her, trying to remove the restaurant's specials from her trousers with both hands. I heard rather than witnessed the slap as her hand caught him full in the face presumably for the liberties he was unintentionally taking with her lower anatomy.

I turned my attention back to the saltcellar, focusing on Linda's careful attempts to refill it, and hoping the harassed staff wouldn't notice. Ordinarily I might have tried to take a grip of the situation and remain calm but my delicate system and pounding head were not helping. I felt clammy and sweaty. I was frantically trying to think of a way out before the cause of the commotion was traced back to my table. As luck would have it I was given a lifeline. My mobile buzzed. It was just a text message from my credit card provider to say my statement was on line. I studied it intently.

'Are you all right, Matthew? You look very pale,' Linda said after I had been staring at the mobile for what seemed like an eternity.

'Err, no…my…my mother has had a…a fall. Fallen down the stairs. Broken her leg, I think. I have to go. I am really sorry, Linda. Perhaps you had better go too. No sense in sitting here on your own.'

'Oh dear, I am sorry to hear that,' Linda said, a look of concern in her eyes. 'Looks like your lucky tie hasn't started to work yet then. I am sure it will though. We can do this another time, Matthew.'

'Sure,' I said, anxious to make an exit while the commotion was still ensuing. Perhaps I wouldn't be noticed leaving. 'We'd better go, Linda,'

'I will just clear the rest of this salt up, Matthew. We don't want to leave a mess for the waiter to clear up, do we?'

'Err…I wouldn't worry too much about that, Linda,' I said, catching sight of what appeared to be most of the restaurant staff now attempting to clear up the spillage several feet behind her. 'Look, I have to go. It's an emergency.'

We got up and left, my pace more hurried than was polite, striding ahead of Linda. As I turned out of the doorway I felt a sharp tug on my sleeve accompanied by a piercing shout of 'watch out.' I turned both in reaction to the tug and the shout. Linda's face was aghast.

'The ladder, Matthew. You nearly walked under it. It's very bad luck if you do.'

The decorator had moved his ladder nearer the doorway. I hadn't noticed it in my hurry to get away and almost walked beneath it. Bad luck? The bad luck had already occurred regardless of whether I walked under a ladder inadvertently or deliberately. Linda had also alarmed me more by her reaction to a simple ladder leaning against a shop front than any possibility of further impending doom. It was at that point I decided that perhaps this particular rendezvous was not meant to be.

Cecil was on the phone that very evening.

'How did it go geezer?'

'Not too good, mate. There was a bit of commotion. She's got this superstition thing going on. Ballsed up the whole date.' I blurted out the whole sorry episode much to Cecil's amusement.

'So you won't be seeing her again then,' he laughed.

'Well, I don't think so. I mean I can't be doing all that walking round ladders, saluting magpies, avoiding black cats and crossing my fingers palaver. I'd be a bloody nervous wreck all the time. I knew this wouldn't work out.'

Cecil's voice took on a more serious tone. 'Look mate, it's only your first date. Chill out. There are still loads of birds out there. Ok, so the first one you met is a hocus-pocus freak but they ain't all gonna be like that. Give it another go.'

He had a point. Perhaps I was over reacting. Maybe I shouldn't quit so easily. I was listening to my negative side, which hadn't wanted to sign up in the first place, and after all I had spent twenty-five quid for the privilege of a month's membership. No sense in wasting it based on a first date that didn't quite go as planned. There'd be other opportunities. Back to the drawing board.

6

I logged on again later that night to Cupids Pursuit and was surprised to see that I had six e-mail messages. I am not sure why I was surprised as it was a dating site and the whole point is for people to contact one another. I suppose it was because I was so new to it and didn't know what to expect. There was an email from Linda expressing her concern, hoping my mother was all right and seeing if we could get together once things had improved. I knew it was cowardly but I decided not to answer just yet. I wasn't blaming her completely for the date going wrong. It was partly my fault for turning up with a hangover. If I hadn't perhaps I would have had my wits about me and not have been so clumsy but perhaps Linda's superstitious nature also encouraged unfortunate situations to arise. I decided to stay clear for a while. There were plenty of other guys for Linda on the site. I scanned the other messages.

'You look cute. How are you? I showed your picture to my nine-year-old daughter and she approves. Passed the first hurdle. LOL.'

That unnerved me. This woman sees me as husband and father material already. She has to be unstable if she's letting a kid influence her decision making. I deleted the message. There were another three messages each giving out their personal mobile numbers. They all had the same approach in common.

'I know you may think this is a bit forward and I don't normally do this but you looked nice and I wondered if you want to chat on the phone. I like to put a voice to a face and no sense in emailing all the time. Call me'.

Bloody hell I thought, that is direct. I could be an axe man. Even worse she could be an axe woman. Who gives their number to complete strangers, unless they are desperate? And as for *'I don't normally do this,'* I had a sneaking suspicion that each of the ladies in question did do it, all the time. I decided that maybe I should take some time to see who was on line and then I could take control of the situation myself and select who I wanted to contact. I started to browse the profiles and read them more carefully. It was clear that everyone was selling themselves. All so positive and upbeat about their lives.

'I'm a happy, fun loving, uncomplicated, strong, low maintenance girl looking to meet someone special to spend time with……'

'I would consider myself to be quite a balanced down-to-earth person, lacking that special someone to share good times with….'

'I am confident, outgoing, fun loving, I have a positive attitude to life and a great sense of humour….'

'I am caring, loving, romantic, loyal and trustworthy.'

Another profile caught my eye. She was using the profile name 'Tarzan's Mate'.

'Hi, I'm Jane. I have been single for a while now and even though my life is good I am still looking for the missing link.' An unfortunate choice of words, I thought, since no doubt any dating site would contain its fair share of Neanderthals.

It seemed that everyone was trying to portray themselves in the best possible light and from their own viewpoint. I suppose there was no sense in giving the world a reality check. I mean who would be attracted to anyone who told it like it is.

'I am struggling with the mortgage since my bastard husband buggered off and I can't cope with three delinquent kids. My car is knackered and I need a man to rescue me from my shit life. I am exceptionally nosey and spend too much money on shoes and fags. The photo on here is of my mate who is better looking than I am. I drink too much and I had a restraining order filed against me by my last partner, but we laugh about it now. Oh, and I haven't had a shag in months.'

No, I figured that wouldn't work.

Then there were the profiles that listed what the ladies in question liked doing in their spare time.

'I like nothing better than cosying up in front of a log fire with a good film and an equally good bottle of wine…'

'I like to wander along a moonlit beach and then curl up by a roaring log fire…'

'I like eating out and eating in…'

'I like nothing better than to stay in with a good DVD and a nice glass of red…'

'I like going out and staying in…' Seriously confused, it seemed.

'I love to visit a cosy country pub or walk along a deserted beach under the moonlight…'

'I could debate for hours with the man of my dreams in front of an open log fire…'

'I like to walk along the beach with my dog following happily behind…'

'The man of my dreams, a good DVD, a roaring log fire and a nice glass of

vintage red would be my ideal night in...'

'I like the outdoor life, deserted beaches but snuggling up in front of the fire with a good vintage bottle of wine does it for me too...'

'I love exploring French chateaux...'

'I have an eclectic mix of interests from photography to contemporary ceramics...'

Contemporary ceramics? Well, that's definitely swung it for us guys. What else could we be hoping to find except for someone into fancy, painted pottery. And as for French chateaux, that one was a bit off the wall. Not your everyday hobby unless you live in France.

It seemed there was definitely a common theme running through many of the profiles. Had all these women been brought up on a diet of Mills & Boon? Would I need to invest in a log fire if I wanted to find the ideal relationship? How many homes have roaring log fires these days? And I didn't quite get all the stuff about wandering along deserted beaches in the middle of the night. Not only did that seem like a tall order in the UK where I was more than likely to freeze my nuts off than enjoy a romantic interlude, I also considered that finding a deserted beach was highly unlikely given the possibility they would all be teeming with internet daters. The last time I had been on a beach in the middle of the night was when I was staggering back to my apartment from an Ibiza nightclub in my youth. Not the most romantic experience either.

This was all fantasy. It wasn't real. I had begun to think that perhaps I should update my profile to show that I was tuned in to this romantic whimsy that women seemed to aspire to. How could I be different though and still catch the mood I wondered? How many variations on the theme were there? *I like curling up in front of a glass of red wine with a log fire in my hand whilst watching a good dog and taking a DVD for a walk on the beach.* Or maybe, *curling up in a glass of wine with a red dog on fire whilst nursing a vintage DVD.*

Perhaps I was hallucinating. I had become so engrossed in reading through the profiles that I had forgotten to check the last of the six e-mails messages I had received. I opened it.

'Hi Matthew. I assume that is your real name. I am looking for someone funny, gorgeous, interesting, sociable, intuitive, sensitive and observant. Would you like to chat sometime? Pamela. X'

It was a tall order. Funny, gorgeous and interesting was hard enough but she had a shopping list. I was certainly sociable but was I intuitive? Did I need to be? Wasn't the whole point of the date to find out things about one another, not to do it through extra sensory perception? I wasn't even sure I could claim to be observant having almost walked under that ladder on my last date, much to Linda's alarm. Following my uncertain start to dating again I wasn't confident I could live up to all of Pamela's criteria but we guys have egos so it was a challenge. I clicked on her profile. Long blonde hair, attractive smile and she was on line right now. I took the plunge.

'*Hi Pamela, it's Matthew,*' I typed into the chat screen, *'thanks for your email.'*

Thirty seconds later the computer screen lit up with her response.

'*Hi Matthew. How are you?*'

'*I'm well. Just logged on. Miserable weather here again.*' I was making small talk still unsure of the dating site thing.

A flurry of messages appeared on my screen, one after the other.

'*So, tell me about you? Where do you live? What sort of music do you like? Have you any kids? What do you like doing? What's your favourite food? Have you been married? What do you do for a living? What do you want from this site?*'

Even if I had wanted to answer all her questions I didn't think I could type fast enough to keep up. In fact I was a tad unnerved by them all. If it wasn't for the fact that I quite liked her picture and that she lived just five or six miles away I might have bottled it there and then.

'*Are you a detective?*' I tapped out rather frivolously, trying to lighten the tone and perhaps demonstrate my humour.

'*I am just trying to find outs things about you,*' she responded, somewhat defensively.

'*Oh, I thought I was being interviewed for the position,*' I joked.

'*No. Can you tell me a bit more about yourself? I tend to prefer the simple profiles rather than the CVs, but yours is very basic. You don't give much away.*'

'*Well, I have just joined. I didn't see the sense in writing a whole load of personal stuff straight away. It will all come out eventually.*'

The truth was I wasn't sure about what to 'give away' at all but I wasn't hiding anything either.

'*What are you looking for on here Matthew, casual dating, something more serious, someone to go out with, a family oriented person or a one night stand?*'

I definitely felt I was being interviewed by now. I wondered what the difference was between a family oriented person and a one night stand. Could you not have a one night stand if you chose and still be family orientated? I ignored it.

'*I have no big agenda Pamela. I was just seeing what happens, going with the flow. It's early days yet. If something permanent came up that would be a bonus, of course.*'

I didn't want to sound over eager but none of that sounded convincing.

'*Ok. Well as you don't seem to give away much about yourself just now, ask anything you want about me?*'

That was a killer line. It had the effect of causing my brain to seize up temporarily and my fingers to freeze above the keyboard. I was stumped. I hadn't a clue what to ask. Questions like what are your hobbies, what sort of music do you like, all seemed so dull and lame. It was obviously a woman thing to ask loads of questions, to get to the nitty gritty personal stuff. And, yes, it was like being interviewed. My attempts at humour hadn't made me feel that I had already ticked Pamela's 'funny' criteria box and now I was nose-diving on the interesting option too. I needed to change the subject.

'Look Pamela, why don't we meet for a drink. It's easier face to face and we can find out more that way.'

It was an attempt to save the day. I had plunged in and far more quickly than I had intended.

'I don't actually drink,' she replied, *'do you?'*

'Well I like to go out for a drink with my mates occasionally.'

'Do you? How often?' she quizzed.

'A few times a week.'

'That's quite a lot,' she replied.

I didn't think it was a lot but I tried to play it down.

'Well it's just a social thing. A few quiet beers,' I replied, trying hard to dismiss the images of a typical night out with Cecil.

'Oh, it's just that I am a little wary of drink. My ex was an alcoholic.'

'No, need to worry on that front. As I say it's just a bit of socialising.'

'Ok, let's meet up. It would be nice,' she replied. *'Wednesday night is good for me.'*

'Great,' I typed, *'where would you like to meet?'*

'I live in South West London, near Wimbledon, so if you don't mind coming to me we could meet at Wimbledon Station. Everyone knows where that is so it's a good rendezvous point.'

'No, problem at all,' I replied, *'I am not too far away.'*

We made the arrangements and exchanged mobile numbers. I was suddenly excited about my second venture into the dating game. I resolved to be more open in response to any questions.

7

Wednesday night arrived. Rummaging through my wardrobe I settled on a smart suit as it was the safest bet to make the right impression. It also showed that I had made an effort and wasn't taking the date lightly. Well, at least, that was my thought process. You could never be sure to get it dead right when trying to make a first impression.

I decided to take the train. That way I could relax and have a drink if Pamela wasn't too alcohol adverse and the advantage was that I would also end up at Wimbledon Station without too much effort. It was a fifteen minute walk to the station at a brisk stroll. I had been walking for no more than five minutes when it started to rain. Heavily. After all the effort I had made to look presentable for my date I wasn't going to get soaked now. I decided to call a taxi. As I pushed the buttons on my mobile it suddenly slipped through my wet fingers, bounced on the edge of the kerb and disappeared into the gutter. On any other night it may have just landed on the road and stayed there, but tonight it went straight through the grid of a nearby drain that was struggling to cope with the sudden torrent of water gushing towards it.

'Oh bollocks,' I shouted and then I caught sight of the taxi sign. I practically jumped out in front of it in an effort to attract the driver's attention. Big mistake. The car screeched to a halt right by my feet. In a reflex action I leapt backwards but I was not quick enough to avoid the enormous spray of rainwater that shot up from the tyres and hit me mid thigh, completely soaking the front of my trousers and shoes. The driver didn't seem to notice as he lowered the passenger window and lent across the seat to speak to me. There was nothing that I could say that would have altered the fact that my trousers were now drenched so I left it.

'Wimbledon Station please driver. And I am in a hurry.'

'No problem, boss.'

I jumped into the back seat as quickly as I could to get out of the rain, pulling the door closed behind me. As the door slammed shut the left side of my jacket became trapped firmly between the door edge and the body of the car. Swivelling round on the seat I tried to free it but the door had shut tight against it. Just as I was about to reopen the door the driver put his foot down and accelerated away at speed. The sudden violent movement of the vehicle threw me back into the seat and sideways at the same time. I heard the rip and felt it in the same moment. My suit jacket had torn from top to bottom right along the back seam. It only remained in one piece because the collar was holding the whole thing together. I couldn't believe my luck. I tried to catch the driver's attention to explain what had happened but he had the radio on so loud he couldn't hear a thing. Vigorous tapping on his shoulder was just about to turn into a grip round his throat when he finally responded and turned the radio down.

'I've ripped my jacket in your door,' I said, feeling the pointlessness of my words as they emerged.

'You take it up with big boss, boss.'

As he said it he handed me a business card over his left shoulder. Real Libel Car Services, it said in bold print. An odd name I thought but whatever they were called I'd take the matter up with them later. My immediate concern was to get to my date. I eventually managed to get the driver to slow the cab enough so that I could release the door and free what was left of my jacket. That done, I slumped heavily into my seat trying to peer out of the steamed up glass, hoping my trousers would dry out by the time I reached Pamela in Wimbledon. I'd worry about the jacket when I got there.

Forty minutes later we pulled up.

'There you go boss. Twenty five pounds.'

'Twenty five pounds,' I repeated, 'That's expensive.'

'Petrol boss, that's expensive too,' he replied.

I made a mental note not to use Real Libel Car Services again. Twenty-five pounds seemed excessive for a journey from the other side of Kingston to Wimbledon. I paid up and stepped out into the pouring rain that was still lashing down relentlessly. Looking up to get my bearings I could just make out the silhouette of a large arch in front of me. I peered through the gloom and mist and spotted a sign close by, attached to a lamppost. As I walked forward to get a better look the image became clearer. It was a brown sign with a white border, a prominent arrow pointing upward on its left side with the word 'Wembley' in large bold white letters in the centre. On the right side was a circular logo with an arc. The realisation of where I was came crashing over me with heart sinking clarity. It didn't need the additional sign that announced 'Welcome to Wembley Stadium' to confirm what I now knew. That the cab driver had made an almighty cock up and delivered me some fifteen miles away from where I needed to be. Wembley Stadium. No wonder it had cost twenty-five pounds. I had paid all that money and I was still bloody miles from Wimbledon Station where my date was. I fumbled in my pocket for my mobile, forgetting that it was now winding its way around the London sewerage system.

The rain was relentless, seeping steadily into the collar of my once crisp white cotton shirt and down my neck. Pulling the lapels of what remained of my jacket tight around me and fighting off the wave of alarm that was threatening to take over my reasoning, I trudged off looking for another taxi. Out of the gloom a car appeared. It pulled up next to me.

'You want taxi cab, boss?'

I did want a taxi cab and a fast one at that. I jumped in making it clear where I was going.

'Wimbledon, South...West...London, please. And I am in a hurry.'

Relieved to be out of the rain and on my way, I slumped heavily into the seat. As I did so a sharp, stinging prod to my rear end caused me to recoil almost instantly, pulling me back off the seat to an accompanying, familiar ripping sound. The top of a metal spring was protruding from the seat right underneath me and it had torn half the backside out of my trousers. I stared down at it in disbelief. Well at least I now had matching jacket and trousers although I knew the ripped, distressed look was not meant for suits. Half-heartedly I tried to get the driver's attention but given that my suit jacket was already beyond repair, I decided there was no point. The outfit would have to be ditched anyway. At that point I wanted to call it a night, pack up and go home but I felt bad about letting my date down. I couldn't even let her know where I was without my mobile. I decided to persevere. Perhaps she'd understand. Maybe she would even be impressed by my determination to overcome adversity and get to her no matter what the obstacles. My spirits lifted. Something positive could come of it yet.

I finally got to Wimbledon. The rain was incessant. Thunder was now rolling above me as I stepped out of the mini cab. I looked around for a sign that would indicate which way I should go and that would tell me if I was anywhere near our rendezvous point at the station. People were rushing around, their heads bowed, their pace hastened by the need to get out of the foul weather. Ahead of me I saw a solitary figure standing by the kerb, an umbrella in one hand, the other hand clutching a dog lead, on the other end of which a large Alsatian was sniffing the gutter and straining to get home. No weather to be dog walking, I thought, but I guessed the man would be local and decided to ask directions.

'Excuse me,' I said as I approached, 'could you tell me where the –'

My question was cut short by the cataclysmic crack that fractured the heavens. A sheet of lightening tore across the black night sky illuminating the darkness, in a sudden ear splitting detonation of light and noise. Alarmed out of its wits the dog leapt at me hysterically, as if I were the cause of its sudden terror. The abrupt force of its forward movement caught me totally unawares, its muddy paws trailing down the front of my shirt, propelling me backwards towards the road. I tried to maintain my balance and at the same time push the crazed beast away from me but managed neither. I hit the pavement in a heap. The Alsatian followed immediately behind, landing on top of me in a mass of wet fur and drooling slobber dripping from its open mouth onto my face. For a moment we stared at each other eye ball to eye ball, both man and beast temporarily immobilised by the shock of our predicament. It was the dog that reacted first. A mournful whimper signalled its delayed reaction to its terrifying experience which I now felt as a warm trickle of wet liquid as it peed itself all over my legs. I tried to push it off succeeding only because its owner, who hitherto had displayed the reflexes of a sloth on sleeping pills, finally came to his senses and managed to pull his traumatised pet away from me. It just wasn't to be my night. As I rolled onto my side in an effort to get up I caught sight of a brightly illuminated articulated lorry speeding towards me. There was nothing I could do to avoid the blast of wet sludge that spewed up from each of its four sets of tyres, hitting me full in the face as it cut through the rainwater. Momentarily blinded by the polluted puddle I stretched out a hand to steady myself and almost cut it on what turned out to be a discarded Bacardi Breezer bottle. As I staggered to my feet, soaked, disorientated, my clothes practically shredded and still clutching the bottle, I heard a voice that sounded familiar. Pamela.

'Good Evening, Matthew. You finally made it then, did you? You couldn't even be bothered to turn up on time.' She glanced towards the bottle in my hand. 'And I see you decided to start your night out without me too. You said you liked a drink but I didn't expect to find you rolling around in the gutter like a vagrant. You should be ashamed of yourself, you...you...drunk! How could you do this to me? I have been looking forward to this date. You blokes are all the bloody same.'

With that she turned on her heel and was gone. I slumped back down onto the kerb, too astonished to even notice the Alsatian, a calmer temperament now restored, eagerly licking the rainwater from my face.

I stepped out of the hot shower relieved to be home. A steaming cup of coffee with a shot of brandy was easing my disappointed state of mind at a wasted night. More out of a need to explain myself to Pamela than arrange another date I logged on to the site. She hadn't answered my calls so I thought I would send her an email by way of explanation, even if I knew my predicament would take some explaining. My landline had gone off once but it was just Cecil. He'd left a message for me to see how the date had gone and to find out why I was not picking up my mobile. I am not convinced his concern was totally about how I had got on as he finished the message with his usual question 'Has she got any mates?' I didn't want to get into a Cecil conversation at that point so I decided he could wait until the morning when I would get a replacement mobile.

The site looked busy as I browsed through the profiles. I clicked on Pamela's trying to decide how I should start the email. I couldn't think straight. Perhaps it was tiredness or the fact that I was still pissed off about the misunderstanding of our failed date but I decided I could compose something better by way of explanation in the morning. I was about to shut down the computer and head off to bed when a message flashed up on screen.

'*Hi. Nice picture! Is your real name Matthew?*'

I clicked on the profile. An attractive smile beamed from her picture. She was brunette, thirty-five according to her profile and based in Regents Park, London.

'*Yes it is,*' I typed, '*what's yours?*'

'*Hi Matthew, I am Julia.*'

I hated this first bit, the introductions. I didn't know how to start. I was still learning how to behave on the site. I didn't want to appear too serious or too frivolous and I certainly didn't want to appear desperate, which I wasn't. I wanted to create an impression, capture attention, make myself seem interesting. First impressions and all that. '*Hi Julia, how are you,*' seemed totally unimaginative, but I typed it anyway.

'*I am very well, thank you. How long have you been on the site then, Matthew? I've not seen you before.*'

'*Only just joined really,*' I replied, '*I am one of Cupid's virgins.*'

As I pressed the enter button on that last statement I had a momentary wave of embarrassment. I was trying to be light hearted, humorous. What if she misunderstood me? Would she think I was a perv?

'*Oh, a new boy! Well you look normal, at least! You wouldn't believe how many weirdoes are on this site. Half of them are married, half of them have pictures they took twenty years ago and half of them say they are at least six inches taller and two stone lighter than they turn out to be when you actually meet them! Five feet eleven actually means five feet four, a few extra pounds translates to morbidly obese and a sparkling personality means dull as ditch water.*'

'*That's three halves, Julia,*' I typed, trying another attempt at light hearted banter.

'*Three halves?*'

'*Yes, you can't have three halves. Only two.*'

'*Oh, you are silly, Matthew. But you sound fun. I hope you don't mind me contacting you. I am a little impulsive I know but I am fed up with waiting around for someone who is normal so I just go right on and say Hi now.*'

I wasn't quite sure whether normal was good or bad. I mean, compared with the weirdoes she had referred to it seemed to me that normal was good. On the other hand I didn't want to be too normal. I wanted to have mystery, sex appeal and be, maybe slightly dangerous, in a roguish sort of way. I was going to have to work on my image and profile I reckoned.

'*No problem Julia. I like impulsive,*' I said.

I wasn't particularly impulsive myself and, being naturally wary of internet dating, was unlikely to start being impulsive now. My experiences so far had not done a lot to make me throw caution to the wind, in any case.

'*Great. Matthew, I am going to be even more impulsive and give you my number. I don't give my number out to anyone but there is something about you that makes me feel it is ok. Why don't we chat right now. Ring me.*'

She typed out her mobile number.

What could I say? Maybe I just had to get used to women dishing out their numbers. Maybe that was the way it was now. I could hardly say no, let's be cool and get to know each other. I mean that wouldn't exactly do much for my image. Even I knew that a roguish, dangerous image doesn't include 'let's get to know each other a little first.' I dialled her number.

'Hi Julia. It's Matthew.'

'Hello Matthew. Thith ith fun.'

'Pardon, Julia... are you Welsh?'

'Oh sorry...I think my 'phone is on its way out... it crackles, gets dithtorted...bad interference. I am getting another one soon. Take my land line number and call me back.'

I called the number. We chatted for ages. She sounded great and we seemed to hit it off. She said she was out of town on business until Friday and perhaps we could get in touch when she returned with a view to meeting up at the weekend. It sounded good to me. I was optimistic. I gave her my mobile number.

It had been a long night. I went to bed and slept soundly.

8

I was driving back to the office from a meeting on Friday morning when my new mobile rang. It was Julia again. The conversation that followed was at best fractured.

'Hi Matthew. How…you? Listen…'

'You're breaking up Julia. I'm driving. Bad reception.'

'Can you hear…Matthew? I haven't… long….just going to catch… tube to… later.'

'I can't hear what you are saying, Julia. Your line is not too clear. Is it a bad signal or do you need to change that phone?'

'Hello. Hello...Matthew...still there? Look just listen…am having.......party tonight… my place. I...in Regents Park. It would be lovely……....if.......... fancy.....dress……There will be plenty of drinks… food. My sister is....from … Africa so....an African gorilla ...theme ...plan. I will text the add…Do bring a friend if you like…. got …go……hope you can come.'

'A party? Tonight. Would love to come Julia. I will see what I can dig out. Hello...hello...Julia?'

'Hello. Matthew?.....text details........you later. Bye.'

Mobiles on the move can be highly irritating. The reception wasn't good and Julia's phone was clearly on its last legs anyway but I got the gist. I said I'd be there, just before the mobile cut out totally. Bit short notice for a fancy dress party I thought but maybe that's what being impulsive is all about. Bring a friend too. Right, I thought. I can kill two birds with one stone. Get a date and get Cecil along to meet her mates.

I called Cecil as soon as I got back to the office. 'Ces. It's me, Matt.'

'How you doing, geez? You up for a beer tonight?'

'No, listen Ces. We have a party to go to.'

'A party. Any birdies?'

'There should be. It's a party. Woman I met on the net...she's throwing a party. Tonight. Trouble is it's fancy dress.'

'Fancy dress? What sort?'

'Some sort of African animal theme. She was going on about gorillas and food and loads of drink. Something to do with her sister coming from South Africa. I expect it's because she lives near London Zoo as well and the African connection probably inspired it.'

'London Zoo. Animals. I ain't going to no party like a fucking extra from Jungle Book mate. Fuck the party. Let's go out.'

'Cecil. Look. I want to go. She seems ok. Good looking woman. She's bound to have loads of mates. And based in Regents Park they could all be the sort of attractive women you'd like to meet. I mean for the sake of a few quid at a fancy dress shop it could be a good night out. And you keep asking whether these women have got mates. So here is an opportunity. And I don't know anyone else there so it will be good if you tag along. Don't blow me out on this one.'

'Ok mate. But if it's crap we jump in a fast cab home get changed and go out, right?'

'Sure. No problem. Let's meet about nine o'clock. She is going to text the address and I will text it to you soon as I get it. But make sure you wait for me there before you go in.'

'Ok, mate. Feel the power within the power.'

'Sorry, Ces?'

He'd hung up. Another of Cecil's inspirational sayings that went right over my head.

It was fortunate that I had a fancy dress shop local to me and I knew they could help. I had been there a few times in the past when Olivia and I had wanted outfits for New Year and Halloween events and over the years we got to know the owner. I gave him a call.

'Hi Jim. It's Matt. How are you doing? Business good?'

'Ticking along, Matt. What can I do for you?'

'Look, I know it's short notice but I need a gorilla suit for tonight. Can you sort something out?'

'No problem, my friend, got just the thing. I will have it all ready for you. What time can you get here.'

I told him I would swing by on my way home from work.

At six o'clock that evening I pulled up outside the shop.

'Hi Jim. You got the outfit.'

'Yeah, it's here Matt. Let me show you.' He reached under the counter, pulled out a green canvas bag and began to open it up.

'Don't worry about showing it to me Jim. It will do I am sure.' I reached over to take the bag.

'Hang on Matt, let me show you how to put it on. It's got –'

'Don't worry about that, mate,' I said grabbing the bag and making my way to the door, 'I'm sure it won't take a lot of working out. It's a gorilla outfit right. I have to run. I've left the car outside on the double yellows and I still have to get home, shower and change. Listen, thanks... I owe you.'

There's not a lot of getting ready to do with a gorilla outfit. The body is an all in one jump suit. You simply need somewhere to put your cash and your mobile once the outfit is on. I found an old bum bag I'd bought in Greece about five years before and strapped it over my Calvin Klein's. Underwear was all I would need under the costume, I figured, since it was likely to be hot dressed head to foot in a furry outfit. Next I placed the gorilla head in position on the top of my head and tugged it downwards. It was so tight my skull just about penetrated the opening. I tugged some more wriggling my head from side to side to ease the entry. I managed to get it in to just above my ears when I had to stop for a breather. More wriggling and tugging got it down over my ears, which were now folded downward in a tight stretch against either side of the mask. A final hard tug on both sides and it suddenly dropped down into position, my scalp tight against the skull. Relieved that the whole outfit seemed to fit I took a step back to admire my King Kong look in the mirror. The bumbag left an obvious bulge in the front of the outfit but, hey, I thought, I'm a gorilla. Fearsome. I was ready.

Earlier in the evening I'd called a London taxi cab to ensure there would be no delays and sure enough at precisely the arranged time, 8.15pm, the taxi turned up, the driver hitting the horn to announce his arrival. I was looking forward to the party and eager to get going. One last admiring look in the mirror to check my costume and I was ready to go. It looked cool. I liked it. Another blast from the cab's horn interrupted my moment of self-admiration. I tugged at the gorilla head to remove it for the cab ride. It wouldn't budge. I tried again but it was a very tight fit. I gave it several tugs once more but it wouldn't come off. I started to feel a hot flush developing under the mask and a momentary sense of panic. The taxi honked again. Placing both hands at the back of my neck I tried to force the mask up and over my head. It was still stuck tight. Sweat ran freely down my face. I didn't know if the human head expanded as you got hotter but what I did know at that point was that the gorilla mask now felt a lot snugger than it had when I first put it on. The taxi honked yet again.

I bent forward from the waist, my head almost down by my knees and gripped myself in a half headlock, one arm almost encircling the front of my head, the other doing the same from the back. I tugged hard, rolling my head from side to side in an attempt to corkscrew the mask off. All to no avail, except that the whole gorilla head felt like it had swivelled sideways and I couldn't see. Standing upright again I could feel that all I had succeeded in doing was turning the gorilla head ninety degrees so that it was now facing completely to the left. That wouldn't look right at all. It would look like I was permanently trying to see if I could cross a road if I went out like that. I managed to swivel it back to face the front again, the eyeholes lining up so that I could actually see once more. Another blast from the taxi horn. I decided to try one more time to remove the head and if I couldn't shift it I'd just have to live with it for now. Bending forward at the waist again, I gripped the head in the same double-armed headlock I'd used earlier and tugged for all I was worth. The effort had no real effect on moving the gorilla mask at all but it did cause me to pitch forward so that I collided, face first, with the arm of my sofa. Fortunately the padding in the mask saved me from any injury and the sudden bump made me realise that it was a futile exercise at that very moment. If I did get it off I would still need to get it on again for the party. There wasn't time to worry about it now. Pulling the front door shut, I ran out to the waiting vehicle ignoring the surprised look of the driver.

'Regent's Park please, driver.'

'I coulda guessed mate,' was his mocking reply.

The journey was quick and I spent most of it still trying to loosen up the gorilla head. With the energy I was expending I was becoming hot and exhausted and still it remained firmly in place. Eventually, I decided it was better to stay calm, cool down and not to worry about it until I absolutely had to remove it. Maybe with Cecil's assistance I would get it off later.

The taxi pulled up in Regent's Park a few hundred yards from Julia's street and in plenty of time. I jumped out and walked to the driver's side, pulling out a twenty-pound note from the bum bag to pay the fare. It must have been the lack of sensation in my gorilla fingers that was the cause of my slack grip on the note. As I reached forward to hand over the cash a sudden gust of wind caught it and blew it straight out of my hand. I watched, trance-like for a moment, as it fluttered upwards over the taxi, coming to rest tantalisingly out of reach on the cab roof. I reached forward in a clambering motion at the side of the vehicle, stretching as far as I could across the roof. The note fluttered towards me brushing the middle finger of my right gorilla hand. In desperation I thrust upwards in a leaping motion that took both feet off the ground, simultaneously bringing my left hand down hard onto the cab in an attempt to trap the note against the top of the vehicle. The massive thump against the metal roof reverberated loudly making me realise that I had completely overreacted. The driver was out of his cab in an instant just as another gust of wind lifted the cash again, swirled it into the air and carried it away in a horizontal direction down the middle of the road.

'Oi, what are you doing on my taxi, you mad fuck? Get off my bleedin cab.'

I didn't comprehend the question fully as I was focused on my fast disappearing money. My reflexes kicked in and instinctively I set about chasing after it scattering passers-by, who, seeing a fully grown gorilla running up the street, were reluctant to come to my aid. A couple of times I got close to the wayward note as it dropped towards the ground and, as it lay there enticingly still, I tried to stamp on it to arrest its progress. But each time I got within stepping distance a teasing wisp of air would lift it and carry it further away. The cabbie was shouting after me, now under the impression that I was trying to run off without paying.

I can understand the sight of what appears to be an angry gorilla running down the centre of the road, stopping every now and then to stamp its feet, would alarm most people so I am not surprised that someone made the call. Next thing I knew, from nowhere I was surrounded by armed police. If I hadn't put my hands in the air I'm sure a tranquiliser dart would have ended my night. I think my reaction flummoxed them. Not many real gorillas would put their hands up cowboy style at the sight of armed cops. They were also a little taken aback when I spoke in English, albeit a bit muffled given the tightness of my mask.

'Don't shoot! I'm going to a fancy dress party,' I blurted out. 'Honest.'

A serious looking older man, who turned out to be a senior officer, stepped forward. The cabbie caught up.

'He's tried to leg it without paying his fare officer. And he has vandalised my taxi. Nick him, he's a bloody nutter,' the cabbie said.

Given what he had said I wasn't sure if the cab driver considered it an offence to be a nutter and wanted that lumped in with the other two perceived offences. I ignored him, took a deep breath and began an explanation.

'Look officer, it's not what you think. It's all very simple. I am off to a party, a fancy dress party, which is why I am wearing this outfit. I went to pay my fare but it is very difficult getting the money out of my wallet with this outfit on. I mean look at these fingers. Then the wind blew the cash out of my hand. I wasn't running away, I was just chasing after my money.'

As I spoke a young female officer came up and stood next to the stern looking older policeman.

'Take the mask off sir,' said the senior officer.

'It's not a mask officer. It's part of my gorilla costume.'

'I can see that sir. Just take it off.'

'I can't. It's stuck.'

I saw the female cop stifle a giggle, clearly amused by my costume and the whole ridiculousness of the situation.

'Stuck?' said the senior officer, his head tilting to one side as his left eyebrow rose vertically.

'Yes, I put it on before I left home to see what the outfit was like and I can't get it off. I wouldn't normally ride around in a taxi like this. I was running late.'

'I need you to take it off sir. We need to identify you.'

My protestations appeared not to hold any sway with the senior officer. I knew that eventually I would have to get the mask off anyway. I bent into the position I had been in earlier, gripped the gorilla head with both arms and twisted. I felt the movement but everything went black. I realised I had only managed to twist the head again, this time turning it round a hundred and eighty degrees to face backwards.

Stifled giggles filled my darkness and then I felt someone clasp my head. More twisting and pulling, this time not of my doing. I was dragged from side to side and forwards by the violent tugging, my lack of vision contributing to complete disorientation until I lost my balance and ended up toppling over. Reaching up I managed to swivel the gorilla head back to the face forward position and found myself looking straight into the eyes of the senior officer who was prostrate beneath me.

'I'm really sorry officer. I told you, it's stuck.'

I got back to my feet and offered a hand to the prone copper, pulling him upright.

'There is only one thing for it then, sir, if it's stuck. I am going to have to call the fire brigade,' he said as he brushed down his jacket and placed his peaked cap back on his head.

The female officer was trying desperately not to laugh. Her hand kept brushing her face to hide the fact. 'I don't think there will be any need to call the fire service out, guv. He's legit. A member of the public has just found his money,' she said. 'She picked up a twenty pound note in the gutter over there. So it seems this gentleman is telling the truth.'

The senior officer looked me up and down, his face displaying a moment's indecisiveness. He turned, surveying the line of uniformed officers behind him, their rifles still pointing in my direction.

'This won't look good in the papers tomorrow - armed police arrest gorilla in Regents Park for doing a runner. I would be a laughing stock. It's been a long day already.'

It seemed he was looking for a way out to spare his blushes.

Turning to the female officer he said, 'PC Penny, give this gentleman the benefit of your advice and make sure he understands me and my crew do not want to see him wandering about in the street like some circus act again. If we do he will be arrested for disturbing the peace or wasting police time or whatever I feel is most appropriate for a lunatic running about dressed as King bloody Kong.' With that he wheeled around jumped into his car and was gone.

PC Penny, turned back towards me, looking me up and down.

'Right, sir. You have caused enough commotion for one night. My Sergeant is none too amused about being called away from his desk to deal with a joker in a monkey suit. I suggest you pay the taxi driver and make yourself scarce.'

'Yes, I am really sorry to have caused all this trouble. I didn't mean to–'

'Can you speak up sir, you are very muffled.'

I could see mischief in her eyes. She was clearly amused by my predicament.

'I am sorry Constable. I just can't get this gorilla head off at the moment.'

'I know that. Let me help you,' replied PC Penny moving towards me.

'No... No...I mean...thank you for offering but I am meant to be at a fancy dress party and I am worried if it does come off now, as it's so tight I might not get it back on again and I would look ridiculous turning up to a party in half a costume. You just saw how difficult it is to budge.'

A hint of a smile played around PC Penny's lips. 'You are wandering about in the middle of London, sir, in a gorilla suit and you are worried about looking ridiculous at a party? Ok. I will spare your blushes. I don't need to know what you look like. You haven't committed any offence, despite having put half of London's response team on full alert. Let's just put it down to experience and you can be on your way.'

'Thank you officer...err officer...erm...'

'Penny. Louise Penny.'

It was probably relief at the situation being sorted out fairly easily and no doubt a bigger degree of relief at not having been shot in the first place that caused me to blurt out, 'Pleased to meet you Louise Penny. I am Matthew.'

'Pleased to meet you too Matthew,' she said, fixing her gaze directly on my gorilla head, a smile playing on her lips. 'No doubt I'd recognise you should you have the misfortune to run into me again. Now, I will say goodnight to you.'

'Thank you, office...err...constable... err Louise... thank you...sorry again.' I turned to go.

'Oh, sir, just one more thing. Are you concealing something under that costume?'

'Concealing something, officer? What do you mean?'

'Well I have to be satisfied that you are not a danger to the public, that you are not carrying an offensive weapon. That bulge in the front of your costume. What are you hiding?'

I felt my face turn scarlet even though my embarrassment would not have been obvious under the mask. PC Penny was now looking straight into my gorilla eyes.

'Oh... no...it's not offensive...I mean... it's just a...just a bum bag. I had to have somewhere to put my money. Gorillas don't have pockets.'

'Are you sure that's all you have sir. I mean you have heard of stop and search, haven't you. You realise I can exercise my powers of search.'

Mischief danced in her eyes, a hint of a playful grin again. I couldn't call it and couldn't afford to misinterpret it. After all she was a police officer in full uniform and on official duty.

'Don't worry. That won't be necessary. It's just somewhere for my money. Like I said, a bum bag. It's nothing –'

'It may be nothing to you sir, but I have to satisfy myself that you have nothing offensive in there. You will need to show me.'

I didn't know if she was playing with me or deadly serious.

'You really don't want me to carry out a search now do you sir?' she said.

I opened three of the buttons on the front of the suit to reveal the black bum bag complete with its yellow piping.

'It's just got my cash, mobile and keys in it officer. That's all.' I felt exposed, vulnerable, foolish even.

PC Penny grinned at me again. 'I will take your word for it this time sir. Pay the driver and be on your way. You are free to go...King Kong.'

I did as I was told, handed the taxi driver his cash and set off to look for Cecil.

Approaching Julia's road I spotted Cecil about a hundred yards away. His profile was unmistakeable. As I got nearer I realised he was wearing some sort of orange looking outfit. He was carrying something long under his arm too. I called out to him, mostly so he wouldn't be too surprised at a gorilla approaching on the pavement.

'Cecil. It's me. Matt'.

He turned in the direction of my voice.

'Matt? Matt. Where you been mate? I've been here twenty minutes.' He was peering intently at the spectacle heading towards him.

'Don't ask Ces. I'll tell you later. Let's just get to this bloody party.'

Cecil's intense stare gave way to loud laughter as I got closer. 'Fuck me. What have you come as geezer?'

'What do you mean what have I come as? A gorilla. Can you not tell? African theme? You get it? A gorilla. Isn't it blindingly obvious?' The tension from my earlier encounter was still gripping me. 'More to the point, Ces, what the bloody hell are you?'

'A giraffe,' and with that he produced from under his arm the neck and head of a giraffe.

It was at least four foot tall. I wasn't sure if it was Cecil's little man psyche that had led him to choose one of the tallest outfits you could possibly get into or whether he had gone to great effort and was just being highly imaginative for the party.

'Bloody hell, Ces, that's big.'

'Of course it's big. It's a fucking giraffe, mate. Hang on while I get the head on.'

With that he placed the giraffe neck and head over his own head and it matched up perfectly with the lower part of the costume. The only problem, it seemed to me was its height. Cecil who, at five feet eight inches tall, was usually a good four inches shorter than me, now towered four feet above me. Fortunately there were eye holes at the base of the neck through which, I assumed, he could see enough to be able to negotiate his way.

'What made you pick a giraffe Ces?' I asked mainly to see if I could ascertain his thinking.

'Well, it's African ain't it. And it was the only fucking animal I could get my hands on last thing on a Friday night.'

Oh well, I thought, no one can say we didn't make an effort. We walked the rest of the way to the address and rang the bell.

My first reaction was delight at seeing Julia. My second was total puzzlement as she was in a cocktail dress. Her reaction was slightly different. She screamed and keeled over. Her shriek brought several people out to the door, every one of them dressed in a variety of cocktail dresses and evening wear. Each had a look of utter bewilderment at seeing a full sized gorilla and an even fuller sized giraffe standing on the doorstep. I was not quite sure what Cecil was seeing given the position of the eyeholes but a party to Cecil was a party. Ignoring the gob smacked guests he strode forward into the hallway. 'Let's get a beer mate,' was the last thing I heard him say.

He had remembered to duck his way through the doorframe but the proximity of possible beers and perhaps the restricted sense of his surroundings that the tunnel vision his giraffe head was offering him, temporarily caused Cecil to forget about his newly acquired loftiness. As he stepped purposely forward, the top of the giraffe head hit the ornate pendant light fitting that dominated the centre of the hallway. On contact the whole unit swung upwards, the gold pleated shades and ornate crystal petals hitting the ceiling with a resounding crash. The heavy impact caused the delicate glass and crystal to shatter and fall to the floor in a shower of splinters and fragments of metal. In a swift evasive reaction to the pieces of glass and fragments of bulbs that were cascading about his person, Cecil leapt forward only to connect with the other matching fitting with precisely the same result. Several of the women began screaming in shock as the debris fell around them. Most of the men stood stock still, frozen on the spot by indecisiveness and utter bewilderment as the chaos unfolded in front of them. In an instant I knew our party was over.

I sprung forward and grabbed Cecil by the arm dragging him back through the wreckage of Julia's hallway towards the door. I wondered why all of the guests were reaching for their wallets and purses and throwing them towards us as I pulled Cecil to the exit past a clearly distraught Julia, who had managed to regain her feet but looked as though she wouldn't be staying upright for long. In the urgency of the moment Cecil forgot to duck as we reached the doorway. His giraffe neck caught the wooden frame and bent backwards at right angles as I tried to pull him through. The impact caused him to lose control of his legs, which were now trying to take him in the opposite direction to his upper body, and he almost keeled over on his back in the hallway. If I hadn't had hold of his arm he almost certainly would have done. To ensure he got out in one piece I jumped behind him, grabbed the neck section and pulled it back even further so that it was bent in the middle with the head pointing to the floor. I then managed to shove him through the door with the aid of my right foot in the small of his back. Once out I legged it up the road dragging Cecil with me.

Cecil wasn't happy. 'What the fuck are you doing geezer? You almost pulled my fucking head off. And the party hasn't even kicked off yet? Have you not seen the birdies? Let's go back. Their insurance will cover the damage.'

'Cecil, in case you didn't notice, firstly it wasn't a fancy dress party, secondly the guests all think we are muggers and will be calling the police this very second and thirdly we are now wandering the streets like two escapees from the zoo and, even you must agree, we are both highly visible and identifiable. So as for going back to the party, that's not happening Cecil.'

It was night over. We flagged down one of those illegal, dodgy cabs that roam the streets of London looking for desperate customers. The driver didn't seem to bat an eyelid at the two peculiarly attired passengers. He probably just wanted the fare, no questions asked. On the way I tried to tell Cecil about my earlier run in with the police but he just laughed at me.

'Mate. Let's get out of this stupid gear and go and get a beer somewhere proper.'

'Not me Ces, I've had enough excitement for one night already. Can you help me get this bloody ape head off before I boil up.'

'Just pull it off geezer–'

'I can't pull the stupid thing off Ces. It's stuck and now it's starting to choke me. God knows how I got the friggin thing over my head in the first place. Give me a hand.'

I bent my head forward towards Cecil and he tugged at the head with exactly the same outcome as before. It wouldn't move.

'See I told you Ces, I am going to have to cut it off when I get home or walk around for the rest of my life like an extra from Planet of the Apes.'

'Hold it geezer. Stop the panic. Turn round.'

I turned so that I was facing away from Cecil and felt his hand delving into the fur at the back of my neck.

'Thought so. You twat. There's a fucking zip.'

I dropped Cecil off at his place and made my own way back home. As I struggled out of the rest of the monkey outfit I noticed the flashing red light on the answering machine. I hit the 'play' button and waited. New message, at 1.35pm.

'*Hi Matthew. Impulsive Julia here again. I thought I'd leave you this message in case it wasn't clear when we spoke earlier. My mobile is definitely on its way out. Anyway, what I wanted to say was that I'm having a cocktail party tonight at my place. I live in Regent's Park. It would be lovely if you could come along, if you fancy it. The address I can text to you later. There will be plenty of drinks and food. My sister is over from South Africa so an African grill or a barbecue seems to be the plan. As I say I will text the address. Do come and bring a friend if you like. Would be so good if you can make it.*'

I flopped down on the sofa. A cocktail party. A bloody cocktail party. It suddenly dawned on me. An African grill, whatever the hell that was. A grill. Not a gorilla. Not a gorilla at all. She'd never mentioned gorillas. It wasn't even fancy dress. I felt like a total moron. Why hadn't I listened to the message before I went out especially after the garbled mobile call. I was usually so systematic. Normally I would double check if I wasn't sure. I had let myself get carried away with the prospect of the party. Julia's impulsiveness must have been catching.

9

The following day as soon as I woke up the anxiety hit me. The evening had been a total catastrophe. The sounds of screaming, shouting and breaking glass filled my head and I had to know what had happened. I picked up the phone and dialled Julia. I tried to sound nonchalant and breezy. She didn't.

'Hi Julia. How did the party go? So sorry I couldn't make it…err…something came up.'

'It was a disaster Matthew. We were burgled by–'

'Burgled,' I interrupted, in what sounded like a voice a couple of octaves higher than my normal range.

'Yes, burgled, mugged. Call it what you like. Thugs. Robbers. They burst in. Demanding my guests' money. Threatened us and…and...and trashed the place.'

'Sorry, Julia? Calm down. They did what? Burst in?'

'Yes, Matthew, burst in…and...trashed the whole place. Destroyed my light fittings. Robbed us.'

Even with the benefit of the viewpoint that I had experienced on the night I still thought this account of what actually took place was a little hysterical. I waited until she had calmed down a little.

'Are you sure they demanded money Julia? Did they take anything?'

'No, it all happened so fast. My guests gave them their valuables and wallets but they just ran off after wrecking the place. They must have been high on drugs. I called the police and they are on the look out.'

'You did what? Called the police? Did you have to call them?'

'Well of course I did Matthew. They were robbing us.'

'Err…did you get a description, Julia…you know...for the police?'

'I did, yes. But they were in disguise. It was obviously a well planned robbery.'

'Disguise?' I questioned, trying not to let the anxiety creeping into my voice betray my concern.

'Yes. Disguise. Like animals. One was dressed as a gorilla and the other was a giraffe...or an antelope or something.'

'Are you certain?' I replied trying to take in what she was saying.

'Don't be bloody stupid Matthew. Of course I am certain. I know what a gorilla and a giraffe or an antelope look like.'

I ignored the fact that Julia's inability to distinguish clearly between a giraffe and an antelope could be construed as an indication of her lack of certainty.

'No, I meant, are you sure they were robbers? I mean it seems odd to break in somewhere and then, when people are giving you their valuables, to run away without taking anything.'

'Well they must have panicked or something. I don't know. It was horrible,' she said her voice beginning to crack.

I didn't want to push it too hard but I had to know where I stood. 'And you have told the police all this Julia? About the disguise?'

'Yes,' she sniffed.

'Well, they should have no trouble finding them then. And you told them it was a robbery but they didn't take anything. The police may not think it's a robbery if nothing was taken.'

'Of course it was a robbery, Matthew. They just burst in. Why else would they turn up at my cocktail party in disguise? They obviously didn't want to be recognised. They must have been watching my guests arrive and decided to attack us, wreck my house and steal our valuables.'

I was beginning to be unnerved by Julia's spin on the whole unfortunate event. I decided not to pursue the matter further as I was not convinced Julia was in the frame of mind to apply logic. Even if I had pointed out that it is highly unlikely that a couple of opportunist muggers would be walking around with wild animal disguises at the ready in case they saw some rich pickings, Julia's perception of what had actually happened was unlikely to change. Of more immediate concern to me now was the fact that she had involved the police, particularly as I had already had the encounter with them on my way to the party.

'Look, Julia, I am really sorry that this has happened. I do have to go now. Something has come up. I expect you will be busy with the police anyway. I will call you.'

As soon as I came off the phone I called Jim at the fancy dress shop.

'Jim, I can't explain now but if anyone enquires about the gorilla suit that I picked up last night you know nothing. I will drop it back shortly.'

Jim was nothing if not discreet.

'Don't worry mate. I hadn't booked it out officially anyway as it was so last minute. You know how it is, a bit of cash in hand always comes in handy. How did you get on anyway. The outfit all right? Did you find the zip? Everyone has trouble with that.'

The zip. I'd forgotten about the zip such was my alarm at Julia's account. I ignored the question.

'Yeah, great thanks Jim, but, you know, not a word about the outfit, ok?'

My next call was to Cecil. I gave him a quick low down on Julia's flight of fantasy.

'Stupid bitch,' was Cecil's summary. 'So the old bill are now on the lookout for a gorilla and a giraffe in Central London.' He was laughing aloud.

'Ces…it's not funny. You don't seem to realise, if they check on fancy dress shops in London and then trace your outfit back to you, at the very least we will face a charge of, I don't know, criminal damage or something or intent to rob or whatever they call it and on top of all that my cover will be blown with Julia and another potential date goes down the pan.'

'Geezer, are you having a foam bath? You still want a date with a bird who cocks up her own party invite and then gets herself in a hysterical state over a robbery that never happened. Are you sure? I would stay well clear of her. She's off her trolley, mate.'

'You're right Ces. Maybe I should for a while. But what about that incident I had with the police? It won't take long for them to put two and two together. I mean there can't have been too many blokes dressed as gorillas in precisely the same vicinity last night. I am in deep shit.'

'Take it easy mate. First of all did the police get your details?'

'No, I–'

'Did they get a proper look at you?'

'No…no, they didn't…I had the gorilla head on.'

'Ok. So no details and no description. So –'

'Hang on Cecil.' My one error suddenly dawned on me. 'I introduced myself to the policewoman.'

'You did what? Are you fucking nuts? You don't say nuthin to Old Bill. And you decide to introduce yourself. Where did you think you were? The fucking Royal Variety Performance?'

I had to stop Cecil before he went off on one. 'Ces. Ces. All I said was that I was Matthew. I mean she introduced herself to me. It just came out. That was all I said. Just my first name. Nothing else.'

'You sure you didn't flash your passport at her too? Ok. Look. All she knows is some mug called Matthew was wandering about in Regents Park dressed as a gorilla. If she wanted full details she would have got them. And all that dopey bird at the party has got is that one of the so called robbers was dressed as a gorilla. She's got no description either. So what have the Old Bill got? Nothing except two sightings of a gorilla in Regents Park. And guess what mate? You ain't done anything either. You ain't committed an offence. So she had her bloody lights busted. That's an accident. By the time she's calmed down she will realise the Old Bill have got nothing to go on, they will lose interest and she has to claim on her insurance. Mind you I'd like to see the insurance company report. Two chandeliers busted by a runaway giraffe.'

'But Ces, I just thought, Julia, knows my name is Matthew.'

'Who's Julia?' Cecil asked.

'The woman who's party it was, Ces. From the dating site. I told you that. She invited me.'

'Yeah, I was thinking. Look. That don't matter. Her complaint to the Old Bill is that two muggers broke in, right? Dressed as animals. Why would she even think of you when she is focussed on two muggers? She is not going to assume that her date thought he'd dress up as a gorilla and decided to rob her as a surprise, is she? I mean you have just spoken to her anyway, and she told you what happened. It'll all blow over geezer. No crime's been committed. Yeah, definitely an insurance job. Old Bill won't even be interested.'

There was some sense in Cecil's thinking. He had a point. Maybe it would all calm down once they all realised the futility of searching for one or even two people in gorilla suits. But what about Cecil's incriminating giraffe outfit.

'Ok Ces, maybe you are right. But what about the giraffe suit? How are we going to sort out your outfit? It's a direct link to us.'

'Calm down mate. It's not a problem. I didn't get it from a fancy dress shop. There was no time,' he said.

'You didn't?' I said, hoping that, even worse, he hadn't stolen it.

'No, mate. It was in my loft. You remember when my sister worked for that theatre company that went bust? Well, she had a load of stuff off the costume designers and the giraffe outfit was with it. I remembered it. You didn't think I was going to spend good beer money on an outfit for some dumb arsed party that was always gonna be shit anyway, did you?'

'No...err, no of course not Cecil. Good thinking.' I felt a momentary wave of gratitude towards him.

'And listen mate. When you take your outfit back do yourself a favour. Slip the geezer a little *how are ya* and he will keep his mouth shut too.'

As soon as I came off the telephone to Cecil I drove down to the fancy dress shop with my gorilla suit completely concealed in the green canvas bag and my own appearance obscured by dark glasses and a baseball hat. When he had finished laughing at my predicament Jim assured me that he would get the suit back in storage and no one would ever know it had been out of the shop. 'After all, mate,' he said, 'one gorilla looks pretty much like another and there are loads of shops in London who stock them. Your secret is safe.'

A twenty-pound tip helped seal the deal.

I spent the rest of the day quietly, pottering around the house, trying to do normal things that people do on a Saturday afternoon. Since I'd split with my wife I had gradually got back into certain domestic routines despite the odd riotous night out with Cecil. I needed a bit of fresh air so decided I'd give the lawn what surely must be its last cut of the year. It was a tedious job but it had to be done. And anyway I thought it would take my mind off the party fiasco. It was a small lawn so it took me thirty minutes. I piled the cuttings into two black bin liners and took them to the end of the garden. There were three bags there already from the last time I'd cut the grass. I was only putting off the inevitable trip to the recycling centre so I took all five bags and stashed them in the boot of the car. Might as well get the job done now, I thought. My good intentions were interrupted by the shrill of my mobile. It was Cecil.

'Did you get it sorted mate?' he asked.

'Yeah, no problem, Ces. Jim's cool and I think the little tip helped.'

'Told you, geezer. You should listen to your mate Cecil a bit more,' he said. 'So, what you doing tonight? Fancy a few liveners in town?'

I didn't fancy any liveners at all. I actually fancied a quiet night in. I'd had enough excitement for one night and risked Cecil's disapproval by declining his invitation. I went back in the house and put the kettle on. May as well chill for the rest of the day. I'd do the recycling in the morning.

I was feeling a little more at ease now that I knew that both fancy dress outfits were safely tucked away. My thoughts turned back to Julia. Maybe I should give this a break. I'm not having much luck on the dating site. Maybe it's not meant to be. I logged on. I was half intending to delete my profile and cease my membership but I had almost another three weeks of it left to go. My mind was in turmoil. If I deleted myself then I could go back to normal dating, meeting women in bars. But then I hadn't had much luck there mainly, I reckoned, because I usually went out with Cecil and evenings with him tended to get messy. On top of which when we did meet women I didn't usually get a word in edgeways as Cecil was usually in full flow with his brand of chat up lines. The trouble with him was that he was a mine of information. He had a retentive memory and knew something about everything because of it. His modus operandi in the chat up game was to bombard the lady in question with a barrage of facts as soon as any subject came up at all. The effect of this was to leave the hapless lady in question either with a glazed look that suggested she had lost the will to live and was contemplating hanging herself, or a look combining total bemusement and astonishment. Neither of these looks gave me the impression that Cecil's chat up was going to result in anything other than the object of his attention going off to call a psychiatrist to treat her newly created condition or to help Cecil unravel the complexities of his psyche. Certainly the path to true love or even unbridled lust was not being smoothed by his techniques. Consequently, our evenings out usually ended up in a gin fuelled mess in some expensive bar at 5am in the morning, with no women and Cecil and I wondering where it had all gone wrong. I wasn't ready to go back to that just yet.

Having just turned thirty it was blindingly clear to me that Cecil was not yet ready to relinquish the party lifestyle whereas I had now had my fill of it. It could only go on for so long and perhaps it had now served its purpose for me. Approaching forty, I could see the need to move on. So, while I still had the alternative lifeline of the dating site I reckoned that perhaps I should cling to that until at least my membership expired. It was the festive season in a few weeks anyway and things could only get better I reasoned.

With a newfound optimism I rejected the idea of deleting my profile and started to browse the site again. There were loads of potential contacts. All shapes and sizes. Some of the profiles were quite detailed with all the personal attributes filled in. Others were a little more flimsy in the information given. I quickly realised that someone who had declared their height as five feet two inches but had not filled in the *'what do you weigh'* box, which now read *'not given'*, may not in real life have matched my idea of the perfect woman I had visualised in my head. I decided to ignore the *'weight not given'* profiles. I had an idea of my type. Yes, I liked blondes, preferably tall, hopefully with a sense of humour, sexy too, maybe even with a bit of a naughty streak. If I could get that package then it would be all worthwhile. Wishful thinking maybe. I couldn't really go on a dating site and be that precise as it seemed likely, from the brief knowledge I had gained so far, that I would be narrowing the potential candidates down to about ten people. I realised that to take that approach would be reducing my chances of finding a date to almost insignificant odds. I decided to be open-minded and go with the flow.

10

A photograph caught my eye. Her username was 'Sexyblueeyes'. The name conjured up something alluring. I took a look. Her details were all complete: 5ft 8in, 9st 7lbs, thirty-eight years old, brunette and, of course, blue eyes. I clicked on her photograph. I was getting used to the more elaborate photos the ones posed with cars, dogs and cats and even dolphins and the ones riding elephants and camels. Of course everyone was trying to sell themselves but a picture riding an elephant in some remote part of India was not really telling me anything about their real life in Chelmsford. Everyone was trying to make themselves much more interesting than they really were which made me wonder why I had uploaded a picture of myself which would have barely been accepted as a passport photograph. I let the thought go and watched as 'Sexyblueeyes' picture appeared on the screen. It was only a facial one so we had something in common. I risked an opening line.

'*Hello, how's life treating you on here?*' I typed, rather unimaginatively.

'*Helloooooo to you too. God, there are some cretins on here,*' was the reply.

It crossed my mind that I may have inadvertently joined the rank of cretinism with my uninspired approach but I persevered.

'*Really. Well it takes all sorts I suppose. What's happened?*'

'*Nothing has happened. That's just it! And some of the chat up lines are so corny!*'

I was glad I had stuck to a straightforward conversational tone rather than risk a smart arsed chat up at that point. '*So no luck then with the dating game,*' I ventured.

'*Oh no. I've been on loads of dates. I don't believe in hanging about. But there are so many weirdoes on here.*'

'*Well, I am not too weird,*' I said, hoping that my response didn't sound as weird as it felt the moment I'd pressed the 'enter' key.

'*Oh present company excepted!*' she typed, '*I do like your picture. You don't look weird at all. Lol.*'

Encouraged by the fact that I didn't look weird I became a little more adventurous. '*And I do like your picture too. Have you got sexy blue eyes in real life?*'

'*Of course! Even better in the flesh!*'

At that point the conversation started to get a little flirtier. I was enjoying it. It was light hearted, no pressure. None of the 'interview' questions. Her approach was relaxed and humorous. '*Make me laugh, Matthew, and you are halfway there,*' she typed.

I wasn't sure where halfway there was and I wasn't going to ask at this point but it sounded appealing. We spent the next couple of hours chatting on line. Her name was Sally. At almost midnight she finally said goodnight, saying she would be back on tomorrow.

I woke up in a good frame of mind. I popped out for breakfast and stopped off at MacFadden's bar for a coffee on the way back home. Carlos was behind the bar as usual but thankfully Cecil was nowhere to be seen. When I got back home I logged on. Sexyblueeyes Sally was on line.

'*Hi Sally,*' I typed, '*how's things?*'

We continued our internet exchange for nearly an hour. Then we moved onto mobile numbers and a proper chat. The subject of a date came up. I was keen. She suggested a meeting, Tuesday or Wednesday.

'Tuesday will be fine. Lunch maybe? Where would you like to meet?' I asked.

'Well, Matthew. I am really keen on history. It is a passion of mine and, well...there is actually an exhibition I would really like to go to. Do you know Lord Rufus Hemmingwell?'

I hesitated for a moment. 'I can't say I do to be honest.'

'I don't mean personally but you must have heard of him. He is always in the papers. A peer or something. He owns Hemmingwell Halls in Sussex.'

I still hadn't heard of him but I pretended I'd seen him in the papers.

'Well, he has one of the largest private collections of armour in Europe and–'

'Armour?' I interrupted, 'Armour as in knights and jousting and that sort of thing or tanks and artillery?' I wasn't sure where this was leading as we had been discussing a date. I then found out we were still discussing a date.

'Yes, armour for knights and soldiers. He has this fantastic collection of body armour, gauntlets, swords, shields and chainmail. Most of it medieval and the thing is he has opened it to the public earlier this year for only the second time in the last twenty-five years. I'd really, really love to see it again. We could meet at Hemmingwell Halls and then find a nice quiet country pub for a late lunch. What do you say Matthew?'

The first thing I said was, 'Again? See it again?'

'I meant in real life. I have been looking online,' she said hesitantly. 'It would be so good to see it. I know it is not the usual place for a date but at least we'd have something to do. And if we didn't hit it off at least we could focus on the exhibition…all that armour. It is very interactive too. So much to explore.'

I was beginning to wonder whether it was going to be a date or a history lesson. I'd envisaged a nice wine bar, a few relaxing glasses of wine and a long lunch. An armour exhibition didn't seem like a bundle of laughs for a Tuesday afternoon. But I liked her picture and in view of my recent date experiences this seemed positively sedate.

'Ok. Hemmingwell Halls it is then.'

'Good. I will meet you in the exhibition at two o'clock. I will be wearing my favourite yellow jacket, the one in my picture, so you can't miss me.'

I got to work earlier than usual on the Tuesday and finished just before midday. I made some excuse about a family commitment that I couldn't get out of that afternoon. The last thing I wanted was my work colleagues knowing I was on a dating site. I had looked up the location of Hemmingwell Halls on their website that morning and bought a ticket on-line. I estimated that the journey should take me about ninety minutes in the car. My work suit seemed presentable enough for a lunchtime date.

There wasn't a great deal of traffic on the road that day and it wasn't long before I saw the signs directing me to Hemmingwell Halls. I turned off the main road and onto a minor country road that took me to a tree lined driveway that eventually opened out into a spacious gravel car park enclosed on three sides by farmland. It was already over half full with cars and at least three coaches. People were making their way to a brick arched gateway that was marked 'House and Grounds.' I had arrived about half an hour early and since I already had my ticket I thought I might as well kill time by having a quick look around to see what it was all about. I had no real interest in history but I figured if I familiarised myself with some of the exhibits I could surprise my date with my knowledge and a few well-chosen comments. I followed the crowd, through the arch into an open courtyard. To one side a gift shop was proudly displaying the usual array of postcards, books, pictures and homemade jams. On the other side a small office jutted out from the main building where our tickets were checked. The assistant stamped them with the date and said that they would have to be shown again in the main house. From the courtyard another pathway led up through the trees out into a clearing where the main house that was Hemmingwell Halls stood in full view to my right.

Hemmingwell Halls was a truly impressive building. A typical English stately home set in ornate landscaped gardens. Rectangular in shape with two extended wings on either side of the main structure, the building had rows of high windows along both storeys and a row of dormer windows set into the roof. The front of the house was dominated by a projecting porch supported by two sturdy columns. It had a low pyramid roof that proudly displayed what must have been the family coat of arms as its centrepiece. The grounds at the front were split by a long gravel drive that led to a broad stone stairwell, set deep into a grassy bank. At the top of the steps a stone balustrade ran parallel to the honey coloured facade of the building as far as the eye could see. From the top step rows of slabs formed a wide Yorkstone path that took the visitor straight to the columned entrance and a large oak panelled door, which was fully open.

I started to walk towards the house, every step making a satisfying crunch on the golden gravel of a semi-circular pathway that curved around to merge with the central driveway. I climbed the steps and stopped for a moment to take in the view. All around me the landscape was perfectly formed with beautifully manicured lawns edged with wide borders filled with a vibrant display of winter flowers and shrubs that strained to catch the watery November sun. Mature oaks and tall pines helped to break the vastness of the terrain that lay beyond the gardens. I was no horticultural expert but even my untrained eye could appreciate the planning and care that had gone into the remarkable vista that lay before me.

I made my way to the front entrance and walked in. Ahead of me was a sign pointing the way to the armouries exhibition. I paused to take in my surroundings. The main entrance hallway, its highly polished marble floor glinting under the lights, had several rooms leading off from it in all directions. In the centre of the rear wall a fine ornate staircase rose on both sides to the first floor, its wrought iron balustrade embellished with intricate metal carving and engraving. The walls were lined with family portraits ascending with the incline of the stairs towards a high vaulted ceiling rising above the top floor. It was certainly a most unusual venue for a date but I was beginning to think that the house might be worth the trip alone.

The hallway was rapidly filling with visitors as I walked towards the armouries sign. An improvised ticket check had been set up, a velvet rope barrier with brass fixings stopping the eager public gaining access without their credentials being checked again by a security man in a navy uniform. I took my place in the fast forming queue. My ticket was checked and the stub removed. Once past the rope barrier there was a short wood panelled corridor, its walls lined with a series of paintings depicting mediaeval battle scenes, which led to the main exhibition room.

I wasn't really prepared for the enormity of the exhibition room. It was huge. A soaring ceiling of intricate geometrical patterns, edged by ornate mouldings painted in fine gold leaf and lapis lazuli. To be honest I didn't know it was lapis lazuli at all until I overheard a much more informed visitor explaining the architecture to her companion. Before that I just thought it was painted blue and gold. Enormous wood panelled walls, hung with colourful tapestries, bordered the room on three sides. On the fourth side the main exterior wall was punctuated with three tall, rectangular round headed windows each framed with long red Venetian damask curtains. The whole effect was one of opulent regal splendour.

If the overall presentation of the room was impressive what it housed was even more eye catching. Divided up into six raised platform sections, three each on either side of a central walkway, a dazzling display of body armour, weaponry and regalia covered the whole of the vast floor area. Each of the platforms was further divided by a smaller walkway that allowed viewing access, with a blue rope barrier surrounded each unit. Full suits of armour gleamed under the shimmering spotlights that picked them out in all their majesty. Rows of fighting equipment, shields, swords and lances stood resplendent under the lights. Another section displayed metal breastplates, chainmail, gauntlets, visors and helmets of all shapes and sizes. At the front of the room, standing as if to engender a sense of grandeur and stateliness in the visitor, the exhibits were introduced by a row of heraldic flags, standards and pennants each presenting a multitude of different crests, insignia and coats of arms. A truly inspiring display that filled the mind with a sense of history, power and chivalry.

The room was filling slowly and was already quite crowded. They must all be tourists I thought. No one else could be here for a date. I wandered along the central aisle between the exhibits. Up close they were even more impressive. Rows of helmets with fascinating names - pig-faced helmet, barbute combat helmet. Full faced helmets with visors or partial face coverings with central t-slots. Metal gauntlets that stretched along the forearm with leather hand and finger interiors. Long chain mail shirts, with matching hoods to protect the head. Steel leg protectors, called greaves that covered the leg from ankle to knee. Most impressive of all were the suits of armour. Three of the display areas at the back of the room were totally given over to full-length complete sets of body armour. Like a phalanx of soldiers they stood polished and gleaming in the spotlights. There must have been sixty separate items, an image of power and force, all with full face helmets, heavy shoulder protection, breastplates and leg irons. The most eye catching were a mixture of steel and bronze, the golden glow of the bronze emphasising the central breastplates and the jointed areas of the arms and leg fronts.

In the short space of time I had been in the main exhibition area it had filled up quite quickly. Most of my attention was now on the exhibits but I was still mindful of keeping an eye out for my date in her yellow jacket. And then I spotted her. Well I assumed it was her as I spotted the bright yellow jacket immediately but the person wearing it bore very little resemblance to Sexyblueeyes Sally at all. She was still some way off in the crowd so I had to do a double take. It was definitely that jacket from the picture but the woman wearing it had to be almost sixty years old. It said thirty-eight on her profile. I don't mind a bit of poetic license with a woman's age and could almost expect it but this was more than license. This was bordering on a full blown liberty. She hadn't seen me yet because of the tourists and as she got closer I could see some vague resemblance to her on-line photograph but more in the way you can see a resemblance between a mother and her daughter. I considered for a moment that Sally may have bottled the date at the last minute and sent her mother instead.

Whether it was the unsuccessful dating experiences I had had so far or whether it was a sudden attack of sheer cowardice that I knew would prevent me from telling her straight what I thought, I don't know, but I panicked. I decided I was bailing out. Standing her up. It wouldn't matter too much. She liked it here I reasoned. She'd said as much. She'd have her history for the afternoon and I'd have my sanity. I'd been out of the dating loop too long to think rationally about what was the best way of extricating oneself from a date I didn't fancy and no immediate solution was springing to mind. Bailing out seemed the only option. My mind was racing as I tried to justify my intention. She had misrepresented herself. That was not fair. I couldn't take the risk of ending up stuck with someone I didn't want to be with all afternoon. On the other hand I didn't want to hurt her feelings. It made sense not to go through with it, for both our sakes. It was entirely her fault anyway. My mind was made up.

I knew I couldn't get past her as she approached without her spotting me, not even in the melee of tourists. I backed off a little and found myself almost at the very end of the room with the two most extreme display sections of armour on either side of me. I stood still for a moment, thinking. There were five or six people in front of me but all facing away. Over their shoulders I could see Sally's distinct yellow jacket looming larger.

My next decision was probably an impulse one, inspired by the fact that each of the display items was free standing and not encased in cabinets. I sidled across to my right, stepping over the blue rope barrier and onto the raised platform until I was in amongst the display. Since each suit of armour was roughly the same height as an adult, I reasoned that I could hide amongst it until Sexyblueeyes sidled past. Then I'd slip out from my hiding place and, frankly, leg it.

She was approaching now and seemed to be with two elderly ladies, who I assumed to be tourists. They were walking slowly towards my position, chatting animatedly as Sally pointed at the exhibits. She was obviously giving them the benefit of her historical knowledge. Every now and then they would stop to admire different pieces. I was feeling more than a little unnerved standing amongst the armour not knowing if I was fully concealed but hoping that I may see an opportunity to slip away when they were not looking my way. No such opportunity arose. They moved nearer, slowing down, pausing again in front of particular exhibits that caught their attention. I began to feel cornered.

Any escape route I had considered was slowly being blocked off as they got closer. I could hear them chattering. Sally's new companions were American. I thought again about just taking advantage of the fact that she was distracted, in full flow with her tourist companions and just striding boldly past to freedom. But I remained transfixed, rooted to the spot by the dilemma of my making.

As they got closer I could see Sally's features more clearly. She was definitely a lot older than she had portrayed herself and the lashings of pale powder caked onto her face did not do a tremendous job of concealing her age. In fact it made her look even more dated. If I was feeling any pangs of conscience about deciding to bail out of the date, the visual impact of Sally's deception only served to overcome those feelings of guilt and reinforce my desire to get out of there. But how was I to do it, I wondered, without a full on confrontation. Maybe I could have dodged past them without her noticing who I was. But I'd lost my nerve. I decided that I definitely couldn't risk just stepping out from amidst the exhibits and being seen. That would just look dumb now. My reaction to my growing confusion about what to do was to back away further until I found myself at the back of the display with pretty much nowhere to go. And then I spotted the hinges on the back of one of the steel suits that was closest to the walkway.

I know it was stupid but I couldn't help myself. Feeling the urge to hide completely, I eased open the back of the armour. It was all one piece from the shoulder to the base of the spine. It was only a matter of stepping in. With a hand either side of the waist, I raised one leg and slid it into the metal casing that formed the leg protection. It slid in easily, all the way down to the foot. I then lowered my head beneath the shoulder plates and eased it up into the cavity that formed the mask that was the face protection. Then it was simply a matter of stepping in with the other leg and I was inside the armour, my left arm sliding almost naturally into place into the left sided gauntlet. It was obviously some sort of special exhibit to have the hinged back. With my free right hand I pulled it to and then slipped my arm down into the right gauntlet. I was now facing the front and totally encased in the heavy metal exhibit, unable to move but with no intention of going anywhere. I'd just stay there until my date had seen enough and moved on. Narrow slits in the facemask gave me just enough of a gap to see through but only straight ahead. I had no real peripheral vision. Sounds from outside were muffled but I could at least hear. The inside of the suit smelt metallic and musty. How did people go into battle encumbered with this lot let alone ride horses in it? More to the point, what the hell was I now doing inside it? I started to realise the enormity of my decision. I was inside but how was I to get back out? I stood stock still, not that I had much choice given the rigidity of my confined space, and tried to collect my thoughts.

Sexyblueeyes and her new American friends were getting closer, close enough for me to hear their muffled voices. They were in the aisle that ran between the rear wall and the very last display platform. Then they stopped.

Right beside me. I felt my heart pounding. I imagined it could be heard all over the gallery. It was hot and dusty inside the suit. There were beads of sweat trickling down my face. I wasn't sure if my perspiration was induced by the heat or by unbridled fear at my predicament.

Something light and feathery dangled down onto my nose. It felt suspiciously like a cobweb. There was not much I could do other than stand in my rigid state. The cobweb like thing brushed over my mouth and nose again, its movement caused by my breathing. It tickled. I felt the urge to scratch my face and brush it away. But I couldn't. I couldn't really raise a gauntleted hand up to a metal mask and achieve the required satisfaction of getting rid of the irritating article. I was sure I felt the spider who owned the dangling material crawl across my brow but I realised it was just some more beads of sweat. I had to stay calm.

'Isn't this armour wonderful,' drawled one of the American women, reaching out a hand to touch the breastplate of my suit.

My instinct was to recoil but I managed to stay put.

'They are so life like.'

Her hand was now stroking the helmet visor. Sexyblueeyes was looking directly at the mask, inches from where I was. I practically had eye contact with her from where I was standing. Close enough to see that whilst her eyes were indeed blue, I didn't at that moment consider them at all sexy. Her proximity was unnerving me. I could even smell her perfume. I was convinced she knew I was in there. But she couldn't possibly know that. I tried to stay calm. Tried to keep my breathing under control. The cobweb fluttered over my nose again causing it to tingle. Please do not let me sneeze, God, I prayed. I can't sneeze. I mustn't. My eyes began to water. The dust and the cobweb causing the irritation. I was wet with sweat now.

'Would your boyfriend mind if we toured around the gallery with you?' one of the tourists asked. 'You English must know so much about all this stuff and it would be such fun to be guided by a genuine English couple.'

Boyfriend! Couple! God, what had she told them?

'What time did you say he was coming?'

'Oh he is a little late. You know what boyfriends can be like,' I heard Sexyblueeyes reply.

The word boyfriend was beginning to worry me. It hadn't taken her long.

I felt the sneeze building up. A tickling sensation that made the inside of my nose prickle as if thousands of tiny needles were being prodded into me. I tried to ignore it but the sensation was getting too much. I had to stifle it. I stuck out my bottom lip and blew upwards towards my nose. A warm breath of air fluttered the cobweb. I couldn't blow too hard for fear that the sound would be heard. The warm air temporarily eased the sneeze sensation. I did it again. Staring straight ahead and concentrating on stifling my impending sneeze. The sweat ran freely down my face. My hands were clammy in the gauntlets. My shirt was now glued in a sticky sensation to my back. I blew some more. I had to stay calm. How long were these women going to stay there? Sexyblueeyes was at that moment out of my line of vision. Maybe she was moving on and her companions would follow her. I hoped so and focused on controlling my sneeze. I blew upwards again.

I should have thought of it. Obviously I had not been thinking clearly at all up to that point. And it happened. My mobile went off in my pocket. Four loud rings that echoed through the armour sending a jolt of disbelief to my brain. I heard myself shout, 'Shit! Shit!' The two American women were staring aghast at the armour. They were beckoning to their left as if calling someone over just as my answer phone kicked in.

'Hi Matthew. It's Sally. Sexyblueeyes. Where are you? I am–'

Horror, panic, alarm and disbelief all hit me in one swoop. The effect caused an involuntary spasm to course right through me. I instinctively made a grab for my mobile. In my confined and restricted garb this sudden move only caused the armour to keel off balance to the right. It all seemed to take an age to happen as if time had suddenly been stretched. But there was nothing I could do to stop it. As I toppled I caught a fleeting glimpse of Sexyblueeyes, her mobile still clasped to her ear, her mouth wide open in astonishment. My suit of armour crashed sideways hitting its immediate neighbour. It in turn went the same way catching another exhibit to the side, which then clipped another one slightly to its rear. The process escalated, a domino effect of crunching, crashing iron suits each smashing against its neighbour in a deafening surge of noise and metallic collision.

Pandemonium ensued. There were screams, shouts and, most worryingly of all, the shrill high-pitched whine of an alarm siren. Shit…I am in big trouble now, I thought. I could hear the sound of people starting to run and staff ushering them to the exit, trying to control the chaos. I had ended up on my back amongst the pile of exhibits, some half on top of my prone body. In an effort to get up I rolled onto my front and rammed my elbow against the hinged back of the armour. It wobbled but remained shut. I hit it again, this time harder, wincing at the jolt of the hard metal against my elbow. Another wobble but it didn't budge. Dread and fear started to take hold. Fear of being trapped or fear of being caught, I didn't know which but my main thought was to extricate myself from the pile on the floor and get the hell out of there. From my face down position I could hear that the room was still in uproar. I pushed my right arm forward as far as it would go into the gauntlet and jerked it back hard. The sickening crunch of my elbow against the heavy metal sent a searing spear of pain right to my fingertips but the impact had the desired effect. The back flew open on its hinges and crashed loudly to one side. Manoeuvring myself backside first from the armour I pushed back with my outstretched arms until my lower half was sticking in the air. This gave me enough scope to draw my knees up towards my chest and bring my shoulders and head in line with the opening. Gradually getting to a kneeling position, I was eventually able to free my head from the metallic encasement, the cool air giving me a moment's relief on my sweat soaked face.

From a kneeling position I took in my surroundings. It was bedlam. People running towards a fire exit on the external windowed wall of the building were now held up as they arrived at the same narrow point at the same time. All around me a pile of shiny suits of armour were lying in heaps, some appearing to be in a final embrace, others splayed out like corpses on a mediaeval battlefield. I didn't have time to take in the enormity of what I had done. Despite being on the verge of panic myself I quickly realised I had to take advantage of the madness around me and use it to make my own escape. I got to my feet, picked my way through the debris and jumped into the crowd. My heart gave a momentary lurch as I caught a glimpse of the whirring motion of a CCTV camera pointing at the exit. Head lowered, I merged into the mass of bodies squeezing towards the escape door, now just another sightseer trying to get out of the building. The alarms were screeching, their high-pitched distressing wail continuously adding to the sense of unease and disquiet amongst the throng. Slowly but surely the security staff steered us into an orderly procession from the building, down several stone steps and into a courtyard at the side of the house. We were then marshalled into an organised gathering in the appointed emergency assembly area. There were several relieved looking faces in the crowd but most of them still looked completely bewildered. I didn't feel any relief at all, only an increasing sense of trepidation at what was to come.

The Head of Security approached us. He explained very calmly what was happening, that they needed to check the building and that although we could not return to the exhibition, access to the rest of the building would be possible once they were satisfied that it was safe. In the meantime he asked us all to remain in the assembly area. There was no way I was staying. My instinct told me to get as far away as possible not least of all because I knew I was the cause of the mayhem that had occurred but also because the longer I stood in the crowd the more likely I was to run into Sexyblueeyes. And that could not happen. If it did she might put two and two together with the phone call she had made and I was dead meat.

The crowd wandered about, chattering amongst themselves in that anxious but relieved manner that people have when they have survived a shared calamitous experience. Their focus on their perceived near miss was my cue to sidle off slowly. I had not gone more than two yards when I heard a yelp behind me. I turned and found myself face to face with one of the American ladies that had been chatting to Sexyblueeyes Sally.

'You stood on my foot,' she said

'Oh...did I? I am so sorry. I didn't see you. Are you ok?' I had been slinking away backwards trying to keep my eyes on the security staff.

'That's all right, young man, I am fine. Are you ok?' She paused for a moment looking at my lower body. 'Have you hurt yourself?'

I hadn't realised I was clutching my right elbow to my side, seemingly unaware of the pain but sub- consciously protecting what felt like a tender area following my escape attempts from the armour.

'Oh, yes. I am ok. Just a bruise, I think. Bashed it as we were trying to get out.'

'And your clothes. You have torn your trousers and they are all covered in dust. Are you sure you are ok?' she asked, inspecting me from head to foot.

'No, honestly, I am fine. I tripped, as we were all trying to get out…on the steps. Bit of a panic, eh?' I said, smiling in an attempt to lighten her concerned mood. 'How about you, are you ok?' I wished I hadn't asked.

'Well, I seem to have lost my sister with all that commotion. There are so many people here. You haven't seen her have you? She was with an English lady in a bright yellow jacket. She should be easy to spot and they might still be together.'

'A yellow jacket? Err...no...no...I haven't seen anyone like that at all.'

'Oh, perhaps you'd be a gentleman and help me find her then. You English guys have so much class and are so helpful. And we can't go anywhere just yet anyway.'

That's all I needed. Some American tourist who thought all English guys were like Prince Charles. She was probably wondering why I wasn't wearing a bowler hat and carrying a brolly. And the last thing I needed was to help her look for the very woman I was trying to avoid.

'I can't...I can't help you look. I'm…err…I'm…blind.' I had no idea why I said that. It just came out as a logical reason for being unable to look for something.

'Blind? Oh dear, I am sorry. That is probably why you stood on my foot. Maybe I should help you then. These crowds must make it very difficult for you.'

'Colour blind...I mean. I'm not blind blind...err...as in...blind. Just, you know…colour blind. I would be no use to you. I wouldn't be able to see anyone in a yellow jacket at all. I mean, I wouldn't actually be able to see a yellow jacket. Or any colour jacket for that matter. So I couldn't possibly help if Sexyblue…I mean, your sister's friend...was wearing anything in colour...or anybody was in colour.'

She was looking at me strangely now, mouth open as if to say something.

'So, I must go and find my dog. My blind dog…that helps me... err...get about...sorry, I have to go.'

'Your dog is blind too? You poor thing.'

I was about to reply when the flash of yellow caught my peripheral vision. Turning to my right I saw the familiar yellow jacket in the distance. Sexyblueeyes Sally, her back to me at that point, was wandering through the crowd. Next to her was the other elderly American lady.

'Err, no…not blind. I mean…a guide…a guide dog. I have to go.'

'Excuse me, young man. You have a guide dog for colour blindness? That is unusual. We don't have those back home,' said the American lady, a look of astonishment enlarging her furrowed eyes.

The yellow jacket was getting closer. I wasn't even looking at my new American acquaintance now.

'Yes. He helps me get about…in colour. You know…err sniffs colours out…err…so I can distinguish things…like traffic lights and…and…well, you know…things.'

The yellow jacket was now only yards away on the edge of a throng of people all waiting to be given some direction.

I started to back away. 'But he is hopeless with clothes. He can't do clothes…clothes colours. I can't take him clothes shopping. I had better go find him. Sorry…I have to go. Nice to have met you.'

It was her face that got to me. Her astonishment turned to a bewildered, lost look. I knew I wasn't thinking straight. Sexyblueeyes was closing in. I was already bordering on panic following the incident and the possibility of running into my abandoned date was just getting me more flustered. But even so I couldn't just desert a lost and disorientated old lady. I put an arm around her shoulder and wheeled her around on her heels to face in her sister's direction.

'Look why don't you start looking over there. There may be somebody who can help you in that crowd of people. You never know.'

I gave her a gentle push in the back to set her on her way and sidled slowly away. When I was clear of the crowd I legged it towards the car park.

11

I got home and poured myself a brandy. I didn't usually drink brandy and especially not on a Tuesday but I needed a quick hit to calm me down. I had visions of the authorities rapping at my door and being charged with vandalism. I tried to be rational. There were loads of people in the exhibition this afternoon. The chaos had happened so quickly not one of the visitors or staff could have seen what happened. Nobody had mentioned anything as we were being shepherded out and not one of the staff had said anything either. Sure I had noticed a CCTV camera but that was pointed at the exit. Maybe, they'd assume it was just an accident caused by the vibrations of such a large crowd. I knew I was clutching at straws but I was trying to comfort myself by coming up with a rational explanation for a suit of armour moving all by itself.

The brandy was sinking in. A second glass and I began to calm down. I now had the rest of the afternoon off. I fired up the computer and logged onto the Sky News website. I wanted to see if there was anything at all about what had happened at Hemmingwell Halls. There was nothing of course. It was hardly newsworthy in the big scheme of things. I poured a third brandy and sat down in an armchair. I'd chill for a while and not worry. If anything was to happen I guess I'd soon here about it.

I logged on next to Cupids Pursuit . I don't know if I was becoming addicted to the possibility that someone may have contacted me but I found myself drawn to logging on. I also had a slight desire to see if there was any come back from Sally even though it had only been a couple of hours since the incident.

I had one new email. From LegalLady. It said she liked my profile. It said she liked my picture. It asked what a '*good looking guy like you*' is doing on a dating site. It said she was in the legal profession, something I could have guessed from her username. It asked if I would like to chat with her. I clicked on her picture. I was taken aback. She looked gorgeous. Blonde hair, pale blue eyes and a knockout smile. I was mesmerized. There was something sensual about her look. I couldn't put my finger on it but it clearly had hit a deep basic sub-conscious area of my psyche. There were two more pictures. One was a full-length one. A classic black dress and killer heels. She exuded sex appeal and that was just in the picture. I fancied her already. And she had contacted me. I started writing a reply. I wanted to be cool. Take it in my stride but I wanted to get it right. I guess I wanted to impress. I took a sip of my brandy. Take my time. Don't be uncool. Remember she had contacted me. I was off the blocks already. I thanked her for the email. I thanked her for her compliment but didn't answer why I was on the site mainly because I wasn't so sure I knew that myself. I told her I had only just joined. And I said that '*chatting would be good.*' A total understatement but I was still trying to be cool in a very uncool way. I hit the send button. Five minutes later she was on line.

'*Hello. Thank you for your email. So, you are a new boy then?*'

'*Hello to you too. Yes, still feeling my way about.*' I typed rather cautiously.

'*So what are you doing on here in the afternoon? Are you working?*'

'*I have the day off,*' I said, which was now true after my earlier misfortune.

'*And you?*'

'*I have just finished a very long court case and I should be writing a report but I have promised myself an afternoon off for so long that now I have the opportunity I am going to take it.* '

'*What do you do?*' I asked, probably unnecessarily.

'*I buy shoes! On my afternoons off. No, I am a solicitor. All very dull really. Look, why don't you call me and we can chat more easily. My name is Diana.*'

She typed out her number.

I was gobsmacked. I couldn't believe my luck. This gorgeous lady had offered me her number. I told her my name and called. She had an educated, elegant voice, cool and sexy. The sort that should really be on a sex chat line.

'I am surprised that you are on a dating site. You must meet plenty of people in your circles,' I enquired tentatively.

'Oh I do. But they are mostly wankers. Up their own arses frankly. And I don't get an awful lot of free time with my work hence I joined this little community.'

There was a hint of fun and teasing in her voice. I was surprised at her vernacular but it excited me to hear an educated lady use such base language.

'So what brings you here Matthew?'

Critical question I thought. And asked by a lawyer. People are questioned by lawyers all the time. And they know they are possibly going to be ensnared by their reply. But what made it worse was that in this case I fancied her already and I wanted to get it right.

'No agenda really, Diana. Just seeing what happens. No sense in having high expectations as you could get disappointed. So I am going with the flow and if something serious comes up that will be a bonus.'

I'd started the sentence without having a clue where it would end up. The truth was I had no idea why I was on the site. I kind of knew what I wanted to happen but it was what I wanted to happen in real life too. I couldn't really say I joined the site because my mate Cecil thinks it is a great way to 'do more birds.'

'Perfectly sensible approach Matthew. I think I will like you. Now, look. I hope you won't think I am being forward but I don't believe in endless emails, telephone calls and texts. We clearly both want to meet someone eventually, otherwise we would not be on the site. I have a very busy professional life, as no doubt you do, so I like to get to the point. And the point here is that I would like to meet with you. For a date.'

I tried to contain my enthusiasm. 'I'd like that Diana.'

'Excellent Matthew. How about dinner on Friday?'

I was going to say, in an effort to remain nonchalant that I would check my diary but Diana had been so direct and appeared not to want to beat about the bush that I agreed immediately.

'Friday at 8.15pm then. I know a lovely little restaurant in Knightsbridge. I will text you the details…if you want me to?'

There was laughter in her voice. I was only too eager and I think she sensed it. We finished the call. I couldn't believe it. I was excited by her. She was direct and knew what she wanted. My mood was buoyant, looking forward to Friday.

It was brought back to reality with a bump. Sexyblueeyes Sally was the bump. My mobile rang and I made the mistake of answering it.

'What happened to you? You stood me up.'

My mind raced, looking for a plausible explanation. I found myself saying that I hadn't stood her up. That there was some sort of commotion at Hemmingwell and they wouldn't let me in.

'Well, luckily you were late. There was a terrorist incident and–'

'A terrorist incident? Terrorist? What do you mean?'

'There was some sort of explosion in the exhibition room. They evacuated everyone and–'

'Explosion. No, it wasn't an explosion.'

'How do you know that, Matthew?'

Good question, I thought. How did I know that?

'I don't actually know, but it would have been on the news, if there'd been an explosion, wouldn't it?' I said

'There may be a news blackout. MI5 could be involved. You don't know. There were police everywhere,' Sally answered.

I hoped that Sally's view of 'police everywhere' was simply a product of her seemingly imaginative take on the incident.

'Did they say anything… all these police?'

'They were asking questions. Lots of questions before they let us leave. Anyway, you were fortunate not to get caught up in it but shame about our date. I was looking forward to it. Shall we rearrange, let's say for Friday? How about Friday?'

'I can't Sally. I am going to...Scotland,' I lied, 'To Scotland...for a month... unfortunately...for work. Big problems up there with my...my company.'

'Oh, that is disappointing Matthew. Well, perhaps when you get back then.'

'Yes. When I get back.'

As I ended the call I hoped that a month's absence would kill Sally's enthusiasm, that by that time I would no longer be on the site and maybe, if things went well I'd be seeing someone – like Diana.

On Thursday morning I got a call from Cecil at work. He wanted to know if I was up for going out on Friday night. I told him I couldn't. That I had a date with Diana.

'I gotcha mate. I set you up on a dating site and the next thing I know you are blowing your mates out. Who is this Diana anyway?'

I explained all about Diana. He could tell from my voice that I was enthusiastic.

'You sound a bit keen mate. Don't go rushing in. You've only been on the site two minutes. Any other mumbles?'

Reluctant as I was because I could guess his response, I had to tell him about the disastrous Hemmingwell Halls date. It was more to do with getting it off my chest than anything else. I waited for the reaction. He was reasonable for once.

'Look mate. Chill about it. It's one of them things. An accident. That's all. Could be anything kicked it off in their book. One of the exhibits wasn't fixed down properly. The motorway is only a few miles west of that area, isn't it? They'll put it down to vibration or something. No-one spotted you did they? If they had someone would have come forward by now and said they saw some nutter tampering with the exhibits. Just use your fucking head in future. If you don't fancy the bird just tell her right up front instead of getting yourself into a load of hassle. You gotta laugh though, geezer. Henry VIII's full army and you take them out single-handed. Give me a shout Saturday and we'll catch up for a beer then.'

Friday came all too slowly. I stood in front of the mirror that morning. Had I cracked it? A great opportunity. The sort of date I was looking for. Professional lady, good job, clearly educated, independent, stylish and you know what they say about these blue stocking intellectual types...sexy too. Well, to be honest I wasn't sure anyone said that at all. Perhaps it was my own lurid fantasy. Whatever the case I wanted to make a good impression. Dress to impress, clean cut and suave. I decided the hairstyle needed a bit of an update. I didn't have a regular barber and in fact I actually didn't go to a barber anymore. It was usually one of those unisex hair salons. The type of place where they do an interview with you before you have your haircut and where they give you a cup of coffee that you never ever get the chance to drink; there are usually far more female customers than male customers and you feel just a tiny bit weird being in there because you are a bloke. I had seen an advertisement in the local rag for a new place in town called Kutzville. I called and got an appointment for one thirty. It was close to my workplace and I knew I could nip out during lunch.

I pitched up five minutes early. The place was all mirrors and piped music half drowned out by the sound of whirring hairdryers. A white tiled floor, strewn with the remnants of numerous human heads, was being swept apathetically by what looked like a very bored apprentice. On both sides of the room, their hair a mass of tin foil and clips, rows of women sat in high leather chairs either reading magazines or chatting to the assistants. A low ceiling, painted brilliant white and housing far more spotlights than were necessary for normal illumination, completed a clinical effect, making the room seem more like a laboratory than a salon.

I moved towards the reception desk where a young girl with heavily made up eyes checked my appointment.

'Kaylee's free,' she said, 'she's one of our senior stylists. Is that ok for you?'

I nodded, not really knowing whether Kaylee was ok for me at all or whether in fact a stylist was what my hair required. The receptionist took my nod as agreement and showed me to a seat. Looking around as I sat there, I realised I was the only male in the salon. I thumbed through a magazine, not seeing what was on the pages and a slightly nervous feeling in my stomach. I wasn't sure why. Probably out of my comfort zone.

Within five minutes an assistant approached me.

'Hi I'm Kaylee. I am your stylist today.'

Kaylee was about eighteen, fresh faced with a perfect complexion and dark hair tied back severely. Her youthful looks left me wondering how she had gotten to be a 'senior.' She led me to her station deeper into the salon and sat me in front of a tall mirror. She flicked at my hair with one hand, her head tilted to the side as she scrutinised it. Next she started pulling it up through her index and middle fingers, feeling its texture, letting it flop back down again and repeating the whole thing several times. I was beginning to wonder if this was some new holistic approach to hairdressing that dispensed with the need for equipment for the sake of the environment, when she stopped what she was doing and asked my mirror image if it would like a drink. I fancied a coffee and, with a wave of her hand she sent the broom wielding apprentice off to fetch it. Maybe that's why she was a senior, I thought, because she could order even younger girls around.

Presumably now satisfied that I had hair worth cutting, Kaylee sat down next to me and asked me what I wanted done today. Now that I was in the chair I had no idea what I wanted done at all. In fact whenever I go to have my hair cut I have no idea what I want so I always end up saying what I always say, 'err, just a trim and a tidy up will be fine,' when really I want to come out of there with hair like David Beckham and attitude like Dizzy Rascal. So, I asked for the trim and the tidy up. The very badly disguised roll of the eyes from Kaylee was a dead giveaway that her heart had sunk with disappointment at my desire for a trim and now she was not going to get the opportunity to test her creative side on my noggin.

My coffee duly arrived but just as I had finished stirring in the sugar and was about to take a sip, Kaylee promptly whisked me away saying 'let's get you washed.' I wondered if this was something to do with the preparation for my haircut or whether indeed my after-shave was not to her liking and her sensitive nose had deduced that I personally needed a full hose down. I needn't have worried. Or maybe I should have. Yet another assistant appeared with a long black gown that went on back to front and tied up at the back.

'This is Leanne,' Kaylee said, 'She'll look after you and I'll see you when you are done.'

Leanne was just as young as Kaylee but with short, bleached blonde spiky hair, dark eyebrows that contrasted dramatically, bright red lips, the lower one spiked by a silver ring and the proud owner of a pair of very prominent breasts. Between her bright red lips I could see a piece of gum doing some sort of tango in her mouth. She sat me down at a sink that was actually located very inconveniently behind me. That meant I had to tilt my head back at such an acute angle that I could have swallowed Excalibur without it cutting a sinew. The view I now had was of her upside down chest. She then turned on the water and tipped it over my head.

'Is that temperature OK for you, Sir?' she asked.

It occurred to me that there had to be a better way of finding out if the temperature was ok rather than by testing it on my head first. I gave an involuntary yelp by way of response but I would have thought that the skin now practically blistering on my scalp would have given her some indication that perhaps the temperature was a tad too hot at that stage. But, no, Leanne's awareness levels were not that attuned and perhaps the fact that she was also checking herself in the mirror opposite to see how fast she could chew her gum, prevented her from actually using her eyes to see how her customer was reacting to her attempt to parboil his head. As a result I had to direct her, in a voice that was somewhere between a screech and an attempt to suck in vast quantities of oxygen, to add a little more cold water. Her philosophy must have been that the customer is always right because the water then went from Vesuvius molten to Antarctic Ice Cap freezing in a nano-second. My reflex reaction to the massive temperature change was to grip the sides of the seat so hard that she must have heard the wood splintering. As a result she suddenly realised her client was clearly not comfortable and she managed to adjust the two extremes of temperature to a much more tolerable cool. I certainly didn't want to be turning up for my date with a blistered head.

With my hair finally washed and my ordeal over, Leanne led me back to Kaylee's station and the leather chair in front of the tall mirror. Kaylee sat me down and once again, ran her fingers through my hair, examining it closely. She stared at me in the mirror for a moment, a quizzical look crossing her features. I thought she was about to try to persuade me to have a Mohican or some other outrageous style that would not be at all suitable, such was her expression.

'Are you alright, Sir?' she asked, 'You look very red.'

I told her I was fine. I didn't feel like telling her that she too would look red if she had just been through Leanne's hair washing technique.

'Must be the temperature in here,' she said, 'it can get very warm under all these ceiling lights.'

She then gripped my wet hair between her fingers, and began to clip it enthusiastically at a pace that made me wonder what the rush was.

'Are you doing anything nice this afternoon, Sir?' she said as she clipped.

My honest reply might have been that I would be visiting casualty immediately after my haircut to see if they could graft some skin back onto my scalp but I settled for a less confrontational answer since my upper body was covered with the gown with no arms and she was in possession of a very sharp pair of scissors.

She continued to cut at the same furious pace. The hair wafted down and settled on my nose making me feel the need to brush it away. However with my hands now undercover that was not possible. Nor was it possible to reach out and pick up the tantalisingly close cup of coffee that was still where I had left it and which I was beginning to get emotional about. Emotional because I realised that that cup of coffee, which had been made especially for me and was within touching distance, would never reach my possession.

Kaylee finished the haircut and picked up a mirror. Holding it behind me she said, 'How's that?'

I wondered for a moment if my head now resembled a cricket ball given her choice of words and the earlier scalding.

'It's fine, thank you,' I said.

I always say that. I mean it's only ever the back of my head. I worry that if one day someone creates the Bayeux Tapestry on my head I will still say it's fine.

'Do you put anything on your hair in the mornings, Sir?'

The word '*anything*' confused me. Did she mean a blancmange? A copy of the Washington Post? And why in the mornings? My failure to react inspired her further.

'Products. Hair products…do you use any, Sir?'

'Oh, yes. Products. Yes...yes, I do,' I said hesitantly, not wishing to appear dim.

'And what do you use?'

'Well, I use...you know... stuff. Stuff for your...well, for your hair. Like... err...shampoo.'

It appeared that my lack of hair product knowledge was just what she needed to hear.

'Well today I am going to use these. This one will thicken your shaft and–'

'Will do what?' I asked, a little taken aback.

'The hair shaft, Sir. Gives it more volume and texture, strengthens it, making your hair look thicker. Then I will put some wax on to give it shape and hold.'

This she did after blowing all the wayward hair off my face with what felt like an aircraft engine.

'There you are Sir. You should do that every morning.'

Doing that every morning not only meant I would have to buy a hair dryer with a Rolls Royce motor but also seemed like an incredibly long palaver. I then made a silly mistake.

'I don't have those products,' I said.

'You can buy them here, Sir,' was Kaylee's instant retort, 'I'll pop them in a bag for you.'

It sounded very helpful but I was now wondering what had happened to 'would you like to buy some, Sir?'

Kaylee beckoned me to follow her to the till. My debit card was poised.

'Oh and you will need the shampoo too Sir.'

'The...shampoo?'

'Yes. The special shampoo that goes with the products.'

Special shampoo. I wondered what could be special about it but I bought it. I paid. Seventy-two quid. I was gobsmacked. I had only had a trim but I didn't want to make a fuss. After all, there were all these women in there who probably thought nothing of spending two hundred quid just to have their hair looked at. They'd probably expect to pay the seventy-two quid for the coffee alone, that they never get to drink. It wasn't until I went back out on the street and looked at my receipt that I realised where it had all gone wrong. Thirty pounds for the haircut and forty-two for the products. The products cost more than my haircut, which was ironic since I left with less hair than I went in with and a stack load of products to treat what was left. I hoped that Diana would notice the seventy-two pounds benefit and the rest I would put down to experience.

12

I spent the afternoon willing the clock to go around faster. I don't think I did any useful work. My mind was occupied with the evening ahead and the anticipation of a new romance. I mentally prepared my outfit and thought about how I'd get there. Should I drive? Or maybe get a train and a tube to Knightsbridge.

At five o'clock I was out of the office in my car and heading home. I was no more than fifty yards from home when I felt the tyre burst. A bloody puncture. I limped the car the rest of the way home and onto my driveway. No time to worry about that now, I'd change it in the morning. My travelling decision had been solved for me. I'd get a train and a tube tonight. At least then I could relax and have a glass of wine or two. I called up the journey planner for London on the internet. A train from Kingston then two tube journeys, one on the Victoria Line and another on the Piccadilly Line. It looked a bit more complicated than I had thought. I decided a taxi would be a better option. Yellow Pages gave me no end of local options but each one I called was fully booked. It was almost six o'clock and I still had to get ready. Concern began to creep over me. I had to be on time. I had to make the right first impression. I flicked through the directory more hurriedly realising there were no more local cab firms left for me to call and cursing myself for not booking something earlier in the day. The only option left was the train again. I raced up the stairs to my bedroom pulling off my shirt as I ran. A fast track shower and I would be on my way. It was then that I spotted the mini cab card the one I had thrown on the bedside table when I emptied the pockets of my wet clothes, after my disaster date with Pamela. I had completely forgotten about Real Libel Car Services. I called them.

'Is that err...Real...Libel Car Services,' I enquired, as the controller, with his casual telephone response of 'Yo boss,' hadn't really confirmed that I had rung the correct number.

'Yes, it's Real Libel Car Services, boss,' he said.
'But, don't you mean reliable?' I asked, checking the card again
'That's what I say boss,' he said.
'Oh, you are Reliable,' I said.
'Thank you, boss. Very nice of you to say.'
'No, I meant...look your card says... real...libel–'
'Yes, boss, that's right, Real Libel. You can rely on us. You want cab?'

I did want a cab and didn't see there was anything more to be gained by discussing the nuances of the English language any further. They had a car available and, it turned out, the company was local. I gave him my address, details of my precise location and was promised a car for ten past seven. Feeling slightly more relaxed at having secured transport I showered, shaved and got dressed. A Paul Smith grey micro check suit with a black open neck shirt, a subtle hint of Acqua Di Parma fragrance, black leather shoes shined and buffed. I tugged at my shirt cuffs so that the cufflinks just peeped beneath the jacket sleeves. One final mirror check from several different angles to boost my confidence and I was ready. Nervous, but ready for my date with the delicious Diana. A quick gin and tonic would ease the initial nerves as I waited for the cab.

Ten past seven came and went. No taxi. I waited another ten minutes and rang Real Libel enquiring as to the whereabouts of their driver. The controller informed me that the driver had got lost. I asked him what he meant by lost. I mean we are talking about a suburban town in which the cab company was based, not the Amazon Jungle.

'Your road is not on his satnav, boss,' he replied, 'but he will be there in five minutes.'

I live in a new road. I'd told them that. I'd also told them exactly where it was. I'd given them exact directions including local landmarks and seeing as how Real Libel Cars were based less than half a mile from me I considered that being on time was not too much to expect. Another fifteen minutes went by and the cab still hadn't turned up. I rang the office back.

'My cab still hasn't turned up? Is your driver still lost? Have you reported him as a missing person yet?'

Anxiety was creeping through me. It was now seven thirty-five and I had less than one hour to get from Kingston to Knightsbridge.

'There is no need to be like that boss,' came the defensive response, 'he will be there any minute.'

'Well any minute is not what I asked for. The minute I actually asked for, which you said you could do, was the tenth minute past seven. It is now almost the fortieth minute past seven and you say he will be here any minute. Did you have any particular minute in mind?'

I would have cancelled at that point but having waited this long I had no choice. Searching around for another cab on a Friday night, as I had already discovered, was not an option. I decided to hang on a bit longer. The minutes slipped by. At each sound of a car engine I ran to the door. My anxiety levels were increasing. If I was late Diana may not wait. It wouldn't be good to be late. I went outside to check how flat my car tyre was, thinking that maybe I could get it to a garage and get some air into it so I could drive. I felt it in the dark. Flat as a pancake. Down on its rim. No chance.

Finally after another ten minute wait the cab rolled up. It was now forty minutes late and it only had one headlight. I was fuming. I got into the passenger seat. The whole vehicle smelt of cigarette smoke.

I stated the obvious. 'You are late.'

'Sorry boss. It was not on the satnav.'

'Yes, I know it isn't on the satnav. I already told your controller that when I booked earlier on. In fact I explained exactly how to get here, told him all the landmarks on the incredibly difficult half mile journey you have from your office to my house. And you still roll up forty minutes late.'

'It not my fault boss, it was not on the satnav.'

'Look, you are a cab driver, right? So, as a cab driver, the one thing you need to do is know where you are going. That's all. At the very least you have to know an area a half a mile around you. But you think a satnav is going to do it for you. That's why you are forty minutes late. Because you think your satnav drives the car. So, it is your fault... and if you don't mind and you are sure you, or even your satnav, can find your way to Knightsbridge can we go now?'

We drove off. He switched the radio on. It was a foreign music radio station. To say it was dull was putting it mildly. I wasn't sure if it was some sort of funeral dirge but it certainly wasn't helping my mood.

'Can you turn the radio off, please,' I said as politely as my mood would allow.

'I like this song, boss,' was his reply.

Like that song. It wasn't even what might pass as fitting the category of song. There were no words. It was just some sort of cacophony of instruments competing to see which could make the loudest wailing noise. I did need him to turn it off or I had the distinct feeling I may end up throwing myself from a speeding cab. I took a deep breath.

'Well, since I am the customer and I am paying for the wonderful privilege of sitting in your sumptuous Real Libel limousine with its one headlight, I just thought that perhaps it might be quite good if you were to consider my wishes.'

'Sorry boss?'

I realised that this was not an apology. He just didn't get sarcasm. I tried the less subtle approach.

'Can you turn the radio off.'

'I like this song, boss.'

'Look it's not a song. I wouldn't even call it a tune. Perhaps it isn't either.

Perhaps your radio is malfunctioning. Whatever it is, I'd prefer it if we could turn off the noise and get a bloody move on seeing as how you have already made me forty minutes late and I am supposed to be in Knightsbridge at 8.15, which seems highly unlikely at this stage unless this vehicle, which is masquerading as a taxi, suddenly develops wings. Understand?'

I was not sure which bit of my exasperated sentence had the desired effect but he promptly reached forward and turned off the wailing. I sat in silence. Until we hit the queue of traffic. It was bumper to bumper.

'Do you not know any back roads,' I asked. 'There are short cuts. I will show you.'

'I follow the satnav, boss.'

By now it was too late to get out of the traffic and take another turning.

'Go into the bus lane then,' I said, 'it's clear.'

'No, boss, I get nicked by police.'

'No you won't. It's almost ten past eight. The bus lane stops at seven o'clock. See...four pm to seven pm it says on the road signs. You do read road signs don't you? I mean, if you are a qualified driver then you will have learnt to read road signs. So get in the bus lane. We will pass this bloody line of cars. That way I might have some semblance of a chance of getting to the place I am going to before they turn the lights off and lock the doors.'

'But boss all these cars, they not in the bus lane. I must follow them.'

I could feel my irritation levels rising, out of frustration at not being in control of my own destiny and because of my growing anxiety that Diana may not wait.

'They are not in the bus lane because they are all cretins. They clearly all went to the same driving school as you, where they don't tell you to read signs. They are all suffering from buslaneitis. They have become so used to staying out of the bus lane that they never bother to look at the times they can drive in the bloody bus lane, and then cause the sort of jam that you feel happy to join. They are sheep!'

'Sheep? Where sheep boss?'

With that I yanked the steering wheel hard to the left causing the cab to veer out of the queue into the bus lane.

'What you doing boss? You get us killed.'

'What I am doing is doing what you should be doing and that is driving this thing you claim to be a taxi. And getting us killed, right now, seems infinitely more attractive than spending another minute in this heap with you and your brand of popular music. So now get your foot down and get on with it.'

I think I scared him. He accelerated straight down the empty bus lane past the queue.

We arrived at our destination at 8.35.

'How much?' I asked.

'Nineteen pounds boss.'

Nineteen pounds seemed about £18.99 too much for the experience I had just had, but I was glad to reach my destination at last and was now in no mood to argue. I handed over a twenty-pound note.

'Thank you very much boss. Goodnight.'

'Err... my change please. One pound change.'

'Oh, I thought that was the tip boss.'

A wave of exasperated rage overwhelmed me.

'Tip! Tip! You thought I was giving you a tip! You are forty minutes late in a car that would barely get through an MOT, I practically drive it for you, I tell you the bloody route and you think I should be giving you a tip. What bit about customer service are you not getting? A tip is given when someone exceeds that which is the basic expectation of the customer. Since I expected to be driven from A to B in comfort and on time, as my basic expectation, you have singularly failed to meet that, let alone exceed it. Therefore you should be giving me a tip. In fact a refund might be more appropriate.'

I opened the door and went to get out.

'Boss, boss.'

I turned around.

'You want my card in case you need taxi later?'

I decided that my energy was better served in trying to compose myself rather than kicking out his one remaining headlight. I was twenty minutes late. Not a good start. I was flustered and anxious on top of the degree of nervousness I felt about meeting Diana in the flesh.

As I entered the restaurant. I spotted her immediately. She was seated at the bar, legs crossed, one elbow lightly perched on the bar surface and what appeared to be a Martini held delicately between her slender fingers. Tall, elegant, immaculately dressed in a simple black evening dress that stopped just above the knee, her legs, toned like a dancer's, sheathed in black stockings. (I automatically assumed they were stockings. I am a man. There was no other consideration.) She looked stunning. Her pictures did not do her justice at all. I was almost speechless.

'Err, Diana? Matthew. So sorry I am... a little late... delays on the tube.'

I had no idea why I mentioned the tube since I had come by taxi. I obviously still had the tube map in my head and I was clearly disconcerted by her cool elegant aura and the heady scent of her perfume. I held my hand out in greeting. She offered her hand and in the same instant pulled it back. To my horror I realised my palm was covered in dirt and oil. Dirt from my stupid flat tyre that I had been checking. The wheel must have gone through an oil patch too.

'Oh sorry. A puncture. I had a puncture.'

'A puncture? A puncture on a tube train?' she repeated, her brow furrowing slightly.

'Err, not a puncture exactly. A problem with a wheel. Had to help the driver.'

'Sorry Matthew. You helped the driver with a wheel on a tube train?'

'No, a problem with the taxi driver.'

'But I thought you said you came by tube?'

'No. I meant by taxi.'

'You sound confused? You can't tell the difference between a taxi and a tube train. I would have thought there was a fundamentally noticeable difference.'

'Sorry Diana. I meant I got a taxi after I had decided not to get the tube and he turned up forty minutes late.'

'Oh I see and he was late because he had a puncture?'

I could tell she was mocking me now and in lawyer mode.

'No, he got lost. A problem with his satnav. I was going to get a tube but then got the taxi.'

'So who had the puncture?'

'I did. On my car, earlier...and I was going to change it but...look, shall we get a drink Diana. I think I need one.'

She smiled broadly at me, clearly amused at my disquiet.

'I have already ordered some champagne, Matthew.' Her gaze lowered to my waist. 'Oh, and what have you done to your trousers?'

There was a large oily handprint at the top of my right leg, where I had rested my hand during the cab ride. So much for first impressions. I needed to clean up. I spotted a member of staff, a tall haughty looking man with thick bushy eyebrows and a Hitleresque moustache, who appeared to be giving instructions to two other restaurant staff.

'Excuse me, waiter. Could you show me where the gent's toilets are?' I asked.

For a moment he stood still, his back towards me as if he hadn't heard my request. Then, turning slowly in the direction of the voice, he caught sight of me, his hands clasped tightly together in front of his chest. There was no immediate response to my question. He simply looked me in the eye, his gaze then lowering slowly in a deliberate assessment of my appearance, before returning to eye level again.

'Sir, I am the maître d' of this establishment and the lavatories are in that direction.'

That was all I needed, to hack of the head man before I had even sat down. I headed off in the direction he had indicated and cleaned up as best I could but there was a limited amount I could do with my oil stained trousers and I returned to the restaurant.

It was a very grand, superior establishment, all oak panelling and elegant mirrors and subdued lighting with an air of exclusivity. It was not the type of place I was able to frequent on a regular basis. Diana was waiting at the bar. The champagne had been poured. We spent the next half an hour getting to know more about one another. Diana had been a solicitor for several years specialising in civil litigation and was now a partner in a successful law firm.

She was clearly well connected and used to the high life. She had a cool, calm manner about her that radiated confidence and refinement with that instinctive ability to know how to deal with any situation that arises. I began to relax but felt the need to demonstrate my own savoir-faire. I turned to the maître d' who was looking me up and down again in a self-important manner.

'Are all these tables reserved?' I asked.

'Some are but others get quite excitable as the evening wears on, Sir.'

All I needed was a comedian waiter.

Diana laughed. 'Don't take any notice of James, Matthew. He has been here forever and I think you may just have started off on the wrong foot by referring to him as a waiter. He can be very snooty and he is very protective of me too. Anyway, we already have a reservation. Shall we sit down?'

James led us to a discreetly placed table in a corner and handed us some menus. He gave me the wine list. I detected the hint of a smirk.

'Do you have a preference for white or red Diana?' I asked.

'Oh the Bordeaux is very nice here,' she replied, 'I'd recommend the Chateau Cheval Blanc Premier Grand Cru, St.Emilion.' It rolled off her tongue effortlessly with an authentic French intonation.

I lowered the wine list.

'Well, I will be happy to go with your recommendation then,' I said.

I was pleased that the decision was made so quickly and it saved me exposing my limited knowledge of wines. Then I saw the price - £450 a bottle. I nearly had a blue fit. She had expensive taste. I could hardly go back on it now and James was hovering. I ordered the bottle and he removed the wine list.

'May I say, an excellent choice, Sir,' he said, his smirk growing slightly more condescending.

Diana scanned the menu. 'So what are you having, Matthew? I am torn between the asparagus in lemon butter and the avocado & crayfish tails, to start,' she said.

Torn? What rent asunder, ripped to shreds? I thought that torn was a little descriptive but perhaps that was just her way. I wasn't torn at all. I wasn't sure what to have. Having just ordered a four hundred and fifty pound bottle of wine I was now considering a plate of chips and peas. I examined the options seeking out the least expensive starter as price was now my priority not that anything on the menu appeared cheap.

'I am going for the leek & potato soup, I think.'

We ordered the first two courses. James took the menus and left.

'So, Matthew, what do you like doing? What are your hobbies?'

'What do I like doing? Well…' I was momentarily stumped. My mind was a blank. Perhaps some sort of wariness factor had kicked in given her profession and my earlier inauspicious start but now my brain was over processing even the simplest of questions.

Diana noticed my hesitancy. 'You know, hobbies, sports. You look very sporty and your profile says you like tennis and football.'

'Yes, it does, I like all sports. I–'

'Do you play golf? I absolutely adore golf.' Her hand stretched out across the table, her red tipped fingers resting gently on my arm.

'Oh yes. I love golf.'

I had no idea why I said it. It must have been the confusion I was experiencing at the thrill of her touch. I had never played golf in my life.

'Fantastic. What's your handicap?' Diana asked, her enthusiasm plain to see.

Despite my limited knowledge of golf I had at least heard of the handicap system. 'Well…I don't have a handicap…I mean, officially…err…because I don't currently belong to a club.'

I knew I shouldn't have used the word currently. Not with a lawyer sitting opposite me.

'I see. So you used to belong to a club. Which one, Matthew?'

'No…no, I have never actually belonged to a club. Mainly because I was too busy playing tennis and football. It's hard to fit it all in.'

She wasn't letting go.

'So where did you play then?' A slight frown crossed her brow giving her a serious look, an expression that was more suited to the courtroom.

'Oh you know. Just with friends. The odd round here and there. Just for fun.'

James returned with the wine, a welcome interruption since the distraction allowed me the opportunity to change the subject. He displayed the label in my direction. I nodded my approval. I could hardly comment or reject it. A moment later it was uncorked and with an expert flourish he poured a small portion into my glass and stood back expectantly. I lifted the glass, catching Diana's gaze as I did so.

'I am sure it is a fine wine,' I said, not wishing to go through the ritual of tasting it under scrutiny, 'thank you, James. You may pour it.'

Diana smiled her approval. A lady indeed but not one encumbered with too many airs and graces it seemed and, after all, the wine had been her recommendation. I sensed that I had somehow paid her a compliment.

'It's very good Diana,' I said savouring the rich, fruity sensation that glided over my tongue. 'An excellent choice. A favourite of yours?'

'Thank you Matthew. Yes, it is. One of my golf partners introduced me to it. Anyway, you were saying that you play with your friends.'

'Oh, yes…yes, I do…err…have…have played…but not for a while.'

So much for trying to change the subject. I was kicking myself. I wished I had just said that I didn't play golf. I am sure it wouldn't have mattered. Relationships can't totally depend on having everything in common. I was starting to feel warm. I could see it coming. I just knew she would ask and I knew it was my own stupid fault.

'Splendid. How about a round on Thursday? I have a long weekend off and it would be great to get out on the course with you. My girlfriend is abroad and can't play this week so it would be ideal. Just the two of us.'

I could feel the situation getting out of control. What I should now be saying was that I couldn't play this week, because I am working or doing charity work with animal welfare groups or flying to Houston to give NASA some advice on their space programme. Maybe I should just be saying I couldn't play, full stop, and leave all the reasons off the end of that sentence. Anything but agreeing to play golf.

'Well, we could but when I say I haven't played in a while I mean I haven't actually played in years, Diana,' is what came out. 'I am so out of practice I would spoil your game.'

'Don't be silly. You will be fine. A few holes and you will be back into it.'

I had already got myself into a hole and it was getting bigger every time I opened my mouth. I didn't want to disappoint her and possibly miss out on a second date. But there was no point in putting myself into a pressure situation. Time to bite the bullet and come clean.

'Look Diana, when I said I haven't played, I–'

'Matthew. I have an idea. I know it's hard to get back into a sport when you haven't played for some time so why don't we pop along to the driving range tomorrow afternoon and hit a few balls. It will be like a second date.'

A second date. The words burned into my mind eroding my sudden resolve to come clean.

'Well…I think…I'm not –,' I stuttered to find a response and was stopped by her interruption.

'No excuses now Matthew, it won't take you long to get into the swing again. It will be fantastic. And we can have a nice relaxing drink afterwards. What do you say?'

Her radiant smile left me no choice. What could I say? It sounded like the better of two options. It got me out of a round of golf where I had no doubt I would seriously embarrass myself and end all hopes of developing anything with Diana. The driving range sounded like the best solution to a situation that could be getting out of hand. It also solved Diana's desire to play golf and at the same time secured me a second date, even if it was not my ideal scenario. Anyway, how hard could it possibly be to hit a small ball up into the air with a stick?

The rest of the evening was superb. The food was excellent. Diana's company was captivating. I was beguiled by her charm. We finished our meal. James brought coffee for her and a pot of tea for me with two glasses of Armagnac to round off the meal. I poured my tea. Why is it that in restaurants the spout of the teapot always leaks the tea down the side and into your sleeve? The first warm trickle missed the cup completely. Diana laughed. My shaking hand hadn't helped. The prospect that I would be presented with the bill very soon had begun to unsettle me. What if I had reached my credit card limit? How embarrassing would that be? No use worrying about it. I nodded in James's direction and he duly presented me with the bill. All seven hundred and twenty five pounds of it. I tried to contain the inward shock with an outward display of indifference and rummaged in my pocket for my wallet.

'Matthew. I am getting this.' Diana reached out and picked up the silver dish that contained the bill.

My surprise didn't stop my protest. 'Oh, no, Diana, I wouldn't dream of it…I –.'

'Matthew, I invited you remember so it is my treat.' Her serious face emerged again. 'And anyway, I can put it on my office account, so please. You can treat me to the driving range and some lunch tomorrow.'

I couldn't argue with that. Seemed like a very good deal to me. My desire to be the gentleman was quelled by the fact that she would be claiming the bill as a work expense. She had a taxi arranged. We parted company. I was looking forward already to my golf date.

13

'Cecil. Cecil. Listen.' I called him the minute I got in.

'Geezer, what do you want? It's twenty past one in the morning. What's wrong with you?'

I thought that was a bit rich coming from Cecil who was the king of drinking and dialling at ungodly hours of the morning when he was partying in some dive.

'Well, what are you doing in bed at this time on a Friday night? You are normally out partying.'

'I've been out. Mates leaving do. Started at eleven o'clock this morning,' was his groggy response to my question.

'Look Ces, sorry to wake you. It's an emergency...I need some golf clubs.'

'You need some what? Some fucking golf clubs? At this time of the morning? You going to play golf in the dark?' Cecil seemed more alert all of a sudden. 'Mate, you must be pissed. And what sort of emergency is that? You don't even play golf. Anyway, aren't you supposed to be on a date with some lawyer tart?'

Cecil had a way with words and only he could blend two such diverse professions into one entity.

'No Ces. You don't understand. I don't need golf clubs right now. I need some for tomorrow and I have no idea where I can get any at short notice and I thought you might know, or be able to help. I mean what are mates for?'

Maybe I shouldn't have asked that question because he decided to answer it.

'I'll tell you what mates are for geezer. Mates are there for you on a Friday night. When they get a bird they hook you up with her mate. They–'

'Ces, I don't have time for this now. I am really sorry to wake you but Diana...the lawyer tart...I mean, my date, wants to go to the driving range with me tomorrow. She seems to be under the impression that I can play golf and –'

Cecil's laughter stopped me in my tracks.

'Let me get this straight geezer. You pull some rich, classy lawyer bird and you arrange to play a game of fucking golf, a game that you don't even play, and then you are on the dog to me at nearly two o'clock in the morning when you should be at her place giving her one. You gotta sort yourself out mate.'

'Ces. I don't want to mess this one up. I'd be stupid to let this one go. I know I don't play golf but it's only down the driving range, not an actual game…an hour, then who knows. All I need is to get hold of some clubs. I can't very well pitch up without any gear. That won't look right at all. I mean I have already dug myself a hole by making her think I play the game in the first place.'

'What did you do that for? You should have just plied her with champagne and you'd be getting the old hashmadishmalacka by now. Instead you are scrambling around for golf clubs to play some stupid game that you are going to fuck up anyway.'

Cecil wasn't actually doing my confidence any good at this stage.

'Yeah, I know Ces. But I have done it now. I can't get out of it now. I mean I can hardly say I lied about the golf, can I? She is a lawyer. She hears lies all the time. So she is going to take a dim view of it. She will just lump me in with all the other crooks and villains she comes across and bang goes another date for me.'

The phone went quiet. 'You there Ces?'

'Yeah. I was thinking. Look leave it with me mate. My old man has a set of clubs. Got them a few weeks ago for his birthday. Not even used them yet. He's away this week and I am keeping an eye on his drum. I will drop them off for you in the morning.'

'Cecil, you are a legend. Cheers mate.'

'And don't smash 'em up either. They're brand fucking new. You owe me one geezer.'

Good as his word Cecil pitched up with the golf clubs the next day.

'Get them back to me by Monday, geezer. I don't want the old man knowing they been out of the house.'

'No worries, Cecil…and thanks.'

'Yeah, well get the job done, mate. And remember, you owe me one.'

I gave him a rueful smile. I owe Cecil one. The number of scrapes I had got him out of, I reckoned he owed me two hundred and twenty one and this was just reducing the deficit.

'Oh, Ces. Just one more favour mate. You couldn't give me a lift to the driving range could you? My car's got a puncture.'

'You are taking the piss now, geezer. Go on. Jump in.'

By midday Cecil had dropped me off at the driving range. As I walked across the car park I saw Diana pull up in a brand new Mercedes. She clearly had it all. Good looks, great figure, top job and all the trappings of success. She waved at me cheerily as she got out of the car.

'So glad you made it, Matthew,' she whispered as she gave me a peck on the cheek. Once again I caught a whiff of her perfume and the sensation made my head go light. A frisson of excitement electrified my body. Suddenly I could play golf or at least I'd give it a bloody good try.

'Let's have a quick coffee Matthew and then hit some balls.'

I followed her to the cafeteria. I watched her tanned, toned legs stride purposefully ahead of me and I just knew I wanted to be at this driving range no matter what happened. Over coffee I relaxed. Diana was bubbly, cheerful and enthusiastic, the soft touch of her hand on mine as she emphasised a point sent a thrill through me. I was mesmerised.

We finished our coffee and set off to the upper level on the range. I had Cecil's dad's bag of clubs slung over one shoulder, the contents rattling with each step as it bounced off my right hip. Diana was carrying a slim, lightweight bag containing approximately half the amount of clubs that I had.

'Nice clubs Matthew. How long have you had them?'

'Err...not long at all, Diana. They are new.'

'Ooooooo, keen aren't you.' She smiled and pointed in the direction of the golf ball dispenser. 'Why don't you get the balls and I will go and get us a bay.'

She handed me the token and I set off in the direction of the dispenser. Perhaps it was because I had never been to a driving range before or it might have been that I was focused on returning to Diana. Whichever it was I somehow failed to notice the stack of baskets that are supposed to be placed under the dispenser to catch the balls. The metal token clinked into the slot. I pressed the button next to the 200 balls marker. In one thunderous eruption a flurry of golf balls spewed from the machine, hit the ground and bounced, like a storm of giant hailstones, in every direction. In a reflex action I dived forward in a hopeless attempt to catch them all. I was so engrossed in scrambling around on my knees trying to stop the avalanche that at first I did not notice the fat bloke walking towards me, golf bag dangling from his shoulder. He was clearly a regular at driving ranges and obviously so used to the sound of balls being ejected from a ball dispenser that he didn't bother to look in that direction. His gaze was fixed firmly ahead, out across the green expanse of the astro-turfed range, no doubt figuring that he would tube his first shot way past the 250 yard marker. By the time I was aware of his presence his foot was about to come down on top of two of the errant golf balls. My warning shout choked on my tongue. Too late. He went down like a stricken airship, arms flailing at some imaginary lifeline, his golf bag ejecting golf clubs in a myriad of different directions as he hit the ground hard. I ran towards him.

'You...you ok, mate?' I stuttered.

He was struggling to get to his feet, cursing under his breath. I tried to help him up but he was a big lump. He winced hard as he put his substantial weight onto one foot, which, judging by his contorted face, had sustained a painful injury.

'My bloody ankle. Shit, that hurts. What the hell was that?' he said, his face reddening.

'It was the balls…the balls from the machine…I am so–.'

I didn't get to finish the sentence. It may have been shock, embarrassment, or both but he started to rant.

'Bloody machine! It never bloody works properly. I am going to sue the bastards. Health and safety…bloody sue their arses off. Bloody liability. I could have been killed.'

A slight exaggeration, I thought but I was relieved. He wasn't blaming me. He can't have seen what really happened. Nobody had. They had all been looking the other way, hitting golf balls or selecting clubs or whatever golfers do when they are on driving ranges. He can't have seen my cock up. I was suddenly aware of Diana standing behind me.

'What happened, Matthew? Is this gentleman all right?'

'Err... he had a slight accident. The balls from the –'

'Slight!' he fumed. 'I nearly broke my bloody neck. It's negligence. That's what it is negligence. I will sue them, sue the lot of them.'

'Calm down Sir.' Diana's assertive, even tones seemed to have the desired effect. 'Are you injured.'

'I've hurt my ankle. Sprained it I think. I was playing in a competition tomorrow too and now I am going to miss it. Bloody menace these people. I will report this. I want compensation.'

A row of chairs lined one of the back walls. Diana beckoned at me to pull one over for the stricken golfer. He waved it away, perhaps preferring to limp to emphasise his pain. I offered to call a first aider but he refused that too.

Diana took charge again. 'Look, I am a solicitor. Here's my card. Go home and get your ankle seen too and when you feel better give me a call and perhaps we can discuss what you can do. I have colleagues who deal with injury claims and we can look at the circumstances and see whether you might have a claim.'

Diana's words seemed to hit the spot. He took the card, placed it in his pocket thanking her, and limped off. Shit, that's all I needed. An investigation by my date. Suppose somebody had actually seen what happened.

Diana turned to me. 'Did you see what happened, Matthew?'

'Well, yes, I did. The balls just poured out of the machine. I pressed the button and –'

'Oh you did see then. A first hand witness. Excellent.'

'No….no I didn't...I mean I am not a witness…the balls just...when I pressed the button–'

'You mean the balls that caused that gentleman's accident were the ones you were getting?'

'Yes...but...I didn't actually see what–'

'Why did they not go into the basket, Matthew?'

Good question. 'Well, because...because there must have been a hole in the basket,' I said, frantically trying to think of a feasible reason why two hundred golf balls would spill all over the walkway of their own accord.

'There must have been a hole in the basket Matthew or there was a hole in the basket?'

'Must have...well, I mean there had to be.'

I was flustered. I didn't want to appear completely stupid in front of Diana and I certainly didn't want an accident claim against me by some pissed off fat bloke. Anyway, he seemed to be walking ok even if it was with a limp. I reckoned a bit of ice and rest and he would be fine and once he'd calmed down he wouldn't bother thinking about suing anyone. After all if he was a golfer he wouldn't want to put his local driving range out of business, I reasoned. Feeling better about the whole thing, I saw a way of saving my embarrassment and letting things cool down.

'Yes, Diana, there was a hole in the basket. I mean how else would the balls have spilled out all over the pathway?'

'Oh good. Faulty equipment, poor maintenance, negligence. Sounds like a perfect case for suing whoever is responsible.'

I cringed. She did seem a little enthusiastic.

'Do you have the basket, Matthew?'

'What...what basket,' I answered, trying to buy time while I thought of a good reason why I didn't have it.

'The one with the hole in it. The one that the balls fell through. It would be helpful as evidence.'

'No...no, I don't...I think it was picked up...picked up by someone else. Anyway, Diana, let's not let this spoil our day and, after all, it is your day off. Relax. The guy has your card. If he calls you can take it up then. He probably won't bother. He was just embarrassed...you know, because he fell over and couldn't get up. Why don't I go and get another token. Let's hit a few balls, what do you say?'

'You are right Matthew. Yes, I should not be thinking about work. Ok. Hurry back.'

My apprehension had only subsided marginally when I got back with a full basket of balls. We took two adjacent bays, Diana's to the left of mine. I took a club from my bag.

'What are you hitting, Matthew?'

'Err...the ball Diana.'

'No silly, what club?'

'Oh, of course. Only teasing. I am hitting a...erm....' I stared down at the club hoping for some indication of what it was and caught sight of the symbol at the very bottom. '... a 'b'... a 'b' club.'

'A what?'

'A 'b' club. Oh, wait a minute.' I turned the club and examined the end more closely.

'It could be a 'P'. Yes, a 'P' Club.'

'Oh you are a one Matthew. You had me going there. A pitching wedge,' she giggled.

I giggled back, nervously. A pitching wedge indeed, whatever that was supposed to do. 'Go on then. You first,' I said hoping I'd pick up a tip from watching her.

Diana placed her ball and proceeded to swing her club in a smooth arc sending the ball cleanly up into the air. I figured I had an advantage seeing as how we were both facing one another in our bays and I could see what she was doing. I just needed to copy it now. I placed my ball on the tee. I drew back the club, swung it forward and completely missed the ball in a wide swinging air shot. I looked up at Diana sheepishly.

'Best to have a practice swing, I always think,' I said, but not convincingly.

I tried again. The club came swinging down, catching the ball at such an angle it flew off the tee to my right hand side, bounced off the partition behind me, shot forward and hit the other partition in front of me and then dropped lamely into the safety net on the edge of the bay. I saw Diana's look of puzzlement.

'Bit rusty…takes a while to get back into it, don't you think,' I said, feeling my discomfiture increasing.

Another ball. Perhaps making a complete tit of myself with my first two shots somehow reinforced my resolve to get the next one right. I swung the club at the ball. However, it seemed that putting all my energy into swinging at a stationary ball whilst my body was as taut as a steel cable did not translate itself into a good golf shot. The trajectory of my swing coupled with the power I was trying to generate caused my body to pivot almost in a three quarter circle. The clubhead again missed the ball completely and in doing so my momentum launched the club right out of my hands, over my right shoulder and straight into the viewing mirror behind me. There was an almighty crack of splitting glass as the mirror fractured from top to bottom. It was my good fortune that it was toughened glass and it did not shatter. I heard Diana shriek with astonishment. Two members of staff rushed forward.

My embarrassment crawled over my skin from the neck up. 'I am sorry. It was an accident. I will pay for the damage. I slipped. I'm really sorry,' I said to the two employees.

My apology and offer to pay seemed to sort the situation out. They took my details. I turned to look at Diana.

'Matthew, what were you doing?'

'I said I was a little rusty Diana. It's been a while since I held a club. And I haven't got the right shoes on either,' I blurted out lamely.

'I can see you are rusty Matthew. I have never seen such an odd stance or grip. Tell me, are you left handed?'

I thought she was being facetious just because I hadn't quite managed to hit a ball properly yet.

'No,' I laughed, 'I am right handed.'

'I thought you were. When we were out last night everything you did was right handed, and you carried your golf bag on your right shoulder too which was why I was more than a little puzzled when you turned up with left handed golf clubs.'

'Left handed golf clubs? What do you mean?'

'I mean those clubs you have are made for a left handed player. They are completely opposite to those used by a right handed player. Here, look at mine.'

She reached into her bag, withdrew a club, and then handed it to me. 'See, the club head faces the other way, to the left. Yours faces to the right, which is why you were standing facing me when you were trying to hit the ball.'

The blood was draining from my face as I listened. I was also considering what method I might use to murder Cecil.

'Oh that. Yes...yes, they are left handed. Yes. That's because, although I am actually right handed I like to play golf left handed...which is why I have these left handed clubs.'

My mind buzzed, frantically trying to come up with a plausible reason why a supposedly competent right handed person would be trying to hit a ball with left handed clubs. I heard the nonsense that was emerging from my mouth but I could not do a thing to stop it.

'I don't do everything right handed. I mean, for example I...err, swim left handed. I read the paper left handed.'

'Swim left handed, Matthew? How do you swim left handed?'

'Well, you know, I always start the stroke with my left hand, if I am doing front crawl of course. Yes, I swim left handed. So you see, just because I am right handed doesn't mean that I have to do everything that way.'

Diana looked sceptical. She didn't seem convinced by my explanation.

'We still have nearly all the balls left Diana. Do you want to carry on,' I asked, optimistically in the circumstances.

'Look, maybe we have had enough excitement for one date Matthew. One wounded casualty and a shattered mirror before we have hit a ball properly, suggests that perhaps this just isn't our day.'

'Well, we could do something else. No sense in wasting the day,' I said.

'Like what, Matthew? Swimming, perhaps? Maybe you'd like to show me your left handed technique.'

She picked up her golf bag as she said it. I realised that there was no point in trying to convince her to stay.

'I'll call you,' was her parting message.

'Cecil. Cecil. Open up. Are you in there? I have brought your clubs back.'

I banged hard on Cecil's front door. I'd driven straight round to his place from the driving range.

The door opened.

'Left handed clubs Cecil! They are bloody left handed clubs. The golf clubs you gave me are left handed!' I slung them on the floor in front of him.

'What the fuck are you going on about geezer,' was Cecil's response.

'You've screwed up the whole date for me Ces. The clubs are left handed! I couldn't hit the ball with them.'

'Hold on a minute geezer. It sounds to me that if you go on a golf date and you can't hit a golf ball that you screwed up the date, not me. You've never even played golf so picking a fucking driving range to go on a date is just about the stupidest place you could pick. And somehow you think it's my fault. You're a fucking snob mate. You think because she's some upper class lawyer you'll impress her by playing golf cos you think that's what they do. And what the fuck are left handed clubs anyway? Golf clubs are golf clubs. I helped you out cos that's what mates do and then you give me all this shit.'

'Is your dad left handed Cecil?'

'Yeah, but what's that got to do with anything?' Cecil said, scratching the stubble on his chin in puzzlement.

'Left handed golf clubs are for left handed people Cecil. That is why your dad has left handed golf clubs. Because he is bloody left handed. Tumble? They make right handed clubs for right handed people and left handed ones for–'

'Alright, alright. How the fuck am I supposed to know that? You didn't even know it. And anyway, you can't play golf so what difference does it make.'

'Well, for a start Ces, it might have given me half a chance and looked like I knew what I was doing if they had been right for me. If they'd been the right way round for a start. As it was I looked a right dick head and cocked the whole thing up.'

I relayed the full story of my calamitous golf experience to Cecil. When he'd finished laughing he came up with his usual solution.

'Put it down to experience geezer. She'll get over it. Let's go get a couple of cold ones. Carlos is having some sort of social event bollocks down at Fad's that he's calling a gourmet night but he's got a band and some pole dancers. I was there in the week and he's trying to drum up some business. We could stick our heads in there and if its crap we can move on. Keep the dream alive.'

I was struggling with the concept of a gourmet night and pole dancers but after my hair raising dating adventures I was even considering that a night out with Cecil may even be relaxing by comparison. No sense in me sitting at home hoping Diana would ring.

14

It was about 7.30pm when we got to MacFadden's. Carlos served up a couple of cold beers. We sat at the bar. It was still fairly quiet, just a few occupied tables at the far end of the room. 'How's the dating going Mateo? Carlos asked, as he wiped away the circular puddles left by the cold glasses on the bar surface.

'Not very successful so far, Carlos. Anyway,' I said, changing the subject, 'where are the pole dancers and what's this gourmet night?'

'Pole dancers? No pole dancers. Two new pole bar staff. Nice lassies from just over from Poland. Started this week. Hanka and Janka. They will be in later.'

'I thought you said there'd be pole dancers, Carlos?' Cecil said.

'No, Cecil. I said pole bar staff. You were pissed.'

'And the gourmet night, Carlos? What's that all about,' I asked.

Carlos stopped wiping, slung the cloth below the bar top and leaned forward as if to share a secret.

'Aha, it's my little brain wave to bring more business in. The gourmet night is a typical Scottish South American evening, excellent food…haggis, anticuchos, empanadas, stovies, tatties and music from the Gastric Band.'

Cecil and I looked at one another. I don't think either of us could quite see the cultural harmony between Scottish and South American recipes but Carlos had a foot in both camps and at least he was trying. Neither did I want to be the one to point out the irony of promoting a food-based evening with a group called the Gastric Band.

I turned to Cecil. 'Ces, tell me. You recommended that I try the internet dating thing and yet you don't use it. But wouldn't you like to meet someone permanent, you know, maybe have a girlfriend?' I asked.

'I'm not looking for a relationship mate.'

'So what are you looking for then?'

Cecil looked away for a moment and stared into his glass as if expecting the answer to my question to be floating in the froth of his beer.

'Nothing geezer. I don't want a bird in tow all the time. Relationships only ever end up in one place.'

'They do? Where's that then.'

'Tesco's.'

'Tesco's? What do you mean by Tesco's, Ces?'

My lack of understanding seemed to galvanise Cecil. He stopped examining the contents of his glass, raised his head and fixed me with an intense gaze.

'Look mate. You gotta make your choices. Do you want to live the dream, take down as many birds as you can or do you want to end up in Tesco's?'

'I'm not getting you, Cecil,' I said, still slightly puzzled by Cecil's train of thought.

'Tesco's geezer. Pushing a fucking trolley around Tesco's every Thursday night with some bird you don't fancy anymore. That's where relationships get you.'

'That's a very specific view point Cecil. I mean, it doesn't have to be that way –'

'Mate, look at it this way. Every kid sticks up two posters on their bedroom wall when they are young. Right. One's a Ferrari and the other is a blonde page three stunner with tits like melons. Images of their aspirations. But what do they settle for? Some overweight bird who can't be bothered no more and a Tesco trolley. What happens between the poster stage and the growing up bit? I'll tell you what happens, mate. When they get out in the real world they get scared. That's what happens, mate. They get scared of going after what they want cos it's hard and cos you gotta compete. They lower their sights and go for the easy option and easy options don't give you the rewards. They let the dream die. And then they settle for something they didn't want. Once you get scared you lose your edge.'

'Blimey, Ces, I only asked if you would like to meet someone. That's a bit of a bitter and twisted view.'

Cecil ignored my remark, which had clearly hit a nerve, raising the memory of his own lost love. He had definitely gone for what he wanted back then and lost it through his own stupidity. I left it at that. I knew he didn't like to talk about it. He was staring back into his beer.

'Yeah mate. Yeah. That's what happens. Me, I am keeping the dream alive. I'm out there... competing.'

'But Ces, I have done that with you and we nearly always end up rat arsed in some bar with no birds at all.'

'Yeah. Ok, I know we do. No one said this relationship would be easy,' he said, his face cracking into a grin, breaking the serious focus the conversation seemed to be taking. 'I'm a man of extremes, mate. I know that. Sometimes it goes tits up sure and I end up kicking an empty coke can all the way home in the early hours. Shit happens but you have to feel the power within the power.'

I didn't ask what he meant by that. I had become used to Cecil's mysterious adages.

'Well, anyway, I am only giving the dating thing a try until Christmas,' I said. 'If it doesn't happen then nothing lost. I know what you mean by keeping the dream alive but sometimes perfectly decent, presentable people can't find a suitable partner for whatever reason so it's just another option. I mean I am not going to get desperate and sign up for years. I like bars and the chance that I might meet some decent women but it's very hit and miss and so I will just see what pans out with the internet thing. I can assure you I am not looking for a trip around Tesco's every Thursday and as soon as –'

'What about those two over there mate?' Cecil said, interrupting my thought process.

'Sorry Ces?'

'The two birdies in the corner. Over there,' he repeated, nodding his head to emphasise where he wanted me to look.

I looked over my shoulder in the direction Cecil was indicating. Sure enough there were two girls seated at corner table, absorbed in their own conversation, a bottle of wine standing in the centre of the table. One of them was facing away from us but she had blonde shoulder length hair and her companion had dark hair, cut a little shorter.

'Let's give them a bit of the old mumble, geezer,' Cecil said, his eyes twinkling at the thought.

'Hang on, let's just finish this one and get another beer first Ces,' I said, stalling.

It wasn't nervousness about speaking to women in bars that was making me hesitate. It was more to do with the fact that I had been in this situation with Cecil before and the likelihood of me getting any chatting done at all when he was in full flow was slim.

'Ok mate. You get 'em in and I'll go over and break the ice. I'll need a good wingman here. Don't let me down,' Cecil said as he got up from the bar stool.

Cecil's 'breaking the ice' technique was more akin to starting a full blown avalanche than anything as subtle as a few well-chosen words that would initiate a nice slow thaw. I was only too happy to hang back finish my beer and order some more, especially as I expected him to be back again within five minutes complaining that they were 'lesbo troglodytes' and frigid ones at that.

I sat back cradling my cold beer and glanced over at Cecil as he set about his task. Five minutes went by and he was still there. The two girls seemed to be laughing and responding to the interaction. I was not surprised. Cecil could be amusing, funny and very knowledgeable. It was just that sometimes he could also be overpowering. Another few minutes went by. Carlos was busying himself around the bar preparing for his exotic extravaganza of food.

I sipped my beer, glancing over occasionally at the corner table to see what was happening. Cecil had pulled out a chair and had placed himself between the girls. It didn't occur to me to go over and join them simply because I was expecting Cecil to come back to the bar especially as I had a full pint waiting for him. To my surprise when I next looked up he was waving me over in what can only be described as an excitable fashion. I picked the two beers up and made my way across the floor to where they were all seated.

'Mate. Let me introduce you to Sheryl and Louise.'

The two girls turned to look at me. I nearly dropped both pints right there on the floor. The blonde was PC Penny. Louise Penny. The police officer from the fancy dress fiasco.

'This is my mate Ma–'

'Michael!' I shouted before Cecil could announce my name.

Cecil, shot me a puzzled look but said nothing.

'Yes, I am Michael,' I said again a tad too loudly.

'Well very pleased to meet you, Michael. I am Louise and this is my friend Sheryl,' the blonde one said.

It was definitely her. Definitely PC Penny who had all but arrested me in my gorilla outfit. The only difference, apart from the fact she was out of uniform, was that her hair was down now and she wore slightly more make up. I stood there, still clutching the two pints.

'Would you like to sit down, Michael,' said Sheryl. She had a North American accent.

I sat down. Louise on my left, Cecil on my right and Sheryl opposite me.

Your friend has been telling us all about you, Michael,' Sheryl said.

'Err... has he...what did he say?' I glanced over at Cecil. 'What did you say Cecil?'

'It's ok. Nothing incriminating,' laughed Louise, looking directly at me.

I had just taken a sip of my beer when she uttered the word incriminating. At the best of times the word has overtones of guilt and blame but coming from a woman I knew to be a police officer, and in my heightened state of alert, it hit me right in the solar plexus. It was exactly the wrong moment too. I coughed and spluttered as I choked on the mouthful of beer. The gassy liquid squirted from my nose and mouth simultaneously.

'Are you ok?' inquired Louise.

'I am fine. It just went down the wrong way. I am sorry,' I said through my coughing fit.

Louise took a tissue from her bag and handed it to me.

'Sorry about that. Too big a mouthful, I think,' I said, as I dabbed at my face with the tissue. When I had wiped away the liquid I scrunched the tissue and, unthinkingly, offered it back to Louise.

A slight frown creased her brow. 'You can keep it, Michael,' she said.

'Oh, yes...err...sorry. And, sorry about that. Got a little excited. I haven't been out much lately. Err, not at all in fact. For weeks. No socialising, parties nothing. Not used to it the...err...to the beer.'

'Well, good to get out now then I guess,' said Sheryl. 'Louise and I are just catching up. I am over here from Toronto in Canada for six months and we thought that we would –'

'Toronto? You're from Toronto?' Cecil was off. 'Did you know that the CN Tower is the largest free standing structure in the world?'

'Well, I guess I'd kinda heard something about that but it's not something I'd thought about too much,' Sheryl said.

'It's 1,815 feet high and weighs 130,000 tons,' added Cecil for good measure.

'Has somebody weighed it then?' queried Sheryl mockingly.

'And it houses the world's highest wine cellar.'

As uncomfortable as I felt I didn't want Cecil to get into full flow. 'So what do you do Sheryl?' I asked.

'I am a forensic scientist. I am over here working with the Metropolitan police for six months.'

'What about you? What do you do Louise,' Cecil asked.

'I am a police officer. That's how Sheryl and I know each other. We have been working on some stuff together. We hit it off so socialise from time to time,' she replied.

That was all I needed. How did I end up sitting next to the police officer who had nearly arrested me, even if she didn't know it? I tried to remember Cecil's rationale that I hadn't done anything and that even if I thought I had the police had nothing to go on. Louise stared at me for a moment and placed her wine glass on the table.

'Michael, I hope you don't mind me saying so but you do look familiar. You are not on television or anything, are you?' she said smiling mischievously. 'What do you do?'

The smile was the same one that I had seen before from my monkey suit. My hands felt clammy. Maybe it was just her way. Maybe my imagination was running away with me.

'I work in leisure, for a health club chain as a marketing manager. Nothing as glamorous as being on television,' I said.

'Sounds exciting. It means you should be fit,' Louise replied. 'No, I don't know anyone in that business. It was just your eyes. I have a thing for eyes. I used to have a part time makeup artist job when I was working my way through university and my specialty was eye make-up.'

'Eyes? Well, I have always had them...the eyes. I mean, well, everyone has them, I suppose... and I am no different I have eyes too. Yes, two...two of them...like everybody.'

I had to get a grip. I was panicking myself over the slightest thing. Yet I felt so unnerved. I had seen her stare into my eyes when I was in the gorilla outfit.

But I was being ridiculous. It was impossible for her to recognize me. I had been covered from head to toe in an ape suit. Completely concealed. It was surely only because I recognized her that I felt she knew me.

'You are funny Michael,' Sheryl remarked.

'Well well, the long arm of the law then,' piped up Cecil. 'I bet you two have seen some sights?'

'You wouldn't believe what I see in my job as a copper,' Louise said. 'From the sublime to the ridiculous. Only the other week I was called to –'

'Anyone for another drink?' I stood up abruptly. As I did my arm connected with the bottle of wine the two girls were sharing. It pitched across the table spilling its contents right across the surface, the bottle rolling sideways towards Louise. She was on her feet in a flash, her swift movement saving her from a soaking. She was taller than before. It was the heels and she looked stunning. I couldn't have apologised more. Sheryl pulled away from the table to avoid the drips now trickling over the edge onto the floor.

'I am so sorry. It was an accident. I don't know what happened. Let me get you both another bottle,' I said.

'It's ok Michael,' Louise said, 'don't worry. You are obviously a little excited about being out tonight. Listen, Sheryl and I were moving on soon anyway. I am working tomorrow so mustn't be out late. It was nice to have met you guys. You have a good evening.' She glanced briefly in my direction. 'And chill.'

With that they were gone.

Cecil started. 'What the hell was all that about geezer? We could have been in there. You screwed it right up. What's up with you? I need a wingman and you are like a nervous fucking puppy. Anybody would think you never seen two birds before.'

'Ces. It was her. The bloody police woman…from the other week…with the gorilla thing.'

'Who was her? What are you talking about?'

'You know. The fancy dress night. That Louise was the policewoman who cautioned me when the cops came out after me in Regents Park. I was in the gorilla suit.'

Cecil started to laugh. 'You mean that blonde bird was the copper who nearly nicked you. So that's what all that 'Michael' bollocks was all about. That's funny.'

'No, it's not funny, Ces. Far from funny. Suppose she recognized me. If she recognized me then she only has to put two and two together and then we get landed with the robbery charges at the party. And I couldn't take any chances with my name, you know, after I'd told her I was Matthew that night.'

'Hang on a minute geezer. Sit down and take a large slug of your pint. First of all, I know you are having to try and pull birds off a dating site these days but you ain't that ugly that some copper is immediately going to clock you for a gorilla she cautioned in Regents Park. Secondly, there was no robbery.

And anyway, how the fuck is she going to recognize you if you were in fancy dress?'

'The eyes, Ces. The eyes. She looked into my eyes. You heard her mention it. And her mate is a forensic scientist.'

'Get a grip mate. She is a copper not a psychic and her mate ain't Sherlock Holmes. Nobody gets stuff pinned on them because of their eyes. Look at it this way. She thinks you are called Michael, she has never actually seen you before, ever, and all you had to do was blag it and you might have got yourself laid. You fucked up mate. And I could have taken her mate down but you screwed that up too.'

'But Ces, what did you say to them? That Sheryl said you were telling them all about me.'

'She was winding you geezer. Trying to put you at your ease cos you'd been standing there like a fucking twat gripping two pints like you were gonna do some juggling act. Anyway, I wasn't talking about you. All I said was that my mate was at the bar just before I called you over. I was just giving them the old mumble. Doing the legwork that you were supposed to back me up on as a wingman. Remember.'

'Look, I'm sorry Ces. It rattled me seeing her…the policewoman. I mean of all the bloody birds to come in here.' I was starting to feel guilty now for wrecking Cecil's chances, but secretly grateful that the two girls had left. 'It's livening up a bit now. We can still have a laugh.'

Cecil still didn't look too impressed. 'Let's get outta here mate. This place is doing my head in now…and there ain't no pole dancers.'

Carlos saw us about to leave and asked where we were going.

'Out Carlos. Where there is a bit more life,' Cecil said, grumpily.

Carlos looked disappointed. 'It's early yet Cecil. The party is about to start. The band will be here any minute. Here, have a drink...on the house.'

Placing his empty glass on the bar, Cecil was dismissive. 'Look Carlos. Nice try mate but I ain't hanging around waiting for a load of geezers in kilts to turn up riding llamas. Tumble?'

Saturday night turned into Sunday morning. Another night on the town Cecil style. We ended up in a sleazy, late night drinking den at four o'clock in the morning in Central London. It appeared to be inhabited by criminals, gang lords and a lot of heavy looking blokes. The sort you didn't want to make eye contact with. There were only three women in the whole place and they all seemed very connected to some of the villains. I had no idea what we were doing there or even how we had got in. Probably a Cecil 'how are ya' hand shake. Now the night had slipped by and really it was time to go home. I sat nursing a large gin and tonic at the bar wondering how I could get things back on track with Diana. Tiredness and alcohol were blurring any rational thinking. Maybe I should get some clubs and learn to play golf. If I was to do that it was going to have to be quick or the initial attraction Diana had had for me would be gone. Could I learn to play golf in a week? At four o'clock in the morning I believed I could. Maybe I could just spend every evening at the driving range. Practice makes perfect after all they say. Whatever I was thinking I realised that it was not the best time to make any impulsive decisions. I looked across at Cecil who was soaking up the reflected light of being seen around what I can only describe as mobsters. It wasn't as if he was a villain himself. He just liked the image. I just didn't get it myself and it certainly wasn't helping me on my quest for love.

    I slipped quietly away.

15

I got up about midday the next day. The first thing I did was check my mobile. No calls from Diana. Nothing from Cecil either but that was not unusual. He always got himself home in the end. I resisted the immediate temptation to switch on my computer and log on to the site. Instead I made a late breakfast of scrambled eggs, toast, bacon and a large mug of tea. I'd just chill today. I didn't fancy changing the car wheel at all. That could wait until later when I felt more energetic.

Despite the idea having formulated in my head under the influence of alcohol and lack of sleep, I had resolved to give the golf a shot. I would get some lessons that very week and practice every night at the range. Then I could get involved with Diana in something she loved. A shared mutual hobby. It could undo the bad start and I'd have a great excuse for spending some time with her and building a relationship. I knew it could turn out expensive but I felt it would be worth it. I had a cupboard under the stairs that I had been meaning to clear out for some time and I convinced myself that I might find some stuff worth selling and make a bit of cash towards some golf clubs.

It seemed like a plan. I dived into the cupboard. Shoes, a couple of old tennis rackets, a few CD's I hadn't played in years but nothing that appeared worth anything. As I dug deeper I found an old camera, a radio and a clock. The pile was growing but nothing of value appeared. I pulled out the bumbag that I had last worn on my fancy dress night. Another bit of junk. I had no more plans to dress up as a gorilla any time soon and bumbags were very eighties so that could go too. I slung it on the pile and carried on rummaging.

The knock on the door came at about one o'clock. I opened it. To my utter astonishment PC Penny was standing on my doorstep in full police uniform. A white long sleeved shirt was covered with a navy vest that bulged at the front, almost like a bulletproof vest. Matching navy trousers were held up by a black leather belt complete with metal handcuffs on one side and what looked like a holster on the other. From the top of the white shirt, at her neck, a chequered cravat protruded. A radio perched on her right shoulder hummed quietly, a digital display floating over its screen. Her hair was pulled tight into a ponytail but most of its blonde colour was concealed by a bowler style hat with upturned edges. Around the base of the hat ran a band, with a similar black and white check pattern to the one on the cravat. In the centre of the hat sat a gleaming silver badge that announced she was Metropolitan Police with an ER logo portraying allegiance to the crown. She looked quite taken aback too. I felt an involuntary nervous impulse in my arm that urged me to slam the door but somehow I kept my composure.

'Michael!' she said.

'Michael...,' and then I remembered. 'Yes, Michael...that's right, Michael.'

'You don't recognise me do you?' she smiled. 'The uniform I guess. It's Louise. We met last night. In that MacFadden's bar. What are you doing here?'

I recognized her all right.

'Oh yes...Louise. I remember,' I said feigning lack of concern. 'Yes, the uniform threw me there...although it's a very nice uniform. I live here. What are you doing here?' That was the information I really needed to know.

'Well, that's a co-incidence. Small world, Michael. Can I come in?'

I didn't realise it but I was unintentionally easing the door back towards a closed position in some sort of sub-conscious attempt to put a physical barrier between us.

'Oh sorry...of course.'

She waved at her colleague who was in the police car parked in the road to signal that all was well.

I opened the door fully and let her in. We sat down in my front room. She took her hat off and placed it on the arm of the sofa.

'So, what are you doing here Louise. You didn't say?'

'I am working Michael. I–'

'Oh I thought I may just have got lucky with a kiss-o-gram,' I said flippantly, hoping to ease my tension and somehow side track her. My mind was racing. Obviously Julia had complained about her alleged burglary and somehow, I didn't know how, it had been traced back to me.

'As I was about to say Michael, I am looking for a Mr Matthew Malarkey in connection with some routine enquiries we are making regarding an incident at Hemmingwell Halls, a stately home in Sussex the other day.'

I felt the blood drain from my face and my hands become instantly wet and clammy.

'We are contacting all visitors on that day as a matter of course to ask a few questions. We traced Mr Malarkey to this address from his debit card details.'

Bollocks, I thought. Why didn't I pay cash? More to the point why did I agree to go in the first place. A bloody stupid place for a date. You are meant to have wine and food on a date not history lessons.

'It's a bit of a surprise to find you here Michael, I must admit. Do you know Mr Malarkey?'

I couldn't deny it. She had the address and I needed time to think. 'Err, yes Louise. I do. He is my lodger. But he is away at the moment. Long weekend somewhere.'

'I see. Well perhaps you could give him a message to contact me on his return.' She handed me her details.

'Could I ask Louise…has he done something? Is he in some sort of trouble? I mean you can't be too careful…with...with lodgers.'

'No. It's just routine at present Michael. I shouldn't worry. We just want to eliminate him from our enquiries.'

Eliminate. Do away with. Get rid of. The word was bouncing around in my head.

'Anyway, I will leave you in peace. You look like you are busy. Are you having a clear out?' She pointed to the pile I had hastily formed on one of the spare armchairs.

'Yes, some old junk. It's quite therapeutic to have a clear out. Out with the old, in with the new. How was your night out anyway?' I asked trying to ease my tension.

'Very nice Michael. Good to let my hair down with a friend once in a while. I quite liked that bar, MacFadden's. Maybe I will see you in there sometime.'

'Yes, you never know,' I said.

She walked to the front door and I held it open, relieved to see her go. I stood and watched as she paused for a moment to put her hat back on. As she did she turned back towards me.

'Oh by the way Michael, did you know your car has a flat tyre. Bye for now.'

I closed the door. I had to think. The whole incident at Hemmingwell replayed in my head. Then I remembered the CCTV camera. But Louise had said that I was traced through my debit card. The CCTV camera had been pointing at the exit. Yes, it had been. I remembered seeing it as I clambered from the debris of the scattered armour. So my face wasn't seen and there was such a melee to get out that it was not clear who exactly was there. Anyway, I was sure that identification from the back of your head is not considered by a court to be sufficient proof that someone was in a given place at a given time. At least I hoped not. I could just come clean and tell everything to Louise but then she would wonder why I had pretended to be Michael in the first place. And why had I? Because of the stupid gorilla incident. I couldn't really tell her I was the guy dressed as the gorilla too. It wouldn't take long to connect me to Julia's complaint after that. She'd think I was a complete lunatic. I had to give myself time to think. This could get serious. I had no idea what level of damage there had been at the Hemmingwell but it hadn't looked like a mop and a bucket would sort it out when I'd left. Some of that armour had to be worth a fortune. I could be in for some heavy legal action. I'd never be able to reimburse them and I'd end up doing time. And if they associated me with the incident at Julia's place too, I would be considered a serial vandal and do an even longer stretch.

I called Cecil. Maybe we could meet for a beer and a chat. I fancied a distraction. His voicemail kicked in so I left a message. I even thought of calling Carlos at MacFadden's to see if he fancied a drink but I thought better of it as I really couldn't spend my whole night listening to endless stories of his imaginary conquests.

With nothing else to do and by way of distraction I sat down and logged on to the site. Nothing from Diana. I browsed through some of the profiles.

'*I love running in the rain, seafood, high heels, red wine, walking the dog on a windy day, the smell of fresh cut grass, gentle teasing, chocolate cake and cream, exploring somewhere new, kicking leaves, jumping in puddles and relaxing in familiar surroundings.*'

Nice profile, all seemed wonderfully rosy in her fantasyland but no picture. What was she hiding? I wasn't in the mood for jolly, jolly.

'*I'm the sort of person who loves going out and staying in. I'm looking for something more.*'

Going out and staying in. I guess that if that's all you do you would want something more.

'*Calling all sincere, honest, affectionate, witty men, who'd be interested in getting to know an independent, romantic, fun-loving woman. I would love to find someone who will laugh with me and cry with me.*'

I was almost interested until I read the cry bit. Did she have issues? Did I need any more things to cry over? My life was starting to get complicated enough now without getting involved in someone else's blubbering. I definitely didn't seem to be in the mood for cyber dating tonight. I was secretly disappointed that I had not heard from Diana. She had set the standard for me in my mind. I had the feeling that everyone else would now be a disappointment and my enthusiasm for the site, such as it was, had waned significantly.

An email message flashed up on the screen. I opened it.

'*Hi handsome. Don't know how long you have been on the site but I was wondering if you might like to meet for a coffee or a drink and a chat. We seem to be local to each other. My membership expires tomorrow. Why don't you call me.*'

Her name was Abigail and she'd left her mobile number. I clicked on her profile. She was 42, a bit older than me. I had no problem with that. She was attractive, dark hair, nice smile and sexy eyes. She was still online so I messaged her. She responded by asking me to call her. What the hell I thought, I will go for it. I called the number. We chatted for ten minutes, small talk to start. Then she got straight to the point.

'Well, are you going to ask me or not?'

'Ask you? Ask you what?' I said.

'Ask me out, of course. For that drink, I mentioned in my email. And I don't mean in several weeks. I mean tonight. How about it?'

Well that seemed to be the asking taken care of but for the sake of it I asked anyway. She lived in Richmond so we agreed to meet there later. It was the distraction I needed and I had nothing to lose. It was the whole point of being on the site. Meet people. Go on dates. See what happens. Even if it was all done in record time.

I got ready. Smart casual this time, jeans, shirt and jacket. I grabbed the keys to my car my mood lifted by the anticipation. My mobile jangled as I was going through the door.

'Geezer. I'm up for it. Where? What time?'

'Oh, Ces. Sorry mate. I've got a date now. I can't.'

'So what did you call me for?'

'Well, a drink but I hadn't arranged the date then. Oh, bollocks!'

'Mate…It's cool. No need to be like that.'

'Sorry Ces. Not you. I just realised I forgot to change that bloody wheel on my car. Look I got to go sort this out.'

'Ok mate. Give her one for me.'

I wasn't going to play the mechanic now. It was only a short bus ride between Kingston and Richmond. Ignoring the stiff breeze and hint of rain in the air I set out, a spring in my step.

Abigail was bubbly, fun and very tactile. Dark hair cut short, her dark lashes emphasised by precision grooming. Her lips were full and glowing, the perfectly applied gloss so shiny I could practically see my mirror image. She was also petit and very buxom. It was impossible not to notice her boobs and she knew it. They were creatively presented in a red top, the first two buttons of which were casually left undone. The desired effect was clearly achieved and I found it difficult not to gawp every time I looked at her.

We sat in a cosy pub by the river. She said she'd liked my picture and my 'normal' profile. Apparently many blokes uploaded pictures of themselves bare-chested or engaged in extreme sports. Many of the male profiles were bordering on the fanciful and did not seem realistic. She was surprised just how many blokes had declared their love of cooking, housework and romantic nights in. I had to confess that I had yet to browse the male section and, as I was unlikely to do so, I'd have to take her word for it. As the drinks flowed Abigail became even more tactile and was cosying up ever closer to me. Her hand was resting on my leg, her ample boobs pressing against my arm. I don't know why but I wasn't completely comfortable. I'd only connected with her a few hours ago and now here we were sitting in a pub, her presence very intense, space between us practically non-existent. And I knew next to nothing about her. She was making all the moves. I felt that I had lost control of the normal dating interaction; the thrill of the chase had been taken away from me by her very positive body language. She was calling the shots and it had unsettled me.

'Do you dance, Matthew. I just love to dance.'

'I can dance, but only really at parties, that sort of stuff.'

'Oooh...that's good. I am having Salsa and Ceroc lessons at the moment. I just love all that sensuous Latin dancing. It is so sexy. Do you like it, Matthew?'

As she said it her thigh, tightly encased in a black skirt, pressed almost imperceptibly against mine. I explained rather lamely that I had never really tried that level of dancing. I offered to get more drinks.

'Not for me Matthew. I have had enough. I feel a little tiddly. I'd really like a coffee.'

'Ok. Cappuccino, Latte...maybe just a plain one? Sugar?'

'Not here silly. Why don't you come back to mine. I make a lovely cup of coffee. Nice and frothy,' she said, stroking my arm, a subtle wink fluttering her dark eyelid.

I couldn't say no. In fact I wasn't sure I wanted to say no. Wasn't this the point of dating? Get to know someone and if you are getting on take it a step further. And we were getting along fine. I liked Abigail. She was easy to get on with, vivacious and attractive. Most guys would be very happy to be in this position – an invitation for coffee back at her place by an attractive woman who was clearly giving out positive signals that she fancied me. On top of all that the date had gone smoothly, none of the disasters that had thwarted my previous attempts.

Her flat was comfortable, warm colours, rugs, big sofa with lots of cushions, subtle lighting, very feminine. I sat on the sofa taking it all in. Abigail went to the kitchen to make the coffees. I had that feeling of being in someone else's territory. A feeling of contradiction. I was in warm homely surroundings where I should feel relaxed yet the person I was with was a total stranger. Should I get up and walk around looking at the photographs that were on display, feigning a laid-back, casual attitude? Or do I sit still and behave myself until invited to 'make myself at home'? While my brain was processing my position she returned with the coffees.

'Oh Matthew. Relax. Make yourself at home. Let me take your jacket.'

I handed over the jacket and she turned to place it on the back of a chair. I had just taken my first sip of the coffee when I heard what I can only describe as a blood curdling scream coupled with the expression, 'Oh my God.' It sent a shiver down my spine and made me jump to attention tipping a substantial dollop of hot coffee onto my jeans. Abigail had leapt straight onto the sofa and was exhibiting all the signs of a human being in sheer terror, screaming and pointing at the floor. I experienced a sudden transformation from the relaxed state that Abigail had suggested to a heightened state of adrenaline fuelled, warrior like aggression by the terrifying commotion. My whole body was now in a state of attack readiness – but for what? I looked around and could see nothing except Abigail standing on the sofa, still pointing at the floor and shouting 'Oh my God, Oh my God', repeatedly. At first I thought that she was a member of some strange religious sect and it was now prayer time. However, my eyes were naturally drawn to the pointing movement and I realised the object of her sudden madcap attention was in fact a spider. What is it with women and spiders?

'Can you see it...can you see it...look!' she wailed.

In fairness I could only just make it out, as it was not exactly a Godzilla like mutant brute. In fact it wasn't much more than a money spider and an atomic powered microscope might have helped me identify it more easily.

'Get rid of it, get rid of it,' she shouted.

I wondered briefly why women under duress say everything twice but I got down on my hands and knees onto the carpet to try to remove the scurrying spider. It was clearly in a state of shock itself at the domestic disturbance that it had caused. I tried to get it to run on to my hand by placing my palm flat on the floor but, as is the way of spiders in these circumstances, it preferred to make a number of hand brake turns to avoid contact with what must have looked like the mother of all monsters.

'What are you doing, what are you doing...don't touch it,' came an anxious cry from the sofa.

'Err...you want me to get rid of it but not to touch it,' I asked bemusedly. 'What shall I do then? Hypnotise it so it walks out the front door and goes to live in Scotland? Or perhaps I should sing it a lullaby until it falls asleep and we can get the SAS down to remove it? Or how about I call a meeting with it for Tuesday and negotiate a way out that is acceptable to all parties?' I was amused by Abigail's disproportionate reaction, given the miniscule size of the creature.

A cushion flew extremely close to my head and I realised that this tactic of trying to soothe the situation by making light of it was not helping. Eventually the by now confused, and probably dizzy, money spider decided that it had less to fear from my hand than it did from the deranged woman towering above it on the sofa and decided that it was probably prudent to take the free ride out of the danger zone. I lifted it up gently.

'Don't bring it near me,' she screamed.

That was the last thing on my mind. I was never going to take it anywhere near her. If I had been able I would have moved it to a location at least one hundred and fifty miles away from her presence so that we could just return to a quiet sociable evening. I put the misbehaving spider outside the front door. No doubt the poor mite didn't stay there long given the ever increasing breeze level, which seemed to have reached gale force proportions.

Now that the rescue of both parties had been achieved Abigail got back down onto the floor and picked up her coffee.

'Oh Matthew. Thank you so much. You are such a hero. I do like a man who can take charge of a situation. I am not too keen on spiders.'

Not too keen. That was a bit of an understatement given Abigail's vigorous reaction to a creature that was barely visible to the naked eye. As for heroes, if praise were being dished out I would have recommended the money spider as being more deserving of such an accolade since he had chosen to live on the same premises as a woman prone to apoplexy at his appearance.

'Your jeans. Matthew. I have made you spill your coffee on your jeans.'

I had forgotten about my spillage in the heat of the turmoil but clearly there was a rather large wet patch on my right thigh. Abigail began to tug at the jeans with both hands.

'Take them off. I will soak out the stain and dry them on the radiator.'

'It's ok Abigail. They are fine. It's only coffee and they are just jeans. Don't worry.'

'It's no trouble Matthew. Come on. That stain will dry in and your jeans will be ruined. Take them off.'

She began tugging at my belt next. She was insistent. Before I knew it my jeans were off and she had taken them out to soak. I felt like a complete idiot, embarrassed beyond belief. I was now sitting on the sofa in just my boxer shorts, shirt and worst of all my socks. Most men are now aware of the absurdity of being seen in underpants and socks. But I could hardly take them off. What message would that give out? Discarding my socks on the floor and sitting bare footed in my pants on the sofa would seem to be taking relaxed a bit far.

'That's better Matthew. Your jeans are in soak. Now you drink your coffee while I make myself more comfortable.'

For a split-second I contemplated more comfortable. It hadn't exactly been comfortable since we got here. My deliberations on what more comfortable might be were put into sharp focus on Abigail's return. She was stark naked. Not a stitch of clothing. Her boobs standing proud and resolute. I almost spilt my coffee again. I was dumbstruck.

'So are you going to shag me or not Matthew?' She fluttered her eyelashes as she said it.

Again I couldn't speak. I went to say something, I am not sure what but nothing came out. I sat there in my shirt, underpants and black socks with my mouth wide open in an almost catatonic state.

'You don't fancy me do you?' Her face crumpled. 'I can tell.' Tears started to roll down her face. 'You men. You are all the same. I wish I hadn't joined that stupid dating site.' Her words became incoherent, lost in her sobbing.

I jumped up. I wanted to console her. I put my arm around her. She sobbed into my shoulder.

'Abigail, let me get you something. Something to put on. Sit down.'

I found her dressing gown in a bedroom and brought it out. Once it was on her tears dried up and she calmed down.

'Of course I fancy you Abigail. You are very attractive. It's just that it's all a bit quick. You took me by surprise. I am not used to it being so…well...so blatant. And what with the spider and me sitting here in my socks and pants and all, I felt a bit strange. You know. So it's not you. Honestly.'

She had regained her composure now. She explained that she had been on the dating site since her divorce had come through three months ago and in that time had been through a variety of experiences. She had been stood up, let down at the last minute, plagued by creeps and weirdoes. Guys had showed up looking absolutely nothing like their pictures and then explained it away by saying they had used a mate's or a brother's picture. She had been groped within thirty seconds of meeting by guys who assumed she was after sex because she was on a dating site. She had even met one potential date that showed up with only one leg and had conveniently forgotten to tell her about it. It had all been a bad experience for her and I had been the first person she had met that seemed normal. She apologised to me.

'There is nothing to apologise for Abigail,' I said. 'I am completely flattered that you fancy me. But a good-looking woman like you doesn't have to try so hard. Honestly. Just because you have had some bad dating experiences doesn't mean you should, if you don't mind me saying, throw yourself at anyone. Men will only take advantage and you will never meet anyone really nice who will respect you. Sorry…don't mean to lecture you.'

'Now you are apologising Matthew. Thank you. I appreciate what you said.' Her face lit up with a smile, a small tear still hovering below her right eye.

I wiped it away.

'So, remember Abigail, if you go on a date and it's not what you want or the person is not how he portrayed himself call it a day. Make your excuses and leave.' My own drastic and extreme evasion tactics with Sexyblueeyes Sally flashed briefly through my mind. I dismissed the thought as quickly as it had come. 'Well, look, I had better go now. Thank you for a nice evening. Will you be ok?'

'Yes. Thank you Matthew. Thank you for the advice. And thank you for the spider too. I will call you a cab.'

I stood up and went to get my jeans. I found them. In a washing up bowl totally immersed in cold water. Terrific.

'Abigail. My jeans are totally soaked now. I can't wear them.'

'Oh, yes. Well at least the stain will be out,' she said smiling as if this was the key point.

'Great, that's great…but I can't get in a cab with no trousers on.'

'Hang on then, I may have something you can wear.'

I couldn't quite see how any of Abigail's jeans could fit me since I was six feet tall and she a good seven inches shorter than I was. She came out with a pair of black leggings.

'Put them on. They'll do for a cab ride. It's all I've got. They stretch,' she said handing the entirely unsuitable item of clothing to me.

I seemed to have no choice. I struggled into them. She was right. They did stretch. They stretched, just enough so that the bottom of the legs came down as far as my calves. If I wanted them covering my modesty that's the best I could do. I was a dead ringer for Max Wall in his heyday.

Abigail wrapped my wet jeans in a supermarket carrier bag and handed it to me. 'Hurry Matthew. Your taxi will be here soon. Real Libel Car Services. They are very good.'

16

I spent most of the morning at work reflecting on my previous night's experience. Abigail's story had made me think. It seemed to me that all of us, both men and women, were going through the same frustrations when looking for love. The dating site thing was just another option. Just another way of putting men and women together. But like real life it had no guarantees. On signing up we were all full of optimism that this was the answer. This was a way of putting like-minded people in touch. This would set us on the course to find our soul mates. It cut out all of the randomness of being in the right place at the right time to meet the love of your life. Well, no, it didn't. It just provided more selection but it was still a gamble. It was still the roulette wheel spinning and you hoped the ball would land on your number. But most of the time it didn't. It was just randomness on a bigger scale and in the comfort of your own living room. Now you had tens of thousands of potential partners to view. In a bar you were limited to maybe ten, twenty depending on where you went, but you had first hand, direct interaction. You could see the body language. You could pick up the sub-conscious signals. You could stare into the eyes of your potential match. All of the programming that nature had hard wired into the human psyche was dependent upon receiving that data. So it was easier to make that decision about whether to take the next step. And even then that still didn't guarantee success.

On the dating site there was no body language, no eye contact and no subtle signals to work with. Your decision on whether to turn that initial contact into reality was based on the photograph that someone else wanted you to see and your own judgement of what all of the emails and messaging banter was trying to say. Once you had assimilated that lot and had decided to take the reality test, you then end up at the very same 'bar stage' that you were trying to eliminate by signing up on a website in the first place. The difference now being that you were then stuck with your date if you decided you were not suited. Stuck because you were dependent upon one another now for your night out. The only reason you were there was to meet the real person. You didn't show up with backup in case it went pear shaped. At least in conventional bar meetings you had your friends to return to if the 'chat up stage' was not working.

Dating sites were a step back in one respect. Like a qualifying stage in a sports event. If you got through that you entered the competition proper. No wonder it was so hard for men and women to succeed in that indefinable pursuit of cupid. Perhaps we were not meant to go looking for love. Perhaps we were meant to just shut our eyes and wait until we stumbled over it. Maybe it was a mixture of both. A frantic desperate search was not going to yield results but a helping hand in pursuing what you wanted could never hurt.

I still had the best part of two weeks left on my membership, which would take me more or less into the lead up to Christmas. With the festive season looming and everyone in relaxed party mood perhaps my fortunes would change. I was still determined to pursue my chance with Diana but I decided to keep my options open too for the remaining few weeks. My optimistic thoughts were cut short by my office telephone. The head of the sales department intent on giving me stats. Work was getting in the way of my daydream.

I began to feel the curiosity arise in me even as I put the telephone back down. Had there been any contacts today? Had I received any emails? Had fate intervened to send me the woman of my dreams? I knew I shouldn't really log on to the site from my office computer but my newly optimistic mind-set was getting the better of me. A quick look wouldn't take long. As the site materialised on my screen, fear of discovery and schoolboy excitement combined to supercharge my focus on the monitor. The naughty kid in class was not paying attention to what he was supposed to be doing.

It took no more than half a minute for the computer to fully fire up the site but apprehension fuelled my impatience. My fingers drilled out a beat on the desktop as I waited. Once in front of me I was confronted by the log on page. I dragged its edges horizontally and vertically to reduce the page size to that of minimum detection risk and logged on. A full gallery of female faces materialised on the screen, sixteen to a page. Blondes, brunettes redheads, smilers, sultry poses, a whole sweet shop of choices. I went straight to my profile. Five emails in my inbox, two from Indonesia, one from Nigeria and two from women without photographs. Nothing from Diana. I deleted the first three instantly. No sense in even reading emails from abroad. We are unlikely to be able to meet up. The next two were similar, simple one line 'hello, how are you' messages. I deleted those too. No pictures and no content meant nothing to go on to me so no basis for interaction. I scrolled back to the main gallery intent on browsing the pictures to see if a face would catch my attention.

The sound of a human voice cut through my concentration drawing me back into my surroundings with a jolt.

'Hi Matt. How are you doing. I've got the new joiners lists for you.'

I hit the *minimise screen* icon in a spontaneous reaction to the sudden shock. The image disappeared into a corner as I swivelled my chair away from my desk to face the voice.

'Oh, hello Jasper. Good thanks...the lists?'

Jasper Kane from the sales team. A young, dynamic twenty three year old, who had only been with the company three months but was already making a name for himself. He had sold a record number of club memberships in the short time he had been with us, mostly to female members. It was easy to see why. His dark good looks were a throwback to the thirties Hollywood idol era. Errol Flynn meets Clark Gable. A gleaming toothy smile beneath attentive grey eyes probably sold more memberships than any sales patter. He certainly didn't need a dating site.

'Yeah, the lists of this month's joiners for your marketing campaign. Do you want me to email them over? I can do it later if you are busy right now.'

Busy? What did he mean by that? What had he seen? 'Err...no...I'm not busy. Well, I mean...too busy. Yes, email me. Thanks Jasper.'

'So, what are you working on at the moment then Matt? Looks exciting?' he said, nodding towards my pc.

Negative thoughts zipped through my mind as my discomfiture grew. He had seen something. 'Nothing...I mean...nothing special. Just some...you know... ideas...for...for a...err, targeting campaign. Promotions, that sort of stuff.'

I felt my posture shift to my left as I was speaking but could do nothing about it. Deliberately trying to adopt a relaxed pose in front of Jasper, I stretched my legs out and crossed my feet at the ankles. My upper body, however, was doing its own thing. My left elbow had perched itself on the edge of the desk, splayed away from my torso, with the arm reaching up so that the forefinger and thumb of my left hand was resting casually against the side of my face. The effect of this strange pose was to incline my upper body heavily to the left so that it was obscuring the pc monitor behind me. Not that there was anything to hide now that I had minimised the screen. But clearly my sub-conscious had gone into protect mode.

Jasper gestured towards the pc. 'Ok. Looked like you've developed quite a target audience already Matt. Need any help on the sales front?' he asked.

He'd seen more than I thought.

'Oh no. No, just early days. Building some...err...some databases. Just... you know, trawling around looking for...for marketing opportunities,' I said, feeling myself lean more to the left.

'You targeting the female market then,' Jasper said, his teeth gleaming as the thought switched on his full beam smile. 'Seemed to be quite a few ladies there.'

I had to get rid of him now. My discomfort was becoming unbearable and if I leaned any more to the left I would be horizontal.

'Women? No, anyone really. Just...you know...grouping them all together. There are a lot of potential female prospects out there. Equality and all that. I'll give you a shout if it goes anywhere, Jasper.'

'Ok. Let me know. I can work on the ladies for you,' he said, a conspiratorial wink flickering across his face as he turned and walked away.

'Send me those lists, Jasper,' I called after him in an attempt to make it seem like I had been focussed on my job. I wheeled my chair back round to the pc. Bloody idiot. What was he doing creeping up on me anyway? I logged out and shut down the site. I resolved to be more careful in future.

The lack of activity on my profile brought my thoughts back to Diana. I'd made my decision. I needed to go for it. My first step was to ring the driving range and book a crash course of golf lessons. I booked four nights of one to one two hour lessons, the first one that very evening.

Learning to do anything new in four days is not easy but mastering a new sport that requires coordination, technique and control is almost impossible. Nevertheless I was so determined to use the golf angle as my access to Diana that I made rapid progress. The golf professional had tried to dissuade me from booking two hour slots at a time suggesting it would be too intense a learning experience but I was single-minded in my desire to master the basics. By the end of my sixth hour I felt confident enough to buy my own set of clubs. Right handed ones this time. The whole lot, lessons and clubs, cost me almost fifteen hundred quid. Money well spent, I considered, if it got me close to Diana. After the third evening of lessons I plucked up the courage to call her.

'Diana. Matthew. How are you?'

'Hellooooo Matthew.'

She seemed pleased to hear from me.

'Any luck on the site?' I asked.

'I haven't been on at all Matthew. I have been very busy. Lots of new cases coming in. How about you? Any dates?'

'Not really Diana. I have been practicing–'

'Not really? Oooh. Are you hiding something from me Matthew? Who's the lucky lady.'

'No-one Diana. I just went for a drink. A friendly drink....a lady from the site. Look, Diana I was wondering. I have been brushing up on my golf for the last few days and I wondered if you wanted to try again.'

Perhaps it's a woman thing, a desire to compete with one another, but the fact I had said I'd been out for a drink with another woman seemed to focus her.

'I see. Looks like I have competition then, Matthew. Okey Dokey. Let's give it a try. What about Friday morning. At my club. We will play a round and then have some lunch. The weather forecast is surprisingly good for Friday. I will email you.'

Friday. A bit soon to be playing golf but not too soon for a date. I had been thinking more of going back to the driving range together to show off my new found skills rather than a full-blown round of golf but my judgement was clouded by my eagerness to get another date, no matter what the circumstances. I had two more hours of lessons booked and had been making reasonable progress so by Friday I figured I'd be in much better shape to play than I had been during our last golf encounter. I agreed to the game.

'Excellent. I will book the day off.'

17

After my lesson that evening I stopped by MacFadden's. Cecil was sitting at the bar nursing a bottle of Bud and chatting to Carlos. I greeted them both.

'What the fuck happened to you, Saturday night? I turn round and you've gone,' was Cecil's form of greeting.

'It was Sunday morning by then Ces. It was late. That place was a bloody dive. I'd had enough.'

'Mate, not even a see you later Cecil, I'm sodding off. Leave me standing there on my Jack Jones. The place was full of heavies and you do I'm all right Jack on me. Nearly got a pasting for looking at some villain's bird. Where'd you go?'

'Home Ces. It was over. And I don't know why you're complaining about the clientele. You took us in there. You wanted to go in.'

Apparently Cecil had no recollection of how he got home at all but woke up in bed in the morning lying on the kebab he had bought on the way back.

Carlos threw back his head and laughed. 'You two cucarachas. It's very simple. You should have stayed here. It was a great wee night. The band brought the house down. Hanka and Janka were dancing on the tables.'

'Shouldn't they have been clearing them, Carlos, if they are bar staff? Maybe they are pole dancers after all geezer,' Cecil responded. Turning to me, he said, 'You fixed that puncture yet then or you going to be expecting a chauffeur for your little golf games from now on?'

He seemed unusually moody. I decided to avoid the subject of golf while he was in a mood and just said that I had fixed the puncture.

'So, Mateo, how's your luck then with the dating game?' Carlos asked.

'No luck at all I'm afraid, Carlos.'

'Wait a minute geezer,' Cecil interrupted, 'what do you mean no luck? What about that date you had on Sunday? You know when you blew me out after ringing me up for a beer?'

Cecil was clearly miffed with me on two accounts. Leaving him on the Saturday and not following through on the Sunday with my invitation for a beer. I felt bad that I had called Cecil up and then let him down so, I took him to one side and I told him the full story of my episode with Abigail. The least I could do was let him know what happened but I didn't want the whole bar knowing.

'Hang on mate. Let me get this straight. You join a dating site to do more birds. You don't even have to try and get the white ones down with this bird cos she's done it for you already, and you go all fucking social worker. You are losing the frigging plot, mate?'

'It wasn't like that Ces. In the first place I haven't joined a dating site to do more birds, as you put it. That is why you would join a dating site. Not me. I'm looking for something a bit more meaningful than that now. I've done all that. She was a person having a bad time. I couldn't take advantage of that. I am older than you. I am nearly forty, mate. I am tired of the partying not least of all because I can't cope as well as I used to. I gave it a good shot after my marriage went down the pan and I have to say, you have been legendary in keeping an eye out for me, making sure I got out and about and all that. Now I just need some calm and stability in my life. It doesn't mean I won't fancy the odd night out with you at all. You will always be a great mate, a true friend.'

Cecil drained the last of his bottle, placed it firmly on the table and looked me in the eyes. His frown softened.

'Geezer. We are mates, comrades, brothers, right? Always mates. No matter what happens. I know we are two different people. You're Ali, I am Frazier. But we have a bond. Don't you forget it. You might be hanging the gloves up, geezer, but if you need anything I'm there. Right? Trust me. You hearing me?'

He reached over and gave me a hug. A massive back slapping hug. Typical Cecil.

'All the same mate, you should have taken her right out of the equation.'

I saw the glint in his eyes. He was up for getting the beers in but I had to decline. His mood had lightened from the earlier dark intensity so I decided it was safe to mention my golf date.

'I got a golf lesson tomorrow Ces and then I am playing golf with Diana on Friday so I'm behaving myself tonight.'

'You still trying to blag that lawyer tart, then? Mate, she doesn't want no golf playing, lick arse creep fawning over her all day. She's got enough of them at work. Why do you think she's on the dating site? She wants a proper geezer. A geezer with hairs on his chest. A geezer who will go medieval on her. Birds like that with high-powered jobs where they have to make all the decisions and compete every day in man's world just want a fucking caveman. And now you're playing fucking golf with her. Don't tell me. You've even bought golf clubs.' He looked directly at me, the question in his gaze but didn't wait for a response. 'No need to answer mate, I can see it in your eyes. You can't fool me. You ain't gonna take down some high class totty by giving her what she can have already.'

Cecil's little diatribe wasn't helping matters. I knew I was trying hard with Diana but I took comfort in the fact that she seemed to like me. I'd play the round of golf, chill and let my own personality emerge. I changed the subject.

'Ces, listen. I need to talk to you. I don't have much time now but I had a visit from that women police officer, PC Penny. She's investigating the incident at that exhibition I went to in Hemmingway Halls.' I explained the whole discussion to him.

As usual he was cool in his reaction. He could be when it came to serious issues. After some consideration he said, 'Just play it cool mate. She has your address so won't let it drop until she has closed that line of enquiry. So, very simple solution. Call her up. Say you've been given a message to contact her. Tell her you are about to leave the country again on business so if you can be of any help on the phone you'd be glad to assist. That way you have shown willingness to cooperate.'

'But Ces, if I call up that's blown it completely–'

'Mate. You pretend you are you. Get it? You are ringing up as you but she doesn't know it's the geezer she knows as Michael. Blag it mate. What are you? Your policewoman then eliminates another off her list and she doesn't come back around your gaff putting you on the spot with you having to pretend to be somebody else. If you ignore it you open up a whole new world of pain, geezer. So, get with the programme.'

I must admit Cecil had a way of making it sound very straightforward. One simple call would sort it all out. PC Penny would then move on to something else. Worst case I'd at least get to know what the situation was and whether in fact I was in any sort of trouble. I told Cecil I'd call up tomorrow.

'One more thing mate. If I were you I'd put a bit of a swerve on your voice. You know disguise it a bit. Remember she has spoken to you and these coppers can be a bit cute.'

Great, I thought, now I had to be an actor too.

Thursday night's golf lesson went well. I was hitting the ball fairly straight most of the time. The pro said I had a natural swing but I would need to keep practicing it. I told him I was playing my first ever round of golf tomorrow. He told me just to keep on doing the things I had been doing all week and I'd be fine.

Back at home I decided to bite the bullet and call PC Penny. I was put through to her immediately.

'Hello, is that PC Penny? This is Matthew Malarkey. I understand from my friend Michael that you wanted to speak to me.'

I tried to disguise the nervousness in my voice and hoped that having dropped the pitch a couple of octaves along with adopting a more sophisticated business like accent, I could carry off the deception.

'Mr Malarkey. Thank you for contacting me. I wanted to meet with you to discuss some matters relating to an incident recently at the Hemmingwell Halls. When would that be convenient?'

'An incident? What type of incident,' I asked remembering Cecil's instruction to 'blag it geezer.'

'I am afraid I can't discuss details with you on the telephone Mr Malarkey. We should speak in person,' PC Penny replied.

'I am terribly sorry but I am leaving for Buenos Aires tonight on business and I am likely to be away most of this month. Is there nothing I can help you with right now?'

'Well, as I say, I would like to see you personally as you are one of the last people we need to speak with. However I am anxious to move on with this, so in the circumstances perhaps you could answer a few questions for me?'

Relieved, I agreed to answer.

She explained that the incident that had occurred had caused damage to a number of exhibits and that she was making general enquiries to see if there were any witnesses. I held my breath waiting for the first question. I needn't have worried. I was only asked to give my account of what I saw on my visit; whether I saw anything that may have led to or caused the incident. Needless to say I had nothing of any significance to contribute. PC Penny thanked me for my co-operation and said that if she needed to speak to me again she would be in touch.

I assumed the police always finished the discussion like that and I felt a weight had been lifted from my shoulders. But that feeling didn't last long. I had to ask. I had to know what the worst case was.

'By the way officer, the damage you mentioned, how erm...how bad was it?' I asked, in what I hoped was a detached and offhand manner.

'Well, as I say, several of the exhibits were damaged but it is too early to say to what extent. However, initial estimates are in the region of tens of thousands of pounds.'

Tens of thousands. The figure reverberated in my head. Tens of thousands. That could be ten thousand or ninety thousand. Either way it was out of my league. The shock of the figures prevented me from speaking. It was just as well, as my disguised voice would have transformed into a high pitched falsetto in an instant had I been able to utter anything at all.

'As I say, Mr Malarkey, if we need any more assistance I will be in touch. Good night.'

18

On Friday morning I loaded my new clubs into the car and headed off to the golf club. I might have known it would be plush. Set in acres of lush green Surrey countryside, even this late in the year, it looked immaculate.

Diana was waiting for me at the entrance. She looked stunning even in golf attire. Perfectly made up, her blonde hair tied back and her smile radiating a welcome that made me realise why I had gone to so much bother.

'Matthew. Lovely to see you. I will sign you in and we will go and have some coffee first. We are on the tee at nine. Oh, nice new clubs again. Right handed this time I see,' she said with the merest hint of a raised eyebrow.

At five minutes to nine o'clock, fuelled by caffeine, Diana and I walked out to the tee. I was nervous. I had tried to convince myself that there was no need to be nervous following my four days of intensive lessons but now that I was about to set foot on the course the nerves kicked in. As Diana would be playing from the ladies tee I was due to play first. I stepped forward, pushed the wooden tee into the ground and placed my ball on it. It fell off. I stepped back fully aware that Diana was watching my every move. I felt the tension mounting in my body. If I had been standing on the high diving board in the Olympic freestyle final I would have felt less pressure. I managed to place my golf ball on the tee peg at the fourth attempt. It sat there, almost mockingly, daring me to swing and hit it. My legs had now turned into something probably resembling blancmange and I was not sure that they would reliably hold me upright until I had completed the shot. Stay focussed. Do what you have been doing all week on the range.

I went for broke and swung the club. The clubhead connected with the ball and it set off on a bullet like trajectory out into the open. For a moment it flew through the air, a brilliant white orb against the blue sky. Then, as if programmed by a higher power, it suddenly arced off wildly to the left in an almost perfect curve towards an area of dense woodland. Its flight path was terminated abruptly by a collision with a giant oak tree midway along the fairway. I just knew that the way my luck was going it was not going to bounce back onto the fairway. I was right. It cannoned straight into the trees.

'A little wayward…I'm warming up still,' I said half-heartedly as the disappointment of my opening shot sank in.

Diana then proceeded to smack her ball straight off the tee right down the middle, another eighty metres further on from where mine had landed. We headed off. I found my ball, off the fairway in the trees resting against a twig. I bent down and moved the twig. My ball moved slightly forward, maybe about two millimetres.

'That's a penalty stroke, Matthew,' Diana called out.

Penalty stroke? I looked across at her standing in the middle of the fairway, her ball perfectly placed at her feet. I wanted to say that it was supposed to be a relaxed, friendly game of golf and I realised that she wanted to be competitive, but did she really think I had gained a huge advantage because my ball had moved forward two millimetres when the hole was still 180 metres away? Did she not realise that I still had to hit the shot out of where it was now buried and that two millimetres further forward actually meant that it was still 179,998 millimetres away from the hole and, in the big scheme of things, two millimetres is so infinitesimally small, it would make absolutely no difference whatsoever. The tension in my body and fear of failure in front of Diana had made me edgy and tetchy. I took a deep breath and accepted that I would lose a shot because of the major misdemeanour of gaining a full two millimetres and got on with it.

As a result of my apprehension and turmoil my next shot, which had to travel over a wide brook that was guarding the front of the green, landed right on the far edge of the waterside bank. Diana hit her second shot with deft precision straight onto the green and we made our way towards where the balls had landed. Hers perfectly placed, mine requiring me to perform what seemed to me to be some sort of trick shot. I stood over my ball, my left foot on the upper part of the bank and my right on the lower part nearest the water. I swung, connected with the ball and watched as it lofted beautifully into the air and flew towards the centre of the green. At the moment of impact my lower foot slid down the bank with the momentum of my swing. It was one of those irreversible moments. You know what's going to happen but there is not a damned thing you can do to change the outcome. My whole body weight shifted onto my sliding foot and down I went, tumbling in an undignified heap right into the brook. To add to my embarrassment I landed flat on my back in the water.

'Great shot,' were the first words I heard. Unbeknown to me my ball had travelled the remaining sixty metres straight into the hole. I didn't know whether to laugh or cry. Somehow I had managed to par the first hole.

As I managed to scramble on to my knees in the water to get up I could see Diana looking around in puzzlement to see where I had gone. She hadn't seen my misfortune at all as she had been watching the flight of the ball. I considered that this was an opportune moment to crawl along the brook into the undergrowth and disappear no questions asked. However I was sure to be spotted. As she turned away I managed to clamber out, in my soaking wet state, to one side and to her rear. Got to style it out I thought.

'Thanks Diana. Yes, tricky pitch shot, I have to say, but they are the ones you have to make to save par,' I said, as nonchalantly as I could.

She turned in the direction of my voice and did a double take.

'Matthew! You are soaked! How did you...oh...my god...you fell in the brook? How funny.'

It didn't feel too funny from my point of view. I was wet through and despite the sun shining it was still a chilly winter's day.

'You can't continue the round like that, Matthew. Look, I will wait here while you go back to the clubhouse and get some fresh clothes. There is a shop there that has lots of stuff.'

I had no choice really. I was soaked through to my underpants. As quickly as I could I legged it back to the clubhouse. It cost me almost a hundred and fifty pounds for new trousers, a shirt and a jumper. Fortunately I hadn't had my windproof on so I was spared that expense.

I caught up with Diana at the second tee and apologised profusely for keeping her waiting. We played on. By now though, I was resigned to something else going wrong on the remainder of the round. It seemed that the path to a romantic ending with Diana was going to be difficult with many an obstacle to be surmounted before I could rest easy. It may have been my acceptance of this state of affairs that caused me to relax, more in a 'sod it, it's all gonna go tits up somewhere' kind of attitude than any real loosening up on my part, but for the next nine holes I played reasonably well.

It was after we had teed off at the eleventh that she dropped the bombshell. I'd played well enough to feel that I could attempt to chat about something other than how well Diana was playing and had casually asked how business was. She gave me a very broad run down of her hectic week and then almost as an afterthought, she casually gave me the news.

'Oh, Matthew, I meant to tell you. That chap we ran into at the driving range is suing.'

My mouth had obviously dropped open and my expression must have conveyed some sort of astonishment, as she felt compelled to clarify the situation by refreshing my memory.

'You know. That chap that slipped on the golf balls.'

I really didn't need reminding. The incident, along with all the other mishaps that had befallen me on my search for love were all firmly imprinted in my skull. I could only utter a feeble, 'Oh, really' by way of a response.

'Yes. He is claiming damages, personal injury, loss of earnings, negligence, medical expenses and loss of enjoyment of the facilities during his period of injury. We are doing it on a no win, no fee basis.'

Is that all I thought. Why doesn't he throw in attempted murder, assault by spherical objects and loss of weight through being unable to feed his fat face whilst bed ridden.

'Has he got a case, Diana?' I mumbled.

'Well I am not going to prejudge these things Matthew until I have examined the facts fully but if it can be demonstrated that the driving range is at fault by supplying defective equipment then he may well have. Oh, and I will need you as a witness at some point since you saw first-hand what happened. It would have been useful if we had managed to retrieve that faulty basket.'

Terrific. That's all I need. To be a witness in an accident claim which I knew to be false, which I was actually responsible for and which was now being pursued by a woman who I fancied like mad and was trying, very unsuccessfully, to impress. I was grateful that no faulty basket would ever see the light of day.

'Err...can't you put him off? I mean who needs the inconvenience of legal action,' I blurted out without thinking.

'Put him off, Matthew? Why would I want to do that? He is a client and it is my job to advise him correctly. On top of which he is a highflying corporate type who is unlikely to be fazed by a court case. And, as it happens, I quite like the inconvenience of legal action, as you put it, since it pays my bills. Now, are you going to hit that ball? Lunch is calling and I am absolutely ravenous.'

No win, no fee. I was the one in the no win situation. If I went along with the case and lied, sooner or later I would be caught out. That would completely finish my chances with Diana. If I confessed all to her it would completely blow my credibility and that would completely finish my chances with Diana. My appetite for both lunch and golf had suddenly waned. I shanked the ball straight into the tree on my next shot. The remainder of my round was a disaster. I might as well have gone around the rest of the course with a scythe in my hand. Divots, grass, earth all flew in a multitude of directions. The one thing that failed to fly with any sense of real direction was the ball.

Back at the clubhouse we changed and sat down to lunch.

'Thank you for the game Matthew. You had, shall we say, an interesting round. Now what are you having to drink. A gin and tonic must surely be in order, don't you think?' She giggled as she spoke and placed her hand on mine.

The sensation of her slender fingers seemed to energise me, give me an immediate rush of positivity. I knew she liked me. She wouldn't be here otherwise. She found me different from the type of men with whom she normally associated. I found her very different too. Elegant, sophisticated, intelligent and beautiful with a sensuous, soft quality beneath the surface that she was clearly used to keeping under wraps by the demands of her job. Why would a woman like Diana need a dating site? I didn't know but obviously she was not meeting the kind of guys she wanted to. Maybe I was her type. This was after all our third date even if the second one had not gone the way I had wanted it. So something was right. My positive thoughts were beginning to evolve into full-blown optimism. The second gin and tonic was helping in that regard too. The conversation was relaxed. I started to find out things about her. She told me that she had been married to a lawyer. It had lasted nine years until the pressures of their careers pulled them apart. We had something in common there. She had achieved a level in her career that had satisfied all of her professional ambitions but now she felt it was time for her to focus on her personal ones. There had been plenty of opportunities for dates or indulgence in casual flings, but now she wanted something that would lead to a permanent relationship. Her social life revolved around after work wine bars, at which more often than not she would be the object of the drink-fuelled advances of some up and coming legal executive or solicitor, or dinner parties where invariably she would be the only single there. She had encountered a few potential relationships that never quite got off the ground mainly because things were not always what they had seemed. One guy revealed the fact that he was married after three weeks of dating. Another had been a con artist who liked to prey on professional women. The dating site had been the recommendation of a friend of hers, she told me, who had actually met someone on there and was due to get married in six months' time. So it did work.

Our lunch orders arrived and the conversation flowed.

'So, tell me about you Matthew. What's a good looking, charming man like you doing on a dating site?'

My life story was about to be revealed but first I had to clear up the one issue that was still troubling me. I had made my decision. I knew I could not embark on a potential relationship whilst there was deceitfulness lurking in the background.

'Diana, there is something I have to tell you.'

I saw a brief look of dismay cloud her expression.

'The case. The one with the fat guy and the driving range. There is something you should know.'

I told the full story of the incident. I told her that it was all my fault. That it had happened because I had never been to a driving range before. That in fact I had never played golf before either. That the left handed clubs were borrowed. I apologised for not telling her straightaway. I watched her face. I waited for her reaction. She seemed calm. I guessed that in the legal profession you got used to people changing their stories.

'You had never ever played golf before?' she said finally.

Of all the things that I'd said I thought this was the oddest one to pick up on but I soon found out where it was going.

'Why? Why did you make out that you could play golf and then cause all that havoc? No, let me guess. You were trying to impress weren't you Matthew. Trying to make out you are something you are not. For what? To get into my knickers? Was that it? Why are you men such shits?'

I wasn't sure I could answer any of these questions but I made an attempt to explain my motive, not least of all because I was wounded by the 'knickers' jibe.

'Shut up Matthew. Why can you not just be who you are? That is all us women want. A straightforward, no nonsense, down to earth guy who is comfortable with himself and honest. I don't know whether you realised it or not but I liked you. You were refreshingly different. All you had to do was be yourself. I really don't care whether you play golf or not. It is not a problem to have different interests. In fact it's healthy. But what I do not like is deceit. I see enough of it every day. How can I trust anyone who perpetrates such pretence just to create an impression? How would I ever know who you really are?'

I felt battered now. I tried to justify my actions by blaming the dating site environment. Not knowing how to behave. The whole culture of being who you wanted to be. The need to compete and get an advantage. The golf was just a way of gaining an advantage with a woman I found attractive, with a woman who I knew would be inundated with requests for a date. My justification did not seem to be going down too well.

'I have choices Matthew. Just because I am on a dating site and may get a lot of attention does not mean I cannot exercise those choices. I am not taken in by any of the nonsense I get on that site. I am selective and, if you recall correctly, I selected you.'

I tried to lighten the mood. 'I am sorry Diana. It was a mistake. A huge mistake. I know I am hopeless at golf but I love tennis. Do you play?'

'What would you like me to say Matthew? That I do play tennis? Would that make you feel better? Actually, I have never played so I have no idea of whether I could share your enthusiasm. Does that make you like me less? I thought not. That's the point Matthew.' She got up to leave.

'Will I see you again, Diana?'

'I will be in touch. We have that legal issue to resolve, have we not?' And she was gone.

I slumped into an armchair at home. What a day. My emotions had done the full Blackpool Big Dipper experience. And like the Big Dipper I had finished at the lowest point. Clearly I had messed up. My chances of seeing Diana again, other than to sort out the legal claim against the driving range, were remote. And now it was likely that Mr Corporate High Flyer Fat Man would be suing me instead once Diana had updated him. On top of which, in the back of my mind, I was worried sick about the incident at the Hemmingwell Halls. It had also cost me over a thousand pounds for a newly acquired golf hobby. What else could go wrong. I fell asleep where I sat.

I was awoken by the shrill ring of my mobile.

'Matthew! It's Julia!'

'Julia? Julia! Oh, shit...you–'

'I beg your pardon Matthew?'

'Sorry. Sorry Julia. Bit of a cold. I sneezed. Sneezing a lot. What's up?'

'Nothing's up Matthew. I just wondered if you fancied meeting for a drink or something. After all we didn't get to meet properly the first time did we, what with all that horrid robbery thing.'

'How is that Julia? The horrid robbery thing. Any news?' I had almost forgotten to add Julia's damaged property to my list of woes.

'Not yet. The police are still looking but they don't seem to be trying very hard. They said that as nothing was actually stolen it may be difficult to press charges even if they do trace the muggers.'

'Wait a minute Julia. If there was nothing taken then there can't have been a robbery and therefore we are not muggers. I mean they...they, whoever they may be... they can't be muggers. So the police shouldn't be chasing them. Maybe you should drop it...don't you think?'

'Drop it? Whose side are you on Matthew? You are not one of those liberal do gooders are you that thinks muggers should be sympathised with and given holidays in Majorca? They destroyed my chandeliers. They were worth over one thousand pounds each. I have told the police I want them pursued. Now what about that drink?'

To be honest I did feel like a drink now but not with Julia. Not that there was anything wrong with Julia apart from a tendency to exaggerate, blow things out of proportion and be the owner of a crap mobile that was the cause of my horrendous party error in the first place. Add to the fact that she seemed to want to hound me to the ends of the earth over two stupid chandeliers, although I suppose she wasn't to know it was me personally, and I thought I'd rather steer well clear at this point. I explained to her that I was away on business for a while and tried as best as I could to sound as if I might be interested in doing something at some point in the future. I saw the opportunity to manipulate the situation.

'Perhaps we could get together when all of this...this, err...robbery thing, has died down Julia. It must be a lot to contend with for you at the moment. But it's only a couple of lights. Nobody is hurt. The sooner it's over the sooner we could meet up I guess. I can think of far better things to be doing than worrying about what's happened. We all have to move on, look on the bright side. Build a bridge. Get over it.'

Julia didn't seem too impressed with my flippant dismissal of her situation but the hint of a future drink seemed to cheer her and we left it at that. I hoped that she might consider my advice and let the matter go. If she did I would gladly buy her a drink.

I made a cup of tea and sat down in front of the computer. A promotional email from MacFadden's popped up. Carlos was having a wine tasting evening. Tonight. I hadn't checked my emails in days. I then logged onto the Cupid's Pursuit site. There were a few messages in my in box. One from a lady in Brighton.

'Hi. Like your profile. If you like mine, let me know and we can go from there. Sue.'

One from a lady in Aberdeen.

'Hello, any luck with the ladies so far? Let me know if you would like to meet.'

I was finding out that a lot of time on dating sites is spent filtering out who is not suitable. I liked the look of the lady in Aberdeen but it was obvious that she suffered with shortcomings in the geography department and clearly she may not have considered that the small matter of the five hundred and forty two miles between our separate localities could be an impediment on the path to true love. Sue from Brighton looked very appealing in her picture, auburn hair and a beaming smile. Brighton was manageable and so that I could keep my options open, I sent back a 'maintenance' reply thanking her for her email, saying that I liked her profile too.

The one that caught my eye was from a twenty six year old. She said her name was Delita Popov. She was Russian but living in London. Apparently she liked my picture and liked older men too. She asked me to get in touch. I was flattered. I wasn't looking for a younger woman, well not that much younger anyway. But she was very attractive. Short black hair, green eyes. Her second picture can only have been uploaded just to emphasise how long and shapely her legs were. Even though she did not fit my relationship criteria I felt a rush of excitement as I dispatched my reply.

Now for that drink. I called Cecil.

'Cecil. Are you going to that wine tasting at Fad's tonight?'

'The geezer has lost the plot mate. Fucking wine tasting. What's he trying to do to the place? He'll have it full of wankers and snobs banging on about some shit South American wine he's bought on the cheap in a friggin cash and carry.'

'Chill Ces. He is trying. There are some good wines around from South America. Give it a chance. It could be laugh and we don't need to stay all night. Look mate after the day I have had I wouldn't mind a beer or a glass of plonk.'

After telling him all about my latest disaster with Diana I wasn't sure if Cecil was sympathetic or taking the mickey. It was clearly more of the latter, as he made no attempt to stifle his involuntary laughter.

'Ok, see you in Fad's later then, mate,' he said.

19

'Mateo. Cucaracha. Welcome. Drink for you. On the house.' Carlos handed me a small looking glass that contained a clear liquid. 'Down in one.'

I did as he suggested. 'What was that, Carlos?'

'Pisco Puro.'

'Pisco? Pisco what?' It tasted much better than the name suggested, very smooth, almost non-alcoholic.

'It is the little bird. The drink of the Incas. It's a spirit, a brandy and we drink it all the time in Peru.'

'Yeah, but isn't this a wine tasting evening Carlos?'

'Mateo. Sure it is. But the Pisco is made from the Quebranta grape so it is ok. It's a grape juice. Just like wine. And as a special promotion everyone who comes to my wine tasting tonight gets a free Pisco - on the house, no charge, gratis.'

'Well, it's very nice Carlos. Can I try another one?'

'No problemo Mateo. But it is very potent so you must not drink it like the natives. Now you go and sit down. It is table service tonight. Hanka and Janka will be taking your orders.' Carlos walked round the bar and put his arm around my shoulder, leading me towards one of the tables. Raising his hand he pointed at a middle-aged man wearing black trousers, a white shirt, a black bow tie and a long black apron that stretched down below his knees. 'That gentleman over there, Mateo, is our guest sommelier this evening. He specialises in South American wines so if you want to know anything just ask him. The featured wines are all at twenty-five per cent off tonight.'

'Sounds cool, Carlos,' I said. 'You should do some good business.'

'I took your advice Mateo. You know, promotions, freebies.' He patted me on the shoulder and turned back towards his bar.

I took a seat and sat back to savour my Pisco, this time more slowly. The place was filling up. The crowd was mid-twenties to late thirties with a few either side of each age group. Carlos clearly had done a good job of the promotion. For once he'd thought of some background music, a mix of Latino cafe grooves and funky house classics. The lighting had been subdued in the right spots. The effect was to give the place a Friday night, the weekend starts here, feel good factor. With a bit more enthusiasm and a bit more advertising Carlos could have the place buzzing. My thoughts were brought to an abrupt conclusion by a hefty slap between the shoulder blades.

'Geezer. How you doin?' Cecil's entrances were never subtle.

Within ten seconds Hanka or it may have been Janka was hovering.

'You like Pisco, Sir?'

Cecil looked bemused. 'Do what, darling?'

'You want to take a Pisco?'

Cecil turned towards me, his eyebrows raised.

'A Pisco, Cecil. Off the tray. It's the drink. A freebie from Carlos.'

Cecil immediately grabbed two of them and necked them both. 'Not bad. What is it?'

I explained that it was a brandy, like a shot and that it was part of the promotion. Cecil grabbed two more.

'Easy Ces. We got all night. Sit down. What do you want to drink?'

I browsed the wine list especially prepared for the event. Cecil wanted beer.

'Ces, let's have a bottle of the wine. It's twenty five per cent off and it will be showing a bit of support for Carlos. He's gone to a lot of trouble to get this together. I will pick a bottle.'

'Yeah, it's all right mate. Some birdies in for a change. Might be a bit of a mumble on tonight geezer.'

I chose a bottle of Tacama Gran Blanco, for no other reason other than I liked the label. The guest sommelier arrived holding the bottle at an angle in front of his body, in both hands so that we could read the label.

'Excellent choice Sir. The Gran Blanco has a beautiful intense colour. It is a bright, neat, fresh white wine with citrus notes. It is lightly bodied yet well balanced, denoting finesse and it is a great complement to fresh, lightly seasoned foods.' He removed the cork smoothly. 'Would you like to taste Sir?'

I jumped in before Cecil could reply offering my wine glass.

'What do you think Sir?'

'Err...yes...very nice,' was my amateurish response.

'Yes, a fruity bouquet with a hint of summer flowers and a light lemony palate, don't you think?' the sommelier added, as he poured some more of the contents of the bottle into my glass, finishing with an extravagant flourish.

With my embarrassingly limited knowledge of wine and my total lack of familiarity with any South American wines at all, I resorted to nodding my head and sucking the roof of my mouth simultaneously by way of agreement.

Cecil grabbed the bottle from the sommelier's grasp. 'Don't be shy geez. Fill us up.'

The sommelier left us to it.

MacFadden's bar had suddenly taken on a new lease of life. The bar was full. The music was pumping and Carlos was now in the middle of what had become an impromptu dance floor, twisting and rotating in his own unique dance style, arms flailing above his head, body gyrating in what appeared to be a mix of Latin salsa and an Apache war dance. His expression had set into something resembling that of a salacious sex fiend with significant learning difficulties. But in all fairness to him he had three delectable looking ladies surrounding him. To a bystander it would not have been clear whether they were mesmerised by the unveiling of a new dance genre or they were all paramedics who recognised the signs of an impending medical emergency. Either way he was getting more attention than Cecil and me.

We had almost finished the bottle of Gran Blanco when I suddenly found myself looking up at PC Penny.

'Michael. Cecil. How are you? You remember Sheryl. From last week? Do you mind if we join you?' They were both holding the freebie Pisco Pura.

Cecil was straight on the case. 'Grab a pew, ladies. Let me get some more drinks.'

I managed only a nod such was my shock at seeing Louise, not only because of the complexities of my double identity but also because she looked gorgeous. Her blonde hair was down and she was wearing a pale pink blouse over a tight short skirt. She sat down next to me.

'Oi. Geezer. Smellihead.' Cecil wasted no time in attracting the wine expert's attention.

'You liked the wine, Sir? Maybe you would like to try the Gran Tinto? It's a very nice red,' he said to Cecil.

'Dish it up geez. And another bottle of that blank stuff. Yeah, and four more of them piss shot things too.'

I was cringing. Sheryl appeared amused by the wide boy cockney that was Cecil.

Louise smiled and looked at me. 'So how have you been Michael?'

'Good. Good. Thanks. Yes Good.'

'It's ok Michael. I am off duty now. You don't have to pretend to be good all the time,' Louise laughed.

I couldn't decide whether Louise was flirting with me or whether it was the effect of the Pisco Pura that made me think she might be. I'd drunk three of them already, and half a bottle of wine too. She had that mischievous look in her eyes, the one that I'd last seen up close and personal through my gorilla mask. The wine arrived along with the shots. The red was opened first.

'Would you like to try Sir?'

This time Cecil jumped right in. He sniffed it, waving it in an exaggerated fashion beneath his nose, pausing briefly to let the aroma penetrate his senses. Next he sipped it, savoured it, and ran it around his mouth, his tongue clearly relishing the liquid. He swallowed. The sommelier, entranced by probably the first person to show some consideration for his beloved wine, awaited the verdict.

'Hmmm. Woody, rich bouquet. Overtones of pluminess. Smokey but dry palate. Hints of…octopus,' was Cecil's response, a huge grin on his face.

Louise and Sheryl burst into fits of giggles. The sommelier's face dropped as it dawned on him that Cecil was taking the mickey.

'Just pour it geezer. It's plonk, ain't it. Right ladies. Get these pissos down you and let the party begin.'

Two more Pisco Puros followed in quick succession.

Carlos appeared on the scene. 'How you doing, you cucarachas? And who are these lovely lassies? Senoritas, I am Carlos MacFadden, laird of these premises.'

Carlos was now in full-blown ScotSpan, a hybrid language that indicated that he had entered an alcohol inspired identity crisis.

'Geezer. Why have you not got any Scottish wines going on?'

I wasn't sure whether Cecil's question was designed to throw Carlos or test him.

'Do me a favour Cecil. Us Jocks only make wine out of trees, brambles and gooseberries. You Sassenachs would never stomach it. It's all you can do to stomach our whiskey! Now ah dinnae ken why you two senoritas are sitting here with these two cucarachas when you should be dancing wi' me. And go easy with the Pisco Pura or you'll be mad wae it.'

The girls seemed highly amused by Carlos.

'Pleased to meet you Carlos. I am Louise and this is my friend Sheryl. It's a very nice bar you have here.'

'You lassies have very good taste. Let me get you a drink on the house. On Carlos MacFadden. Tell you what…let's try the Tacama Selección Especial. You will like this one.'

The sommelier approached with the wine, a little more tentatively this time but seeing Carlos still at the table, he went straight into expert mode. 'Ladies, Gentleman. The Tacama Selección Especial.' He gave the bottle an exuberant flourish and began to pour. 'An intense and complex bouquet. It brings to mind plums and liquorice with peppery notes to enhance its richness. A taste of Selección Especial is unforgettable, a rare–'

'Well if you cut the bullshit geezer maybe we will get to taste it,' Cecil interrupted.

I never did understand why Cecil needed to be so boorish sometimes. He was far from ignorant, had an active and informed mind and, when he wanted to be, could be very charming. It's just that most of the time he didn't want to be. He wanted to be the centre of attention and it was easier for him to do that by adopting an unrefined manner that was not constrained by the niceties of polite society.

We now had four bottles of wine on the table, two whites and two reds plus several shots of Pisco Pura. Carlos pulled up a seat in between Sheryl and Louise. It was clear he wasn't being the convivial host anymore but was fully intending to join us.

'So what do you two lovely lassies do then?'

'They are the long arm of the law, mate. So you better make sure you have your licence up to date cos once they drink your wine they'll nick you...and then deport you back to South America or Scotland or some other god forsaken place like that for being an illegal.'

'I'm no illegal Cecil. I've been here longer than you!'

'Only cos your older, geezer.' Cecil liked the last word.

Carlos turned to the girls. 'Are you the polis?'

'Well I am a police officer and Sheryl is a forensic scientist.'

Carlos topped up our glasses with the Tacama.

'I am very happy then to welcome the police to my humble establishment.'

'Cut the bollocks, Carlos. So, Louise, what's new in the world of fighting crime?'

I felt a shiver of unease as Cecil asked the question.

'Nothing too exciting at all, Cecil,' Louise said, 'I am afraid it is all very mundane. The life of a Metropolitan police officer, especially at my level, is not that glamorous. I get passed down all the crap jobs.' It must have been the wine or the South American brandy that was loosening Louise's tongue. 'I don't really discuss my job when I am off duty but I must tell you this. It's so funny. I had a job land on my desk just before I left tonight. Some woman is complaining about being mugged by two blokes dressed as a gorilla and an antelope, would you believe?'

I literally choked. The wine spewed out from my mouth and nose in a coughing, breathless stream straight down the front of my shirt. Even Cecil looked temporarily surprised. All eyes were on me now. I apologised.

'So sorry,' I wheezed, 'too big a gulp.'

Louise began to slap my back to help me recover. 'You seem to have a problem with that Michael. Estimating how much liquid you can get in your mouth.'

Sheryl started to giggle. I regained a bit of composure and kicked Cecil under the table. He got the message. Cecil was quick on the uptake. I caught the stealthy wink he gave to Carlos who seemed puzzled when Louise called me Michael. Cecil had seen my reaction to what Louise had said and realised that it was time to change the subject. Unfortunately Carlos didn't.

'How do you know they are blokes? If they are dressed up, I mean?'

I intervened as I wiped down my shirt. 'Carlos, the ladies don't want to talk about work. They are off duty.'

'It's ok M...err...Miguel. Maybe I can help them solve their crime. My brother is a police officer in Peru.'

I breathed a sigh of relief that, even though he was getting inebriated, Carlos had the savvy to pick up on what was going on. I guessed that because he'd known Cecil and me for so long he realised that things were never always what they seemed. Well, especially where Cecil was concerned, anyway. But I wasn't sure that he'd keep it up now that he was in inquisitive mood. I didn't know how to tell him that because he had a brother who was a copper in the Peruvian police force, that didn't make him and expert crime investigator. I beckoned to Hanka for more brandy. Anything to divert attention onto something different. I raised a glass.

'Here's to the future success of MacFadden's bar and a big thank you to Carlos for his hospitality.' I raised my glass in the toast and we downed the shot in one. 'Now get out there and strut your stuff Carlos.'

It never took much to encourage Carlos onto a dance floor and with a somewhat bizarre quiver of his pelvis he was off and running.

'Thanks Michael,' said Louise, 'It really didn't bother me but I really shouldn't be talking about my work to total strangers. So you rescued me there. From myself. These shots do go straight to your head. Oh by the way, I know it's work again but I thought you should know. Your lodger, Matthew, has been in touch. So thanks for passing on the message.'

I was tempted to ask how it was going but thought it best to drop it at that point. I'd had a few drinks by now and did not trust myself to get anything right at all. The fact that Louise had received Julia's complaint just served to make me want to keep quiet in case I totally incriminated myself. The girls got up to go to the ladies.

'Cecil. Listen. We have to talk. You heard her. You heard Louise. She's now looking into that stupid bloody incident. I am in the shit now.'

'What is the matter with you? I have already told you. Nothing has happened and even if that brainless bird whose party it was thinks that she has a complaint, the cops have got nothing. Mark my words the whole thing will be dropped. Even Carlos MacFadden, who doesn't know whether he is a fucking jock or a gaucho, can see they have nothing to work with. Just stay cool, well as cool as you can be with half a bottle of red down your shirt.'

'But Cecil. How long do you think it will be before she will put two and two together? She stopped me on the way that night. In the bloody gorilla suit. You know, with the taxi driver.'

'And? What has she got? She doesn't know anything, stupid. If she knew it was you she wouldn't be sitting here knocking back Carlos's freebies, would she? Now get a fucking grip and let's party. I am gonna make a move on this Sheryl bird. She's all right. And she's giving me the eye.' He shoved his wine glass disdainfully to one side and pointed towards the bar. 'I'll tell you what you can do, mate, to take your mind of all this bollocks. Get me a beer. I'm getting fed up drinking all this poncey wine.'

Table service was focused on the wine promotion so I made my way towards the bar. A crowd had developed and I joined a line of eager revellers spread along the length of the bar, their outstretched hands picked out in the downlights from the ceiling as they vied for attention. Behind the counter staff flitted from end to end in a buzz of activity, mixing cocktails, plucking fruit from trays to embellish colourful drinks, trying to service the ever increasing demand. My turn came eventually and I ordered two pints of Peroni. I felt a tap on my shoulder.

'Hellooooooo, fancy seeing you here!'

At first I didn't register who it was. It was probably because it was all out of context. MacFadden's was my local. I knew most of the usually sparse crowd that frequented the place.

'It's me. Abigail. How are you Matthew?'

Abigail. The spider date. The one who had stripped all her kit off in front of me. Just last Sunday.

'How am I? I am fine, Abigail. Fine thanks.' In the corner of my eye I spotted Louise and Sheryl returning to our table and Cecil waving at me to hurry up.

'I am so pleased to see you. Is this your local then?' Abigail said, a broad smile on her glossy lips.

'Well, no, not really...well sometimes. I mean it's local in that it's not far to go. I am just here with my friend who comes here sometimes,' I said deliberately trying to block Abigail's view of Cecil in the background.

'What's happened to your shirt? Did you spill something?'

It crossed my mind that that should have been obvious. It was unlikely that I had bought a white shirt with a red wine stain motif. She started to dab at it with a tissue.

'Don't worry Abigail it's nothing. It will be fine. Great to see you. I was just getting a drink.'

'Matthew, let me get you a drink. You were so kind to me the other night. Look, why don't I bring my friends over and join you. We can have a nice drink all together.'

'No!' I almost shouted it. 'I mean...no...I have to...to go. I have to change this shirt. It's soaked. I can't stand around like this. Good to see you Abigail. Bye.'

'That'll be £7.50 please mate,' said the barman, one of a number who had been hired especially for the evening. The two beers were placed firmly in front of me. I fumbled for my wallet. As I did Abigail picked up both drinks.

'I'll give you a hand Matthew. Is that your friend who is waving?'

'No. No...don't worry. It's fine. No... it's not...wait, Abigail.' I turned to take back the beers. I was interrupted by the insistent barman.

'That's £7.50 mate.'

By the time I had paid, Abigail was walking in the direction of Cecil's table. I rushed after her and got alongside her just as she was about to place the beers on the table. In an ill-judged, hasty movement, I made a grab for both glasses, intent on getting them off Abigail and directing her away from the table. Unfortunately at that precise moment she turned towards me obviously surprised by my sudden appearance. My left hand hit the beer nearest to the table sending half of the contents straight over Louise's pink blouse.

'What the fuck you doing geezer?'

Cecil was almost as shocked as Louise was at the sudden arrival of half a pint of cold lager down her front. I lunged forward to Louise's aid. It was purely a sub-conscious need to make the whole situation disappear, rather than any real practical measure to clear up the mess on Louise's blouse that caused me to start frantically wiping down her top with both hands.

Louise was calm. 'It's ok Michael. Don't worry. I will clean up in the ladies.'

She got up, accompanied by a stunned looking Sheryl and headed off to the ladies again.

'What's with throwing the fucking drinks around tonight, geezer? What's all that about?' Cecil's eyes betrayed his annoyance.

Abigail was still standing by the table, her face a mixture of confusion and amusement. 'Are you Michael? I am Abigail.'

'No, I am not fucking Michael, lady. And who are you anyway?'

'Cecil. Stay calm. Abigail is a friend of mine. I will explain later.' I turned to Abigail. 'I am sorry about that Abigail. Let me get you and your friend a drink.'

I led her back to the bar. 'Look Abigail, my friend Cecil is an undercover detective and...and...well the two ladies who were at the table are suspected drug traffickers...and I am sort of helping him so I have a different identity and...well, she thinks my name is Michael. So you must call me Michael otherwise it would blow the whole operation.'

'Ooooo, that is very exciting Matthew...I mean...Michael.'

She had that look in her eye again, the one that I had seen in the bar on our date and she was moving in closer.

'Oh, but that was a bit unfortunate spilling your drink over her.'

Explanations tumbled around in my head, my anxiety at the way the situation had developed causing my mind to search for a rapid response.

'Well...well, that was just part of the cover. Erm...Cecil wanted me to check her for... for a...a wire. You know...a bug. A microphone bug. So I had to think of something fast so I could...well, search her, without it being too obvious.'

'Wow...that was a clever ruse with the drink then, but isn't it usually the detectives that carry the bugging devices?' Abigail asked, her face full of wonderment. She had a point.

'Well. Yes...usually, but in this case...sometimes the criminals...err...like to do the bugging because ...look it's complicated Abigail and could be dangerous.

I can't say too much more. I have said enough already. And it's best you stay away. In fact now you have been seen with me it might be best if you left.'

Abigail leaned forward, put one arm around my neck, her other hand tracing her fingers over my chest, pushed her boobs hard against me and whispered in my ear. 'Oh it is exciting. I think you are so brave and sexy. If you want to come over when you have done you know where I am. And if you want to come as 'Michael' don't forget your big pistol...mmmm.'

Before I had time to think of an answer Carlos was on the scene.

'Hey, Mateo... err... Miguel. Another lovely lady, eh? You should be out there dancing.'

'You know me Carlos, I don't dance much –'

'Not you Miguel. The lovely lady.'

Abigail was grinning like a Cheshire cat, her expression telling me that she was concocting some mystery in her head about my newest pseudonym, Miguel. I winked at her and put my index finger to my lips in a conspiratorial gesture. Carlos, grasped her hand. As he turned to lead Abigail to the dance floor I grabbed his arm, temporarily halting his progress.

'Keep her away from my table Carlos.'

'Do me a favour. She's dancing with me now. She won't want to go near your table. No problemo.'

I turned to see that Louise and Sheryl were back at the table with Cecil. They were all staring directly at me. I said goodbye to Abigail and went to join them. I started to apologise profusely to Louise.

'Don't worry about it Michael. Clearly your lady friend is a distraction.' Her friendly persona now had a hint of detachment. 'It's best we go now, anyway. I need to change this top. It's been fun. Thank you for the drinks.'

With that they were gone.

'You did it again then mate. You screwed up the evening.' Cecil's verdict was about to be delivered.

'I am sorry Ces. It wasn't my fault. I –'

'Who's fucking fault was it then mate? I told you to stop panicking. You are making a mountain out of a friggin molehill. You ain't done nothing. Well you hadn't until you tipped half a fucking pint of cold lager all over your policewoman and then started groping her tits in front of the whole bar. She's got more on you there than anything else. Common assault and sexual assault.'

Cecil noted the alarm in my eyes.

'I'm winding you geezer! The more you fucking panic and behave like some sort of half-witted imbecile the more you draw attention to yourself. You'll start making her suspicious and she won't even know why. She'll start thinking she should suspect you of something cos you behave like a twat every time she sees you. I mean that's the second time you've spilt booze in her direction. The first time you missed. This time you didn't. It's the second time you blew half your drink out through your nose as well. She'll start thinking your some sort of half man, half dolphin. Imagine it from her point of view. She's run into you twice in the very same bar and both times you can't even manage to keep your drink either in your glass or in your mouth.'

It did sound disastrous the way Cecil told it.

'I know. It's all this dating thing. It's not happening Cecil. It's all gone wrong since I signed up. It's the pressure. I am going to pack it in.'

'Well, mate, I'm beginning to think maybe you should. It's starting to go wrong for me too. I was on a dead cert tonight with that Sheryl. The white ones were coming down geezer and now I'm sitting here with you, looking like a couple of sad sacks. And who is that Abigail bird anyway?' I explained to Cecil about Abigail.

'You mean that bird with the massive tits is the bird you told me about that stripped off and wanted you to give her one and you didn't? You are a roll and butter, geezer.' Cecil caught the eye of one of the waitresses. Ignoring the fact that she was carrying a tray with a bottle of wine and two glasses, he clicked his fingers at her. 'Janka. Two large Bombay and tonics please darling. And plenty of fresh mint.'

The two drinks arrived in clear ice blue logoed Bombay Sapphire glasses, the crystal clear gin, ice and splash of tonic contrasting enticingly with the bright green crispness of the mint. I savoured the aroma before taking a generous mouthful, the sharp tang of the gin followed by the almost sweet after taste of the mint. The hit was almost immediate.

'Cheers mate.' Cecil clanked his glass against mine. 'I can't believe you let that Abigail slip through your fingers. She serves it up on a plate...you gotta get a grip mate. You should be out there partying like a legend. Taking down the birdies. Life's too short to be worrying mate. You don't want to be lying on your deathbed thinking I should have shagged more birds. Chill. Keep the dream alive You hearing me geezer.'

'But Cecil, I've told you, I've done with the partying. I am fed up with waking up with the hangover from hell and then wasting the whole of the next day trying to get myself back to normal. Fed up with the merry go round of trying to meet women, spending shed loads of money and ending up shitfaced on my own in some bar at four in the morning. I am getting older Cecil. We all are. I don't want to be on my death bed, alone with no one there for me and all I have is vague drunken memories of women I shagged whose names I can't even remember. Laying there at the end of it all with no one looking out for me. No one loving me. The party stops somewhere Cecil, even for you. And then we look around and what have we got for the partying? Nothing. Not a fucking thing. Just missed opportunities. Wasted days. And who remembers us for it? Nobody. I want somebody to remember me, Cecil. I want someone who wants me for who I am. For me. Who doesn't mind if I am not partying. I just want something...someone a bit more solid in my life. But where am I gonna get that Cecil? Where?' The gin was starting to kick in.

My maudlin outburst was cut short by Carlos and Abigail. They were clearly in high spirits, energised by the dancing. I had had enough by then. I was tired. Exhausted from the nervous energy I was using up.

'Did you catch them Matthew...I mean...Michael?' Abigail was flushed and breathing heavily from her exertions on the dance floor.

'Catch who? And don't you start with this Michael bollocks too,' Cecil interrupted. He was looking at me for an explanation. I stood up. I drained the last of my Bombay, put the glass down on the table and headed for the door.

20

I woke up hot. Thirsty and hot. The winter sun was streaming through my half-open bedroom curtains, its warmth focussed straight onto my face. I looked at my watch. Eleven forty five. Another day in danger of being wasted. My head was fuzzy, my eyes bleary. I raised myself into a sitting position, fumbled about for the remote control and powered up the television. Flicking through the channels I could see life was going on around me no matter what my state. Cheery weather forecasters enthusiastically explaining what a great day it was going to be even though it was half over already. Celebrity chefs churning out recipes that were impossible to follow and then pointing out that you had to log onto websites to find out how to do it yourself. Each programme interspersed with advertisements for the festive season's round of TV programmes, shopping and gift ideas.

As my brain began to come to terms with the fact that I was now conscious and would have to start dealing with everyday life, it started sending out messages that my head was hurting and I was very dehydrated. I assumed this was normal survival stuff designed to get me back to some sort of post alcohol equilibrium but right now it was an inconvenience. I wanted to curl up again under the quilt and sleep but my head was telling me I had to take a variety of actions in order to be able to deal with the daylight world that weather forecasters and celebrity chefs were now presenting to me. That meant Berocca, paracetemol, breakfast of some sort and copious amounts of water. I struggled downstairs. Loaded up on the Berocca, sparkling water, toast and tea. I checked my mobile for messages. Nothing. I switched on the PC. I had two messages on the site. One from Sue in Brighton, again asking if I'd like to meet up at some point and another from the young Russian stunner, Delita. I sent a message to Brighton Sue.

'Would love to meet sometime Sue. Shame we are not a bit closer.'

It was another maintenance message, keeping my options open. Delita was a different matter. My hangover was creating a devil may care attitude. Any caution, tact or good sense was being seriously suppressed by the influence of alcohol withdrawal symptoms on the controlling centre of my nervous system.

'*Thanks for the reply Delita. Would love to meet up. Anytime! Love your pix too. Call me.*'

I'd never done it before. I had always been a very private person. I am not sure what possessed me to do it then other than a logic malfunction, but before I had given it any thought at all, I had typed out and sent Delita my mobile phone number.

By one thirty I was showered, dressed, and still not sure what to do with the day. I was tempted to call Diana to see if she'd like to meet for lunch but I thought better of it. Her curt and hurried exit the day before left me feeling I should let the dust settle. I figured that a walk down to town for the papers might help clear my head.

The chill winter air cut sharply through the fuzziness in my skull as I walked back with an armful of papers. My head cleared but not sufficiently enough to stop me deciding to call in at MacFadden's as I passed the doorway. Hanka, or it may have been Janka, was behind the bar. There were already several lunchtime drinkers scattered around. I was about to order a coffee when Carlos suddenly appeared from nowhere.

'Hey, Mateo. How you doing this bright sunny morning? Or are you Miguel today?'

A conspiratorial wink flickered in his eye. He seemed inordinately cheery. I told him how I felt since he had asked.

'No worries, amigo, I have the perfect hangover cure.'

Within minutes a large Bloody Mary with a stick of celery and a cherry tomato garnish appeared on the bar.

'Compliments of the house, Mateo. I owe you one for introducing me to the lovely Abigail. A real firecracker.'

Whatever pyrotechnics Abigail had been the cause of I didn't feel inclined to ask at that stage. I stared at the tall red concoction placed in front of me. The last think I wanted was an alcoholic drink and especially one with vodka in it. Carlos could see the queasy look on my face.

'It will do you good Mateo. Kill you or cure you. It's full of vitamins and it's a good hair of the doggie.'

The prospect of the possible relief of my hangover encouraged me to take a swig. It was palatable, almost appetizing. I took another mouthful. It was refreshing I had to admit.

'So, what happened with Abigail, Carlos?' Curiosity had got the better of me.

'She knows how to rumba, man, I'll tell you that much. She has grace, rhythm and style, a real dazzler on the floor. Where did you find her?'

I shrugged off his question with a smile. I didn't feel up to going through my brief history with Abigail right at that point. I also knew that I shouldn't take Carlos's assessment of Abigail's dancing skills at total face value since I had seen his own unique attempts at the Latin style and he had imbibed his fair share of the Pisco Puros the previous evening too.

'Two more of them and one for yourself Carlos.'

The last person I needed to run into was Cecil but there he was, large as life, calling in the Bloody Marys.

'You look like shit, mate. What you been up to?'

I considered that Cecil's question was a tad unnecessary seeing as how he had spent most of the previous night drinking with me. I sipped my drink and didn't answer.

'I had a little text from the Canadian bird this morning, mate. Looks like the little mumble swerve didn't go to waste after all last night,' Cecil said as he pulled up a stool next to me.

I couldn't believe it. Here I was, hung over, fed up, harassed, stressed out and considerably out of pocket in my pursuit of love and my two closest acquaintances seemed to be setting themselves up nice as you like with two dates without the slightest bit of aggravation at all. I took another large slurp from my Bloody Mary. Sod's law, I figured. The harder you try, the less likely you are to succeed. Don't bother looking for something and it turns round and whacks you around the head to let you know it's there. Now Cecil was moving in on Sheryl who just happened to be a good friend of a police officer who, unbeknown to her at this stage, was on my case. I didn't want to think about it right now. It seemed to me that both Cecil and Carlos were full of the joys of spring and the Bloody Mary's flowed as a consequence.

By four o'clock my speech was slurred. I tried remonstrating with Cecil as he ordered a seventh straight Bloody Mary, arguing that it was my understanding that this particular cocktail was meant to be a hair of the dog and not meant to form part of a full on booze up. Cecil referred to me as a 'pussy' and got the seventh one in. There was no real point in arguing with him when he was in party mood. In any case I was getting beyond caring now that my hangover had eased and the Bloody Mary's had kicked in.

As I sat there, listening to Cecil in full flow, contemplating where the day was going to end up my mobile lit up with a text message. It was Delita Popov and she wanted to meet. Tonight. I suppose I shouldn't have been too surprised. I had said anytime but of all the times she could have picked she had to choose the moment I was sitting getting hammered with Cecil. Sod it. What the hell. May as well go for it, I thought. My mind-set had crossed over all the way into devil may care territory. In any case my two friends were getting themselves lined up with women, so why shouldn't I? It wasn't a competition but I had decided I wanted to meet her.

I made my way outside the front door of the bar for some privacy and called

Delita straight back. Her voice was mysterious, velvety and sexy with a strong east European accent. Mine was slurred with a hint of vodka but she didn't seem to notice. In my slightly intoxicated state I dispensed with the niceties of making an effort to arrange to meet her. I told her where I was and told her to meet me there. She didn't seem at all put out by my candid manner and if anything seemed excited about meeting.

One hour later Delita made an entrance. And what an entrance. She paused, framed in the doorway as she scanned the bar area. Her legs looked even better than they did in her picture, their impossible length now exaggerated in vertiginous heels that were surely not designed to walk in, their shapeliness emphasised in a diminutive tight leather skirt that embraced her hips almost severely. A fitted, short style leather jacket with distinctive inset zips and white contrast stitching, zipped tightly over a black lacy blouse completed her bold fashion statement. Her pause was fleeting. Her intense gaze alighted on me almost immediately.

'Matthew. Hello. I am Delita. I recognise you from picture. You look like you.'

I was pleased about that. She kissed me on both cheeks and then leaned back to look at me. The green of her eyes was accentuated by a hint of black eye liner. Her short black hair, scarlet lips and the stern darkness of her outfit gave her an air of mystery. Her Russian tone only served to enhance this impression.

'You like me? You like how I look?'

I wasn't sure if she was seeking my approval or establishing that she looked like she did on the site. I assured her I liked her very much. I was aware of Cecil and Carlos both looking at me from the far end of the bar as I led her to a table.

'Let me get you a drink Delita.'

Back at the bar I could see Cecil was dying to ask.

'She's my date Ces. From the internet site. So I need some space. Ok. Just me and her.'

'Alright geezer. Keep your hair on. Bit young for you, though, mate. Where you been hiding her? How old is she anyway?'

'Twenty-six. And I haven't been hiding her.'

There was still plenty of the Gran Blanco remaining from the previous night so I took a bottle back to the table. Too young for me. Maybe. But I was secretly pleased to be seen with a twenty-six year old. Especially one as striking as Delita. It wasn't doing my ego any harm after all the knocks. Every man in the bar, and all of the women too, had noticed her. You couldn't help it. And I was the one sitting with her. I knew she was unlikely to be the long-term love I was looking for, but right now she was a bonus. The copious Bloody Mary's had done two things. Cured my hangover, which was the point, but left me feeling slightly intoxicated, which was not the point. However, my tipsy state meant I was a lot more relaxed on this date than I had been on any other.

We chatted freely. Delita was from Moscow and a dancer, a classically trained ballet dancer. That perhaps accounted for those shapely legs. I was curious as to why she contacted me on the site. She explained that she had liked my picture and my straightforward profile that wasn't trying to impress but was simple and to the point. I refrained from telling her that I had been trying to impress but that I was just crap at it, especially where women were concerned. She said she liked older men and that most of the guys that she had met that were her age were immature. They didn't understand her art and she had nothing in common with any of them. She liked the more sophisticated type. I hoped that my indulgence in Bloody Mary's that afternoon had not dulled the debonair and cultured persona that was now struggling to make an appearance.

In an effort to impress I tried to recall what little I had ever heard about the ballet. The truth was that I knew nothing about it at all but somewhere in the deep recesses of my sub-conscious there were snippets stored on the Bolshoi Ballet, Nureyev and Nijinsky. Probably stuff I had picked up from playing quiz machines in pubs. I dropped what little I knew into the conversation. Delita seemed impressed. She stretched out a long slender hand and traced her red tipped fingers gently along my face.

'I knew I'd like you, Matthew. You are elegant, very sophisticated. Do you like Pavlova?'

Her touch sent a tremor through me but despite the thrill of it I wanted to remain cool and composed and play up to the refined image she was creating of me.

'Pavlova? Well, yes, I do, Delita. Pavlova definitely appeals to my taste.'

'Really, Matthew? How wonderful.'

I wasn't completely sure where Delita was going with this but I decided that it wouldn't do my chances any harm to have something in common with her. Her sensuous presence fuelled my imagination.

'Yes, I like the soft moistness, and the crisp, firm exterior,' I said, trying to be as creatively descriptive as my brain would allow after spending all afternoon in MacFadden's.

'You are very imaginative Matthew. I have never heard her described this way, but maybe I see what you mean.'

'Perhaps even with cream and...' I stopped in my tracks as the word 'her' registered in my head.

'Her? Did you say her?'

'Yes. Anna Pavlova. I model my dancing style on hers. She is such a great classical ballerina.'

I'd never heard of her. Ordinarily I'd have been mortified but the Bloody Marys and Gran Blanco had left me temporarily incapable of embarrassment. I realised that since we were about to get totally out of my depth on the subject of ballet that I should move the conversation along.

'More wine, Delita?'

I poured the last of the wine and, echoing from memory the comments of the previous night's wine expert, remarked on its fruity bouquet, hint of summer flowers and light, lemony palate. Delita smiled, looking at me from beneath her lashes.

'You very classy man, Matthew. You like wine. It is your hobby, no?'

Classy. It was yet another compliment. I was flattered that she thought I was classy, the older knowledgeable man.

'It's just a little passing interest. I like to try nice wines from time to time. Not really what you would call a hobby,' I said as I contemplated the pale yellow liquid in my glass.'

'So you have other hobbies, Matthew? You like games?' Delita asked.

She held the stem of the wine glass between her fingers and thumb, the forefinger of her left hand tracing a circle gently around the rim of the glass.

'Games. Yes, I do...football, tennis.'

'Tennis? Is good game. Playing games is good. I get spanked.'

'Oh I am sure you don't always get beaten, Delita,' I remarked sympathetically.

'No. Not always but sometimes spanked. I like.'

I thought of suggesting a game of tennis with her but considered that if she was always being beaten then perhaps I would wait until she had improved first.

'I am member of club, Matthew. Perhaps I take you there. You like?'

A gentle game couldn't hurt I thought and if she belonged to a club she couldn't be too bad. 'Yes, I'd like that, Delita. It would be fun. Look we have finished this bottle. Would you like some more of the Gran Blanco, or perhaps maybe try something different?'

'I get caned, Matthew.'

'Well, we can make it a small glass this time if you like.' I didn't want her to think I was trying to get her drunk.

'No, you no understand. I like to get caned.'

A bit of an odd admission I thought from a woman but no harm in letting your hair down occasionally. I'd been caned myself a few times especially on a typical Cecil bar crawl and if I drunk any more wine there was a strong possibility of getting caned tonight.

'I must admit I have got hammered the odd time myself, Delita. Never hurts...too much.' I laughed.

'Hammered? You brave, Matthew. I just get caned.'

Well whatever she called it I didn't think either of us should over indulge on a first date.

'So you want to play game, Matthew. Maybe you thrash me.'

'Sure. That would be great Delita. But as I am more experienced I would take it easy to start.' My tennis was far better than my golf, so a game with a date didn't hold any fears for me this time.

'Oh. You experienced. So you whip my ass.'

I had to laugh. It was funny listening to her attempts to use street language with her broad Russian accent.

'Well. No need for us to play too seriously to start. We can build up to it. Shall I get that wine then?'

'Why don't we have drink at my club, Matthew. I show you around. You might like to join. Then you and me play regularly.'

Delita seemed keen. Thinking about joining a tennis club with someone I had just met was a little premature but I agreed to go for a drink anyway. Tennis club bars could be very quiet at seven o'clock on a Saturday night so I assumed we would get a quick drink and then I could take her for dinner somewhere.

I knew that something wasn't as it should be when the taxi stopped where it did. We were in a main high street and parked up outside what looked like a nightclub. I paid the driver.

'Come Matthew. This way,' Delita said.

She led me up some stone steps to the main entrance. An intimidating bouncer in a long dark coat with fists clenched in black leather gloves, barred the way. The street light glistened on his shaved head. He glared at me as I approached but on seeing Delita he stepped to one side to let us pass. It crossed my mind that it wasn't usually necessary to have such security measures at the average suburban tennis club. We entered a foyer, my eyes immediately assaulted by lurid pink walls and shimmering blue pinpricks of light streaming from the ceiling, the mix of colours merging in the senses into a vivid purple haze. As I attempted to adjust my vision from street lit pavement to the gaudy psychedelia of the colour scheme, I became aware of someone coming towards us. She seemed to be dressed from head to foot in a crimson rubber cat suit. I thought at first that it was my eyes playing tricks with the colours again but as she got nearer I realised that she *was* actually dressed in a crimson rubber cat suit, which was perhaps a tad ambitious for a woman of her age and build.

'Hello darling.' She greeted Delita with kisses on both cheeks.

I made the mental observation that this was unlikely to be a tennis club after all and that the person in the cat suit was probably not the ladies singles champion.

'Lucy. This is Matthew. He is new. My guest. Lucy is club night organiser.'

Lucy must have been in her late fifties, the blonde dye in her hair not fully disguising the grey peeping through at the scalp and the tight cat suit doing very little to constrict her obvious bulges. Her face was heavily made up, dark eyeliner, long lashes and pink lips that were glossed so deeply they practically clashed with the lights. She put her hands on my shoulders and kissed me on both cheeks too. I could hear the rubber suit squeaking as she moved.

'Mmmm. Some new blood. Very nice. Pleased to meet you Matthew. Yes, I am Lucy or Loose Lucy as the members like to refer to me, ha ha.'

She leaned back, hands on hips and wiggled her boobs at me. Her nipples were forcing the rubber at the front of the outfit into two points, like glace cherries on an ice cream sundae. She turned to Delita.

'But darling he is not dressed properly. Do you want me to find him something. Why don't you both have a drink at the bar and I will have a look?'

I wasn't sure what Lucy had in mind but the rubber suit she was wearing didn't bode well. We entered the bar area. If I had been clinging to any illusions that this was Delita's tennis club and that maybe tonight was a fancy dress theme night, these were abruptly and very firmly eliminated as I surveyed the bar. If Lucy's mode of dress had been a surprise then the rest was an eye opener. Rubber, leather, PVC, transparent lace, chains and uniforms of every description. No one was in street clothes and not a tennis skirt to be seen. I was very much the odd one out. There was a girl in a black PVC nurses uniform; a guy in leather trousers, bare-chested but wearing what appeared to be a gas mask; another guy was being led around by a dog collar and lead, hands tied behind him, his mistress wearing fishnets, heels, a micro skirt, a German officer's hat and completely topless. There were two girls, who appeared to be twins, in outrageously short and revealing police uniforms; a she-devil in red basque, golden horns and red fishnet stockings, waving a cane. I turned to the bar more out of a need to collect my senses than to get a drink.

'You like my club, Matthew? You want to play?'

'It's not…err…not what I expected Delita…I thought that–'

'But I told you. It's a fetish club. I know you like. You said you like to play.'

I hadn't meant that sort of play at all and Delita hadn't said that it was a fetish club either. Whatever I had said or whatever she had said there was clearly a misunderstanding, maybe encouraged by the amount of Bloody Mary's I had downed that afternoon and the copious amounts of South American booze I had consumed the night before. Although I didn't need it I decided to get a beer. It would give me thinking time, something to hold onto and even place a small barrier between me and Lucy should she return with something outlandish for me to wear. Another date gone tits up I thought and this time practically literally given the amount of bare boobs on display. As I ordered drinks for myself and Delita, Lucy returned.

'Here we are Matthew. Best I could do I'm afraid but at least you won't feel out of place.'

'What is it?' I asked, trepidation creeping over me at an accelerated rate.

'It's a baby outfit. Loads of guys are into it,' Lucy said, looking at me as if we were simply discussing a new suit.

A baby outfit. And I won't feel out of place. Had this woman suddenly lost all sense of reality? Loads of guys may well be into it but I wasn't one of them.

'It's ok Lucy. Thanks for looking but it's just not me.'

'Lighten up Matthew. It's fantasy. Fun. It takes you out of your reality. Explore the other side for once. It's nice to dress up.'

Lucy had not convinced me.

'It won't look right at all, Lucy. In fact it will look completely wrong,' I protested.

Lucy grinned at me mischievously. 'There is no right or wrong, Matthew, just impulse. That's my motto.'

Lucy's motto seemed an ideal way of excusing all sorts of behaviour but I didn't think it was sufficient justification for making me look a total twat by dressing up as a baby. In my book there was right and wrong and dressing up as an infant was not only wrong, it was also an impulse I had no desire to indulge. Delita could see my hesitancy and the doubt in my eyes.

'Matthew. It will be fun. Come on. Don't be spoilsport. We have fun, you and me.'

She fluttered her eyes and licked her lips suggestively. I protested that I'd look totally stupid. By way of response Delita and Lucy both pointed out at least two other stupid looking adult babies in the club.

'Pleeeese Matthew. Just half hour. We have drinks and then you change and...we go back to my place,' Delita pleaded, mischief flickering in her eyes.

Lucy thrust the outfit into my arms and then delved into a garish leopard skin handbag that was dangling from her shoulder. Producing a small tube she handed it to Delita. Delita placed it under my nose and popped it.

'Sniff it Matthew.'

An intense rush of giddiness invaded my mind. My face seemed to flush and I felt very light headed. My perception of time began to slow down completely.

'What is it Delita?' I heard myself ask.

'Just popper Matthew. You go change and we have some more when you come back.'

Lucy showed me to a small changing area, sending me on my way with an overly extended pat on my backside. 'Have fun Matthew. Remember no right or wrong in here.'

I left my shirt, jeans, jacket and shoes on a bench. The baby outfit was no more than a giant nappy with an oversized safety pin, a frilly bonnet and a very large pair of pink fabric baby shoes. It must have been the effect of the popper but my sense of the ridiculousness of the whole situation had completely gone. I seemed more aware of the towelling fabric of the nappy against my skin, a sensual awareness that took me by surprise. I walked back out in to the bar area, with a sudden feeling of belonging. Delita was all over me.

'You look so cute Matthew. Here. Drink for my baby,' she giggled, handing me a Goldschläger shot.

I wasn't expecting what happened next. I experienced an abrupt crashing mood swing as if I was being dragged back down to earth, my mental state seemed to go through the floor. I suddenly felt exposed, vulnerable and ridiculous. Delita clearly noticed the change.

'You need more popper, Matthew. It only last ten minutes.'

I didn't need any more poppers. I needed to get my clothes and go. The whole evening seemed to be beyond my control now. I had to get a grip. My momentary bout of rational thinking was abruptly interrupted by the ear splitting shrill of a fire alarm. Pandemonium seemed to ensue. Staff immediately went into evacuate mode ushering the revellers towards the exit. I was fighting against the exodus, trying to get back into the changing room to retrieve my clothes. My endeavours were swiftly terminated by the leather gloved hand of the club bouncer. He spun me around in one rapid, effortless movement so that I was now facing in the same direction as the fast departing crowd.

'I just want to get my clothes...please.'

'Sorry, Sir. This is an emergency.'

I tried pleading even as he was manhandling me towards the door. He wouldn't have it.

'Fire alarm, Sir. Everybody has to leave immediately. Regulations. Health and safety. No exceptions.'

Within seconds I found myself on the pavement on a frosty winter evening in nothing more than an overgrown nappy. Since many of the clubbers were also scantily dressed a huddle began to form. I couldn't believe my ill fortune. Twice in just over a week I had been involved in an evacuation and, although I hadn't caused this one, I wasn't sure which predicament was the worst. I looked around to see if I could see Delita. At least she would be a familiar face. I needn't have worried. I did catch sight of a familiar face. Unfortunately it wasn't a familiar face I wanted to see. A police patrol car, its flashing blue light bar illuminating the crowd, had pulled up next to the scene. Sitting in the front passenger seat was PC Penny. Our eyes locked in recognition. Not in a pleasant, pleased to see you recognition. More a kind of astonished, astounded, gobsmacked, horrified recognition. I felt the blood drain from my face as I caught sight of her colleague emerging from the car. I turned away and tried to blend into the throng on the pavement. I heard the police officer's voice calming and reassuring the crowd. He wasn't being judgemental just doing a job. PC Penny never emerged from the vehicle. Maybe she didn't need to since the fire brigade had now arrived to take charge of the scene. Or maybe she had been rendered temporarily immobile by the trauma of seeing me in such bizarre circumstances. Whatever it was I was relieved that she had stayed in the car. I stood stock still facing into the huddle, not daring to move. Like a child who has woken up from a nightmare and doesn't dare turn around to see what is at the window.

By midnight order had been restored. We were allowed back into the building. I recovered my clothes. I didn't even take the time to say good night to Delita and to be honest at that point in time I didn't really want to see her again.

21

I slept most of Sunday, thankfully. The few times I did wake up during the morning I just pulled a pillow over my head and I hid. I didn't want to contemplate the embarrassing predicament I had gotten into the previous night. Each time the fetish club image popped into my head I felt the waves of shame creep over me. And the fact that I had been spotted made it worse. Although there was an explanation for my appearance in an outsize nappy, there was no explanation that could do it adequate justice. How could I begin to explain it with any semblance of credibility at all? However hard I tried, it would always seem like an excuse, a cover up for my shame. I just hoped I would never have to see PC Penny again.

The following day I had a much clearer head and I sat at work contemplating my experiences. The last one seemed to be confirming my reservations about internet dating. It was all too random. You made your choice and you had no idea what you would get. It made me realise that if you meet someone who comes close to your criteria, who ticks the boxes, who appears relatively normal then that might just be the person to go for. I thought about Diana.

A few days had passed since our brief abbreviated lunch and perhaps she had had time to calm down. Surely a telephone call wouldn't hurt. I could use the pretext of enquiring about progress with the driving range complaint. I tried to convince myself that it was a reasonable excuse to call on that basis. Yet I knew deep down I was harbouring hopes of reviving my romantic dreams and that was the real reason I wanted to call her.

I waited until lunch time to make the call. The last thing I wanted was anyone in the office overhearing a personal call, least of all Jasper Kane, who, with his charm and Lothario image, was unlikely to have ever been in the situation I now faced. As I stood in the car park behind the building I started to dial Diana's mobile number, then stopped, doubts creeping in. Would I seem needy? What if she was simply business like and kept the conversation to the legal issue? How could I move it on to arranging another date? Perhaps I shouldn't call. If I called and I didn't get the outcome I wanted I'd be disappointed. On the other hand if I did call and we kept the discussion to the legal issue, at least I was back in her thoughts. Sod it. I decided to call.

Nervously I punched in her number on my phone. It rang four times and went to voicemail. I pressed 'end call'. I needed to speak to her direct. I couldn't risk leaving a garbled message. On the other hand, if I kept it simple and left a message at least she would know I had called and could call me back. I called again. Her smooth, professional tones invited me to leave a message or to call her office number. I tried to memorise the digits but my brain was not taking in the information. I ran upstairs to my office, grabbed a pen and message pad and raced back down to the car park. I dialled again and this time managed to scribble the office number down. I felt a curious mixture of relief that she hadn't been there and edginess about still having to make another call. Calling her mobile seemed more personal but calling her office in her professional capacity was making me apprehensive. Suppressing the true motives I had for calling I reasoned that my enquiry, as the potential victim of legal action, was perfectly legitimate. I called.

'Twist, swivel and spin.'

'Excuse me?'

'Twist, swivel and spin. Good afternoon.'

'I'm sorry. What did you say?'

'You are through to Twist, Swivell and Spinn, legal partners. Good afternoon, Sir. How can I help?'

'Twist, Swivell and Spinn. Partners,' I said, as I absorbed Diana's professional status.

'Yes Sir. Diana Twist, Martin Swivell and Jacob Spinn. How can I help you?'

'Oh, I see. Sorry. Good afternoon to you. Diana Twist...as in Oliver? Oliver Twist?' It was the first time I had heard Diana's full name. It hadn't arisen before.

'Yes, Sir. I suppose so. Now how can I help you?'

I could hear the impatience creeping into the receptionist's voice.

'Could I speak to Diana...to Diana Twist please.'

She put me through after enquiring as to who I was.

'Matthew. Hello. How can I help?'

Diana's voice was business like, the previous welcoming tone replaced with a much more direct quality. It threw me and for a moment made me wish I hadn't called but I reasoned that as she was at work, that was her normal modus operandi and I shouldn't read anything into it. However, it caused me to tense up and I dispensed with any familiarity. I explained that I was just calling to see if there had been any progress with the driving range incident.

'Yes. There has. My client has decided not to pursue the matter any further.'

'Your client? The fat guy...that is good news.'

'Mr Henderson is my client Matthew and I do not think it is helpful to refer to him in a derogatory manner.'

'I'm sorry Diana. I didn't mean to be rude. I am just relieved that there will be no further action. I mean it was a dubious claim in my opinion and he has just wasted everyone's time by even considering it. Frankly, he struck me as a pompous arse anyway–'

'Matthew, I am the legal counsel. My client had a very valid claim since he sustained some painful injuries for which you may have been directly responsible. However, on this occasion he has decided not to pursue the matter. You should be grateful that he has taken that decision.'

'I am grateful Diana. I really am. But I don't understand. If he had such a valid claim why did he decide to drop it?'

'I managed to convince him that it was in no one's interest to take it further. He is a prominent businessman and a keen golfer and the publicity would not have been helpful to either him or the driving range. No evidence of defective equipment has come to light, despite your claim that the basket you used to collect the balls had a hole in it. So it would seem the accident was clearly not the fault of the driving range but in any case it would not have been good for them to be associated with any negative publicity. So taking all these factors into account, Robert...ah...my...client... agreed that the best course of action was to let the matter rest.'

'Well, that is fantastic news Diana,' I said, trying to ignore the reference to my faulty basket claim, 'thank you for helping me with this. I owe you. Perhaps a drink. Some champagne by way of celebration?'

'You don't owe me anything Matthew. I was acting on behalf of my client, not you. And the matter is now closed.'

I sensed the finality in Diana's words but I had to ask. 'Look Diana, now this nonsense is over perhaps we could meet up again. For dinner. It's a weight off my mind and we could have a little celebration. A nice relaxed date. Start afresh. I would love to see you again.'

'I am sorry Matthew. That won't be possible. Look I will be straight with you. I told you I appreciate honesty and for that reason I must be honest with you. I am seeing someone. I am seeing Robert. Robert Henderson. We have a lot in common. We have been out to dinner and we have arranged to play some golf together so I am going to give it a chance. I am so sorry Matthew. You are a very nice and likeable man and I am sure you will meet someone suitable.'

I returned to my office in a daze. I couldn't remember how I had ended the conversation. My mind was buzzing, my stomach churning. Diana's words pulsing in my head. Robert. Bloody fat pompous Robert. Her client. She was seeing him. No wonder he decided not to pursue me. He had a bigger prize. And I had, inadvertently, through my own stupidity, put them together. I couldn't understand what she could possibly see in him. And I was 'likeable' and 'nice.' Bloody nice. What was nice anyway? I didn't want to be nice. I wanted to be edgy, exciting, roguish, even dangerous not bloody nice. And what did she mean by someone 'suitable'? Diana was suitable in my book. Very suitable. Was that a put down? Was I not good enough, not up to her standard but fat bloody Robert Henderson was good enough. So he played golf. But you can't play golf forever. There has to be more than a common interest. She had liked me at first. I knew that. I had just been stupid. Too eager to please. I should have just been me. I had blown it myself. Robert Henderson, fat pompous businessman and golfer, had not taken Diana away. I had plopped her straight into his lap.

I sat at my desk, my mind going over the errors I had made with Diana. Too late now. Nothing I could do to undo them. I had blown my opportunity.

'You ok Matt?'

I spun round on hearing my name. Jasper Kane, his face a mix of concern and curiosity, was standing by my desk.

'You look like you've seen a ghost. Everything alright?' he asked.

'Oh yes, everything is fine Jasper. Just some news. You know,' I said, trying to feign some composure.

'Bad news? Anything I can do?'

'No…just women, you know.' I blurted it out without thinking.

Jasper flashed his charismatic smile and perched himself on the edge of my desk. 'Oh them. Yeah, they can be a pain in the arse. Great when it's going well, a bloody nightmare when it goes wrong.'

I looked up, surprised to hear that a ladies' man like Jasper might have had the odd nightmare. 'You don't have any trouble though, surely Jasper? You have yourself quite a reputation in the office.'

'Not usually Matt but we all have our moments. It isn't all plain sailing with women.'

'Maybe not but it probably is most of the time for you. What's your secret?'

Jasper laughed, his toothy grin spreading from his mouth to his eyes in an instant. 'Just be natural, be yourself and have some confidence. Simple as that. Women love a guy who is confident. And if none of that works, move on. There are plenty more ladies out there who'd appreciate a guy like you Matt. Be cool.'

He stood up, dropped a brown folder on my desk and walked off. I sat and watched him for a moment. Simple as that then. Be yourself. A recurring theme. Bit late now with Diana. As for confidence, that had definitely taken a hit after some of the disasters I had encountered. I needed to get some of that and quickly.

I had two meetings that afternoon. I breezed through them both in a haze of unfocussed thoughts. Work had temporarily taken my mind off the conversation with Diana but now it was time to go home. I left the office at

6.30pm. Straight into rush hour traffic. It was bumper to bumper. Stop start all the way. An hour later I had had enough. Sitting in traffic gives you time to think and my thoughts were in disarray. I was on a dating site, my mates were lining themselves up with women without any effort at all and now the one date I really fancied I'd practically given away. I turned off into a side street and took the back roads to MacFadden's. I didn't really need a drink after the excessive number of nights I had had on the tiles in the last few weeks but I didn't want to go straight home either and the traffic gave me just the excuse for a detour.

MacFadden's was empty. Just Carlos minding a lone bar.

'Mateo. How are you doing.'

'I got a headache Carlos and I've had a shit day.'

'Let me get you a stiff drink, amigo and tell me all your troubles.'

I declined the offer of a stiff drink and settled for a strong coffee. For the next two hours I sat and poured my woes out to Carlos. I told him all about the dating site mishaps, the incidents with Diana, the stuff at Hemmingwell Halls, the total embarrassment of my night out with Delita (although I couldn't bring myself to mention the nappy thing and thought it was prudent not to elaborate on the full details of my encounter with Abigail either), the complexities of my identity issue with PC Penny and the fact that I had now had enough of looking for love. I told him too about the concern I had that I could be the subject of a police enquiry. He was a good listener. He needed to be. I swore him to secrecy. I wasn't really looking for advice. I just needed to talk.

'Mateo. You need to slow down. You need to stop looking. It will come to you when you stop looking. You are getting yourself into too many mix ups. Too much trouble. You are a good looking boy. Calm down and be yourself. You are hanging out with Cecil all the time and it's not good for you. Cecil is a good lad but you are not Cecil. He needs to live life fast. Too fast for you, now. You need to relax a bit more. Slow down. Then you will find a good woman… and then don't let her go. Start by getting yourself off that dating site. And stop looking for love...love will find you.'

As he spoke he reached for a bottle and poured two large whiskeys. He pushed a glass towards me. 'Here drink this. It will help you sleep when you get home. You need a good night's sleep.'

'I can't Carlos. I am driving. And I've been hitting it too hard lately, in any case.'

'Mateo. It's only one. You've been drinking coffee. You'll be fine. Drink it up and be off with you.'

I knocked back the sharp liquid. 'By the way, Carlos. How are you getting on with Abigail?'

He winked at me and said goodnight.

The road was clear now. It was 10.45pm and I wanted to get home. The petrol gauge was showing empty. I spotted the lights of a petrol station. I was tired after the events of the day and tempted to leave it until morning but I decided I'd fill up there and then and get it done. Fatigue was making me impatient and I stopped the pump at thirty pounds so I could get away. As I walked into the shop area a bloke in front of me was walking up to the only cashier on duty with three very full baskets of shopping.

'Excuse me mate, could I just pay for my petrol quickly and I will be out of your way,' I asked him politely.

'I was here first,' was his reply.

'I know, but as there are only two of us and I only have the one transaction I am sure it would only take a minute, if you didn't mind.' My polite tone remained intact despite the fact I was feeling tired and slightly irritated by his response.

'Well, I do mind. I have been in here ages,' was his response to my respectful request.

Of course he had been in there ages. He had single-handed bought almost the entire contents of the shop. Perhaps he was a buyer for Sainsbury's and was doing the night run to stock them up. As he only had two free hands he was now carrying two of the over laden baskets and pushing the other one along the floor towards the till with his foot. I tried again.

'I won't take long...I–'

'You'll have to wait your turn like everybody else, get in the queue,' he snapped back.

What queue? There were only two of us. How many people does it take to constitute a queue? And who was *everyone else* who had to wait their turn? The shop was deserted. I was the only other person in there. I decided to appeal to the better nature of the cashier.

'Excuse me. Would you mind if I just paid for my petrol quickly.'

'Sorry boss, this gentleman was first in the queue.'

What was this? A conspiracy? Now the cashier was taking sides. Working in the job he did, he must know what a queue looks like and, from my point of view, this was not a queue. And to add to my irritation he had now sided with the unreasonable, manic shopper.

'It's just that I am in a bit of a hurry...and I would be really grateful if you could just take my payment quickly.'

'You should pay at the pump, boss, if you are in a hurry.'

'Look, I can't pay at the pump now, can I? I pressed the *pay at the kiosk* button so I can't do that now. Ok.'

'Sorry, boss, you have to wait in the queue.'

I resigned myself to getting nowhere. What queue? The cashier and the shopper had obviously now formed some sort of self-righteous bond that had me branded as some impatient motorist teetering on the verge of road rage. What happened to civility, consideration and customer service? And what was this guy doing shopping for that much stuff at nearly midnight in a place whose prime function is to sell petrol? And was this place meant to be a garage or a supermarket? And why was everyone suddenly referring to me as *boss*? All these thoughts were racing through my head. I was tired. I wanted to get home. And then I saw the contents of the three shopping baskets.

The cashier was very carefully and deliberately passing them through the scanner one by one as the shopper slowly lifted them from the baskets and handed them over. Biscuits, broccoli, string, a birthday card, a fan belt, asparagus spears, four large packs of potatoes, a packet of scone mix, hair dye, envelopes, cough mixture, Sellotape, two tins of beans, jelly, a can of WD40, organic orange juice, eye wash, three tubs of double cream, baby wipes, two L plates, a box of cake mix, a frozen black forest gateaux, three puzzle magazines and a walnut whip. I had never seen such a diverse array of shopping items. None of them seemed to fit together or complement one another at all. And why would you suddenly need all that stuff at midnight on a Tuesday? I mean sure, pop out to the garage and get a pint of milk, I can understand that. But was he expecting a nuclear war and was heading for an underground bunker? Or maybe he was about to start work on a homemade bomb. Whatever reason the maniac had for going out at midnight to a garage to shop was no real concern of mine but as each item was passed through the scanner I was getting more and more irritable. He could easily have let me pay and go. I had now been in the garage for fifteen minutes while he conducted his own version of supermarket sweep.

At long last the scanner gave its final 'bleep' as the final item went through. The shopper then painstakingly packed everything into about nine carrier bags. I was standing there like a racehorse in the stalls ready to go. Just as he was done and about to leave he turned back.

'Could, I have one of them cigars, please,' he said.

A cigar. Was he celebrating now? And then he was gone.

I went straight up to the till.

'Pump number boss?'

An unnecessary question since I was the only car on a pump in the whole garage. 'Err...five...no hang on... six, yes...pump six.'

'Thirty pounds boss. Do you want a VAT receipt?'

I didn't want any kind of receipt. I just wanted to pay and get the hell out of there. I reached for my wallet. It wasn't there. I went to another pocket. It wasn't there either. I tried my trouser pockets. Not there. I then started to search them all again but this time at twice the speed, slapping the outsides to feel for the wallet and still putting my hand into what I knew was an empty pocket that I had already searched. I could feel my face getting hot.

'Err...I...I seem to have...well, seem to not... to not... erm, to not have my wallet...hang on. It must be in the car.'

I raced out to the car and after a frantic search I found the errant wallet tucked down between the driver's seat and the central gear column housing.

Obviously it had fallen from my pocket and lodged there. I ran back in to the cashier and shoved the thirty pounds across to him. I left immediately out of both my eagerness to get home and embarrassment. Putting my foot down, I sped out of the garage. I had travelled less than a mile when I saw the blue light in my mirror. Slowing down, I eased over to the side of the road to let the vehicle pass. To my consternation it pulled up in front of me, blocking my path. A police patrol car. A burly looking officer walked up to my window.

'Good evening Sir. We have reason to believe you have just left a garage without paying for your fuel.'

'What? No...no, I didn't. I paid.'

'Do you have the receipt Sir?'

'No. I don't have a receipt but I paid. Thirty pounds. I gave it to the cashier.'

'No receipt Sir?'

'No. But look, I can explain.'

I described what had happened but it seemed that when I had run out to the car the cashier had automatically assumed I was running off without paying and had called the police. I hadn't hung around long enough after I gave him the money for him to let me know he'd called the cops.

'Perhaps you could call the garage, officer. If you did I am sure the cashier will clear this up and confirm that I have paid for my fuel and that it is all a misunderstanding.'

The police officer signalled to his colleague in the car. 'My colleague is checking with the garage Sir. In the meantime I need to check some details.'

He took my name, address and the vehicle details. I cooperated fully. I even had my driving licence and insurance details with me. A few minutes later the other officer appeared.

'It all checks out. He's paid.'

I let out a long sigh of relief.

'Have you been drinking this evening, Mr..,' he checked his notebook, 'Mr Malarkey?' the burly officer asked.

I couldn't believe it. Relief to dread in a split second as I recalled Carlos's large whiskey.

'Drinking? No. No, not drinking. Just a whiskey, but not drinking.'

'So you have been drinking then Sir?'

'No. I mean yes. But not drinking. I had a whiskey. Just one. Which is not drinking. And coffee.'

'You sound confused Sir. I am going to have to breathalyse you.'

I had no choice. Why had I not just said no, I hadn't been drinking. They couldn't do me for lying. An electronic device that looked like a radio with a tube sticking out of it was produced. I blew into the tube and waited. The light on the front went amber. I felt a wave of doom.

'The test shows you have had some alcohol Sir but you are fortunate. You are not over the limit on this occasion.'

'I just had the one whiskey officer. I wasn't drinking. That's all.'

'Sir, one whiskey is drinking. You are very lucky. You could have been over the legal limit.'

The second officer then felt the need to get involved. 'Have you indulged in any other intoxicants?'

I thought this was a very odd question and didn't consider that the coffee I had drunk with Carlos would come under the category of intoxicant, so I said no.

'Do you have anything in the boot of your car Sir?'

'No, nothing officer,' I answered.

'Nothing at all Sir?' The officer asked.

I then remembered the bags of grass that had been in there for some weeks awaiting delivery to the dump.

'Well, only some bags of grass officer,' I said.

From looking absent-mindedly around the car he suddenly focussed his full attention on me. 'Bags of grass? Are you being a smart arse now, Sir?' he said, his eyes narrowing.

I hadn't thought I was being smart at all particularly as I had just confessed to a traffic cop that I had been drinking. I was just being straight in an effort to get away as soon as I could and get home. 'I'm sorry, officer. I am not sure what you mean,' I said.

'Oh, I get it. You dope heads are all the same. Trying the old double bluff so I send you on your way. Well, it don't work with me. I'd like you to open the boot.'

Even if I hadn't seen the change of mood in his eyes the fact that he had now dropped the word 'Sir' and had referred to me as a 'dope head' suggested things had changed slightly. I fleetingly remembered my rights from some crime documentary I had seen on TV and realised that I could have refused him permission to search my car but I didn't want to inflame the situation and anyway I had nothing to hide. I unlocked the boot and stood back. The police officer clicked the lid catch and it flew open. A farmyard shockwave of rotting manure hit us head on. The stench of rotting grass metamorphosing into warm compost was overpowering, gripping the throat and nose in a toxic assault on the senses. The three of us reeled back in an involuntary synchronised two-step, hands instantly clasping our faces in an attempt to preserve whatever oxygen remained in our lungs. The bolshie cop recovered first.

'Jeez, man, what have you got in there? Something's dead in there.'

'It's grass officer. I did say so. I was meant to take it to the dump but I guess I forgot about it. It must have gone off.'

The cop clearly saw that as understatement. 'Gone off? You could use it to fuel the bloody car, man. I should get the bomb disposal people down here. Shut that lid quick before we are all gassed.'

I did as I was told. I could tell he was slightly peeved at not being able to charge me with something. I was then dismissed with a completely unwarranted 'Now be on your way before we charge you with wasting police time.'

As soon as I got in I sank into the chair and clicked on my computer. I wanted to go to bed, to rest. I was exhausted. A combination of a hectic social life, nervous energy and the stress of my dating experiences were wearing me out. I needed sleep. But I figured Carlos was right, I also needed to get off the site. His advice was sound. He had made me see sense. The dating site maybe just wasn't for me. It hadn't done me any favours so far. I was no nearer to finding love than I had been when I signed up just over three weeks earlier. I was also disappointed, humiliated and angry at how it had turned out with Diana.

I watched as Cupid's Pursuit loaded up, gazing at the screen for what seemed like an age, my head swimming with tiredness, my eyes fixed in an unseeing stare. Minutes must have passed before I regained some semblance of alertness. I had made my decision. I would remove my profile from the dating site and end my membership. I hovered over my photograph and hit the delete button.

'*Are you sure you wish to delete this picture*', the programme asked me. I was very sure. I clicked on '*yes*'. I watched as the site processed this information. '*Please wait*', appeared on the screen indicating that my picture was being consigned to the bin.

It was three thirty in the morning when I stirred. For a moment I had no idea where I was. As I shook myself from my stupor and clambered back to consciousness my exact location became apparent. I was slumped back in the leather chair in front of my computer, a line of dribble seeping from my open mouth. My computer had gone into 'sleep' mode and clearly so had I. I struggled to my bed.

The following evening I was back on the computer. I realised that I hadn't completed deleting my profile and logged on to finish the task. The email inbox was highlighted in bold, indicating that I had a message. It was from the lady in Brighton, Sue.

'*Hi Matthew. Brighton's not that far. Would be nice to meet with you sometime. I hope you don't think I am being forward but as it's nearly the festive season perhaps we could meet for a Christmas drink. I quite understand if you have loads of offers already. But if you could squeeze me in let's go for it. Life is for living.*'

Her message had an air of positivity, an upbeat devil may care resonance. It was no more than a few lines but it made me think that Sue sounded like someone who just took the dating site for what it was. No agenda, no illusions. Just go for it. Make it work for you. Maybe I should just chill about it all. I had another few days of membership to go, which I had paid for so what the hell, I'd let it run its course. I emailed Sue back.

'*Hi Sue. Thanks for your message. No major plans for the Christmas period. No party invites yet. Not even doing anything Christmas day. How sad is that? So it would be good to meet up for a drink. It is Christmas after all.*'

22

For the next few days I put all thoughts of dating, dating sites and the accompanying troubles out of my head. I needed to. I had to focus on my work and that proved to be a distraction. By Friday night I was feeling fresh and rested. I hadn't heard from Cecil since the previous Saturday, which was very unusual. However, I wanted a quiet weekend for a change and decided that if he wanted to get in touch he would. I'd leave it to him.

I left work at five looking forward to my quiet weekend. I stopped by MacFadden's for a coffee. I felt I had to thank Carlos for listening to me when I was banging on about my troubles on Monday night and I wanted him to know that I valued his advice. It had just turned five thirty when I arrived. Four early Friday night post work drinkers were seated around a single table. Carlos saw me approach. I took a stool at the bar.

'Hola Carlos.'

'Hey, Mateo. How are you? You are looking well. You look like you've been sleeping at last, hombre.'

'Yeah, I took your advice. Got some early nights.'

'You come off that pick up site now?'

'No. Not yet Carlos. I only have a week or so to go so I may as well let it run out, you know. And anyway, it's not a pick up site. It's for dates. It's all above board.'

'Ok. I believe you. What are you drinking? Beer?'

'Oh no, no beer Carlos. I'm not staying. I just popped in to say Hi and to say thanks for listening to me the other night. I must have gone on a bit. I was very pissed off.'

'It's no problem Mateo. What are amigos for? Anyway, it's Friday night. You cannae go home without a wee dram.'

'Just a coffee Carlos. I am taking your advice. Remember? A latte will be fine.'

Carlos turned away, clinked a cup onto a saucer and pressed a button. The espresso machine hissed and splurted as it frothed out my coffee.

'Have you seen, Cecil at all Carlos?' I called to the back of his head. 'I haven't seen him all week and he hasn't been in touch at all.'

'Yes. He was in here on Wednesday. With that American girl,' he replied over his shoulder.

'American girl?'

'Yes, the one you were both talking to with her friend the other night.'

'Sheryl. Cecil was with Sheryl? And she's Canadian, Carlos. What, Cecil was in here...with her? On his own?'

Carlos turned back to the bar and pushed the frothy coffee towards me.

'Sure. He was taking her out. On a date. He don't need anybody else with him on a date. Three's a crowd.'

'I didn't mean that Carlos. I meant Cecil was on date? With Sheryl? By themselves. He was taking her out?'

'Yes, that is what I said, Mateo,' he replied, turning away again to wipe down the coffee machine and pour a coffee for himself.

So that's why I hadn't heard from Cecil. Crafty bugger. He'd mentioned that he'd had a text from her but he kept the rest quiet.

As I sat there quietly sipping my latte and contemplating Cecil's latest manoeuvres, I caught a glimpse of a familiar profile walking by the front window of the bar in my peripheral vision. Instinctively I turned to look. It was Louise Penny. And it looked like she was coming in. I abruptly turned my body sideways to the bar, my head bowed, chin resting on my left hand, my elbow on the bar. It was a classic evasive position in plain sight and I just knew it wasn't going to work.

'Carlos! Carlos!' I hissed, but I was in competition with the espresso machine, which did hissing better than me, and he didn't hear me. In the mirror behind the bar I could see PC Penny hesitate in the doorway. She was in civvy clothes.

'Carlos!' I practically shouted at him. He turned away from the machine and placed both elbows on the bar, chin resting on his cupped hands.

'What's up, Mateo?'

'Look Carlos. It's the police officer. The one I told you about on Monday. Listen. Whatever you do, don't call me Matthew or Mateo or any variation of my name at all. I am Michael. Remember that...Michael. And don't use my surname either. Just Michael or even better nothing at all.'

My tone was clearly over hushed and the fact that I had my head lowered towards my coffee was not helping Carlos's grasp of the situation. He looked bemused.

'I am Michael, Carlos. Remember? Monday night. What I told you. Oh shit, I think she is coming in.'

Sure enough the mirror showed PC Louise Penny walking in and heading for the bar. She stopped at the bar, two stools away to my left. I kept my back turned gazing into the far end of the bar. Why the bloody hell didn't Carlos have Sky Sports showing on one of the TV screens? It would have looked more natural for me to be watching something. Carlos moved towards her, I heard their brief greeting and she ordered a coffee. The espresso steamed and gurgled again. I sipped my coffee and continued to stare ahead, now affecting an air of nonchalance. Perhaps she hadn't noticed me and would just take her coffee and go sit at a table.

'Michael?'

I heard her call the name out with an unusual heightened clarity. I turned around as if surprised to hear my name.

'Louise. Fancy seeing you here,' I said trying even harder to do surprise. 'What are you doing here on your own?'

'Oh, I had a tough day to day. A long shift last night and then one of those days. I just needed to get out of the house so I popped down to the shops and then fancied a coffee. And you?'

'Just on my way home from work. Same really. Fancied a coffee.'

'Are you out tonight partying?'

'Oh no, a quiet weekend for me. Been partying too much of late,' I said sheepishly.

'Really. No bars, clubs or anything?' I saw the twinkle in her eye.

'Look Louise. I need to explain –'

'Hey, there is no need Michael. What people do in their private lives is their business. You don't owe anyone an explanation.'

'But I'd like to. Louise, it wasn't what you think. Not what it looked like. I thought I was going to play tennis.' I was almost apologetic.

'Tennis!' She laughed aloud, immediately cupping her hand over her mouth to stifle it. 'Tennis,' she said again, 'in that outfit? An outsized nappy is not the normal attire for a tennis match Michael.'

I was blushing furiously at the very mention of the nappy. Louise saw my rapidly reddening complexion.

'I am so sorry Michael. I don't mean to embarrass you. I shouldn't comment on what other people choose to do with their evenings. Forgive me.'

I am sure she was sincere but I could see she was struggling to keep a straight face.

'I thought I was going to a tennis club that night.' I said again.

'Ok. Let me get this straight Michael. You were going to play tennis and decided to wear nothing but a giant nappy? Why?'

'No. Look, I wasn't actually playing tennis. I was at a club on a date. And I thought that the club was a tennis club. I mean, I didn't think that that club, the one you saw me outside was a tennis club. I thought my date was taking me to another club…a tennis club.'

'I see. But you still wore the nappy thinking you were going to play tennis?' she said, her eyes twinkling at my bewilderment.

'No. My clothes were in the club –'

'In the tennis club?'

'No, Louise. There was no tennis club –'

'No tennis club? You sound confused Michael. There was no tennis club but you were going to play tennis?'

I wasn't sure if she was being deliberately obtuse or just having a quiet chuckle at watching me squirm.

'Let me start again Louise. I had a date. I thought she wanted to play tennis. Not right then but at some point in the future. I completely misunderstood what she meant mostly because she is foreign...Russian. She said we should go to her club and it turned out that the club was not a tennis club at all but in fact was a...well...a...sort of fetish club.'

'Well from the way the clientele were dressed on the pavement that night it looked completely like a fetish club,' was Louise's helpful observation.

'Yes, it turned out that it was but I didn't know that before we went there.'

'What made you think you were going to a tennis club anyway?'

'Can we forget the tennis bit Louise. It's a long story,' I said, trying to hide the exasperation rising in my voice.

'Ok. Sorry Michael. So, your Russian girlfriend is into fetish clubs?'

'She's not my girlfriend. We were just on a date.'

'Bit of an odd date. Have you known her long?'

'We had only just met that night and –'

'Wow. Only just met and she got you to dress up in a nappy.'

'It wasn't like it sounds Louise. And can you keep your voice down. Carlos doesn't know that bit...about the...the...err...baby thing. It wasn't my idea. It was the club. They said I had to wear something appropriate and they gave me the nappy. I know it all sounds odd and I haven't explained it too well but it all went a bit pear shaped that evening.'

'So, your date. Where did you meet?'

That was the tricky question. Given the experiences I had been through already and the difficulties that had caused a few brushes with the law, the dating site was not the answer.

'We met here,' I blurted out and to a degree there was a certain amount of truth in it since the first time I had seen Delita in the flesh was in MacFadden's.

'So are you seeing each other now Michael?'

'Oh no. It was a one off. I mean...not like that. I don't think it worked out the way it should so it will be best left as a one off.'

'Would you like any more drinks, Sir?' Carlos was hovering.

Sir. That was overdoing it a little since Louise knew that I knew Carlos.

'Another coffee for me please, Carlos and whatever the lady would like,' I said, glad of the distraction. Louise had a coffee too.

'Let me get these Michael,' Louise said.

'No, my treat, Louise. Carlos, I have no change. You ok with a card?'

He waved the card machine at me and I handed over my debit card. I punched in the pin and waited for the receipt.

'So Michael, do you date much then.'

The question was innocuous enough especially since I had mentioned going on a date but it made me defensive. After all it was asked by a policewoman, albeit an off duty one, who was enquiring into my so-called lodger.

'Date? Oh no. Never.' The minute I said it 'never' seemed a bit reactionary.

'Never? You never date at all?'

'I mean I don't really get the time Louise...err...always busy.'

Carlos put two fresh cups of coffee on the bar. Louise picked hers up and took a sip, placing the cup carefully back in its saucer. She looked directly at me in the way she did when she felt she had something meaningful to say or ask.

'I know the feeling Michael. I haven't been on a date in ages. I never get out too much to meet anyone. I am lucky that Sheryl is around at the moment so at least I can go out with her to bars. You never know, I may meet someone eventually. Oh, by the way, did you know Sheryl is out with your friend Cecil tonight? On a date, coincidentally.'

'No, I didn't,' I said. 'I knew they had been in touch. That explains why he hasn't been in contact with me then. Seems everyone gets a date except you and me.'

She laughed. 'Seems that way. I have even thought of joining one of those dating sites, although it seems a bit desperate.'

At the mention of dating site I felt beads of sweat appear on my brow. I picked up my coffee cup, more as a sub-conscious need to have physical barrier between me and the questioner than for any great need of its contents.

'Have you ever thought of doing that Michael?' Louise asked.

I needed to buy some time to answer. I took a slow sip from the cup.

'Thought of what? A dating site? Well, yes, I suppose it has crossed my mind but as you say it does seem a little desperate.'

'Yes, I suppose it does,' Louise laughed, 'and I have heard all sorts of stories about weirdoes on there. People putting photographs on there that are twenty years old. Guys pretending to be someone else.'

That struck a sensitive chord.

'Pretending to be someone else. Like what?' I asked.

As Louise began her reply I stared intently at the bubbles in my coffee not wishing to make direct eye contact.

'Oh I don't mean literally. I mean making out they are taller, richer, younger, have better jobs and are action men, hang gliding, bungee jumping and parachuting every other weekend. I didn't mean they have some sort of secret identity,' Louise giggled.

I liked her giggle but I didn't like the subject matter.

'At the end of the day, Michael, all us girls really want is a normal man. A knight in shining armour to sweep us off our feet.'

Shining armour. What did she say that for? I really didn't want to be discussing knights or mediaeval dress with Louise Penny. I dragged my gaze away from the coffee cup.

'Normal?' I enquired rather unnecessarily.

'Yes. Normal. You know...honest, loyal, caring, able to show his emotions and with a sense of humour. That would do me.'

She blushed as she said it realising that perhaps she had revealed slightly more of a personal view than she had intended. At that moment she looked very vulnerable. And very attractive. I had been so busy trying to cover my tracks and protect my own skin in every encounter I had had with PC Penny that I had really not noticed how attractive she was and that she was a woman with normal feelings, aspirations and desires like the rest of us. I wanted to say that I was an honest, loyal, caring guy and I did have a sense of humour too but I didn't. How could I say anything like that when I had completely hidden my true identity, had never been relaxed enough in her company to show my natural personality and the last time she saw me I was wearing an overgrown nappy. On top of all that I knew that I had stared into her eyes from behind a gorilla suit and was, unbeknownst to her, the perpetrator of the mad incident at Hemmingwell Halls into which she was carrying out an investigation. So I said nothing, except to ask her if she would like another coffee.

'Oh no, thank you Michael. Two is enough for me right now. I really ought to be going. I only popped out for some air really. I am working tomorrow. Listen, thanks for the coffees and the chat. It's been nice. You know, talking of dates, you could say that this was like a date really. For us. Two people who seem never have time for dating. So thanks. Anyway, see you around.'

She got up and walked towards the exit. Then turned back. 'Oh by the way Michael, if you happen to see your lodger, could you tell him to get in touch. I need to talk to him again. A couple of things have come up that I just want to clear up.'

Oh, terrific I thought. A couple of things to clear up. Great.

'Yes. Sure Louise. I will tell him...err... leave him a...a note...or something.'

She smiled and disappeared into the night.

I got home about seven thirty. My positive mood slightly knocked by the meeting with Louise. Well, not so much the meeting, more the fact that there was unfinished business. I put the kettle on, made a cup of tea and sat by my computer. I had intended to have an evening watching television but the lure of the site was nagging at my sub-conscious. Perhaps it was the fact that I knew I was now approaching my final days of the month's membership and that made it slightly more appealing. I switched on the PC. I had two emails.

Sue in Brighton had written, *'Hi Matthew. How are you doing? Hope your weekend goes well. I was thinking about what you were saying about being alone at Christmas. I know we haven't actually met but why don't you come to me for Christmas day. I am alone too. It could be fun. Why not take a chance. Life is too short not to. Let me know. And I will understand if you say no. By the way, what have you done with your picture? I did like the look of you!'*

I was quite taken aback by Sue's email. Not just because it was quite a gesture to invite a complete stranger for Christmas but also it summed up the loneliness of many people out there in cyberland. But I was also one of those people. I was lonely. I was looking for someone to be with. As simple as that. Just to be with. To be with at Christmas and all those other important times. I was running into brick walls all the time with my search for true love and I genuinely had no plans for Christmas. Ever since I had split up with my wife I hadn't really celebrated Christmas. I had been very close to her family and we had always spent Christmas time together. And that had all been taken away when we parted. I had found it hard to adjust. That first Christmas after the split had been very difficult. I did nothing. I sat at home with bacon and eggs for Christmas dinner, feeling sorry for myself. I had sat and looked out of the window and watched people passing by, visiting friends and family, laden with gifts and wallowed in my misery. In the years since I had begun to realise that it was simply a reaction to being abandoned. The solitariness of sitting alone at home with just bacon and eggs for Christmas dinner probably reinforced my sense of injustice at my wife leaving me. It emphasised that all that had been good had been removed and this was what was left. It somehow made it seem that it was her fault. It gave me a focus for blame and my Spartan Christmas celebrations helped fuel the loss. It also felt right, for to do anything else that first Christmas would have been an acceptance that it was over, that life had moved on and was now different. Clearly I hadn't wanted to move on and although I didn't resort to anything quite as austere in the subsequent Christmas periods, I still did not celebrate in the normal way. So, what the hell, life was for living. I'd take up Sue's offer. Who knows what could come of it.

I started typing. *'Sue. Thank you for the invite. Why not! Let's do it. You are right. Life is too short. Give me a call and let's talk. Would be good to get to know you.'* I typed out my mobile number. I'd committed myself. I felt good about it. Nothing could go wrong this time. It wasn't even a date. The second email was from a lady called Amanda. I had seen her picture on line before and she did look attractive. Short red hair cut in a bob style. Nice eyes. She was thirty-seven and lived in Banstead, Surrey. Her email was to the point.

'Hi. Liked your profile and your photo, although it seems to have gone now. Shame. This is my last few days on the site and I am not renewing. I am not usually this forward but if you'd like to get in touch you can call or text me on my mobile.'

She had left the number. I was still surprised at a woman giving a total stranger a mobile number. I just figured that perhaps they made judgements based on the way you looked and felt that a mobile number was quite safe. Her last few days she had said. Maybe I would call or text her. She could be 'the one' and I may miss out if I didn't at least try.

Over the weekend I took it easy. I decided that I would continue to catch up with my rest and stop worrying about things. I'd felt good during the week and wanted to continue feeling that way. I went to the gym on Saturday morning, the first time I had been there in weeks, had lunch afterwards and then called into the local council recycling centre to off-load the festering contents of the car boot. With that job out of the way I spent the rest of the day watching sport on television at home. My normal routine on a Saturday night was to go out but I wanted to avoid drinking. For that reason I stayed clear of MacFadden's even though I felt quite lively and energetic and actually fancied a night out. It was for the 'no drinking reason' that I also avoided contacting Cecil, even though I was curious as to why he had been laying so low over the past week.

As the day wore on I decided I would text Amanda. Over the next hour we exchanged texts and eventually got round to a possible meeting. At that point I called her. We said we would do lunch for a first date and the following Saturday was good for us both. She said she was learning to drive at the moment and it wasn't easy for her to get around as she lived out in the sticks so we would need to meet somewhere local. I told her that I would be happy to pick her up.

The rest of the evening I spent at home watching stuff I had on Sky Plus that had been clogging up the box for weeks. Before I went to bed I checked on line to see if I had any messages from the dating site but there were none. It seemed that once you remove your picture the messages dry up.

23

It was about midday on Sunday when the doorbell rang. PC Penny was standing on the doorstep in full uniform again.

'Hello Michael. How are you?'

'Louise. Hello. I'm fine. This looks a bit official,' I said nervously.

'It is Michael. I actually popped by to see your lodger, Mr Malarkey. Is he home?' she asked.

'Err...no, no he isn't. I haven't seen him. He must be abroad again,' I stuttered.

'Can I come in for a moment?'

I opened the door and let her in. I offered her a coffee. She declined.

'Look Michael, I need to speak with Matthew Malarkey and if you can get a message to him I would really appreciate it.'

'What has he done Louise? I mean has he done anything? It all looks a bit worrying...you know...the police...you...turning up.'

'Well, we are not sure he has done anything but it appears that he may have been connected to another incident that we are keen to talk to him about.'

'Another incident? What sort of incident?' I tried to hide the growing tension in my voice by clearing my throat with a cough. Deep down I guessed that the incident she was referring to was Julia's party, especially as she had mentioned it at the MacFadden's wine tasting night.

'I am not at liberty to discuss it Michael. Do you know when he will be back?'

'He is often away for days...weeks...sometimes...I haven't seen him at all.'

'Well it appears he was in the UK earlier this week. He was stopped by a patrol car last Monday night in a black 'S' Type Jaguar exactly like the one parked on your drive. And quite coincidentally it has exactly the same registration.' The radio on her shoulder crackled with messages. She paused to reduce the volume and then looked at me for an explanation.

It was my opportunity to own up, to confess to my misdemeanours and clear them all up in one outpouring of truth. I would clear my conscience, relieve myself of the burden of anxiety that I was carrying around and face whatever consequences were to come.

'Well, that is his car, Louise. I mean he is my lodger so he is entitled to leave it there. He often does when he is away.'

I'd failed to take the opportunity. I looked into Louise's eyes and saw her puzzlement. I don't know what she expected to hear but that is what came out. In my head it all seemed too complex to unravel on the spur of the moment. I needed time to think. I liked Louise. I wasn't sure how that had happened but I just couldn't bring myself to tell her the truth for fear of her disapproval. I remember that feeling as a little boy. If I did something wrong I hated my dad's disapproval and disappointment in me. He didn't need to do anything else. He didn't need to punish me in any way. The disapproval was enough. Nothing much had changed it seemed. Even as an adult, when my emotions were involved, I could not handle disapproval.

Louise brought me back to my senses. 'When he returns, Michael, can you please tell him he needs to get in touch. It's important that we speak with him.'

That evening I logged on to Cupid's Pursuit. It was my last day. I wanted to check any last minute correspondence. There was one email. From the site administration team.

'Congratulations. Your membership has automatically been renewed for another month. We hope you are enjoying your membership. As a full member you have total access to all site facilities. Did you know that when you upload a picture you get seven times more response? Why not upload a picture today. Good luck in your pursuit of love.'

I couldn't believe it. Automatic renewal. I hadn't agreed to that at all. I checked the terms and conditions. It was there in black and white. If you don't cancel the automatic renewal you roll over to the next period at another twenty-five pounds. I was now a member for a further thirty days. I immediately cancelled the auto renewal for the month after. I couldn't face three months of the site. I scanned the terms more closely to see if I could find some loophole to get my money back after the renewal had gone through. But there was no option. The small print clearly said that when I had signed up I had agreed to auto renew unless I physically cancelled the payment. I could still remove my profile but I wouldn't get any refund for the month. Maybe it was fate. Maybe there was someone on the site for me but I just hadn't stumbled across her yet. Good luck in my pursuit of love - I needed all the luck I could get.

The week dragged slowly. I went to work and the gym. I was trying to keep myself busy. I had two phone calls. The first was from Amanda checking to see if I was still on for the weekend date. I was. She asked if we could make it dinner instead of lunch as she had a driving lesson in the afternoon. Her instructor had had to reschedule it. I told her I'd book us a nice restaurant.

'What do you fancy?' I asked.

'Surprise me, Matthew. I eat most things.'

I was fine with dinner instead of lunch. I was glad to have Saturday night booked up with something other than a bar crawl. The second call was from Sue. Just checking that I hadn't changed my mind about the Christmas meeting. I told her I was looking forward to it even though I was slightly apprehensive about the fact that it would be a first meeting. I put my previous date experiences firmly to the back of my mind. It could be fun and at least it took care of Christmas Day. She said she wouldn't be cooking a Christmas dinner but would do something nice for us to eat and there would be plenty of wine. I was happy about that. If we didn't get on there would be no fun in sharing a turkey.

I logged onto the site after work on Wednesday. I had one email. Her name was Estelle. She said she had only just joined and was a bit nervous. It was her first time on a dating site and she had contacted me because I was local and my description sounded normal. She said if I liked her profile maybe we could chat. I clicked on her page. It wasn't the best quality picture I had seen on the site but she was good looking. Long dark hair, black framed spectacles that made her look intriguing. Her makeup was a little heavy, perhaps overdoing the eyeliner but it gave her an exotic look. She'd kept her profile simple.

'*I never thought I'd be doing this but here I am. I'm looking for love like the rest of us on here. However, I really need a kind, caring, down to earth kind of guy and I definitely don't need any 'players' as I have been through enough on that front. If you like my profile I'd love to hear from you.*'

Simple as it was I identified with it. It wasn't that far removed from what I was looking for too. I typed out a reply.

'*Hi Estelle. Thank you for your email. I think I am fairly normal. And down to earth too. Sure, I'd love to chat sometime. Nice profile by the way.*'

Although it was just another polite reply her words had struck a chord. Part of me had lost interest in the site now but the other side of me could still be intrigued by someone who caught my eye. I had another three and a half weeks left of my membership, thanks to the auto renewal, but I was still going through the motions to a certain extent. I didn't hold out a great deal of hope that I would find what I was looking for now. At least I had a couple of dates to look forward to with Amanda and Sue and if one more materialised that would just be a bonus.

The thought of the date with Amanda made me realise I hadn't booked a restaurant. Surprise me, she'd said. Bit of pressure there I thought. If I picked anything too down market that may well be a surprise but the wrong type. If I went to the other extreme and we didn't click it could be the evening from hell and I'd end up being stuck with a woman I didn't want to be with and a massive bill for the privilege. No sense in over analysing it. I'd just take pot luck. After all the date was meant to be the point, not the venue. I trawled through Yell.com looking for a suitable but 'surprising' restaurant within easy reach of Banstead where she lived. There were plenty. An Indian restaurant didn't seem like an original option for a first date; Chinese? I didn't fancy the chopsticks thing – if she used them, I'd have to and I just knew I'd get more food on my clothes than in my mouth and if I used a knife and fork I'd run the risk of looking unsophisticated. Too much pressure. A kebab was just out of the question and a sushi restaurant was too fiddly and specialised. I was in grave danger of falling into analysis paralysis, the very thing I had hoped to avoid, when I saw *La Choucroute*.

24

I picked Amanda up at six o'clock in Banstead. She looked fabulous. Her short red hair, cut tight into a bob, and wide green eyes gave her an almost waif like appearance. This was exaggerated by her slender figure, high cheekbones and winsome features. Her lips were scarlet, the carefully applied lipstick accentuating her small mouth. Dressed in a long sculpted knee length black dress that hugged her figure and a neat high-necked red jacket her whole persona was one of style and chic. A pair of expensive looking black leather gloves completed the look. She kissed me on both cheeks, a light butterfly touch, her perfume floating teasingly across my face as she moved.

'Hello Matthew,' she said, 'you look very handsome.'

Her remark was simple but it had an instant warm impact, lifting my confidence. I'd chosen a plain black suit with a crisp white shirt. Nothing elaborate. It was always difficult to decide upon the most appropriate way to dress for a first date. Amanda's elegant style made me glad I'd selected something classic rather than too casual.

I told her I'd chosen an excellent French restaurant in Oxted. Her face lit up.

'J'adore la cuisine Français,' she said, fluttering her long eye lashes, 'that is a nice surprise.'

I led her to the car and opened the passenger door.

'This looks like a fast car,' she said as she buckled the seat belt.

I smiled and slid the keys into the ignition. I loved my Jag and delighted in its smooth response and controlled power.

'So, you are learning to drive then Amanda,' I said, firing up the engine.

'Yes, I am.'

'Well, how's it going?' I eased away from the kerb.

'Ok'.

'Have you had many lessons,' I asked.

'One,' she said.

'Oh, so today was your first one then?' The car was now cruising smoothly.

'Yes,' was all she said.

'How did that go?' I turned the car onto the dual carriageway and it accelerated effortlessly up to fifty.

'Fine,' she replied quietly.

She didn't seem to want to talk about it. She was sitting quite rigidly, a ball of tension, it seemed, the initial self-assured air no longer in evidence. I thought it was just nerves at a first date although I did wonder why both of her hands were gripping the seat. I decided that if she wanted to discuss her driving then we'd have plenty of opportunity in the restaurant. I focussed on the road ahead.

We crossed three roundabouts on the A217 and she still hadn't said another word. At the fourth one where it joins the M25, I turned left and accelerated down the long steep slip road to join the main carriageway. The road ahead was a brightly lit meandering corridor cutting through the shadowy darkness of the adjacent fields, its harsh concrete surface intermittently broken by the twinkling red taillights of the early evening traffic. The eerie glow of the instrument panel was all that lit the interior of the car but I could detect a slight tremor in Amanda's hands. She seemed to tense up even more as we picked up speed. She must have been holding it back in some form of pent up nervous force for as we finally joined the carriageway she suddenly screamed at me.

'Watch out!'

I hit the brake even though I hadn't seen anything to watch out for. 'What is it?' I asked, my senses on full alert as only a sudden unexpected intervention could cause when travelling at speed.

'That lorry...watch out for that lorry.'

I scanned the horizon. The nearest lorry was approximately two hundred and fifty metres ahead of us in the inside lane. She started pointing now, her gloved hand tight, the index finger insistent. It dawned on me that the lorry she was referring to was in fact a tiny speck in the distance, a rectangle of lights that I could just about see. I pointed too.

'That lorry,' I enquired, 'you mean that lorry down there?'

'Don't take you hand of the wheel.'

At least I think that was what she said. She said it so fast and so breathlessly that it was just about coherent.

'It's miles away,' I said as calmly as I could.

'It could jack-knife. And you are going so fast you wouldn't be able to stop.'

'Err... I am only doing seventy. That's ok on a motorway.'

'You are going too fast. You wouldn't be able to stop if it jack-knifed. And it might swerve. It might swerve across the road. You hadn't thought about that had you.'

No I hadn't. But I hadn't thought about what I'd do if an alien space ship suddenly hovered above the road and decided to land in front of us either. I hadn't thought of a lot of unlikely things. Otherwise I'd probably never get in a car again. At that particular point I began to think that perhaps she was taking her driving lessons a bit too seriously or that her instructor was demented.

'Are you a nervous passenger, Amanda? I can go slower if you'd like.'

'I am not a nervous passenger at all. I am just a careful driver, which clearly you are not,' she said.

Driver. After one lesson. To describe herself as a driver so soon was highly imaginative, especially given her reaction to her current journey. Nonetheless, I slowed down to thirty miles an hour, which she seemed more comfortable with but which was ridiculous on a motorway. However, I'd decided it was the best option if I wanted to avoid another date going pear shaped even before it had begun. We eventually arrived in Oxted without further drama thanks to my model driving at a speed that would have enabled me to balance an egg on the bonnet without it being unduly disturbed.

La Choucroute was a smart French brasserie catering for the well to do Surrey set. An open plan arrangement made the best use of the available space whilst creative lighting and tactically placed mirrors gave the room an intimate, elegant ambience. A waiter led us to a centrally placed table covered in a crisp white linen cloth, its gleaming wine glasses and glistening cutlery promising a delightful culinary experience. He eased out the high backed wooden chairs in turn and seated us. With an elaborate flourish a napkin was unfurled onto Amanda's lap. Mine followed with a similarly exaggerated action. A wine list was produced almost by sleight of hand and in a distinct French accent he asked if we would like an aperitif. Amanda had Kir Royale. I settled for a coke, noting her look of disapproval as I considered anything with alcohol in it.

As she sipped her drink Amanda seemed to relax at last. The red tinge of the cocktail matched perfectly the rouge of her lips.

'It is a very nice restaurant Matthew. Is this where you take all your dates,' she asked, a slight fluttering of her green eyes revealing the playfulness of the question.

'Oh, no. Not at all. I mean I have never been here before,' I said.

'So, where do you take them all, Matthew?'

'I don't take them anywhere. I mean I don't have that many to take really.'

'Oh, I am very surprised. I would have thought you would have lots of ladies after you. You are a very handsome man.'

The green eyes fluttered some more. She had gone from freaked out passenger to outrageous flirt. It threw me, as did the flattery. I felt a warm glow course through me again. I fancied Amanda. I wanted to get this right. Absent-mindedly I started poking the slice of lemon that was just breaking the surface of my coke with the blue plastic cocktail stick that emerged between the chunks of ice.

'You have gone quiet Matthew,' Amanda said, 'are you looking for something?'

If truth be known I was looking for my confidence. Since all my dates so far had ended in catastrophe I was cautious about getting my hopes up for a successful encounter. The result was that I was keeping my natural optimism in check and it was affecting my ability to relax and behave normally. I was thinking about saying the right thing and making the right impression. The minute I cared about the outcome my confidence deserted me. And I knew that any lack of confidence would just stop the date developing naturally and the result would be as I had now come to expect. Another disaster. Jasper Kane's words of wisdom flashed through my mind. '*Be yourself and have some confidence.*' I decided I had to overcome my concerns, relax and just go for it. I slipped off my jacket and casually placed it over the back of my chair.

Turning back towards Amanda I said, 'Oh, I was just thinking about what you said Amanda. About the ladies. No sense in hiding my light under a bushel, eh. I've had my moments. The ladies like a guy with a bit of je ne sais quoi. You know how it is.'

I felt like I was speaking in a foreign language all of a sudden.

'I see. You are a bit of a ladies' man. A philanderer.'

Amanda was toying with her glass. Her left hand, palm down, held the base flat on the table, the stem emerging between her middle finger and ring finger, her hand splayed wide, the red nails on full display. The fingers of her right hand were stroking the champagne flute from its thin fragile stem all the way up to the long narrow bowl. Her head inclined slightly to the right, the green eyes looking enquiringly upwards from under the dark lashes.

'Philanderer? Well, I...well, you know, you know how it is...err...single man and all that,' I said aware that that was not exactly the most self-assured response.

'It's ok Matthew. I like a man who is confident with the ladies.' She smiled at me, the green eyes clear and direct.

I was no doubt going to say something completely crass when I was rescued by the waiter arriving with two menus. Having handed us one each, he placed a basket of bread rolls in the centre of the table.

'This looks lovely,' Amanda said, 'an excellent choice and you have really not been here before?'

'No, I did a bit of research on line and found it. They have an excellent website with the menus and wine list easy to find. It made my mouth water just reading them on line. It had some great reviews too so I thought it may well be suitable.'

'Very suitable Matthew.'

She reached her hand out and patted mine. Whether it was for reassurance or congratulations, I wasn't sure but I didn't mind which. It felt good.

'So what do you fancy then Amanda,' I asked as I scanned the menu.

'It all looks so delicious,' she said, 'let's choose some starters and some main courses and then perhaps we can choose some suitable wine. You could leave your car here you know.'

Was that freaked out passenger talking or outrageous flirt? I took it as outrageous flirt and realised that if I handled it well the date could end on a very positive note. I looked up from the menu briefly to respond. I don't know why I was suddenly distracted but to my alarm I spotted what I thought was Louise Penny heading into the restaurant. Perhaps I was seeing things. Perhaps my sub-conscious was playing tricks on me. I peered over the top of the menu and did a double take. It was her. PC Penny and a man. Both smartly dressed. I couldn't believe it. I felt the unease rush in through my veins invading all parts of my body. The waiter greeted Louise and her companion and started to lead them to a table. The table immediately behind my date.

'So, Matthew, I was saying…your car. You could leave it and we could get a taxi together?'

I heard Amanda speaking but I didn't take in the implications of what she was saying. My mind zeroed in on just one word of what she'd said. The car. The bloody car. My car was parked just a few spaces along from the front of the restaurant. The car that Louise Penny had spoken to me about only days earlier and which the police had registered to Matthew Malarkey. Me.

I raised the menu so it was practically obscuring my face.

'Matthew. Are you ok?' my date enquired. 'You look like you are hiding behind that menu. You are not playing hard to get all of a sudden, Mr Philanderer?'

I spoke from behind my leather bound hiding place. 'Hiding, err no I'm not hiding. I am…err...I forgot my glasses...I'm short sighted.'

'Short sighted? Now you tell me after driving me here. We are definitely getting that taxi afterwards,' Amanda said, a look of concern on her face. 'Let me help you.'

Before I could react she grabbed the menu from my hand leaving me facing into the restaurant just as Louise and her companion were being seated at their table. Deprived of my impromptu shield I lowered my head so it was below the level of Amanda's. Since I was taller than her this meant I was now in quite a stooped position, looking more Quasimodo than philanderer.

'Matthew. What are you doing? Are you all right. What are you looking for?'

'Nothing...nothing...I am just...nervous.'

Why I said nervous I had no idea. Perhaps it was in my psyche since Amanda had been a bag of nerves on the journey.

'Nervous? Nervous of what?' she said

'Restaurants.'

'Restaurants?' She sounded incredulous. 'If you are nervous of restaurants why did you take me to one?'

I had no answer to that. I had half an eye peering around Amanda's head to see what was going on behind her. I wasn't thinking about what I was saying. In fact I was only becoming aware of what I had said once I heard it.

'Well, not restaurants exactly...it's the...the...the food in restaurants.'

'You are nervous about food, Matthew?'

'Not all food, no, just some.' My voice echoed back to me like a strange disembodied recording. I knew I was creating myself a hole but my focus was still on what Louise was doing not what I was saying.

'Which foods?' Amanda asked, her voice tinged with incredulity.

I could see that Louise had now settled and was taking in her surroundings. I kept my head down, my posture now leaning heavily to my left.

'The ones on that menu. Yes, that type of food. As soon as I saw it I felt, well...nervous. Everyone can get nervous about something.'

'You are nervous about French food, Matthew? But it is a French restaurant and you chose it. I don't understand.'

My anxiety increased rapidly as I tried to attempt an explanation and at the same time stay hidden. 'It's really very simple, Amanda. Not all French foods. Just some. The ones they now have on that menu which they didn't have before,' I said.

'Didn't have before? But you said you'd never been here before.'

'Err, yes, I mean...no. I haven't. The menus were on the website. And now they have things on the menu that they didn't have when I went on the website.'

'Well which ones?' Amanda asked.

For an instant it crossed my mind to grab a bread roll and stuff it straight into Amanda's red-lipped mouth to stop her asking any more questions. Louise was now looking at a wine list. I picked up the menu again and raised it in front of me.

'Which ones. Well, let's see...onion soup, escargots, foie gras–' In my distracted state I was reading straight from the menu.

'Onion soup, escargots, foie gras!' Amanda's voice had now taken on the high-pitched tone of incredulity. 'But they must be on all French menus.' She practically laughed out loud.

'Well, not this one. I hadn't noticed onion soup and foie gras on this one before. Nor in fact, escargots. So they must all be new. They must have decided that as they are a French restaurant they should have that sort of err...French stuff on the menu. And now I am nervous about them. I know it's silly but well, you get nervous as a passenger and it's a bit like that.'

'But if I analyse my nervousness Matthew, it's really about being involved in a car accident. You are not concerned about being in an onion soup accident are you?'

'No. No. Of course not...I...well...' I was struggling. I could see Louise looking around the room again.

'Perhaps you misread the website menu if you weren't wearing your glasses.

And could you put that menu down. I can't see you.' She grabbed at the menu but I managed to evade the lunge.

'I am sorry, Amanda, it's hard to explain. Look, can you give me a minute I need to go to the gent's washroom. I need to...well you know...when I get nervous I need to... I won't be long.'

I realised I was beginning to lose my grip of the conversation simply because I was mostly focused on avoiding being seen by Louise and my posture had become even lower to the table. A few moments in the gents might help me clear my head. I got up from the table in a swift crouching action, head bowed onto my chest and marched to the rear of the restaurant to the washroom. I leant on the sink staring at myself in the mirror. I couldn't believe my luck. The co-incidences. Why did I keep running into PC Penny? Even when she was off duty? Maybe it wasn't co-incidence. Maybe she was following me, keeping me under surveillance. I splashed cold water on my face and shook it off. No, she couldn't be keeping me under surveillance as she would not be allowing herself to be seen if she was. I wasn't thinking at all clearly as usual. And now I was about to screw up another date that seemed promising. However, I realised that if I walked back out into the restaurant I was almost certain to be seen by Louise. And, if she'd seen my car she'd put two and two together, identify me as Matthew Malarkey and I would be screwed. She would then wonder what the cover up was about and assume I had a lot more to hide, or I wouldn't have gone to such lengths. That would make me look completely guilty and I'd be stitched up for tens of thousands of pounds of damages at Hemmingwell Halls. And for good measure she'd probably get me for vandalism at Julia's party too. Terrific.

I had to think clearly. Maybe she hadn't seen the car. After all she was on a night out with a date. She could even have approached from the other direction and not noticed it. I couldn't take the risk though. It was a very distinctive vehicle and since she'd seen it once on my driveway it may just trigger a connection if she had spotted it again outside the restaurant. No, I definitely couldn't risk being seen. I couldn't walk out into the restaurant again. But I couldn't spend the entire evening standing in the gents either.

Just as I was about to become riveted to the spot with crippling indecision I spotted the open window through one of the toilet cubicle doors. It wasn't the most sensible course of action but then I wasn't thinking the most sensible thoughts. If I could get out that way I could easily call Amanda on her mobile and ask her to meet me at the front of the restaurant. I'd think of some explanation later. I'd tell her I had a panic attack or something. Maybe take her to a Chinese restaurant instead. Anything to extricate myself from what I perceived to be a difficult predicament.

I entered the toilet cubicle, closed the door and climbed onto the toilet seat. I then pulled myself up into the window space and peered through. Outside there was an alley and a drop of about ten feet to the pavement. In the darkness

I could just see a green wheelie bin slightly to the left of the window. I realised that if I could squeeze through the window, lower myself down the outside wall to the bin I could easily clamber off the bin and onto the ground. I estimated the bin to be about three and a half feet high and with me being six feet tall that left a mere six inches to negotiate. At that moment it seemed like a good plan and a way out of my predicament.

The window gap certainly looked big enough to get myself through. It had an old-fashioned metal frame with a window that swung open to one side and a metal arm with several holes along it to fix it onto the spike that protruded from the frame and hold it open. I got back down onto the toilet seat. I grabbed hold of one side of the cubicle wall and heaved myself upwards so that I was high enough to swing my legs onto the windowsill. A few pushes with my arms and pulls with my legs and I had manoeuvred far enough into the window opening to assume a semi seated position. I was then able to twist onto my stomach and hang my legs through the window. I paused to get my breath. The pressure on my midriff from my weight on the window ledge as I dangled half in and half out had begun to restrict my breathing. I wriggled further back and paused again. I was hot with the effort but I realised that now there was only one way to go. The point of no return. I was far enough out to make it easier to drop down than it would have been to try and clamber back through, reach the cubicle wall and drag myself back in.

I worked my way backwards so that I clung on by my upper arms, hands gripping the inside edge of the windowsill. I clung there for a while lining up the top of the wheelie bin with my right foot and contemplated the drop. The flat bin lid was just inches below me and slightly to my right side, with its handle directly in line with my foot. I had to get it right. I let go of the windowsill. My foot made fleeting contact with the edge of the bin but my momentum only succeeded in placing the weight emphasis on the handle that was directly above the wheels. The sudden impact tilted the bin back onto its wheels and propelled it forward at an angle until it keeled over completely, skidding to a halt a few feet away across the alley. At the same time I felt a sharp tug on my left arm, which for a split second delayed my inevitable fall. The gap in my shirtsleeve just above the point where the cuff links held the cuffs in place had caught on the window lever but clearly the fabric of my shirt was not designed to support thirteen stone and four pounds. The buttons along the front of the shirt started to pop off under the strain like mini pellets from an air rifle. Then the sleeve started to tear at the shoulder stitching and in one huge rip separated completely from the shirt leaving me to crash in a heap onto the concrete. I felt the jarring pain in my right ankle as it buckled on the ground. My face had scraped the brickwork as I fell and a warm trickle of blood oozed down my right cheek.

Shocked and slightly stunned by the fall I sat up and took in my surroundings. I was sitting in an alley bare-chested, one arm totally exposed, dirt and grime all over my trousers and what was left of my shirt. There was no time to feel sorry for myself. I had to move my car away from the restaurant before Louise came out later. Leaning over onto my left side I placed both hands on the ground and tried to push myself up but the pain in my ankle wasn't helping. I needed to call Amanda. I searched in my trousers pocket for my mobile. As soon as I found the pocket was empty a wave of panic hit me. I almost knew what I had done but still checked the other pocket. I pulled out my door keys and a small box of Tic Tacs. I placed them on top of the stricken wheelie bin that lay to my left and frantically continued searching. Nothing. Nothing in the back pockets either. It was in my jacket. My jacket that was on the back of the chair in the restaurant. My jacket that also had my car keys and wallet in it.

Shit. I kept saying it to myself over and over. What a total dickhead. It may have been shock kicking in but I began to mentally abuse myself, calling myself all the names I could think of in no rational thought process. I sat there like a vagrant, confused, panic setting in. I had to clear my head. I tried to get to my feet again, this time managing a kneeling position before I became aware of a new source of pain in my hip. I was bound to have bruising I thought. Eventually, with some effort, I succeeded in getting to my feet and was able to place some weight on my sore ankle. It hurt. I began to move with a slow limp towards the end of the alley. Although every step sent a twinge of pain through my leg I could at least walk and I realised it couldn't be broken. I made it to the main street. At the corner of the building I took a deep breath and headed to the front of the restaurant. I managed to climb the first two steps when I was stopped by one of the waiting staff.

'Can I help you Monsieur.'

'I need to speak to someone in the restaurant. Can I get a message passed to her please?'

'I am sorry Monsieur, we cannot disturb our customers when they are dining,' he replied.

'But I am with her. I mean I came with her tonight. We are together.'

'Together? I haven't seen you before Monsieur.'

He looked me up and down. I could see his point. I must have looked a total state in my one armed torn shirt, grubby trousers and blood stained face.

'Well to be honest I haven't seen you either tonight but that doesn't mean I haven't been in your restaurant,' I said rather irritably, the soreness in my ankle not helping my mood.

'I am afraid, Monsieur, that your attire, does not comply with our restaurant dress code. Unfortunately you are not properly dressed to enter the premises,' he responded somewhat snottily.

'Of course I am not properly dressed. I mean do you think I deliberately come out wearing blood? Do you think I spent hours in front of the mirror making sure my shirt was ripped in just the right way or that I rolled in the garden for a while until I could make sure my trousers were grubby enough to visit a restaurant? And anyway where does it say that a customer cannot be bleeding or wearing ripped clothing?' My tone was clearly getting more and more excitable and my antagonist more and more perplexed.

'Calm down Monsieur,' he said, raising his hand in a pacifying motion, 'I am sure you didn't deliberately dress incorrectly and you are actually bleeding–'

'I was mugged,' I interrupted.

I thought I could see a way of getting him on my side by seeking the sympathy route. I needed to get my jacket and mobile and I was feeling the pressure of standing there and drawing attention to myself, the last thing I wanted with Louise in close proximity.

'Mugged? Mugged in the restaurant? You said you were in the restaurant Monsieur?'

'No. No...not in the restaurant. Outside. I...I came out for a cigarette.'

'We should call the police –'

'No! No need,' I almost shouted. 'I will report it myself. I just need to get my jacket.'

'Mai oui, Monsieur. Come in.'

He had turned extremely helpful all of a sudden. I had never actually asked to go in, in the first place and in fact the last thing I wanted was to go back inside with Louise Penny in there.

'I just need to get a message to a lady. The lady I was with. My ankle is too sore to walk up these steps so I would be grateful if you could just ask her to come outside. She is the lady with the red hair sitting on her own at the table with the jacket on the back of the opposite chair. She's wearing a red jacket and black dress. My name is... just tell her that her companion is outside.' I tried to be as descriptive as possible. I didn't want any mistakes.

He went off and within a couple of minutes Amanda appeared at the top of the restaurant steps.

'Oh my god! What happened to you?' She looked aghast.

'Nothing...I had an accident,' I said.

'An accident? What sort of accident? And how did you get out here?' she questioned rather too loudly.

'He got mugged,' said the waiter helpfully.

'Mugged? But you only went to the loo. I don't understand.'

'He was having a cigarette outside and was attacked,' said the waiter displaying a talent for piecing together the bits of information he had been given.

I tried to restore some logic. 'Yes, I went to the loo and then came out to have a cigarette and –'

'He got mugged,' chipped in the waiter again.

'I didn't know you smoked, Matthew. Why didn't you say, I am gasping for one myself.'

Of all the things she could have focused on I can only think it was Amanda's own need for a cigarette that made her pick out the smoking. She fumbled in her bag and pulled out a pack of opened cigarettes.

'Here Matthew. You look like you could use one too.'

I had never smoked in my life and so the last thing I needed or wanted was a cigarette. I tried to refuse but she insisted saying it would calm me down after my mugging. My first puff caused the inevitable coughing and spluttering.

'Are you ok Matthew. Maybe I should call an ambulance,' Amanda suggested.

'I'm fine. The smoke just went down the wrong way. They wouldn't appreciate you getting an ambulance for someone who inhaled a cigarette the wrong way,' I said between coughs.

'No, stupid. For your injuries. You are bleeding.'

I was heartened by her concern, which helped me overlook the harshness of being called stupid, although given what had happened to me, it was a completely justified description.

'Oh no. No need for an ambulance. It's just a scratch. I will just go home and clean up. But I do need my jacket Amanda. I left it in the restaurant.'

'Don't worry Monsieur,' piped up the newly helpful waiter, 'I will retrieve it,' and off he went.

As he disappeared up the steps I apologised to Amanda for the spoilt date. I offered to drive her home.

'You must be joking Matthew. You are a reckless driver at the best of times so I am not getting into a car with you now when you are half-conscious and have a dodgy ankle, let alone the fact that you are short sighted and you have forgotten your glasses. I will get a taxi.'

It hadn't taken Amanda long to arrive at conclusions. She'd barely known me an hour and already judged me to be reckless and now assumed I was half-conscious. She was puffing away at another cigarette but thankfully didn't offer me another one, perhaps because she may have seen my attempt at surreptitiously dropping the first one into the gutter after I had nearly choked on it. I considered she'd be better off putting the wind up some hapless taxi driver. I was in no state now to continue the evening. Maybe I'd get a second chance another time.

The waiter returned with my jacket. I thanked him. He said it was no trouble and if I needed a witness for the police his name was Pierre. I wasn't sure why he thought he was now a witness to an event that never happened and he hadn't seen but I left it at that.

'Do you have a taxi number I could call please, Pierre,' Amanda asked him.

'Hang on Amanda,' I intervened, 'I have one here.' I searched my jacket found my wallet and pulled out a card. Real Libel Car Services.

'They are very good.'

25

As I hobbled back to my car I had resigned myself to yet another dating disaster. It looked like it was fated to be that way for me. Instead of Cupid shooting the arrow of love straight at me, I was pursuing Cupid all over the place and Cupid didn't seem to be interested. I eased myself cautiously into the driving seat, cursing the fact that if I had to injure an ankle it had to be the right one that I needed for the pedals in the car. Why couldn't it have been my left one, if it had to be any, the one I didn't need to use in an automatic. Ignoring the discomfort as I hit the pedal, I accelerated away from the restaurant as quickly as I could. A few streets later I pulled over to the kerb. I needed to get my breath and think clearly now that I was away from the restaurant. I knew I wasn't injured to any great extent. My ankle was very sore and my face grazed, the blood making the cut look worse than it was. I just needed to drive home get showered, clean up and rest. As I restarted the engine my mobile rang. To my complete surprise it was Diana.

'Matthew. It's Diana. How are you?'

I was shocked into momentary silence.

'Hello. Hello…Matthew,' she repeated.

'Oh hi Diana.' I tried to sound detached. 'I'm good. How are you?'

'Very well Matthew. Forgive me ringing you but I wanted to speak to you. I felt bad about the way I treated you and I didn't want any bad feeling between us. Look, it would be lovely if we could speak in person and perhaps I could explain myself. I find mobiles a little impersonal. Would that be possible?'

I wanted to say no, it wouldn't. I wanted to gain the upper hand, to take control and bluntly tell her to sod off. But I knew that it was just my pride talking and my reaction to being rejected. 'Yes, that should be ok, Diana. When?'

'Well if you are free Matthew I was thinking about now. I am actually in the

Kingston area at a bit of a loose end. I have been out shopping with a girlfriend. We were supposed to be going for a drink afterwards but one of her children wasn't well so she has had to leave. Are you free?'

My mind was in turmoil. I was free but I wasn't really in a state to go out never mind meet Diana. I wanted to go though. I didn't want to pass up the opportunity. After all she had called me. She must want to see me I reasoned. I'd find a way to make it happen.

'Yes, I am free. I have to pop home first but I could meet a bit later.'

'Excellent Matthew. Shall we say about eight thirty then? And do you know a nice cosy bar or something, somewhere we could have a chat and a drink? I fancy a glass of wine actually.'

It was now seven fifteen. I could get home in twenty minutes or so, a fast shower, quick change of clothes, a taxi into Kingston. It could be done.

'Yes, I do Diana. There is a bar called MacFadden's. I go there quite a lot and we can always find a quiet table in the corner. I know the owner. It's not far from the station. Ask anyone. I will be there as quick as I can.'

Why I recommended MacFadden's on a Saturday night I had no idea but my focus was mainly on getting home and getting cleaned up. Diana's call had taken me totally by surprise but I wanted to see her. The night may not be quite the disaster it had been turning into after all.

I raced down the A25 to the M25, along the A217 and was home within thirty minutes. I hurried out of the car as fast as my limp would allow me to my front door only to feel a sudden sense of doom descend upon me as I stood on the doorstep. Time seemed to stand still and a weird sixth sense flowed chillingly over me. I took a deep breath and went for it. I plunged my hand swiftly into my jacket pocket, my fingers tingling with the expectation of grasping the familiar bunch of keys that allowed me access to my house. But they were not there. Another frantic search through every available pocket produced no keys. I took another deep breath to quell the feeling of rising panic. They must be in the car I reasoned. Fell out of my pocket, surely. It was desperate optimism that I was clinging to as I limped back to my car. I searched high and low, even in places they could not possibly have been in. They were not there. Nowhere to be seen. I couldn't believe it. It seemed to me that whatever I did recently the fates were conspiring against me to make it go wrong. I stood in the road next to my car and a surge of resigned calm hit me. Almost as if whatever will be will be. It all didn't really matter. Whatever I did, I didn't seem to be in control, so I would just go with my fate. This moment of calm triggered an unexpected process of rational thought.

I tried to think back to when I had last seen my house keys. I remembered searching for my mobile after I had fallen outside the restaurant. I had seen them then, I was sure. I had taken them from the pocket of my trousers and... placed them on the wheelie bin, with the Tic Tacs. That's where they must be.

I called the restaurant and asked for Pierre, the waiter. I told him that I thought I'd left my keys on the bin in the alley. He didn't ask for an explanation but went to look. A few minutes later he called back. He had them. I had to make the decision. If I went to collect them now I'd lose at least an hour with the journey time there and back. It was approaching seven forty five. Then I'd need to get showered and changed and get a cab to MacFadden's. It would be a minimum of an hour and three quarters at least before I could get to the bar which means Diana would have to wait by herself until practically ten o'clock. I couldn't risk calling her and expecting her to hang on that long for me.

I asked Pierre to keep the keys until the morning when I could collect them. Pierre said he would but then he dropped a bombshell.

'Monsieur. I called the police for you.'

'You did what? Called the police? For what?'

'Yes, Monsieur. Because you were mugged I reported it for you.'

For me. Terrific. Thanks a bunch, bloody helpful Pierre. Why couldn't he have stayed unhelpful, like he was when he wouldn't let me near his restaurant. I tried not to allow my earlier calmness to get away.

'Pierre. What did they say?'

'They said they could do nothing Monsieur, unless you reported it yourself. They just took some details,' he replied.

'Details? What details?'

'Just what happened and your name. That is all.'

'My name,' I shouted, 'but you don't know my name.'

'Don't worry Monsieur I was able to get it from your table number. You made your booking by telephone so it was simple.'

Simple. Bloody simple. Great, now Pierre was an amateur detective. Bloody idiot, Pierre. But no sense in overreacting. I had to get things in perspective. Matthew Malarkey was at the restaurant in Oxted and involved in an alleged mugging but no complaint was made. So the police wouldn't bother with it. They were the local cops so it was just another Saturday night call. In fact they'd be glad not to have to bother with another load of paperwork. I was panicking too easily at the mention of police. And the fact that PC Penny had been at the restaurant was just coincidence. She was from the Met anyway and nothing had happened in any case, even if it had been on her patch. I had to calm it down. Think of the date with Diana. I had to sort that. I needed to keep Pierre onside too if I wanted my keys back.

'Pierre. Ok, look thanks. I appreciate your help. Sorry about shouting. Still a little sore. I will be fine tomorrow and I will collect my keys tomorrow.'

It was almost ten to eight already and I had lost ten minutes looking for the keys. I rang Cecil. I hoped I could get shower at his place maybe borrow a shirt, even though it may be a struggle getting the right fit since he was shorter than me and much stockier. There was no reply. The panicky feeling was starting to return. I left him a message and simply asked if I could crash at his place later.

I needed to tidy myself up and get a shirt at least. Even if I could find a shop open at this time of night I was running out of time. I had a brainwave. I called Jim at the fancy dress shop. I knew he would be open.

'Jim. It's Matthew. I need a shirt. I am going out tonight and need a shirt. Have you got anything?'

'Bit short notice mate, it's bloody party season and I am pretty low on stuff. What type?'

'Anything. Well, not anything, but something simple, white, plain. And I have got bugger all time.'

'Blimey mate. No problem. I will see what I can do.'

Next I called a taxi and arranged for it to pick me up back at my place for ten past eight. I had to lose the Jag before going to meet Diana in case there was any comeback from the police. I was lucky to get a taxi and didn't need to resort to Real Libel Car Services. With the taxi sorted I jumped in my car and headed for Jim's shop. It was an option to get me out of a predicament. There was no point in asking to borrow one of his own shirts since he was pushing eighteen stone. I was there in eight minutes. I parked outside on the double yellows, leaving the engine running. Jim saw me coming. He had bag ready for me.

'Cheers Jim. I owe you. I'll be back in the morning.' I grabbed the bag.

'Bloody hell mate. Slow down. Must be bloody good party you are off to. Nice make up by the way. Very realistic.'

I ignored him and limped back to the car as fast as I could. Ten minutes later I was at back home for my rendezvous with the taxi. We pulled up outside MacFadden's shortly after and I was relieved to see I had arrived five minutes early. Pushing my way through a crowd of drinkers I found Carlos behind the bar as usual. His mouth opened to say something but nothing came out.

'Don't ask Carlos. Sorry mate. I need to use your bathroom urgently.'

I went straight through to the men's toilets at the back of the bar. I filled the sink with a mix of hot and cold water. I pulled off my torn shirt in a hurry to get cleaned up and changed and threw it carelessly to one side. It landed right in the middle of one of the urinals just as the automatic flush system kicked in and totally soaked it. I snatched it back out. Torn and soaked now, it was useless. I stuffed it in a nearby bin. Turning back to the sink, I plunged both cupped hands into the basin of warm water and splashed it over my face. Two or three handfuls. The sensation of the water felt good, refreshing and invigorating. I hit the soap dispenser and deposited two squirts of gel into the palm of my left hand. It lathered up smoothly and I washed the blood off my face. Next I washed my upper body, under my arms and my neck. With several handfuls of water I rinsed off the soapy gel. My skin tingled but I felt revitalised. I examined my face in the mirror. The cut was really nothing more than a graze high on my right cheekbone but there remained three horizontal red weals and, although I had removed the blood, they were still very noticeable. I checked my watch. It had just gone eight thirty. I tried wiping some of the grime off my trousers with my wet hands but they would have to do. A quick session under the hot air hand dryer and I was ready to get dressed.

I picked up Jim's bag and delved in for the shirt. I pulled it out and let it unfold. Perhaps I should have half expected the unexpected. Perhaps it should have been obvious that it was never going to be a Saville Row classic number. It was the eyelets and laces that caught my attention first. It was a full-blown satin pirate shirt, complete with long frilly cuffs and a wide ruffled collar that fanned out to sit on the shoulders and went all the way down from neck to waist. There were no buttons. It did up by pulling the laces together that ran from the neck to the mid chest area. The sleeves had ties at the cuffs too. The only thing that could be said to be right about it was that it was white. That's all. I cursed Jim in my head despite the fact that he had only been trying to help with my emergency request.

I had a moment's despair and then a realisation that I had three choices. Fish my ripped, soaking wet shirt out of the bin and wear that or put my jacket on and go outside bare-chested, or wear the pirate's shirt. I had three choices and no choice. I slipped the pirate shirt over my head. It slid over my body easily, frilly cuffs dangling almost to my fingertips, the bottom of it reaching down to mid thigh level. I drew the eyelets together to bring the front collars closer together and tucked the rest of it into the waist of my trousers. The whole shirt billowed at the waist and the voluminous sleeves sat like two deflated parachutes around my arms. I grabbed my jacket and squeezed it over the top of the shirt pulling the lapels up around my neck to try and hide as much of the shirt as I could. It still didn't look right. It looked like I was hiding something under my jacket. It was now twenty to nine and I was late. I had to make a decision. In the circumstances the only real option was to leave the bar, call Diana and tell her something had come up. Reluctantly, I decided that is what I must do.

I emerged from the toilets slowly and started to walk to the exit, looking straight ahead.

'There you are Matthew. So sorry I am late.'

Diana was standing directly in front of me looking gorgeous. She did not appear to be dressed for winter at all in a deep V-neck white dress with cropped sleeves and a wide white band at the waist. It flowed over her figure and ended abruptly mid thigh. A pair of silver high-heeled sandals that showed of her red painted toes completed the vision. She kissed me on either cheek. I managed to mumble some sort of greeting in her general direction. My mind was a mixture of intoxication with her aura and a self-protective desire to hide my embarrassment at the way I looked. Her style only served to bring my half hidden pirate shirt and my soiled trousers into sharper focus. She hadn't seemed to notice my attire but if she had she made no remark. There was no sense in nervously hiding it. That would just make me look timid and ineffectual. I'd just have to style it out and be myself. Confidence was the name of the game.

'Hello Diana. Lovely to see you. You look fantastic. What can I get you to drink?' I said, as assertively as I felt able in the circumstances.

A dazzling smile lit up her face. The compliment had worked it seemed.

'Thank you Matthew. Oh I do fancy some wine. Shall we share a bottle?'

We headed for the bar. As I approached I saw Carlos looking at me as if to say something. Before he could open his mouth I introduced Diana.

'Oh, yes, we met briefly. This is the lovely gentleman who kindly took my coat,' Diana said, smiling broadly at Carlos.

I ordered a bottle of Chablis. Carlos went into full customer service mode, flattered no doubt by Diana's smile and at being referred to as a 'lovely gentleman.'

'Let me show you to a table and I will get my waitress to bring your wine over.' He directed us to a table on the far side of the room.

Diana leaned forward, 'So, Matthew, how have you been?'

I didn't tell her how I had really been. She really didn't need to know. I told her I had been fine and that I had been busy with work. The usual non-committal reply when someone asks how you are. She remarked on the scratches on my face but I glossed over the subject. What I really wanted to know was why she was here. I asked her how things were going for her.

'Oh, I have been very busy. Lots of work coming in. More cases than I can handle actually.'

That wasn't what I wanted to know. I wanted to know why she had contacted me and how it was going with the fat businessman, Robert Henderson. I was clearly going to have to lead the subject.

'Are you still on the dating site?' I asked as casually as I could.

'No, I cancelled my membership when I started seeing Robert. Are you?' she said.

'I am. Still looking for love. So, how's it going with...with Robert'. I hated saying his name but at least I had raised the subject.

'Not so good, I am afraid,' she said.

Not so good. Fantastic. I was overjoyed at her response. I tried not to show it. I asked what had happened.

'I think he is married,' she said. 'Typical. Just like all the others.'

I really didn't care why she thought he might be married. I was just glad that his marriage may well have taken him right out of the equation as far as Diana was concerned. But she seemed to want to tell. So I listened to her stories of him having to cancel meetings at the last minute, furtively looking at texts on his mobile and most damning of all, being spotted shopping with a woman in a high street store on Saturday afternoon.

I tried to be sympathetic despite my inward feelings of satisfaction.

'Well it's only been a few weeks since you met him at the range, Diana. Better to find out now rather than later before you got too emotionally involved,' I said.

'Look Matthew. I am not some silly girl. I am not emotionally involved in the slightest. What annoys me is the deceit. The dishonesty. I don't like it. I need to be able to trust someone, do you understand?'

I did. I remembered it only too well. I poured the wine that had finally been delivered to the table. It was cool and refreshing, with a slightly acid after taste. I decided to broach the subject that was intriguing me most. It didn't need a direct question.

'It's really nice to see you again Diana. I was really surprised to get your call.'

'Thank you Matthew. It's good to see you. I like you. I think we got on quite well and on reflection I was perhaps a little judgemental of you and treated you a bit harshly. I wanted to make amends. I don't think you are actually a dishonest person. I just think you were being a little ambitious and, dare I say it, trying to impress.'

I felt an overwhelming sense of relief. The tension I had felt about meeting Diana drained away to be replaced by an instant feeling of relaxation and delight. So relaxed, in fact that I took my jacket off.

'Interesting shirt, Matthew,' she said, her eyes widening as she took in my fashion faux pas.

I'd forgotten about the shirt. The sleeves now flopped down over my hands and the collar flounced out in all its full glory. I was about to offer an explanation when I heard the greeting.

'Hello Michael. How are you?' It was Sheryl. 'I thought that was you. What's happened to your face?'

I was on my feet in an instant.

'Sheryl. Hello. Hi. Let me get you a drink.'

I bundled her across the floor to the bar. Her complete surprise at being man handled cancelled out any resistance she might have felt.

'Fuck me, it's Adam Ant!' Cecil was standing at the bar large as life and there was mockery in his eyes. 'Where you been geezer and what are you doing in that seventies get up?'

I ignored the last question. All I needed was Cecil.

'More to the point where have you been Cecil? I haven't heard from you. No calls. Nothing. And what are you doing here?'

'A geezer can come out for a beer can't he? Me and Sheryl here have been laying low for a while, if you get my drift.' I detected a satisfied smirk. 'What you up to?'

'I am on a date, Cecil. A quiet night out with someone.'

'Who?' he asked.

'Diana. You know, that I played golf with the other week.' I must have inadvertently nodded in Diana's direction as Cecil spotted her across the room.

'That lawyer bird you been after? You cracked it at last then geezer.' He paused just long enough to check out Diana. 'She looks a bit of all right mate. Right stunner. You'll have to introduce me.'

'It's just a quiet night Cecil. That's all. Nothing more. You off out tonight then somewhere?' I asked, in the hope that he was.

'Nah, me and Sheryl are meeting up with her mate and her brother for a little birthday celebration.'

'Mate? What mate?' I asked but I feared the worst.

'Sheryl's copper mate, you know, Louise.'

Louise. But she is in a restaurant, I thought, the one I had climbed out of earlier to avoid her.

'She can't be. I mean, if it's a birthday you wouldn't come here, would you.' I caught Carlos's eye. 'Err...no offence Carlos. I meant, maybe you'd go to a restaurant or something.'

I was half hoping there had been a mistake. I couldn't run into PC Penny again, surely. It was getting to be too much of a coincidence now. Maybe she was following me, after all, keeping me under surveillance. Hiding in plain sight.

'Oh she's doing both, restaurant and bar,' Sheryl said, 'they should be here any minute.'

'Yeah, we'll come over and join you and your birdie for a drink geezer. Make up a little party.' Cecil didn't seem to grasp my concerns at all. Either that or he didn't care.

'No. No...that's not happening Cecil. I mean, we can't. We are not staying. Another time maybe.'

The words had hardly left my lips when Louise and the guy I had seen her with in the restaurant appeared from nowhere.

'Helloooo everybody,' Louise's greeting was expansive. Kisses on cheeks were exchanged with Cecil and Sheryl and then she spotted me.

'Oh hello Michael. I didn't know you were coming. Fancy seeing you again.'

She looked good, hair flowing, make up perfect. For a moment I was pleased to see her and then the usual disquiet that arose in me whenever I encountered Louise Penny reared its head. I was on the back foot again.

'Hi Louise,' I said.

'Let me introduce you to my brother, Ian. Ian, this is Michael. Michael is a...well, I am not really sure what Michael is...a friend?' She looked me in the eyes, a hint of mischief, the kind I'd seen before, lighting up her gaze. 'Yes, a friend of mine.' She giggled as she said it.

She seemed a little tipsy which was understandable if she'd been out celebrating.

'It's Ian's birthday. We have been for a lovely meal and a few drinkies in a lovely restaurant near where he lives and now we are all going to have champagne,' Louise added.

Well at least that explained who the man was.

'Well happy birthday Ian,' I said. I turned to Louise. 'A lovely restaurant? Anywhere nice?'

'Oh, yes, a lovely French restaurant in Oxted. Le Cheroot or something,' she giggled.

'La Choucroute,' Ian chipped in, 'do you know it Michael?'

'Oh no. Just wondered. Fun night, I take it.' If they had noticed anything out of the ordinary at the restaurant it was likely that in her tipsy state Louise would mention it.

'Great fun. Lovely time,' Louise said, 'ooooh champagne!'

Carlos had opened a bottle and four glasses were perched on the bar. Ian started to pour.

'Would you like to join us Michael?' Louise asked.

I started to explain that I couldn't, that I was going somewhere. I didn't know where exactly yet but I had made up my mind the minute I had run into Cecil that it was best for me to take Diana somewhere else. Maybe another country would be a good idea. I couldn't believe that of all the restaurants I could have chosen to take Amanda to that night, I had just happened to pick one in the same town that Louise's brother lived in.

'Oh that is a shame. You could have kept me company. I am sure Ian doesn't want to be chatting to his little sister all night,' Louise said. 'Where are you off to, in that gorgeous shirt?' She looked me up and down. 'Not another fancy dress party.'

Ian was looking at my shirt with a look that bordered on disbelief.

'Another fancy dress party?' I said, trying not to show my discomfort at the question. 'I have never actually been to any fancy dress parties at all. I–'

'Oh weren't you at a fancy dress occasion the other week when I saw you?'

She winked at me as she said it and sipped her champagne, deliberately teasing me. I didn't actually think she would ever have embarrassed me by mentioning the nappy incident but I will never know because I was spared that embarrassment with an alternative source of embarrassment courtesy of Cecil.

'He's going on a date.'

'A date?' A frown clouded Louise's features momentarily, almost a look of disappointment, but it passed quickly. 'Well, you do seem to be doing well with the ladies lately, Michael. I hope she doesn't scratch like the last one,' she said, pointing to her cheek.

'Oh that.' My brain was racing. I couldn't help it in Louise's company. I'd dug myself a hole with her over the weeks and it seemed the only way was down. She'd been at the restaurant where I was allegedly mugged. I wasn't to know if she had chatted to the waiter, Pierre. I couldn't risk any connections. I was in the hole so it may as well get deeper.

'A domestic accident. I had an accident at home.'

I thought that would suffice but she had to ask. Perhaps it was the policewoman in her.

'An accident? How?'

'How? How...with the...err...with the dishwasher.'

I'd said the first thing that came into my head that could be construed as a domestic accident. As usual when I was under pressure it didn't sound too plausible.

'The dishwasher?' Sheryl and Louise said it in unison, which emphasised their amazement even more.

I wanted to get away. I was standing in the middle of a busy Saturday night bar in a ridiculous shirt. I had a beautiful date waiting for me to return to her. I had just blown another date that very evening and here I was wasting time talking about my face. I decided it didn't matter what I said next but whatever I said I was getting out of there.

'Yes, the dishwasher. I dropped my reading glasses into it as I was loading it and as I was leaning down to try and get them back out, I scraped my face on an upturned fork in the cutlery holder. But it's just a flesh wound. I will be fine.'

Nobody said a word. Cecil, clearly having got bored, had turned to the bar with Ian to buy some shots.

I got back to the table to find Diana sipping her wine patiently.

'Is everything alright, Matthew? Who was that young woman?'

'She's a friend. Well an acquaintance really. A friend of a friend. She's Canadian, works in forensic science.'

'But why did she call you Michael?'

'Well...she called me Michael because she suffers from short term memory loss and keeps forgetting my name,' I said as convincingly as I could.

'She is a forensic scientist who suffers short term memory loss? That must be a dreadful drawback in her profession. In my job I have regular contact with forensic scientists and I can see how it would be problem.'

I must have temporarily overlooked the fact that Diana was a lawyer and asking questions was second nature.

'I don't think it is too bad. I mean she almost got my name right. She knows it begins with an M. Which is a start.'

'You should have introduced her Matthew. It would have been interesting to chat with her a little while.'

'I would have done only there would be no point as she would have forgotten who you were in a matter of moments. That is why I hurried her away. She must have forgotten who her friends were and where she was meant to be. I asked them to keep a closer eye on her. Look Diana, let's go somewhere else.'

We got up to leave. Hanka or Janka brought Diana's coat. As we walked to the door I caught Louise's gaze. Our eyes locked briefly as if we were the only two people in the room. In that moment I felt my stomach turn over. A wave of sadness and disappointment swept over me. It bothered me. I could not explain it.

The rest of the evening should have been just what I had always wanted from the dating site. I was on the date I had wanted with the gorgeous Diana but somehow I couldn't help but reflect on that look from Louise and the fact that I had spun a web of deceit and was now lying to two women. We went to another wine bar in Kingston. I couldn't drink anything and I was worried about not having anywhere to stay. If the fates had been on my side I could have taken the opportunity to charm my way into a night at Diana's place but I didn't have the heart for it. Diana could sense there was something amiss. She commented at last on my limp and the scratches on my face. I dismissed it saying that I had experienced a bit of a fall at home and that I was feeling slightly under the weather, that was all. The combination of continual deception, the recurrent series of mishaps and my fall from the restaurant window that night had dulled my spirit. I wasn't really in the mood for a night out at all, even with Diana. I told her I needed to go home. I couldn't believe I'd said it. She was cool about it, if a little surprised. My apparent reluctance probably did me some good with her though. It made me look less needy than I had been in our previous encounters and made me less predictable. Perhaps something worthwhile had come from my evening after all.

As soon as Diana had gone home in a taxi I called La Choucroute. It was still only 10.45 and the restaurant was still open. I managed to get hold of Pierre. I told him I was coming for my house keys right then.

26

I slept heavily. Nervous energy had no doubt exhausted me. I woke at around 10.30am to the sound of my mobile jangling. A text. I wiped the sleep from my eyes and stared at the phone. It was Diana. It said 'Hope you got home safely. Call me.'

Diana texting me. Things had turned around. I'd call her later. No need to look eager now she was contacting me. I swung my feet to the floor and felt the twinge in my right ankle, a reminder of the stupidity of the night before. I stood carefully, placing my weight on the right side. It didn't feel too bad. Probably just some bruising. I walked to the bathroom and caught my reflection in the mirror. The scratches on my face looked far redder in the daylight but they were only scratches. I'd just have to live with them until they healed.

Stepping into the shower I twirled the control to release a spray of hot water that cascaded over me, its warm needles peppering the back of my neck and shoulders, massaging and refreshing. As I stood there in the confined space of the shower cubicle, the water spraying firmly onto my scalp, I felt protected, shut inside the enclosure, hidden from the world by the rising steam. If I could stay in here I would not need to deal with the disorder of my real world outside. The jet of warm water was refreshing, enlivening, pouring over my body in a protective veneer. But at some point I had to face the day. I finished my shower, loaded up on hot buttered toast and a steaming mug of tea and called Diana.

'Hi Diana. It's Matthew.' I tried to sound cool.

'Matthew. How are you today? Better than last night I hope. You did seem a little under the weather.' Her voice was soothing and sexy at the same time.

'Oh, I am fine Diana. A good night's sleep did the trick,' I said.

'Matthew. I have been thinking. I have this little chalet in the French Alps and a group of us are going out there for our annual skiing trip for Christmas. Why don't you come. I think you could do with a break.'

Skiing. I could no more ski than I could play golf. But I was pleasantly surprised by her offer. This was my opportunity to spend some time with Diana in a relaxed atmosphere, no pressure situation and get to know her properly. No trying to impress her, just being myself. I decided I had to be truthful and tell her I couldn't ski. If that meant I couldn't go then I had at least been honest and I hoped that would go down well.

'I'd love to go Diana,' I said, 'but to be honest I have never skied. I can't ski. Not even left handed.'

She laughed at my reference to my golf blunder. 'That's not a problem Matthew. Everyone has to start somewhere. You can get some lessons and before you know it you will be cruising along. There are plenty of good ski instructors around.'

It was beginning to sound appealing. Then I thought about my bruised ankle.

'When are you going?'

'On Christmas Eve. We are staying for New Year too. It will be lovely. A white Christmas. You must come. I am going with three other couples and I am the only single lady there. You could keep an eye on me, Matthew.'

The last sentence was uttered in a low, seductive tone. Whether it was for impact or not I didn't know but it was definitely the deal breaker for me. Why not, I thought. It was a great opportunity and she seemed to want me come too. I didn't do much at Christmas anyway. I was now trying to conjure up a positive response that would make me sound chilled about the whole thing when I suddenly remembered Sue. Sue, who I had promised that I would meet on Christmas Day. The word 'bugger' sprang to mind.

'Are you still there Matthew?' Diana asked.

'Oh, sorry Diana, I was just thinking about your invite. Sorting my diary out.'

What would I do about Sue? I had never even met her so it wasn't as if it was important to me. It seemed a reasonable excuse to just tell her I couldn't make it as I had been invited skiing. Most people would understand that. I would. But I knew the disappointment I would feel if I had had nothing planned on Christmas Day of all days and I had been looking forward to something different. I knew what it was like to be alone on Christmas Day. That feeling, misguided as it was in my case, of being hard done by, nobody wanting to be with me. My conscience wouldn't allow me to let Sue down.

'I don't think I can make the whole period, Diana,' I said reluctantly. 'How about if I came over for three or four days after Christmas. A sort of taster to see if me and skiing get along. Would that be ok?'

'That would be wonderful Matthew. You will love it I am sure, and have loads of fun.'

'Ok, good. I don't have any skis or any equipment or anything,' I said.

'Oh, don't worry about that. You can hire skis and boots and I am sure between us we have spare jackets and things,' Diana replied. 'My chalet is halfway between La Clusaz and Megève. Text me your email address and I will email you the details. Must go now. Lunch with a girlfriend. So pleased you are coming.'

She rang off. I stared at my mobile in a slight daze. One minute I am chasing the elusive Diana and the next I am going skiing with her. Well, with her and a group of friends anyway. I felt good too. I had been honest with Diana, I had not reneged on my Christmas date with Sue and I was still going skiing. Honesty seemed to be the best policy. I was learning it seemed.

With my newly discovered interest in skiing I logged on to the internet. I knew next to nothing about the sport and wanted to get clued up. First I checked out the general locations of where Diana said her chalet was. Then I googled 'ski equipment'. Ok so I didn't need skis but maybe it would do no harm to look at clothing. There was still a need in me to impress Diana. I didn't want to be borrowing jackets. Always better to show up with your own clothes in any case. I found the 'Snow and Rock' site and clicked on *ski jackets*. I was mesmerised by the array of styles and colours - and prices. I clicked on ski pants. Again the choices seemed endless. So were the prices. Maybe it was the wrong time of year to be buying just as it was approaching the height of the season. What the hell, I couldn't ski so I may as well make an impression in some good quality ski gear. I checked my nearest store and within twenty minutes, I was dressed, in the Jag and heading down to Chertsey.

The store was fascinating for someone who had never set foot in such a place. Row upon row of jackets, ski pants, gloves and outdoor wear bordered the perimeter walls. A central stairwell led to an area displaying boots, skis and snowboards in a myriad of different colours. I tentatively looked through the jackets, trying not to look conspicuously like a newbie amongst what appeared to be a well-informed clientele. A white jacket with blue panelling caught my eye. I lifted it out. It had more zips and pockets than I had ever seen in any coat. Zips around the neck, in the sleeves, on either side to vent it and across the pockets. It had at least fifteen labels hanging off it. Technical info. Water repellent...lightweight...insulated...ultra-thin...breathable fabric...durable membrane. Total mumbo jumbo to a novice. I just liked the look of it. I had one arm completely inserted into the sleeve when an assistant came to my aid.

Forty-five minutes later I walked out of the store the new owner of a Spyder ski jacket, Spyder insulated ski pants, a pair of Gore-Tex gloves, a set of snow goggles and an assortment of thermals, socks and base layers. My credit card had taken a hammering to the tune of eleven hundred quid. I hadn't had a clue how expensive ski stuff could be. I did now. It crossed my mind that things would be a lot simpler if Diana had been into simple activities like ten pin bowling or darts or something. I just hoped that after all that effort I could get skiing. I sent a text message to Diana with my email address.

That evening I had a text from Amanda.

'Hope you are ok Matthew. Shame the evening didn't work out. Let's do it

again sometime when you have recovered. I had a bit of a hair raising journey home in that taxi. Bloody menace, almost killed us. I shan't be using that cab firm again. Amanda. X.'

Over the next two days I felt quite pleased with myself. Ok, I'd spent a grand on ski clothes but I was looking forward to Christmas now and my break. Maybe things would turn out well in the New Year. I dropped the pirate shirt off to Jim on Monday night after work. I went to a small office Christmas lunch on the Tuesday. On Wednesday night Cecil rang me.

'How you doin' geezer. Where you been lately. Avoiding your mates, eh?'

'I'm fine Cecil. It's you that's not been around. What have you been up to then?'

'Just keeping the dream alive mate. You still on that dating site?' Cecil asked.

'Yeah, looks like I am on there a while longer too. They renewed it automatically.'

'Done any birds yet?' Cecil had a way of being direct. 'You must have shagged that lawyer bird by now geezer. She's gagging for it by the look of her.'

I was completely baffled as to how Cecil could arrive at that conclusion simply from staring at a woman across a darkened bar but then there was often no logic in Cecil's assessment of a situation where 'birds' were concerned.

'Err, not exactly Cecil. I am seeing her, yes. Well sort of seeing her,' I said, half apologetically for not having some positive news.

'Sort of seeing her? What's that mean geezer? Like out of one fucking eye or something. You are either seeing her or you are not. If you are seeing her you must be shagging her and if you are not seeing her then you ain't shagging her.' More Cecil logic.

'It's complicated Cecil –'

'There's nothing that complicated about birds mate. She wants it and you ain't giving it to her. Am I right? Yeah, I thought so.'

I had no real response. Sometimes there was no point in trying to explain things to Cecil. He saw it in black and white.

'Anyway, mate, it's that time of year. Friday, Fads. Christmas drink geezer.'

Cecil had a way of making an invite sound like an order. I hadn't had a proper night out with him for a couple of weeks and as it was Christmas I thought we ought to get together. Maybe I could explain myself then. It would also give me a chance to find out what was happening with him and Sheryl and more importantly if he knew any more about PC Penny's thought processes.

'Sure. Friday night it is then Cecil.'

Before I went to bed I logged onto the dating site. I had resolved to limit my use of the site from now on but as I was a member again for practically a whole month I thought I'd check in occasionally. I had one email. From Estelle.

'Hi Matthew. Thank you for your email. It's good to know you are definitely normal! Perhaps we are looking for the same things. It would be nice to see a picture of you. Hope to hear from you soon.'

I suddenly remembered her. She'd been in touch the week before and I'd sent her a brief reply. I checked her picture again. Good looking girl I thought. Those glasses were definitely the sexy secretary look. I mailed her.

'Hi Estelle. Just renewed for another month. Yes, it would be good to find out if we are looking for the same thing. Well I guess we are both looking for love, so that's a start. I'm quite busy now over the Christmas period so maybe we can catch up after that and, who knows, maybe meet up. Yes, I must upload a picture. I did have one on here but removed it as I was going to leave the site. But that's another story.'

Five minutes later there was a response.

'Hi Matthew. Well glad you haven't left the site yet then! Yes, it would be nice to see what you look like. It's a bit like playing Russian roulette on these sites as it is without worrying about who you are talking to. I have been approached by lots of men already most of them with bucket loads of issues. And then there are the players. Those guys will never understand a deep and meaningful relationship so they have no chance of forming one. Anyway, you seem respectful and considerate which is a nice change so it would be good to keep in touch. Have a lovely Christmas.'

Estelle's email was encouraging. I couldn't think what I had done in two emails to warrant her comments but then again I wasn't on the receiving end of contact from the guys on the site so maybe I was 'normal' and normal may well be refreshing for the ladies. I decided I'd keep in touch.

27

MacFadden's Bar was dressed up for Christmas. Behind the bar strings of lights snaked their way up, around and down the many shelves in a multi-coloured lightshow, their reflection twinkling on the display bottles and illuminating the edges of the polished mirrors. Bunches of balloons, partly frosted over with what looked like shaving foam, hung in various nooks and crannies. A bold 'Merry Christmas' message was sprayed across the main window. At the back of the main room to the right of one corner of the small dance floor area stood a large fully decorated Christmas tree. The bar sound system was wishing 'it could be Christmas every daaaayeeyayy'. Hanka and Janka were behind the bar, Santa hats perched on their heads, tinsel around their necks. The room itself was already almost full to capacity with Christmas revellers and the remnants of office partygoers. It was the last Friday before Christmas and the party mood was in full swing. Stupid hats, the type you only get at Christmas, were on full display. Reindeer antlers seemed to be in vogue this year. Girls in skirts way too short for the time of year, guys still in their office suits but with shirts open or ties dangling loosely, evidence of early afternoon partying and an end to work for another year. And it was still only 7.30pm. I felt the buzz of the place and I felt good. A new Paul Smith black shirt, grey Prince of Wales check trousers and a black jacket added to my feel good factor.

Carlos was holding court.

'Mateo. Merry Christmas, cucaracha. You are looking cool, amigo. What you having?'

'The usual Carlos. Merry Christmas to you too amigo,' I said. 'Busy, busy tonight eh?'

Carlos topped a Budvar and placed it on a little white mat in front of me.

'On the house Mateo. Busy, yes. Your advice was good. Appreciate it.' He had a small glass of something in front of him. He raised it towards me. 'Salud. Buen estado de salud. Good health, Mateo.' He necked the contents.

I raised my bottle and replied to the toast. 'Cheers, Carlos.' The cool beer had hardly gone down when I heard a familiar voice.

'Geezer!' Cecil was not so much walking towards me as swaggering, arms outstretched. He embraced me in a bear hug. I was a little taken by surprise but Cecil could be expansive with his affections when he wanted to be.

'Merry Christmas, mate. How you doing?'

'I am good Cecil. What about you?' I said.

'Blinding geezer. No complaints. Carlos, two Budvars mate and have one yourself.'

Cecil was never slow to call in the beers and I still had most of my first one.

'So, what's the mumble then mate? You been pretty low key lately.' He leaned back, an elbow placed deliberately on the bar, marking territory as the room filled with eager drinkers.

'Well, I've been doing this and that. Just, you know, keeping a low profile,' I replied.

'What you up to for Christmas?'

'I have a date Christmas day. From the site. I've been invited round for a drink and –'

'A date Christmas day,' Cecil interrupted, 'that's a guaranteed shag then. Bound to be. No bird invites you round her place on Christmas day without giving out the old hashmadishmalacka. It's dead cert mate. Bloke on his own Christmas Day. A sympathy shag if nothing else. Hey, Carlos. What do you think? Bird invites you round her place on Christmas day. She's bound to be giving out the goodies.'

Carlos was nodding and grinning and trying to serve the queue at the bar all at the same time.

'Hang on Cecil. It's just a date,' I said trying to put it all in perspective, 'I told you I am looking for a relationship and she seemed nice so I thought why not.'

'Talking of relationships, you still ain't drilled that lawyer yet, then.'

Cecil sipped his beer, an inquisitive look in his eye. I had to marvel at his ability to link the word 'relationship' with the with the word 'drilled' as if his crude reference to sexual congress would qualify as forming a deep romantic connection.

'I am trying to form a meaningful relationship with Diana,' I said defensively.

'Hang on mate. Let me get this straight. You are trying to form a meaningful relationship with the lawyer but you are going to another bird's place on Christmas day looking for a relationship there too. How many meaningful relationships are you trying to form?' Cecil laughed out loud, took another swig of beer and said, 'Sounds to me like you are looking for a meaningful shag but won't admit it.'

I started to pick at the Budvar label.

'It's not like that Ces. I am on the dating site to find a proper relationship. It takes time and it might mean seeing quite a few different people until I find someone. Right now I quite like Diana and I think it's got a chance.'

'Got a chance?' Cecil looked incredulous. 'From what you told me mate, it's going nowhere –'

'It is going somewhere Ces,' I interrupted, slightly irritated that Cecil could burst my bubble. 'I'm going skiing with her after Christmas, actually.'

'Skiing!' Cecil spat the word out like he'd just eaten a mouthful of capers. 'Skiing! You don't ski geezer. You are going skiing with the lawyer? After your fucking golf fiasco, you are going skiing?'

We were now completely surrounded at the bar. MacFadden's was packed. A hubbub of chatter filled the air. Carlos had cranked the music up several notches. Noddy Holder was asking if we'd hung our stockings on the wall and if we were waiting for Santa Claus to call.

'Yeah, Ces...I am going skiing. What's the big deal,' I shouted, trying to compete with Slade.

'The big deal mate is that you are still trying to impress that bird. You tried it with the golf and fucked that right up. Now you are doing it with skiing. You aren't after a relationship. You want status mate. A posh lawyer on your arm, join the golf club and mix with the ski set. That's what you are after. I told you. You're a bit of a snob deep down.'

Cecil turned to get Hanka or Janka's attention.

'It's just skiing Cecil,' I protested. 'I was straight with her this time. I told her I don't ski.'

Two more beers arrived on the bar.

'Just skiing? Ok. Tell me this then. Have you gone out and bought all the gear?'

He could tell by my reaction. I picked some more label then raised the bottle to my lips. A long slurp this time.

'You have, haven't you. I knew it. And I bet it's the most expensive fucking gear in the shop. And it's just skiing, Cecil! It's just trying to impress, Cecil is what you should be saying. You can't bullshit me, geezer. How much dough you done now mate cos of this bird? A grand or more on golf clubs and lessons. And probably just as much on ski gear.'

There was not much I could say. It didn't look cool and from Cecil's viewpoint I could see how it would look like a desperate need to impress. And if I was honest with myself it was. The Budvar label was now completely off the bottle and I picked at the sticky residue that remained.

'Alright, Cecil. Look, I like Diana, ok, and maybe you are right. Maybe I have gone over the top a bit. But it's done now. Let's just see what comes of it. If it all goes tits up I've lost a few grand and learnt a lesson.'

Cecil looked momentarily concerned.

'Look mate, you are punching well above your weight, trust me. You are out of your depth with that bird. Yeah, sure you could pull it off for a while. You ain't that bad looking, you're smart, a good catch for some bird. But the thing is she's moving in a different orbit. Soon as it settles down, soon as that first attraction dies down then reality sets in. She's gonna want to go to St Tropez, skiing in Aspen, the best fucking restaurants in town. She's gonna want a geezer that can live the lifestyle. The lifestyle she's used to. And, no offence mate, but you ain't up there. And unless you are drilling her into the middle of next week you're gonna need big bucks to keep up. So, then, when you can't deliver and she gives you the fuck off tablet what you gonna do then? You gotta go out and reinvent yourself all over again.'

Cecil's analysis of the situation made uncomfortable listening. I could see his point but I still hoped that excitement, passion, chemistry, all the things that made two people attracted to one another would overcome status and the reality of our everyday existence. I decided to change the subject.

'Yeah, maybe,' I said, '... maybe you have a point Cecil. I don't know. We'll see. But listen, what about you and Sheryl? How are you doing with her? You still seeing her?'

Not only was I curious to find out how Cecil was doing with Sheryl but I was also keen to know what was going on with Louise.

'Yeah mate. She's all right. We are doing a bit of the old mumble swerve,' Cecil answered.

'Blimey, that's a bit keen for you Ces. You must have been seeing her now for all of, let's see, three weeks. Bit of a record I reckon.'

'She's only here six months in total mate, so might as well make the most of it. She's a good girl. Good laugh.'

Sheryl must have impressed. That was high praise indeed from Cecil and the nearest I was going to get to finding out how he felt about her. I was about to try to find out more when we were interrupted by Hanka or Janka. Whichever one it was she was now dressed in a Stetson, cowboy boots and tight denim shorts, around the waist of which was strapped a bullet belt with two holsters. In each of the bullet compartments there was a small shot glass. In either holster was a bottle, containing a dark brown liquid.

'Jägermeister? You like a shot?' she said.

Cecil was straight in. A shot of the brown fluid was dispensed expertly into a glass. Just as swiftly as it had filled the glass it disappeared down Cecil's throat. Cecil shook his head and squeezed his eyes tight momentarily at the impact of the hit.

'One for him too, Hanka...Janka,' he said.

'I am Hanka. Janka is the one with the dark hair,' Hanka explained.

It didn't seem to make much difference because from where I was stood they both seemed to have dark hair. Hanka handed me my shot.

'Get it down, geezer,' Cecil encouraged.

I downed it. It was thick and syrupy, a sweet taste but bitter on the palate afterwards, a hint of spice, leaving a tingly, warm feeling in the throat.

'Two more Hanka, please.'

Cecil handed over a tenner for the four drinks and Hanka produced two more. Down in one. This time no surprise in the taste and the syrupy consistency. The immediate effect was a head rush, the aftertaste seeming to penetrate my nose.

'Bloody hell...that's got a kick Cecil,' I said.

'It's Christmas geezer.'

Clearly Cecil did not associate Christmas with any orthodox religious connotations.

'So here it is Merry Christmas, everybody's havin' fun...' Noddy was in full flow and it seemed the whole bar had joined in with him. I leaned towards Cecil so I could be heard.

'So, tell me more about you and Sheryl then mate.'

The Jägermeister had had the desired effect on me and was loosening my tongue.

'Nothing to tell. She's alright. Bit of fun. That's it,' Cecil answered.

'What about her friend Louise. Do you see much of her? You were all out together the other week?'

'Seen her a few times, mate, but at the end of the day it's Sheryl that's doing the mumble, so what do we need to see her mate for?'

'Just wondered...if...well, if she'd asked about me?' I said.

'Why would she ask for you, mate when she has the Daddiola right here?' Cecil laughed and swigged his Budvar.

'No, I didn't mean Sheryl. Louise. You know all that palaver with the investigation and all that. Just wondered if you had any inside information.'

Cecil put his beer on the bar. A frown formed on his brow.

'You watch too many fucking movies mate. Investigation? Look, I don't know anything about any of that. Neither of them has mentioned anything. I told you, just let it go. If something comes up, just roll with it. Tell her it was an accident and that's it. It's no big deal. They just want to get some info so that fucking rich twat with all his tin suits can get the insurance sorted. Once that's sorted his lordship will be happy as Larry. Tumble?'

I didn't really tumble at all. I knew what Cecil was saying but he couldn't see it from my point of view. Cecil finished his beer slid the empty bottle over the bar and turned back to me.

'Mind you, now you mention it, that Louise has asked a few questions about you.'

My stomach experienced that sinking feeling that you get when you think you are about to hear something you are not going to like.

'Yeah, she's been asking how long you been single, what sort of stuff you like doing, have you got a girlfriend. I reckon she's got a little twinkle in her eye for you, mate. You should get in there. Her mate's getting it and I reckon she's getting jealous.'

Coming from anyone else I might have been flattered, but coming from Cecil who associated female interest in a bloke with a desire to get in his pants, I was just bemused. In fact I reckoned that any questions from a copper who was investigating any situation at all no matter how insignificant could only mean an ulterior motive.

Cecil had somehow managed to organise another two beers despite the fact that the bar was heaving with drinkers trying to get the attention of Hanka, Janka and Carlos.

'And another thing mate. You got to sort this 'Michael' bollocks. It's doing my head in,' Cecil said as he handed me a bottle.

'I will,' I said, '…it's just complicated that's all. So, you reckon she likes me then?'

'Yeah. She's got no bloke in tow. I reckon she'd be up for it if you made a move. And the beauty of it mate is you'd kill two birds with one stone. Not only would you get the old hashmadishmalacka but you'd sort out your other little issue too. Soon as she's dropping the white ones for you she ain't gonna be asking no more questions about Lord fucking lemming head, or whatever he's called. And she ain't gonna be interested in no silly bird who's had her chandelier busted either. Oh, yeah mate. Trust me on that.'

I could tell the alcohol was starting to affect Cecil. His speech had started to deteriorate and his opinions were becoming even more colourful than normal.

'Anyway mate, you'll get a chance to sort it. Sheryl and Louise are coming down for a Christmas drink later.'

'What here? Tonight?'

'Yeah. They had some office Christmas meal on this afternoon so they're gonna finish off in here.'

'I can't stay Cecil,' I said.

'Why's that? Where you got to go? You are supposed to be having a Christmas drink with me. You can't just fuck off on your mates. Just blag it. I told them you'd be here anyway. So, it's gonna look pretty dodge if you are not.'

Cecil was playing me now. I didn't think it would look '*dodge*' at all but that was Cecil. He was right though. I had arranged to see him for a drink. Blag it he said. I'd been blagging it all along, I suppose, so perhaps now it was just a matter of doing it with confidence.

I called across the bar, 'Two more of them Jägermeisters...Hanka...Janka... please.'

By nine thirty I didn't really care. Cecil had loaded up on the Bombay and tonics and I was in party mood. Louis and Sheryl walked in. Both were dressed for maximum impact - Louise in a simple, stunning black satin tunic dress, the shoulders embellished with an array of sequins that glistened in the light as she approached. Sheryl's pencil dress, a complete contrast in white with a two black bands at the waistline. Heads turned. Spotting Cecil, Sheryl walked towards him, Louise following. Sheryl kissed Cecil on either cheek; Cecil patted her bottom. Louise kissed Cecil too but with her Cecil was restrained in his reaction. They both turned to me.

'Hello Michael, how are you?'

Sheryl greeted me as she had done Cecil. 'How is your leg?'

'My leg?' I queried.

'Yes. You were limping last week when we saw you,' Sheryl said.

'Oh, that. Yes, it's much better. Fine in fact. Just a pulled...sprained...you know, a muscle thing.'

Louise approached. There was no greeting kiss.

'Hello Michael. How are you? You are looking very smart tonight,' she said, looking me up and down.

Up close she looked stunning. Her blond hair hung loose. Her makeup was subtly applied to enhance her eyes and a faint trace of pink lipstick emphasised the curve of her mouth. In her heels she was obviously taller, almost my height, and a clear four inches taller than Cecil. I took a deep breath.

'Hi Louise. I'm great, thanks. You're looking fantastic. Love the dress.'

'Thank you Michael. If you don't mind me saying I much prefer your shirt to the one you were wearing last week.' Smiling cheekily, she added, 'Not another girlfriend dressing you, was it?'

I didn't like the way she placed the emphasis on '*another*'.

'No. Not at all. It was an...an experiment. Didn't quite work for me...got to try these things, you know.'

Cecil intervened. 'Your shout, geezer.'

I turned to Sheryl and Louise to ask what they wanted.

'Well, we've been on the champagne already, Michael, so another glass would be lovely,' Sheryl said.

Cecil immediately saved me the bother of ordering the drinks myself by ordering two bottles of champagne on my behalf.

'I've opened a tab for you mate. Stops all that fannying about with cash. I'll square it with you at the death.'

The bubbles hit the spot. The evening started to get blurry. Cecil and Sheryl started to get smoochy. Louise was being chatted up by a succession of chancers trying their luck. I didn't blame them. She looked highly desirable. For some reason I was acutely aware of her presence. Every now and then our eyes locked, fleetingly, and just as quickly the gaze was averted. My mobile buzzed in my pocket. It was Amanda.

'*Hi Matthew. In a bar in town. Little tiddly. Tooooo much champagne, lol. If you are not doing anything why don't you come and join me. Amanda xxx.*'

I put the phone back in my pocket. I was tempted by Amanda's invite but something was compelling me to stay where I was. I stood at the bar watching the evening unfold. Cecil and Sheryl were wrapped up in a cocoon of their own. Louise stood a few feet away, the stem of her champagne glass held delicately between forefinger and thumb, two young guys giving it large. From behind one of them looked familiar but I took no notice. Louise looked like she was enjoying the attention yet there was a distance between her and her admirers that she was controlling. The opening chimes of '*Do they Know It's Christmas*' rang out through the sound system. The room seemed to blur into a mix of sound, movement, chatter and colourful lights. Carlos appeared at my side.

'You ok, Mateo.'

'I'm cool Carlos. Just soaking up the atmosphere,' I said.

'You look sad Mateo. It's Christmas. What's bothering you?'

'Nothing Carlos. Too much partying I reckon. The champagne and that... you know.'

'You fancy that police lady? You keep looking at her?'

'No. No. Carlos,' I said slightly taken aback and turning towards the bar, 'she's nice, attractive...I was just...you know...people watching.'

Carlos put two small whiskey glasses on the bar and pulled the top off a bottle.

'Here. Try this. A single malt. Good old Highland brew. It'll perk you up, amigo.'

I sipped it slowly. 'So how's things with you Carlos? You've done wonders with this place in the last few weeks. Livened it up no end,' I said.

'Yeah. Business picking up big style. Doing more food now too. New chef started last week. From Slovakia. Good guy, but his English is still crap. You know what he did? He was supposed to order three kilos of Parma ham and he orders three kilos of parmesan. Bloody parmesan cheese. What am I supposed to do with all that cheese? Cucaracha!'

I had to laugh as Carlos gesticulated and pointed to his head with his index finger.

'Bloody nutter...but he can cook. Anyway, cheers Mateo.'

He raised his glass and downed the contents. I did the same and felt the rush of the whiskey hit me between the eyes.

'Anyway, are you still seeing Abigail, Carlos,' I asked.

'Too right Mateo. She's a real firecracker. You should see the tits on her. Magnifico!'

I didn't think it was the right time to tell Carlos that I actually had seen the '*tits on her.*' I smiled at him, ignored the remark and glanced back over in Louise's direction. My smile disappeared in an instant. One of her would be suitor's had turned to face the bar and I recognised the profile. Jasper Kane. Carlos was in full flow now, elaborating on the delights of the lovely Amanda but I wasn't listening. I hadn't noticed Jasper coming in. I couldn't be in the same place as a work colleague. He was bound to see me sooner or later. And he was chatting with Louise.

'You ok, Mateo?' Carlos had noticed that something was wrong.
'I'm going outside to get some air Carlos. Thanks for the whiskey.'
Carlos tipped another large measure into my glass.
'It'll keep you warm.'

28

The front of MacFadden's had a small seating area set back from the pavement. Four sets of matching aluminium tables with wicker-backed chairs were placed immediately in front of the main window. A couple of tall patio heaters cast a red glow and some degree of warmth over the seating area. A huddle of smokers stood some way off at the kerb puffing on their cigarettes and blowing the smoke in a white cloud into the chill night sky. They were visibly shivering in an effort to keep warm. Sharp fingers of frost were beginning to creep over the windscreens of the cars parked in the adjacent road. It was cold. It hadn't been noticeable at first as I emerged from the warmth of the main bar but there was a distinct wintry bite in the air.

I sat down as close as I could to one of the patio heaters and placed my whiskey on the shiny table surface. I slumped down into the chair feet resting against the table edge. The shock of seeing a work colleague in the bar raced through my mind. Another large gulp of whiskey slipped down. I couldn't go back in. Too risky. Jasper Kane and Louise Penny. Apart from the fact that Jasper's amorous intentions were usually reciprocated by the object of his desire, he also knew me and that meant discovery was imminent unless I made an exit. Yet I didn't want to run out on Cecil again. I resigned myself to discovery. It had to end somewhere. Let it be someone else who exposed my dishonesty. It would probably be better that way now, as any attempt I made to explain myself would sound hollow once Louise heard the full extent of my deception.

I took another sip of the warming whiskey and sat back, eyes closed against the world. The dull thud of the music from the bar faded slowly as I drifted into a semi-conscious reverie. A muddle of thoughts fought for the starring role in my head. A jumble of subliminal incidents flitted through my brain, my sub-conscious trying to make sense of the disarray in my mind. Colours swam freely, blending into one another; incidents merged; faces appeared looming up close to me then zooming away into the distance. My face felt warm and glowing.

It was the sound of the metal chair legs scraping across the pavement that brought me back to an alert state.

'You are going to get quite a tan from that heater, Michael.'

I sat bolt upright. Louise was sitting in the chair opposite, coffee cup in front of her.

'What are you doing out here?' she asked.

'Oh...Louise, hi. I was just getting some fresh air.'

'Well, you'll get plenty of fresh air out here. It's bloody freezing. Actually, it looked like you were asleep,' she said.

'Asleep? No, I was...well, sort of meditating.'

'It's not a problem, Michael, if you were asleep. Not surprising. It's been a long night,' She picked up the coffee cup, crossed her legs, and took a sip. 'Oh. It's so cold.'

'Let me get you another one, Louise,' I said, 'No sense in drinking cold coffee.'

She laughed. 'No, not the coffee. It's cold. The temperature. I left my coat inside. I'll go get it.'

I was on my feet in instant.

'No...no...no need Louise. Here, take my jacket.'

I stood behind her and placed my jacket over her shoulders. She pulled it tightly around her, covering her bare arms. I let my hand linger fleetingly on her shoulder.

'Thank you Michael. You are a gentleman.' She turned and raised her head to look up at me. 'My perfume will be all over your jacket tomorrow. I hope you like Coco Chanel.'

'I love it,' I said, even though I wasn't at all familiar with it. I sat back down. 'So how's your evening going? I see you were getting plenty of attention.' I had to know.

'It's good fun. Nice to get chatted up. Good for the ego especially when it's by two young, good looking guys. Bit on the young side for me though,' she said, smiling. 'One of them had a plenty of charm and banter but he can't have been more than twenty two and his friends was just nineteen.'

I felt a curious sense of relief.

'So not happening then?'

'Oh no, I need a more mature man I think. Someone more stable. Those two are fun but they are still sowing their wild oats, out on the town all the time.'

Mentally I began to question myself. Was I stable? Certainly I was mature, in terms of years anyway if not in terms of recent behaviour. I was still out every weekend but at least I wanted to end that lifestyle, an indication of my maturity I felt.

Louise interrupted my silence.

'Lovely Christmassy atmosphere tonight, Michael. Are you doing anything nice for Christmas?' she asked.

'Well, I am just having lunch with a friend on Christmas day and then I am off for a short skiing trip. How about you?' The first bit was almost true. Although I hadn't yet met Sue she was a sort of friend in a cyber way.

'How lovely. A skiing trip too. Much more exciting than me. I am off to my parents in Gloucestershire for a week. I'm looking forward to it though...no work. Will be so glad of the break. Do you ski well, Michael? I have always wanted to try it.'

'It's my first time actually so I am a little nervous but you have to live dangerously sometimes,' I said.

'First time. Wow...It would be so much fun to ski together, don't you think? I mean...not ...together...not us...you and me...I mean, you know...two people going together for the first time who are at the same level.'

It was the first time I had seen Louise perplexed. She sipped her coffee, a kind of shielding mechanism, as if she had said something that made her exposed. I looked at her under the red glow of the patio heater, her blond hair contrasting against the black winter sky, steam rising from the coffee cup and I had a moments regret. Regret that our paths had crossed in such a bizarre way. Regret that things had not been different. At that moment everything seemed fine and I wanted it to stay like that. The silence seemed to last for ages but was not awkward. It was almost an acknowledgement between two people that they had probably shared a similar thought for a fleeting moment.

'So how is work anyway,' I asked, breaking the moment, but not sure why I was asking. Louise's work as a police officer was not high on a list of topics that I wanted to discuss. I picked up my whiskey glass and took a large gulp.

'Same old stuff. Lots going on. Very repetitive. Takes forever to get to the bottom of things, so as I say, I will be glad of the break,' she said.

'That's good that it takes forever.' I realised as I began the sentence that I was reacting to my own concerns about everything that had gone on with me and that Louise's difficulty in getting to the bottom of things was a comfort to me, but not necessarily something she would consider as good. 'I mean...not that it takes forever...that, well, because things take a long time you will always have a job.'

'Oh I guess I will always have a job Michael. There are always crooks. Always people to investigate. Speaking of which, and I hope you don't mind me talking shop for a moment, any word on your lodger?'

I drained the last of the whiskey.

'No...no...I don't suppose I will hear from him much now until after Christmas.' I tried to sound convincing.

'Ok, not to worry. I'm sorry. I shouldn't have brought it up. It's not your problem and we are on a night out. I shouldn't have mentioned it. Sorry.'

'That's ok, Louise. It's no problem. I am a bit worried though...just because I am acquainted with him and if he is in trouble.' I was fishing for information that I really didn't want to know about.

'Ok, but I can only give you brief details you understand. You remember when I called at your place to see Mr Malarkey the first time I told you I wanted to see him as he had been traced to Hemmingwell Halls through his debit card?'

I nodded.

'Well, I was also investigating a complaint that we received roughly three weeks ago regarding some property damage at a private residence and it appears that your lodger may have some sort of loose connection to both incidents. One of the visitors we spoke with from Hemmingwell Halls was meeting your lodger for a pre-arranged rendezvous although it seems he made it to the venue but didn't meet with the lady in question. It also turns out that the property damage complainant had invited him to a party she was hosting although apparently he never actually got to that one at all. However, by coincidence both these ladies are members of the same internet dating site.'

At the mention of an internet-dating site my face suddenly felt like all the blood had been drained from it by a giant suction pump. My whole body experienced a shock wave that deprived it completely of voluntary movement, to such an extent that I felt quite unable to speak. Luckily I didn't need to as Louise was on a roll.

'It may all be total co-incidence but we would just like to establish a few facts. We have spoken with nearly all of the visitors from Hemmingwell Halls, although a couple of tourists are also proving hard to pin down, and the majority of the party guest list have also been available, although, again there are a few who didn't show up on the night that we still need to speak to.'

I managed to ask one question.

'Is he in any trouble?'

'I don't know if he is in any actual trouble at the moment. We always speak to anyone connected with any incident and we just need to speak to your lodger just to find out if he can be of any help to us with either matter. Obviously if it had reached a serious stage we would have put a warrant out for his arrest. But I am sure it will resolve itself after Christmas. Anyway, it's nothing for you to worry about Michael, and I don't mean to get you involved.'

I hadn't really heard Louise's last few words fully as I was still focused on the word 'arrest.'

I was brought back to reality by Cecil. He half walked and half stumbled out of MacFadden's doorway. He took three steps forward, two to the right and then one back to the left. When he spotted Louise and I at the table he performed the same sequence but in a different order. This time it was two steps forward, three to the left towards us and then one back to the right. He had turned into wobbly man. Sheryl emerged behind him carrying Louise's coat.

'Mad, Geezaaah. So…dats where you two luf birds got to,' Cecil slurred.

'I think he's pissed,' Sheryl said helpfully.

Well, thanks for that Sheryl I thought. I'd never have reached that conclusion on my own. Just as well we have a forensic scientist on hand to diagnose Cecil's condition.

'He's been drinking Carlos's whiskey. I don't think it's agreed with him.'

More helpful analysis from Sheryl.

I'd seen Cecil drunk, very drunk in fact but I'd never known him to be incoherent nor to lose the ability to walk. I got to my feet.

'Ces. You ok? Let's get you home mate. I'm going to get you a taxi.' I reached out to take his arm.

'I'maw right. Doan wurreee geez,' was Cecil's response.

He wobbled wildly as he shrugged off my attempt to balance him.

I circled him slowly, watching his attempt to walk. Three steps forward again, two to the left and then three to the right. I tried to get myself between him and the roadway so that at least I could prevent him swaying into the street. His gait had now become a kind of forward totter, the weight shift of his forward lean, as he instinctively tried to head in that direction, propelling him faster than his legs could cope. Every now and then he would lurch sideways either right or left. At each side movement his arms waved in the air in what appeared to be a totally random motion but which was clearly an attempt to balance himself. Louise and Sheryl were now bringing up the rear, concern and bewilderment on their faces at Cecil's deterioration from normal adult to a chaotic, unmanageable life form.

'I'll get him in a taxi,' I called to the girls as Cecil staggered towards a shop window, 'there's a cab rank further along.' By now I'd managed to get a grip on Cecil's right arm in an effort to steer him along the pavement in the direction of the taxi rank. 'Ces, take it easy. I am getting you home, mate,' I said.

'Am goin out, geez, goin out,' was his response.

'That's not happening Cecil,' I said, 'party's over mate.'

'Isneva ova till isova…Mad, neva,' he slurred. He was struggling to release himself from my grip, mumbling as he did, 'I'maw right, maw right, Mad.'

Worrying enough as it was that he had now got to an almost uncontrollable state, I had another concern and that was that he was trying to say my name. Normally he never really used it, referring to me as mate or geezer and as incoherent as his articulation was, I was concerned that Louise might realise what he was trying to say.

'Ces, take it easy, mate. Save your energy. We got to get you home mate.'

'Goin out. Am goin out….come on, Mad….s'go out.'

I ignored him and clung onto his arm. We were barely fifty yards from the line of black cabs when a sudden swerve to the left caught me unawares. He totally lost his balance and went down in a heap. Rolling onto his back he stayed there a moment looking up at the sky. Sheryl rushed over to him, kneeling on the pavement asking if he was ok. Lying flat on your back on the public highway on a frosty December evening is never a good indicator of being ok.

'Leave him Sheryl,' I said, 'I'll get him on his feet. We have to get him in a cab home.'

Cecil was no lightweight. He was a big lump and now a dead weight too. I grabbed his right hand with my own right hand, my left gripping his forearm. I tugged in an effort to budge him but not only was he a dead weight he was also not cooperating. I tried again. This time getting him to a semi seated position but unable to get him to his feet.

'Ces, you got to get up mate. You got to help me here,' I pleaded.

'I'maw right. Maw right...going out, geez, goin out.'

I wasn't getting any cooperation. I placed my left arm further along his arm just above the elbow to give me more grip. This time I managed to raise his bum off the floor and his weight almost onto his feet. I held him there for a second while I took a deep breath and made the final effort to get him upright. Leaning back I tugged solidly. He tilted forward slightly but my efforts were undone by a patch of ice. I saw his foot slip on the glistening whiteness and give way underneath him but I couldn't do a thing to prevent him crashing back to the ground and out of my grip. The sudden release of Cecil's mass from my hands instantly propelled me backwards and totally off balance. As I tried to break my momentum, my right foot caught the extreme edge of the kerb, slipped into the gutter and spun me round to face forward. I felt the thud and the pain simultaneously. I heard a scream as I was spun back around violently in the direction I had just come from. I vaguely recall the squeal of brakes. Louise was instantly next to me.

'God, Michael. Are you ok? Are you all right?' She looked frantic.

I was asking what happened. I felt the ache, more intense now, in my upper arm below the shoulder.

'You've been hit by that van. Are you alright? Listen to me...are you alright?'

'I'm ok Louise. My arm aches.' I hugged it to me. Two men were also standing next to me now asking the same as Louise.

'Are you ok mate? I couldn't avoid you. You just fell into the road,' one of them said.

'I did what?' I said.

'Fell into the road. My wing mirror caught you. Gave you a bit of a whack. You're lucky you didn't fall right in front of us mate or you were a goner. I was motoring.'

I looked up. A few yards ahead of me a white van was parked, exhaust pluming into the cold night air, its big black nearside wing mirror dangling pathetically on the end of a cable.

'I'm sorry,' I said, 'I'm sorry about your mirror.'

'I wouldn't worry about the mirror my friend. I'm just glad you're still standing. You sure you're ok?' the van driver said.

I managed to convince him and his mate that I was fine and they went on their way.

Cecil had somehow got himself upright during the commotion but had started a weird two-step stagger that inexplicably kept him in precisely the same spot. My main priority now was to get Cecil home in one piece and get myself home to bed as soon as that was done. Sheryl was worried about Cecil and now Louise was worrying about me. We made it as far as the black cab rank. None of them would take us because of Cecil's inability to stay still long enough for us to get him into a vehicle. I called Real Libel. They'd take anyone.

A short while later we pulled up outside Cecil's place. It was a struggle to get him out of the cab but after a series of pulls, pushes and shoves we managed to get Cecil indoors. Sheryl stayed to keep an eye on him. The cab took us on to Louise's place next. As it pulled up outside I thanked her for her help with Cecil. She turned towards me and I felt a quiver of excitement shoot through me.

'Come in and have a coffee Michael,' she said, placing her hand on mine.

It was nervousness that caused me to decline at first. I knew I wanted to but I also knew I was getting myself closer to Louise Penny when I still had all the unresolved issues going on. I made the excuse that I wanted to get home as my arm hurt. That was partly true. Yes, my arm hurt but I didn't necessarily want to go home. The sore arm resolved the matter. Louise insisted that I came in so she could look at it and decide whether she would need to take me to casualty.

Her flat was neat, tidy, almost minimalist but cosy. A wide expanse of wooden floor was broken only by a sage green rug and a rustic wooden coffee table. Two lamps in opposite corners cast a warm glow round the room. A wood and glass storage unit stood against one wall, photographs in one section, a row of books in another and a display of candles and assorted ornaments strategically placed on the remaining shelves. The focal point of the room was the sofa. It filled the expanse of one wall, a full four-seater, wide deep seats bedecked with cushions. In fact at a rough guess I estimated there were well over ten cushions strewn across it. There barely seemed room to sit without disturbing the layout. I often wondered what it was with women and cushions. Anytime I'd been in the home of a married friend I'd noticed it. Cushions dominated the sofa. My sofa had two cushions, one at either end. They didn't do anything. They were just there, gathering dust. My sister had told me once that she turns her cushions over every day. What for? Baffled me. Louise's sofa looked like a very comfortable and luxurious sofa. One that you could stretch out on and wile away an afternoon ensconced in its welcoming folds, although I did wonder if it was actually for sitting on or whether it was just to house the cushion collection.

'Take your shirt off.'

Louise's command shook me out of my daydream.

She noticed my quizzical look. 'I want to look at your arm.'

I did as I was told. She had adopted a 'control' aura, the professional side taking over. Directing me to sit, she kicked off her shoes and sat down next to me. She started to examine my arm, her touch sending a tingle through me. I felt quite vulnerable sitting bare-chested but at the same time I felt a pleasant anticipatory electricity between us. Her bare knees touched my right leg. Her black dress rode up as she sat, showing her shapely thighs. Her closeness and my vulnerability heightened the tension.

'Can you raise it up,' she asked.

I lifted my arm above my head. It ached but I could do it with no trouble.

'Good. Move it out to the side.'

My sudden movement to the right almost caught Louise unaware. She giggled as my forearm just missed her face.

'Ok. I think you'll live. Nothing's broken. It's very red and you are going to have a corker of a bruise on there but you'll be fine. I am going to get you some ice to put on it...and that coffee.'

A few moments later she was back with an ice pack from the fridge and a brandy.

'Here. Put that on your arm. The brandy will warm you. Coffee on the way.'

For the next hour we talked. About Cecil, Sheryl, relationships. I liked it. I liked sitting there with Louise. My arm was now numb with the ice but I didn't notice it too much. It was clear that Louise was ready for a proper relationship. She told me about her family, about her past relationships and her dreams. I listened mostly. She asked about me but I was fairly vague. I had to unburden myself before I could open up properly to Louise and I didn't want to spoil the moment. The moment I now had with her that wasn't about her job, her investigations, my alter ego or my mishaps. It was just two people sitting talking in the early hours of the morning. I sensed an attraction between us and I wanted to keep the moment. So, I let her talk.

'Right, Michael. It's three thirty and I must get some sleep. I have lots to do tomorrow to prepare for going away, last minute shopping and things.' She picked up her shoes and stood up.

'Ok, Louise.' I checked my watch. 'Yes, it is late. Thanks for the coffee... and the first aid. I must get a taxi.'

'No. There's no need. You can stay here.' She stood in the middle of the floor, shoes dangling in her hand. She'd read my mind. 'On the sofa Michael. In case you take a turn. Delayed shock and all that.'

'Of course. But what about the cushions? Where will they go?' I joked to make light of the moment.

Louise laughed. 'Just chuck them on the floor. You'll be very comfortable. I'll get you a quilt.'

I was woken by the sound of rain hammering on the window pane. Great streams of water ran in long rivulets down the glass. I wondered what had happened to the frost of the night before. The temperature must have increased dramatically. Wiping the sleep from my eyes I looked at my watch. Ten forty five. I'd slept solidly. As I sat up with the heavy quilt wrapped around me I could hear the sound of pottering in the kitchen. My right arm ached reminding me of the near mayhem of the night before. There was a tap on the door.

'You awake Michael?' Louise's face peeped around the door a white towel wrapped turban style, tightly around her head.

'Hi Louise. Just woken up. How are you?'

She stepped into the room dressed in a white bathrobe with pink trim at the collar and sleeves.

'I'm fine, thanks. A shower soon livens you up. Let me have a look at that arm.'

She sat down next to me and examined the emerging bruising that now ran from just below my shoulder to a point above my elbow.

'Nasty. Let's get some more ice on it. You have been in the wars lately, with your face, leg and now your arm.'

She disappeared back to the kitchen returning with a fresh ice pack and the offer of tea and toast. I pressed the pack against my arm trying not to recoil at the initial coldness that bit into the bruised flesh. The sound of a kettle boiling and a toaster pinging out its contents raised my spirits. My mobile buzzed.

'Geezer. You ok? Sheryl said you got run over.' It was Cecil.

'Well not exactly run over, but a close shave.' I recounted my mishap to Cecil. 'What about you,' I asked, 'You were in a bit of a state.'

'Yeah, took myself right out of the equation, mate. That's that South American nutter Carlos's fault giving me whiskey. I don't drink whiskey.'

Cecil didn't always see that sometimes the fault might lie with him.

'What did you drink it for then?' I asked.

'It's Christmas mate. We were celebrating. I had six of them. That's what did it.'

And the beers, Jägermeister, gin and tonic and champagne had nothing to do with it I suppose, I thought to myself. Louise walked in with a plate of hot buttered toast and a steaming mug of tea.

'It's Cecil,' I whispered to her, covering the phone with my hand.

'Anyway, where are you? What you up to mate,' Cecil continued.

'I'm at Louise's.'

'You did the old mumble then mate, at last.'

'No. It's not like that. Look, I can't talk now. Catch you later.'

Now that I knew Cecil was ok I didn't want the conversation going where he was about to take it. I rang off.

'Is he ok,' Louise asked, 'he was in a state last night. Talking total gibberish in the end. I couldn't understand a word he was saying.'

I told Louise that Cecil was fine, relieved that she hadn't understood a word he said, especially the bit where he had been trying to use my name.

We finished the tea and toast. It was time to go. Louise left me to get dressed. At the door she gave me a farewell kiss on the cheek, handed me an umbrella and I headed out into the rain, pleased it was a blue umbrella and not a pink one. Halfway down the path I heard her call out to me.

'Michael. Take my mobile number...just in case...you know, if you felt unwell or anything...after the accident. You could call me.' She looked up at me, for a moment, her eyes holding mine. 'If you needed to.'

29

Diana had sent the details of the skiing trip. Apparently I needed to book a flight to Geneva, the nearest airport to her chalet. Someone would meet me at the airport and take me to the resort. I spent the next hour searching flight deals eventually settling for one on the Sunday after Christmas returning four days later on New Year's Eve. I sent Diana my flight schedule.

I had a text from Amanda. It was curt and direct, '*Got a better offer then last night did you.*' I ignored it. In fact as far as I was concerned the time spent with Louise was definitely a better offer.

The next few days dragged along. Everyone in the office was on pre-holiday wind down. Nothing much was getting done. On the Monday morning I decided to pop along to Jasper Kane's office. It was small with just four occupants, the sales manager, two middle-aged ladies and Jasper himself. Nothing much was getting done in there either. New Year would see the big push for new club memberships as the guilty decided to shed the holiday pounds in flurry of new year's resolutions, most of which would inevitably bite the dust by February. However, it was my job in marketing to prevent the loss of initially keen joiners by producing exciting and innovative reasons for them to stay interested. My job was closely linked with that of the sales department and it was partly for this reason that I went to see Jasper. The other reason was to find out some more about his night out at MacFadden's.

'Morning Matt. How you doing? Good weekend?' Jasper asked as I walked in.

'Not bad thanks Jasper. You? Do anything exciting?' I asked as casually as I could.

'Nah, just the usual. Went out, partied a bit. Tried some bar in Kingston I'd never been to before. Right party in there. Place was packed.'

My attention focussed.

'Any good? Were you on the pull as usual.'

'You know how it goes Matt, always on the look out. Chatted to a real cracker Saturday night. Bit older than me but I like the more experienced lady. Turns out she's a copper too.'

Curiosity was getting the better of me, my heart pounding.

'Any luck? You seeing her again?'

'Nah...don't think she was that interested. I reckon my mate went on about seeing her in her uniform a bit too much. He can be an arse sometimes.'

I felt like finding out who the 'arse' was and thanking him. Relief washed over me, my thoughts confused as to whether it was because of Louise's lack of interest in Jasper or the fact that my secret remained undiscovered.

'Well as you say Jasper, it isn't all plain sailing with women and there are always plenty more about, eh?'

'Too right Matt. Ended up in a nightclub later on, pulled a right naughty little stunner,' he said, flashing the Jasper smile and winking knowingly.

Having heard all I needed to I returned to the business of marketing.

I finished work the day before Christmas Eve. I did the usual last minute shopping. Gifts for my nephews and nieces, was the full extent of my shopping. There wasn't anyone else to buy for. Cecil and I didn't exchange presents. It was a kind of unspoken thing, *'we're blokes - blokes don't give each other presents.'* I didn't mind. It saved me the time wandering even more aimlessly around shops. Cecil sent me a text to see if I wanted to go out on Christmas Eve but I declined. I wanted to be alert for my date with Sue. Going out with Cecil was never going to end with me being alert the following day. So, I stayed home on Christmas Eve. I thought about all those families preparing for the special day to come, wrapping presents, ushering excited children to bed early with dire warnings that Santa Claus wouldn't visit if they weren't sound asleep. I thought about the tooing and froing around the country at that time of year– people visiting relatives and loved ones. I thought about my own lack of someone special to share the delights and excitement of Christmas day. I had my date with Sue but, despite the spontaneity of it all, it was still a blind date with someone I had absolutely no connection with. I thought about Louise spending time with her family and wondered if I would ever meet someone who would be willing to share their time and their family with me at Christmas. I thought about the time Louise and I had spent chatting at her place just the other night and how it had felt special. And then it hit me. The conversation outside MacFadden's.

'Oh fuck,' I heard myself involuntarily spit out the curse. The internet. The bloody dating site. Louise had referred to my 'lodger' being connected in some way to two women on the same internet dating site. I fired up the computer and logged on to Cupid's Pursuit. I still had a couple of weeks or so left of my renewed membership but I knew it was time to go. I didn't want any connection at all to a dating site now. In any case, I reasoned, things were looking promising on the Diana front so I was best off out of it anyway. I decided to delete my whole profile that very night. I clicked on the main part of my profile and noticed I had one email. From Estelle.

'Hi Matthew. How are you? I was hoping I'd hear from you, but I guess you have been busy. Still no picture so I will have to use my imagination. Why don't we take a chance and meet up. I suppose it would be like a blind date. Well for me anyway. I am going to be brave and give you my home number. Look forward to hearing from you if you are still interested. Estelle.'

At the end of the note she'd typed out her telephone number. I scribbled it down on a post it note and put it next to my computer. I had mixed feelings. I wanted to stay in touch with her as she seemed normal but I decided not to reply. There was no point. I was about to go on a Christmas date and then I was skiing with Diana. My focus now was on deleting my presence on the site. I began deleting.

Several clicks of the mouse later my internet presence was history, my profile text removed and all my personal details obliterated. The penultimate click raised the question *'Are you sure you want to delete your membership? You will be unable to access the site and will not be able to see your contacts?'* It was definitely what I wanted. I hit the button and my profile was history.

Christmas Day dawned cold and frosty but no snow as usual. I made a couple of visits to family members, my sisters, to give their kids their gifts. They always asked me to stay for lunch but I preferred to let them enjoy their own family celebrations in peace. They were pleased I had somewhere to go this year.

Back at home I decided to call Sue more out of reassurance than any necessity. Although we had chatted on and off we had never met and the thought of spending Christmas Day together was scary. What if we didn't get on? What if she didn't look like her picture? I felt the apprehension envelop my body as I dialled her number, a creeping fear that tightened every muscle. I had agreed to the date, but with my departure time for Brighton imminent, I was very nervous.

I needn't have worried so much. Sue said she was just as nervous but was looking forward to meeting me. We confirmed a meeting time. The call had reassured me. Nothing much happened anyway on Christmas Day so we both might as well take the chance. It certainly seemed more appealing than sitting on my own watching yet another pile of dross on the TV whilst nursing a stale mince pie.

I dressed casually, jeans and a smart white shirt. I grabbed my jacket from the wardrobe. A fragrance, like petals soaked in water, sweet and floral, floated into my senses. Coco Chanel. Louise's perfume was still on my jacket. It was if she was instantly in the room, so vivid was the impact, her smiling face a picture in my head. I put the jacket back. I'd wear another. Not because I was concerned about arriving at Sue's place smelling of perfume, although that thought crossed my mind, but because I wanted to save some part of that moment when we had sat and chatted on that frosty evening at MacFadden's.

The one good thing about driving on the motorway on Christmas Day at lunchtime is that there is hardly anyone else on it. I was in Brighton in double quick time, much quicker than I had estimated. I had at least half an hour to kill so pointed the car towards the sea front. I'd fully expected the area to be deserted, after all it was Christmas day, but I was surprised to find it was busy. I pulled up across the road from the pier and walked over to the array of brightly coloured sales kiosks that framed its entrance. Groups of people stood around chatting, eating chips and drinking from plastic cups of coffee and tea. Some Christmas dinner. Were there that many people with nowhere to go on Christmas day? Or was it just a social thing that happened by the sea? Perhaps they were all killing time like me before embarking on a mass of blind dates.

I bought a coffee from one of the kiosks and went and stood to one side of the pier waiting for the piping hot liquid to cool down to a temperature which was drinkable. Leaning on the ornate pale blue railings that formed a barrier between the pebbled beach and the pavement, I looked down into the choppy sea and watched the water crashing in across the stones, the waves emerald green, topped with flurries of white tipped spume. Above my head and as far out as I could see, the sky was almost black, a dark mass of grey blue clouds rising up high above the swell of the sea. As I stood there, the fresh sea breeze whipping through my hair, it felt good to be alive. The whole scene, highly charged and atmospheric, had invigorated my mind and body, creating positive energy within me. I gulped in a few more lungful's of the fresh air, catching site of the time on the clock tower above the pier entrance as I did so. I was ready for my date.

Clutching a bottle of fine wine and a bouquet of roses that I had bought on the journey, I stepped out of the car into a quiet cul-de-sac of newly built houses and looked for the address Sue had given me. I pressed the doorbell and waited anxiously. The door opened.

'Matthew?'

'Hello Sue. Yes, I'm Matthew. Pleased to meet you and a Merry Christmas.'

'Pleased to meet you too Matthew. This is pleasant surprise. Come in.'

Sue was lovely. She was slim, short auburn hair and had a ready smile. She was dressed simply in black jeans and a white top, a silver necklace with matching earrings her only adornments. I felt an inner sigh of relief that I hadn't made a fruitless and disappointing journey. To break the ice she offered me a drink.

'Just a beer will be fine,' I said.

'Are you sure. I am having a vodka and soda?'

I stuck with my beer and she wandered off to get the drinks.

'Make yourself at home,' she said, 'take a look around the house'.

It was a large house, several rooms leading off the main hall with a staircase situated to one side that lead to the upper floor. I didn't feel comfortable wandering around a stranger's home by myself and after a cursory glance around the lower floor I returned to the sitting room The most striking feature in the room was the enormous Christmas tree taking pride of place in one corner, its fallen pine needles forming a carpet-like circle at its base. It was impressive but sparsely decorated, the only adornment being candles. Real candles.

Sue had obviously gone to a lot of effort to create an authentic looking Christmas feel. No modern glitter, baubles or tinsel, just the candles. I had never seen anything like it except on a Christmas card scene. She returned with the drinks.

'I love your tree, Sue, very authentic,' I said.

'Do you? Super. I prefer minimalism. I wanted to keep it simple, natural and traditional.'

As she spoke she walked over to a large leather sofa, sat down and patted the seat next to her.

'Come and sit down Matthew and tell me about you.'

I sat next to her feeling her lean towards me as I did so.

'Lovely to see you. I was very nervous about meeting you but I am so glad we did it,' she said.

'A bit of a strange date don't you think but…well, you only live once.'

I told her that I had been apprehensive too but was just as pleased that I had taken the chance.

And I was genuinely pleased. It was effectively a blind date after all and it could have all gone horribly wrong. We toasted our good fortune.

'Are you hungry Matthew?' Sue asked. 'I've got a cottage pie in the oven. It's not really a typical festive dish but as there is just the two of us I thought it would be nice to keep it simple. I did make a chocolate cheesecake too but the dog ate it.'

She laughed as she told the story.

It crossed my mind the dog had probably eaten it because chocolate and cheese should never be in the same recipe. The dog may well have mistaken the combined odour as similar to that from dog food. The fact that he ate the lot would suggest that it did indeed taste like dog food. I kept my thoughts to myself and simply asked where the dog was now. She told me her mum was dog sitting so that we could have little peace and quiet.

Two more drinks followed. We were getting along. Sue was easy to talk to and had an infectious laugh. The fact that she laughed so readily at my attempts at humour put me at ease and enabled the conversation to flow. There was a mixed bowl of nuts and crisps on the low coffee table in front of us.

'You are not eating any crisps, Matthew,' she said.

'I don't eat crisps often,' I said. 'I don't get all these flavours. Sausage, tomato, prawn cocktail, roast beef. It just isn't possible to replicate any of those flavours in a crisp. They should all be labelled *'Dead Sea'* flavour...with extra salt.'

She laughed out loud and moved a little closer to me.

'So, tell me all about yourself, Matthew. What's a nice guy like you doing on a dating site?'

I told her about me. As much as I thought was appropriate anyway given that we had just met.

She told me about herself. She'd been on the site for six months and had had several dates, none of which had come to anything. The usual tale of weirdoes, married men, guys older or shorter than they had claimed and perverts. It all sounded like a sorry story until she told me that the reason she was on the site was because her best friend had met the love of her life on there. So, she was optimistic that the same could happen for her. Her optimism suited her upbeat nature.

'Anyway, Matthew I have gone on for long enough and your drink has run out. Let me get you another. I should check on the cottage pie too and put those beautiful roses you brought in some water.'

She disappeared to the kitchen. I stood up and walked around the room glancing at the photos that were scattered around. They suggested snippets of Sue's life but we had all night for her to fill in the details.

I heard her call from the kitchen.

'Stick a CD on if you like Matthew. Whatever you want.'

The music was an easy choice. The CD was already lying by the player. One Hundred Greatest Christmas Songs. All the old classics mixed in with a few modern ones – White Christmas, Santa Claus is Coming to Town, Jingle Bells. I hit the button on the player, slid the disc into the tray and waited for the first chimes of Winter Wonderland.

It was at that point I spotted the lighter.

'Sleigh bells ring, are you listening....'

The jolly opening lyrics of the carol filled the room. With the Christmas spirit upon me I decided I could enhance the festive atmosphere created by the music. I picked up the lighter and began to light the candles on the Christmas tree. As each candle flared into life the tree took on a warm, homely glow reminiscent of a bygone Christmas card image.

'Drinks are ready, Matthew. I am just sorting out these roses. Come and get it.'

I lit the last candle and headed into the kitchen to find Sue cutting the stems off the roses. The aroma of cottage pie wafted through the room, the heat from the cooker steaming up the large window that dominated one wall. Outside the sun was setting in the distance below the clouds and the darkness of a winter evening had begun to blanket the landscape. I sat at the table with my drink and watched Sue carefully arrange the flowers in a chunky glass vase.

'The food will be ready in about half an hour and then we can open that bottle of wine you brought,' she said.

I wasn't sure if Sue had given any thought to the fact that I had come to Brighton by car and that I was unlikely to be driving back if I drank wine as well as beer. I put the thought out of my mind. I'd cross that bridge when I came to it. She came and sat at the table, opposite me, cradling her vodka and soda. We chatted for a short while in the kitchen, sipped our drinks and watched the pale remnants of the December sun sink below the rooftops. I felt pleased that I had taken the chance and made the journey. It would have been so easy to let the opportunity slip by. Instead I was in the company of an attractive lady and we seemed to be hitting it off.

'Come on Matthew, let's go back to the sitting room,' she said, 'it's much more comfy.'

As we headed towards the sitting room door, drinks in hand, I wondered what the bright yellow glow was that illuminated the room. It didn't take long to find out. A wave of heat hit us as we walked in. To my utter horror the whole Christmas tree was ablaze, a glowing towering inferno of sparking wood and pines. Sue screamed. I froze on the spot, a dreamlike like state immobilising my capacity for responsive thought. The ceiling was blackening by the second, the paint peeling off the walls already. The horrendous situation was rendered even more surreal by 'Rocking Around the Christmas Tree' blaring loudly from the speakers.

Regaining my senses I ran back to the kitchen. I grabbed the soda siphon and rushed back into the sitting room. The first jet of soda completely missed the tree and hit Sue square in the face, soaking her and her white top. My second attempt had no effect other than to produce a pathetic fizz of steam and I quickly realised the futility of tackling a mini Krakatoa with such a puny extinguisher. Flames licked and crackled through the dry timber until it was a yellow cone of heat. We had to get out. Sue was jumping up and down on the spot, yelling 'fucking hell, fucking hell' at the tree in a hysterical, high pitched tone as Brenda Lee sang '... *everyone's dancing merrily in a new old fashioned way.*'

Sue's rant at the tree had not lessened the impact of the flames. I grabbed her hand and dragged her into the hallway. For some reason she was now trying to beat me up, raining blows with a girly clenched fist in a hammering action on my right arm. Ordinarily it would just have been a mild irritation as I tried to get her out of the house but every blow was landing on my already bruised upper arm. I started to shout at her to try and get some sense into her.

'We've got to get out Sue. Stop punching me for Christ's sake. I am trying to rescue you.'

'You wouldn't have to fucking rescue me you fucking moron if you hadn't set my fucking tree alight..,' she screamed at me, '...that's what you've done isn't it.'

The pleasant demeanour that I had encountered when I had arrived had now given way to an almost demonic hysteria. I contemplated knocking her out with the soda siphon I was still carrying but thought better of it given the chaos that was already ensuing. I yanked her forward by the hand in the direction of the front door. Grabbing the handle I wrenched the door open and pushed her towards it, yelling at her to get out. I followed her but in my hurry to escape, I tripped on the doorstep. As I fell forward the soda siphon shot from my hands high into the air and straight through the windscreen of Sue's car, which was parked on the drive. The wail of the car alarm pierced the tranquil Christmas evening. Front doors opened, neighbours craning to see what the commotion was about.

'Call the fire brigade. Quick,' I screamed at a shocked looking lady in the house opposite, '...it's a bloody emergency.'

She didn't need telling twice. The ominous yellow glow lighting up the front window was a clear indicator that a minor disaster was unfolding. As if to emphasise the seriousness of the situation the glass then shattered spectacularly, sending a shower of splinters and sparks across the front lawn.

Sue began shouting at me again.

'What the bloody hell have you done? My fucking house! I've only been here six weeks. What have you done?'

'I just lit the tree...the candles...I thought–.' I didn't get the opportunity to explain what I thought.

'You fucking cretin. I knew it. You lit the candles. They are not meant to be lit. They were just for decoration. Any idiot would know that. The tree was dry as a bone, you bloody fool.'

Candles that were not meant to be lit. I wasn't going to argue the point. I shut up. Sue's language had deteriorated to that of the dockside and her description of me as a cretin, idiot and fool suggested that this date was now well and truly over although the flames turning her window frames and front door to matchwood were also a strong indication that my Christmas date was now done. Apologies did not seem adequate as I watched smoke and flames emerging into the open air through the shattered window, sucking up the oxygen that the fire needed to do its damage. Tears were pouring down Sue's face. Rage, desperation, helplessness, frustration, each emotion gripping her and emerging in long streams of tears. I felt so sorry for her but I kept my distance. She didn't need my sympathy. Her neighbours gathered around to comfort her. No one spoke to me. They had clearly judged and damned me as an arsonist based entirely on Sue's tirade. To my relief I didn't have to stand in isolation for long. The flashing blue lights and wailing sirens of the first fire engine cut into the night air and within seconds the East Sussex Fire and Rescue Service had taken control.

A crowd had gathered on the pavement opposite, their faces lit by the yellow glow of the blaze. The fire crew herded everyone into a safe area and I stood back and watched as they sprang into action. Long yellow hose reels were uncoiled and swelled into life as water was forced through them to emerge in powerful jets pointed directly at the flames. I could only imagine what additional damage the soaking would do to Sue's house. Within minutes the fire was reduced to a dark cloud of black smoke billowing from what was left of the ground floor window and door. It looked to me like the upper part of the house had been spared except for areas of blackened brickwork where smoke and flame had crawled up the outside. After a while, when the smoke had reduced to a smouldering grey wisp, two of the crew in breathing apparatus entered the house. I had no idea why it crossed my mind. Perhaps with inner turmoil and guilt, the absurdity of life pops up as a relief mechanism to moderate negative emotions. Whatever the reason for it, I couldn't help but think that Sue's cottage pie was now cooked.

It was an hour or so before the fire fighters declared the situation under control. I waited, not sure what was supposed to happen next but I knew I couldn't just walk away. Sue was in deep conversation with one of the firemen who seemed to be in charge. Her tears had stopped but her mood was still one of intense anger and it was not hard to see where it was directed. Her finger was pointed accusingly in my direction accompanied by the description of me as 'that fucking idiot.' The fire chief was trying his best to get her to tell him the facts but with little success. Eventually he came over to me, introduced himself as the station officer and asked me to tell him what had happened, presumably because he felt he had a better chance of getting the facts from a '*fucking idiot*' than he did from an hysterical woman. I explained what I had done. I had nothing to hide. It was an accident. When I had finished my account he told me that the police had been called and I would have to make a statement to them. He also told me to stay where I was until they arrived.

At that moment I felt my mobile vibrate in my pocket. I pulled it out and stared at the text message on the screen.

'*Merry Xmas mate, have a good one. Cecil.*'

I arrived home at one fifteen in the early hours. Nearly five hours waiting around in a police station wasn't the best way to spend Christmas night but at least they had my statement and I was able to go home. I had been questioned as if I had started the blaze deliberately. They'd asked me how I knew Sue and I had to tell them about the website. I was starting to feel like a criminal. I crashed exhausted into an armchair.

On Boxing Day morning I called Cecil. He sounded like he'd just woken up.

'Did I wake you Cecil,' I asked, unnecessarily.

'Yeah, mate. What time is it? What do you want?'

I told him that it was just gone nine thirty and waited for a rant about how it was still the middle of the night but it never came. He still obviously had the Christmas spirit of peace and good will to all men.

'How did it go yesterday geezer?' he asked.

'I burnt the house down Cecil,' I replied in a matter of fact voice as I filled the kettle, the phone propped between my chin and my shoulder.

'Good on you mate. You finally broke your duck. I told you–'

'No, Cecil, I literally burnt the house down.'

I flicked the kettle switch to on.

There was silence on the other end of the phone while Cecil absorbed the full meaning of what I had just said. It was either still too early for him to comprehend or he was not fully awake.

'You did what? Whose house? What are you talking about?'

'I set fire to the house Ces. Actually set fire to it. The woman in Brighton who'd invited me for Christmas day. Her house. It's a right bloody mess. She's had to move out to a hotel.'

'Mate. You set fire to her house? Why?'

'I didn't bloody do it deliberately, did I, Ces. It was an accident.'

I explained the whole sorry saga. When I'd finished he was laughing, uncontrollably. Steam was now spouting from the kettle. I dropped a tea bag into a cup and poured the boiling water onto it.

'It's not funny Cecil, I –'

'It is funny. It's fucking hilarious. You go on a date and burn the bird's house down. What's not funny about that? You give a whole new meaning to getting on like a house on fire, mate.'

Another fit of uncontrollable laughter echoed down the phone line. Cecil was clearly amused at his own wit. I stirred my tea.

'Look Cecil, I'm glad you see the funny side of it, if there is a funny side to burning someone's property so it is no longer habitable and then spending the best part of Christmas night in a police station. And this after I have already caused pandemonium in a bloody stately home on another date and you have practically thrashed some other woman's house I am associated with. Not to mention all the other total fuck up's I have had. I mean the police are now going to think I am a serial vandal who targets women on dating sites and gets his kicks from causing as much distress and mayhem as possible on the actual date.'

'Mate. Shit happens,' was Cecil's considered reply. 'She'll be insured. You told the Old Bill the mumble. They'd have charged you if they thought you were some sort of arsonist. Maybe, it's time you got off that website then. It don't look like it's happening geezer.'

Thanks a bunch Cecil, I thought. It was him who had recommended internet dating.

'It's definitely not happening Cecil. I'm off there now already. Done with it. I don't reckon I need it now anyway. You know, now that I have a chance with Diana.'

'You still chasing that lawyer tart?'

'I'm not chasing the lawyer tart. She invited me skiing. She wants me to come.'

'Mate, she's winding you. If she was interested she wouldn't be inviting you skiing. She'd be hooking up with you right here. Not on some mountain in the middle of France. Mate, it's the middle of winter here. What you need is a beach with the sun on the back of your neck and a cold one in your hand. Not fucking skiing with some posh tart.'

I ignored it. I didn't want to entertain Cecil's opinion. I also didn't know why he felt so strongly about me going skiing. I told him I'd see him later and put the phone down.

30

A flight at eight o'clock in the morning meant being at the airport by six o'clock which in turn meant I had to be up at the crack of dawn. I was tired, irritable and tetchy on the drive to Gatwick. My arm ached as I loaded my suitcase into the boot of my car and the bruising was now a florid pink, yellow and purple mixture. My thoughts were a mix of illogical whinges. If I was catching a bus I didn't have to be at the bus stop two hours earlier than the bus. I didn't have to take my shoes off either before I was allowed on. Mind you, it wasn't practical to take a bus to Geneva. I flicked on the car radio for some distraction. The sound of the Killers, '*All these things that I have done*' put me in reflective mood. It could only get better from now on.

Geneva airport was busy but I saw the sign with my name on it as soon as I emerged from arrivals. The driver led me to a people carrier, loaded my bag and I settled in for what turned out to be a short transfer to our destination. The road grew ever steeper as the vehicle climbed into the mountains. Blankets of white untouched snow lay as far as the eye could see, the pine tree branches heavily laden with fresh snowfall. We turned off the main road into a steeper, narrower track that ran up through a line of trees. At the end of the tree line, the landscape opened out to reveal a huge two-storey chalet standing in stark contrast to the pure whiteness of the snow. Its lower storey was constructed of stone walls that gave way on the next level to a wide wooden balcony that appeared to surround the structure. Above this, the walls were made entirely of wood rising to a vast sloping roof that pitched down over both sides of the frame. The whole of this roof was covered by a thick mantle of snow that sat there like icing on some sort of novelty cake.

At the sound of the car engine the door of the chalet opened and a familiar figure emerged. Diana. Despite the thick fleece, ski trousers and fur lined snow boots there was no mistaking her style. The people carrier pulled up into a space by the side of the chalet that had been painstakingly dug out and cleared of the heavy snow to make a wide parking area. Diana opened the door for me.

'Matthew! Welcome to France. Lovely to see you. How was your trip?'

She kissed me on both cheeks as I stepped out of the car. I gave her a quick rundown of my trip as people do even though there was nothing eventful about it.

'Come inside and let me introduce you to everyone. It's a little chilly out here.'

The interior of the chalet was luxurious. A vast wood floor contained three large sofas, a mix of leather and fabric, each positioned to frame a low marble-topped coffee table. On one wall, behind the coffee table, a stone fireplace held the centre of the room. The high ceiling consisted of a network of long wooden beams each concealing subtle lights that cast a cosy glow around the room. At one end an open plan kitchen seemed to have every modern appliance you could think of, a mix of steel fronted units, wooden cupboards and marble worktops. A long timber staircase at the rear of the room led to the upper floor.

'Everyone' turned out to be three couples and one other guy. Diana was effusive in her introductions.

'Hi everyone. This is my friend Matthew that I have been telling you about.'

I wasn't sure that I was overwhelmed by the reference to me as 'friend' but the fact that she had been talking about me made me feel significant.

'This is Angela and Martin, Elizabeth and James and Deborah and Tom. Oh, and Hans is our ski instructor.'

I'd focussed on Hans the moment I got into the chalet. Three couples I thought and one spare man. And Diana. I was relieved to discover he was just the ski instructor. Tall, tanned, tousled blonde hair and a firm jaw line, Hans had adventurer and ladies' man written all over him.

Diana interrupted my thoughts.

'Right Matthew. You are just in time for some après ski and then we are popping into town for dinner. Tomorrow morning our taxi man will take you down and get you kitted up with your skis and boots. Love the jacket by the way,' she said, casting a look over my new ski attire.

'Thank you Diana. I thought it best to get kitted out. I suppose I only need the boots and skis now after all,' I said.

'Great we will get you fixed up tomorrow then. Oh, and I have taken the liberty of booking you into the local ski school for the day to get you off and running. Once you find your feet you can ski from here all the way down to the ski lift. Now let me show you to your room and then you must join us for that pre dinner drink.'

My room was a spacious, open plan style area in one corner of the building. A large double bed, its quilt piled with multi coloured cushions, dominated the room. Two bedside cabinets sat either side of the bed with a low wooden table in one corner and an armchair positioned by a large window that looked out across the snow covered piste.

I unpacked my bag and thought about what Diana had said. A ski school. I presumed that meant a beginner was too trivial for Hans, although I was not too concerned about that as for some reason I had taken an instant and totally illogical dislike to him. I suppose I had to start somewhere but I also realised that a whole day of lessons meant I would lose a whole day of Diana. Still a group ski school was a chance to meet like-minded people, perhaps some fun thirty-somethings who I could hang out with for a beer at the end of the day. Perhaps even some attractive ladies that would cause Diana to raise an eyebrow.

The chalet group spent the rest of evening in a small restaurant in the local village. Although I was seated next to Diana I did not have her undivided attention as she held court in her role as the holiday hostess.

The next morning I was awoken by the smell of coffee brewing and the general hubbub of activity against the wooden floor. After breakfast the group headed down stairs to a ski room in the basement to get ready for their day on the slopes. I was whisked off by the same taxi driver who had collected me from the airport. Our destination was the village centre and the local ski shop. They appeared to know I was coming.

'Bonjour. Monsieur Malarkey? I am Sebastien. I will be helping you today with your equipment.'

'Oh...err...Bonjour Sebastien. Je suis Matthew. Merci. Je ne parle pas Français...err...tres bien.'

I did try but my French was limited. Fortunately Sebastien's English was very good.

The first thing I needed was ski boots. As a total beginner I knew nothing at all about skis and boots but I was about to learn. I had never really hired shoes or boots before. It's not something you do regularly. My closest experience up to that point was hiring those blue ice skates with the red laces that skating rinks provide, as a child. I was introduced to my first ski boot by Sebastien and I was soon to discover that fitting ski boots required instruction all by itself.

A ski boot is primarily a rigid shell designed for stability, to enable the wearer to transmit movement in the legs into ski movements on the snow. That was the first thing Sebastien told me. His next instruction was on how to fit the boots. A simple enough task it would seem in theory. In practice, when handling a piece of equipment that comes half way up the shin and weighs more than a small island in the South Pacific, the reality is somewhat different. Getting one foot into the boot requires perfect balance on the other leg whilst pointing the toes directly downwards into the boot in the manner of a lead ballerina. Without the grace or balance of the aforementioned artiste, it is a difficult exercise to accomplish in one attempt and I soon found myself staggering around the shop floor like a newly born giraffe. I tried the second boot from a seated position but found that the angle required to point my toe down into the rigid shell was better accomplished by standing up, despite the fact that standing was hampered by the dead weight on my first foot.

Once both boots are on they need to be locked into place. This is achieved by closing four spring-loaded clasps that are so resistant to pressure it seemed that a four month course of weight training was required to gain the necessary strength to secure them. Eventually, with Sebastien's help, I managed to apply enough force to lock them and I finally had a pair of shiny white ski boots in place. I then began the process of learning to walk in them. It crossed my mind that there are not many occasions that you have to undergo walking lessons and my last such experience was when I was two years old. The problem with walking in ski boots is that they are not designed for anything remotely close to nimble footwork. The initial steps I took resembled those of Frankenstein's monster in early black and white movies. It didn't improve much after that.

Relieved at getting the boots on, done up and managing to stand upright in them, I was surprised by Sebastien's next request to take one of them off again. Apparently this was so that he could find the appropriate ski and then adjust the ski binding to the boot size, so that once I was on the slope it would remain attached to my boot. Getting the boot on had proved hard enough and getting it off again proved just as strenuous an exercise. Sebastien gave me a helping hand.

'Ok Matthew,' he said, 'these are your skis. I have adjusted them so that when you have a fall they will come off easily. Ok? Now put your boot back on and I will take you across the street and introduce you to Jerome, your ski instructor for today.'

A fall. I didn't like the certainty of the way Sebastien had said 'when' and not 'if'. I felt a degree of apprehension arise in my stomach.

'Ok, let's go, Monsieur Matthew.'

I dutifully followed Sebastien the short walk across the street trying my hardest not to impersonate Boris Karloff in *The Bride of Frankenstein.*

Jerome was in his early thirties, tall, long dark hair, tanned and rugged with what looked like permanent five o'clock shadow that emphasised the rugged image. He had a wide grin that showed off his gleaming white teeth, their whiteness exaggerated by his dark sun kissed complexion. He had kind eyes which softened the outdoor look and which gave the impression that he was a man of patience. He led us out to a waiting mini bus that had 'Ski Skool' emblazoned across the side in large red letters. I wondered why it wasn't in French but it wasn't exactly in English either. There were six of us. My fantasy that perhaps the beginners' lesson would be filled with Scandinavian blondes or happening people was soon shattered. It wasn't. It was me, two seven year olds, two sullen spotty teenagers and a little old lady who looked like she was approaching the wrong end of her seventh decade. I didn't get the feeling any of us would be hanging out for a beer any time soon. As we climbed into the mini bus to head to the nursery slope I was just grateful that it didn't have a Mickey Mouse logo or a bandaged teddy bear motif to reinforce the ski school, beginners' classification that I was now part of.

The drive took no more than five minutes and we piled out of the mini bus onto a wide open space that was barely a hill let alone a mountain. A large sign said 'Nursery Slope'. Over to my left was a broad stretch of land that led down to a group of buildings that housed the chair lift. A network of pylons marched their way up the ever steepening slope as far as the eye could see, carrying a queue of four-seater chairs fixed at regular intervals to a thick steel cable that pulled them up the mountainside. Each chair was occupied by groups of skiers in multi-coloured clothing, their legs dangling into space, skis suspended in mid-air from their boots. One by one the chairs disappeared over a high tree lined ridge as the cables groaned and whirred in the task of taking their passengers ever higher. Underneath the cables a steady stream of skiers floated across the early morning ice heading towards the base station, keen to get to the bottom and begin the climb back up the mountain again.

Jerome lined us all up across the slope to face him. I thought at first we were about to have a school photograph done but realised we were being put in position for our first lesson. The mini bus driver had placed our skis and poles to one side and Jerome now set about distributing them. He called out our names and we were told to put our individual sets on the ground in front of us. Once all pairs were handed out he began to demonstrate how we should put them on. One of the spotty teenagers, standing to my right, was staring at me or more precisely at my brand new ski jacket. Clad in a baggy snowboard jacket that had wide black, white and green bands across it from top to bottom, he had a look of disdain on his face that showed his disapproval of my more conventional attire. His fur-lined hood was up so that only the very front of his face was visible. I ignored him and focussed on Jerome although I wondered why a spotty teen was having beginners ski lessons if he wanted to look like some trendy snowboard dude. To my left stood the two seven year olds, trying to control their impatience but not succeeding too well as their constant shuffling and fidgeting to get going revealed. On their left the little old lady was almost rigid, her face a picture of abject terror. I wondered why she looked so scared and what horrors were going through her mind. Whatever they were her petrified demeanour was making me edgy too.

Jerome placed his skis in front of him and proceeded, with a ski pole in either hand for balance, to demonstrate how to place each boot into the ski binding and attach the whole thing first to one foot and then to the other. Then it was our turn. We were positioned on an extremely slippery surface, each of us attempting to stand on one leg whilst lifting the other one with what feels like a concrete block attached to it. It was not the easiest of tasks to get the skis on. As soon as you try to lock the ski in place it wants to slide off in the direction that gravity dictates, usually downhill. Once you achieve the task of getting the first ski in place you have the even more difficult task of getting the second ski on. Standing on one smooth plank of wood that is positioned on an icy hill, with the other foot poised in mid-air, its unfeasibly large weight dangling as you try to lock the boot into the other ski, is far from easy. This delicate stance is not conducive to remaining stationary for long.

With the aid of my ski poles firmly planted in the snow either side of me, just as Jerome had demonstrated, I managed on my second attempt to lock my left boot into the ski binding. Then came the right one. Gripping both poles as tightly as I could I angled my toe down into the binding. I managed to position the front of the boot in the front end and in pushing the heel down hard I hoped to feel the clunk of the boot snapping into position. It didn't. The heel was off line and hit the snow pushing the ski slightly forward. I felt my right foot slide. I tried to balance by sliding my left foot out slightly to widen my stance. It didn't work. The skis seemed to have developed a motion completely independent of my intentions. My right foot slid further forward as I tried to shift my weight onto the left side to stabilise myself and keep contact with the ground. I saw my right arm begin an anticlockwise helicopter motion. Perhaps when balance is an issue, the human brain momentarily considers that if it gets an arm to rotate rapidly it will generate enough uplift to keep the body upright. It doesn't work. My left arm started to clutch at thin air in an effort to find a secure grab point. Unfortunately that turned out to be the hood of the seven year old on my left and he wasn't what you could describe as stable. My body wheeled around sharply to the right as my left ski went from under me. As it came down and across me, my right hand involuntarily grabbed the other child by the shoulder shoving him, me and the first kid into a direct collision with the little old lady on our left. With no stable contact with the ground all of us went down in a heap onto the snow. I tried to get up immediately but my foot slid along the surface propelling me directly on top of the old lady so that I now had her pinned to the ground. At that point I thought I heard my name being called. I looked up. Gliding effortlessly across the bottom of the piste, a flurry of snow swirling from beneath her skis was Diana. She waved at me in greeting, a broad smile on her face as she carved her way towards the chairlift base station. In her wake was Hans, the ski instructor.

With Jerome's help we managed to right ourselves. The kids thought it was funny. The teenagers thought I was a prat. I apologised to the elderly lady, who turned out to be called, Mary.

'I am so sorry. I couldn't help myself,' I said.

'Oh, don't worry young man. It's a long time since a man couldn't help himself and felt the need to jump on me,' Mary replied, smiling broadly.

'I didn't mean...I mean...I slipped...are you ok?'

She had a twinkle in her eye. 'I am fine. My daughter said I'd fall over sooner or later. I am just glad to get the first one out of the way.'

Eventually we all had our skis in place and were ready for the first lesson proper. The rest of the morning was taken up with demonstrating the '*snow plough.*' I discovered it was a manoeuvre to slow the skier down and eventually stop. An invaluable skill to have in the circumstances. Jerome gave us a number of short runs on the extremely gentle slope to practise. The two seven year olds were fearless and were shooting down the slope like experts within half an hour. The spotty teenagers thought they were experts already and tumbled and improvised their own way down the slope, high fiving and giggling to each other the whole time. I still wasn't sure what they were doing in the school. Mary, the elderly lady, cut an altogether unique figure. Poised on her skis with her backside sticking out, her knees bent and hands gripping the poles like they had become welded to her gloves, she looked like she had been removed from a freezer having been placed there in that position the night before. Totally rigid and staring straight ahead, her expression remained one of complete terror. Jerome spent so much time picking her up off the snow that she might as well have been on a private lesson. My own first three attempts at negotiating the nursery slope all ended in a face first crash into a bank of soft snow but by the end of the day we had all managed the major step of being able to slow down and stop more or less where we decided to without recourse to using our faces as brakes. But that was on the gentle nursery slope. Having completed day one Jerome considered that we were now proficient enough to venture onto our first blue slope the next day. I was not totally convinced.

31

I returned to the chalet knackered, mostly through the use of nervous energy rather than my physical endeavours. The other couples were back already but Diana was nowhere to be seen. I asked where she was only to be told that she was having an après ski drink with Hans.

As I was absorbing this news I had a text from Cecil. '*How's it going mate? You and the lawyer got the mumble on yet?*'

I tapped a quick reply out on the keypad. '*It's not happening, Cecil! I'll explain later.*' I wasn't in the mood for banter with Cecil.

Elizabeth and James invited me into the village for a drink. I decided to accept. No sense in hanging around the chalet waiting for Diana. I may as well make the most of the place. Elizabeth and James turned out to be lawyers too. I wondered how fate had suddenly caused me to be surrounded with legal people at the same time as I was avoiding the law. PC Penny suddenly popped into my head. I had to stop avoiding her. In fact I wanted to stop avoiding her and maybe get to know the real person. I downed a couple of glasses of vin chaud and resolved to sort it out.

I didn't see Diana until breakfast the next day. I'd had a quick bite to eat the night before and gone to bed early.

'Good morning Matthew,' she said, 'how was your first day skiing?'

'Not too bad. Just getting started really. We are going up the mountain today apparently.'

'Excellent. Well perhaps we will see you at lunch later. There is a lovely mountain restaurant, with fabulous views, at the top of the blue run you will be going to. Ask Jerome to show you. He sometimes takes his pupils there.'

'Sounds good, Diana,' I said, 'so how was your day?'

'Oh my day was fantastic Matthew. Hans is such a good instructor. He took me off piste today.'

I really didn't want to know where Hans had taken her. I didn't pursue it.

'So, looks like you have made a new friend then Matthew,' Diana said.

'New friend?' I asked.

Diana held her coffee cup in both hands, sipping it slowly, looking over the cup as she spoke.

'Yes. You seemed to be getting well acquainted with a lady when I saw you yesterday morning.'

'Oh that. No, that was an accident. We fell over. Slipped...and, you know, just ended up in a heap. It was–'

She noticed my embarrassment.

'I am just teasing you Matthew. You are funny. Now we had better get going so I will see you between twelve thirty and one. How does that sound?'

'Great. I'll see you later,' I said.

The school group assembled at the bottom of the main ski lift as arranged with Jerome the previous evening. I had never been on a chair lift before but by watching how everyone else got aboard I managed to get myself in position for the seat to pick me up and whisk me forward into the air. And I quite enjoyed it. As the chairlift took me higher I seemed to experience a feeling of peace and serenity. There was no sound but the occasional whistle of the wind and a periodic mechanical groan from the cables as they passed through the pulleys on the huge towers that supported them. Suspended high above the magnificent Alpine landscape I felt a sudden freedom, a sense of wellbeing. I couldn't go anywhere but yet no one could get to me. And all around me the mountains stretched for miles. Huge swathes of virgin snow lay beneath my feet. Tall pine trees, their boughs heavily laden with fresh snow, jutted from the white terrain. And above me a cloudless, sapphire blue sky. I was aware of the space that surrounded me and it reinforced the sense of freedom.

My relaxed composure was dramatically altered when the chair reached the top of the ski station.

I raised the safety bar over my head and concentrated on placing my skis firmly onto the snow as the momentum of the moving chair pushed me forward onto the landing area that took me clear of it. From sitting completely stationary I was now a blur of forward movement. My left ski made full contact with the surface in a straight line. The other one decided to go off on a path to the extreme right. As my right foot lost contact with the ground, my weight tipped hard left so that I was propelled forward on the left ski. My right began to perform a bizarre flapping motion in the air as it desperately sought a connection with terra firma. I skidded forward completely out of control on the one ski until Jerome came to my rescue. Not that he knew a great deal about it. He was standing with his back to the chairlift talking to the two seven year olds as I hit him just below the knees. The impact took his legs away completely.

Up he went into the air catching the kids with his skis sending them flying to one side and landing on his back in the snow. I slid a few yards further coming to a halt right at the feet of the two spotty teenagers. I heard a word that resembled 'dork' as they turned away. Jerome was fine about it. Clearly he had seen it all before.

With order restored we started the next stage of the lessons.

The top of the blue run was an altogether different prospect from the gentle nursery slope. The early morning snow was packed and ice-like with a shimmer on its rippled surface as it picked up the sun. Jerome lined us up at the top and told us he wanted us to snow plough our way down to a point half way down the hill where it plateaued out. We stood side on to the slope. Looking over my left shoulder at the route we were to take, the pitch looked steeper than the Big Dipper at Blackpool. In that moment I experienced the gut wrenching realisation that I really did not know how to control the two bits of wood that were attached to my feet and whose surfaces were smoother than an Italian gigolo's chat up lines in a dodgy nightclub. I clearly wasn't the only one having reservations. From the corner of my eye I caught a glimpse of Mary who had adopted her customary frozen rigid, bum out pose. I took a deep breath and began to move forward.

Facing down the hill and spurred on by gravity, I suddenly began, through no meaningful instigation of my own, to be propelled down the hill faster and faster at a speed that would scare a space shuttle astronaut. As the speed increased, a sub-zero arctic blast of wind began to distort my features more than the hall of mirrors in an amusement park. This distortion may also have been brought on by my sudden comprehension of the word terrified. As I was propelled forward I heard a shout from Jerome, bellowing out the phrase '*sno ploo, sno ploo*' in his heavy French accent' as I disappeared into the distance. In my terror, I had visions of a head on collision with a rather large mechanical vehicle that is used to shift snow around but realised it was his instruction to enable me to reduce my momentum and stop my headlong descent. Since at that point I felt I was approaching something like the speed of sound, it occurred to me that 'brake, slow down' or even 'fall over you twat' may have held more clarity and been better instruction for me than *sno ploo*.'

Through sheer chance my rapid descent was curtailed by a completely involuntary turn to my right, brought on by an inadvertent shift of my weight to my left ski. My speed marginally reduced as I traversed the slope at an angle but my next problem lay straight ahead. A mountain restaurant on the side of the piste. I remember shutting my eyes and mentally placing myself in the hands of destiny. I felt the sensation of my skis abruptly stopping as I hit the wooden step, but my body continuing to travel forward, superman style, through the air. The two saloon style doors that formed the entrance gave way easily as my head connected with them, sending them rattling back and forth on their hinges as I shot through them and skidded to a halt on the restaurant floor, just missing a waitress who was carrying a tray of lagers. What turned out to be a middle-aged American tourist jumped up from the bar in surprise at the human projectile that had come to a halt next to his feet.

'You ok buddy? You ok?' he said, a note of alarm in his voice.

I rolled on to my back and stared up at him not fully comprehending where I was for a moment.

'That was some entrance, buddy. I know this restaurant says ski in ski out but that's taking it a might too far, doncha think?' he said, as he stretched out a hand to help me up.

I wasn't hurt, just embarrassed. I grabbed the American guy's hand and clambered to my feet, and tried to stand upright in my ski boots whilst my head cleared from the shock of my sudden nosedive. Before I could say anything to my new American acquaintance, Jerome appeared by my side.

'You ok, Matthew,' he asked.

I ran both hands through my hair from front to back and shook my head, in an effort to clear my senses.

'Yeah, I'm fine, Jerome,' I said, 'I just lost it a bit.'

An understatement indeed. The whole thing had happened so fast that I had lost the ability to think.

'You have to slow down, Matthew.'

Really, Jerome. Is that the big secret? All I have to do is slow down. Now why didn't somebody tell me that? So when I am hurtling down the slope at 273mph all I need to do is slow down. I didn't say any of it. I knew I was slightly delirious with fear. Jerome escorted me back outside to retrieve my skis and we went through the palaver of getting my shaking legs back into them again. I got them back in place just in time to see Mary sliding down the very same slope on her bum. I concluded that perhaps hers was the better technique for getting down the hill.

By lunchtime I had used up so much nervous energy I was ready to refuel. I was also looking forward to hooking up with Diana. I had used up a day and a half of my four day break already and had hardly seen her. So much for this trip sorting out my love life. The immediate problem however was that the mountain restaurant was half way down a blue run that had an upward slope at the end of it. The first part of the downward section looked steep enough but according to Jerome the idea was that we had to pick up enough speed on the downward section to get us to the peak of the next slope and cruise gently towards the restaurant. Cruising was not a word that I could readily associate with skiing just yet. The two seven year olds went first, flew down the slope like Olympic downhill racers, glided up the other side and came to a halt cool as you like at the top. I couldn't believe it. No fear. Jerome decided that Mary's rigid ski style was not conducive to allowing her to hurtle down a hill on her own and he offered to escort her. The two spotty teenagers were busy comparing tracks on their iPods and having a gum chewing competition so it was my turn next. If the seven year olds could do it I could too.

I eased forward hesitantly but within a few metres the slope had gripped my skis and I was careering downhill. In an effort to control the pace I instinctively went into the snow plough position, the front end of my skis pointing in towards one another. The manoeuvre immediately stabilised my pace.

'Go for it. Go for it, Matthew,' Jerome was screaming at me.

I realised I wouldn't make it up the other side if I didn't let myself go. I went for it. Somehow I kept my balance as the velocity picked up. I got to the critical dip where the incline changed from down to up and realised I was not going fast enough despite tears streaming from my eyes and my hair so sleeked back it threatened to pull my eyebrows up to my scalp. My lack of final momentum left me some seventy-five metres short of the top of the upward slope. I wanted to blame the weight of the ski boots – a pack of huskies on steroids would have had difficulty dragging them up a hill in my opinion at that moment– but I knew I had not been brave enough to really let myself go following my earlier scary experience with the mountain restaurant.

Failing to reach the top of the slope meant that I had to 'climb' the rest of the way on foot. As I stood grounded on the snow, the restaurant where I was meant to meet with Diana tantalisingly close, I couldn't help thinking that my situation was ironically symbolic of my whole experience of the dating game. So close, but not quite getting to where I wanted to be. My moment of introspection was interrupted by the sight of Mary being towed by Jerome, via a ski pole, successfully to the top of the slope. Even a little old lady, albeit with some help, had made it. My options were to remove my skis (and given how difficult it is to get them on that was not my preference), walk like a duck - that is, with my feet pointing outwards and wide apart with heels together to retain some grip - or walk up sideways like someone sidling out of a nightclub at 3am in the morning having imbibed a little too much of the firewater. None of them easy on a slippery surface. I chose the 'duck' method. By the time I had reached the top of the hill, such was the effort involved, I felt the need for emergency oxygen and a muscle massage from a fully qualified physiotherapist. My legs were blancmange and my face felt redder than freshly poured claret.

I struggled into the restaurant area, parked my skis in one of the many ski racks and Frankensteined it towards the entrance. Rows of crowded tables were spread across the snow in front of the main building, filled with skiers enjoying the mountain sun. I spotted Diana sitting at one of the tables by a circular outside bar that was covered by a giant blue umbrella. A familiar face sat next to her. Hans.

'Matthew! Come and have some vin chaud. How has your morning been?' Diana asked.

'Fine, thanks. Getting there,' I said.

'Yes...looks like it. We saw you coming down that slope.'

I didn't like the 'we.' I didn't like the smug look on Hans face either. So I was a beginner and he was a bloody expert. And the expert seemed to have pole position with the lady. I was irked.

'I am just going to get some food Diana,' I said, walking towards the bar.

I didn't mean to sulk and I hadn't meant to walk away so abruptly. But I was irritated. I hoped it wasn't obvious but since I had been invited this far by my hostess I had half expected some kind of special attention.

I ordered some tartiflette and vin chaud. As I walked back I saw Mary sitting by herself at a table sipping coffee. She caught my eye.

'Hello Matthew,' she said looking at me squarely in the eyes.

'Hi Mary,' I said, 'what are you doing here by yourself?'

'Just having lunch Matthew. The children have met up with their parents and those young boys are not going to sit with an old lady like me.'

'Well, may I join you then Mary,' I asked.

'Don't be silly Matthew, I see you have a lady friend waiting.'

'It's ok Mary. She'll be fine. She has some company.'

I pulled off my gloves, placed them on the seat and sat down opposite her. She had kind eyes, years of wisdom shining brightly. It was the first time I had seen them clearly now that she had removed her sunglasses.

'So, how is you skiing going Mary,' I asked.

'It's dreadful Matthew. I am bloody petrified. I am only doing it because I am here with my daughter and she suggested I have lessons. I don't think it's for me. I'd sooner be on a beach with a good book,' she said laughing, 'I am too old for this. How about you?'

The vin chaud arrived. I sipped it, savouring its warmth and aromatic flavour.

'Oh, I'm getting there, I think. If I could just get the boots on easily, slow down and stop when I wanted to, turn to the left as well as right and get the skis on within half an hour after falling over I will have cracked it.'

Mary smiled and stared at her coffee. A waiter arrived with my lunch. Mary moved her hat and ski gloves to one side to make room for my plate of food.

'You look glum, Matthew, what's the matter?' Mary asked.

'Oh, I'm fine...this skiing is tough...takes it out of you,' I said.

'You sure it isn't something else? Woman trouble, maybe? I can tell these things you know. I have good intuition.'

'Well...you know, I think I am just tired from all the effort and nervous energy...' My sentence tailed off.

Mary stared at me, looking directly into my eyes. It was a little unnerving. I looked away, down at the plate of food that I still hadn't touched.

'You have sad eyes, Matthew. Troubled even. I saw the way you looked at that lady. You have an eye for her don't you,' she said.

'Well, yes I like her –'

'I don't think she is for you Matthew. I'm sorry to say this but she has eyes for that young ski instructor. I have seen the body language. She is very close with him.'

It wasn't what I wanted to hear but I knew that Mary was probably right. I hadn't seen Diana at all really and each time I did, apart from in the chalet, she was with Hans. I knew she was having ski lessons but all day and into the evening seemed excessive even for the keenest skier. I had hoped that she might have made more of an effort with me since she invited me in the first place. And I had expected to spend a little time with her for lunch but Hans was still hovering around although when I thought about it she had never actually said 'meet me for lunch.' If I recall she'd said something like 'we'll see you at lunch.' Maybe that was why she didn't seem too bothered that I had sat at another table with Mary.

Mary interrupted my thoughts.

'I am sorry Matthew. I hope I haven't disillusioned you. But I say what I see. I don't think the two of you even look suited. My guess is that you have a little infatuation. Would I be right?'

I prodded the tartiflette with my fork. Mary was probably right. I had been totally mixed up since I'd joined Cupid's Pursuit and perhaps a degree of desperation had kicked in. Diana seemed a great catch. Intelligent, smart, sexy, good looking, professional and classy. Most men would have developed some form of infatuation with her. I was no different and perhaps vulnerable too, as I was actually looking for love. I took a sip of the vin chaud.

'Yes. Perhaps you could be right,' I said, finally.

I decided to tell her my situation. I told her about my dates. I even told her about Louise Penny. I didn't tell her all the uncomfortable bits. There was no need. Mary seemed to know instinctively that I was a man looking for a soul mate and that the failed dates were just symptoms of my search.

'Matthew. Sometimes we search too hard for the unobtainable, for ideals. We look so hard we sometimes do not see what is immediately there before us. Are you looking too hard? Yes. I think you are. Maybe you should pause and reflect. Is what you seek there already? I don't know that. Only you will find that out if you give yourself time. Look for a connection, young man, not a desire. Love will find you.'

I felt like Grasshopper in the Kung Fu TV series sitting with his wise mentor.

'Close your eyes. What do you hear?
I hear the water, I hear the birds.
Do you hear your own heartbeat?
No.
Do you hear the grasshopper which is at your feet?
Old man, how is it that you hear these things?
Young man, how is it that you do not?'

Several taps of a spoon against a cup brought me back to reality.

'Matthew. Are you there? You have gone very quiet. What is it,' Mary asked.

'Oh nothing, Mary, I was just thinking about what you were saying. You make a lot of sense,' I said.

'Sense. Of course I do. I am an old lady now but I have seen a lot in my lifetime. But I wish I could make sense of this skiing.' She smiled and placed her hand on mine. 'Come on. We had better get back. Might as well finish what we started.'

That night back at the chalet there was still no sign of Diana when everyone else returned. According to Elisabeth and James, they had seen her and Hans coming off the slope and heading for one of the bars in the main village. I suddenly realised I didn't really care anymore. Whether it was a delayed reaction to Mary's words of wisdom or my own sense of self-worth finally kicking in, I didn't know but I actually felt relieved. I realised that, yes, maybe I had been infatuated with Diana but now it was over. I resolved to go back home the next day and sort my life out. My love life could follow afterwards.

The next morning I saw Diana. She was sipping coffee and spreading jam on a croissant in the kitchen.

'Hi Diana,' I said in as cheery a voice as I could muster. It wasn't contrived either. I actually did feel cheery although the prospect of my last few hours on the slopes was still enough to give me a bit of an edge.

'Good morning Matthew,' she said, 'you are up early. Coffee?'

'Yes please. I wanted to get a few extra hours of practice in before I head home later. There are no lessons today so I am just going to work on what I've done so far.'

'Oh of course it's your last day. Such a shame you can't be here for the New Year celebrations tonight. I do hope you enjoyed yourself. Look, I know I haven't seen much of you, what with the lessons and all that.'

'The lessons? You must be an expert by now Diana.' I laughed to show I meant no ill feeling. 'Hans certainly is very *Hans* on,' I joked, as I helped myself to a croissant.

Diana smiled. 'I have known Hans quite a while, Matthew. He's a sweet guy. I only ever see him when I come here. We are old friends.'

I didn't need to know anymore. I left it at that.

'Listen Diana, I do really want to thank you for inviting me here. It has been an experience. A scary one at times. And fun. And enlightening too. So thank you.'

'Enlightening?' she asked.

'Well, let's just say a bit of an eye opener.'

She sensed from the finality of my tone that there was nothing more I wanted to say.

'I guess I won't see you before I go, Diana. I am being picked up for the airport at two.'

She leant forward and kissed me warmly on both cheeks.

'Take care Matthew...and if you ever need anything just let me know.'

32

I missed seeing the New Year in completely because I went straight to bed when I got back home. I was exhausted. I ignored several texts and two voicemails from Cecil who seemed desperate to get me out partying. I knew that a New Year's Eve with him would only end in typical Cecil style mayhem. I switched off my mobile and slept soundly.

The next morning I awoke refreshed, clear headed on a New Year's Day. I decided it was how I wanted things to continue. I made a pot of coffee and sat down at the desk in my study intending to make some New Year calls to my sisters when I noticed it. The yellow post it note with the number on, pasted to the side of the computer monitor where I had left it. Estelle.

I tried to recall her face from the site. She gradually materialised in my head. The dark haired girl with the heavy black glasses. I remembered her emails and recalled how I had thought that perhaps we had something in common. Perhaps I would give her a call. Then I thought better of it. I had done with dating and the site. It was a new year and a new era for me.

I called my sister. Once we had the happy new years out of the way and I had told her about my skiing trip, it was one of those interminable calls where she told me everything the kids had done over Christmas, what they had eaten, who they had seen. I found myself switching off, occasionally signalling the fact that I was still conscious by adding a 'yeah' and a 'really' to the one sided conversation. My mind wandered to the post it note. Nice name...*Estelle*. I looked at the digits scrawled across the yellow paper. Maybe I should give her a call. No harm in it. She had given me her number to do just that. It didn't mean that anything would happen.

'So what are you doing with your New Year's day then?' my sister asked.

'Really,' I replied.

'Sorry?' I said.

'What are you doing...for New Year's Day,' she repeated.

'Yeah,' I replied, mentally noting Estelle's number. I will give her a call. Get it out of the way. See what happens. I had nothing going on anyway, no dates and no prospect of one. I was back to square one.

'You are not listening Matthew, are you,' my sister said, her voice dropping into a *schoolteacherish* tone.

'Listening? Err...yes...I was...am, I mean. I got distracted by a...a... something. Sorry.'

My sister was used to me. She let it go and we finished the conversation.

I cut the call and dialled the post it note number. I did it quickly before I could change my mind. Pacing the room I waited for a response, a mix of nerves and anticipation.

'Hello.'

'Oh, hello. Is that Estelle.'

'Estelle...Oh, I will just get her for you. Who's calling?'

'It's Matthew...a friend.'

There was a long pause.

'Hello, Estelle speaking.'

'Hi Estelle. It's Matthew. From the dating site. I said I would call. I hope you don't mind me calling on New Year's Day.'

'Oh hello Matthew. It's fine. Happy New Year. How are you?'

She sounded nice, a little wary at first but I put that down to nerves. She told me that she had not expected to hear from me as I had disappeared from the dating site. I told her that I'd left because it hadn't really worked out for me. No sense in over explaining. We chatted about the site and about what we had been doing for Christmas, the usual mundane things. I didn't feel it necessary to tell her that I had been responsible for practically burning someone's house down. After a while she asked me what I was looking for. I told her that I wanted a genuine relationship, someone to be with who was a friend as well as a lover. In short I was looking for love. She asked if I had had much success so far on line. I explained that I hadn't had any success at all. That I had been on a few dates but that none of them had worked out. She asked me why that was. I told her that I didn't know. That somehow circumstances conspired against it. That perhaps the fates were not ready to deal me a hand just yet.

'You don't ask many questions, Matthew,' she said.

'Maybe that's because I am a bloke. We don't ask that many questions. We are not as inquisitive as you girls. We let these things emerge in their own time,' I replied.

The truth was I was wary of dating now and had no expectations at all. I was going through the motions. No longer on the website, I knew that this was my last roll of the dice and that if this one didn't work out I was right back where I started. Except I was worse off than before. I had been spectacularly unsuccessful in my internet dating attempts and now had nowhere else to go. So, I asked no questions because I didn't want the wrong answers. The answers that would suggest we didn't have the things in common that give a relationship half a chance of getting off on the right foot.

Estelle laughed at my answer. 'So, what now Matthew?'

'What now?'

'Yes, what now? What happens next? You sound like the one with the dating experience. Where do we go from here?'

'Well, I suppose we should meet up,' I said.

'That's hardly the most enthusiastic approach, Matthew. A girl likes to feel wanted.'

'Oh...I didn't mean it like that. Sorry. Would you like to meet for a drink Estelle?' I asked lamely, in response to her obvious prompt.

'Yes, I'd like that Matthew.'

We fixed a date for Saturday.

It was cold and wet on the night of the date. The rain had begun in the early afternoon and was steadily getting heavier. I opened the wardrobe door to get my jacket. In the corner stood PC Penny's blue umbrella. The thought occurred to me to call her. I had an excuse at least. Maybe we could meet for a coffee or a drink on the pretence that I was returning the brolly. I was a mix of confusion and indecisiveness. She had been in my consciousness almost all the time since that Christmas meeting. Like unfinished business. I couldn't quite bring myself to consider whether that business was professional, personal or both. Whatever it was, I felt like I would really like to see her again. To share another moment like that one again, just the two of us. On the other hand, I carried my guilty secret and to get rid of it would surely destroy any chance of recapturing a shared moment. There was my dilemma. And I knew I had made it worse the longer it went on. Now it seemed impossible to change. If only I had come clean earlier when it actually didn't really amount to much. I pulled on my jacket and tried to dismiss the thought of PC Louise Penny.

I hadn't really wanted this date to be in a place I knew, but it was simpler to arrange a meeting somewhere I was familiar with rather than spend ages thinking of alternatives. The familiar was easier to control and it took away one more element of the unknown in arranging a date for the first time. So I had suggested MacFadden's and although Estelle had said she didn't know it, we agreed to meet there. If the date went well I fully intended to get out of MacFadden's at the earliest possible point in the evening and move on somewhere more discreet.

Peering through my front window at the driving rain I realised I would need a cab. A number of calls proved futile. Everyone wanted a cab on a wet Saturday night. There was none available. Except one. Real Libel Car Services. It appears I was destined to cross paths with them time and again and have few other alternatives. The lights of the car signalled its arrival. As it pulled up outside I made a frantic dash towards it, trying to avoid the rain, and jumped into the front passenger seat. The blast of warm air had hit me as soon as I had opened the door but now that we had been travelling for a few minutes the heat inside the cab was becoming unbearable. The driver was dressed as if he had just tried on all the clothes in Next and had walked straight out of the changing room without paying. A huge grey duffel coat enveloped him, topped off with a chunky woollen scarf and a beanie hat. I had no idea what else he had underneath but the bulk of his top half seemed completely disproportionate to the two stick like legs that emerged from underneath his coat. The noise coming from the car heater completely drowned out the engine, the hot air unbearable but he seemed oblivious to it.

'Are you not warm in here,' I asked, loosening my jacket. The question did seem slightly unnecessary given the amount of clothes he was wearing.

'It's cold outside boss,' was his reply, which did not really answer my question directly.

'I know it is,' I said, 'but we are inside and there is no air in here.'

'No, boss, there is air bags. Look.'

He pointed at a sticker on the dashboard that said 'Air Bag.'

'No...I mean...oxygen,' I said a little louder in case his misunderstanding was something to do with the noise coming from the heater. I was sweating profusely.

'Oxygen? You need oxygen boss? You sick? I take you to hospital. You have a fever?'

Maybe I would need a hospital if the temperature went any higher.

'No. I don't need a hospital. Nor oxygen. Just some fresh air. You know, air...air that is outside. It's far too hot in here. How do you open this window,' I asked.

I had been surreptitiously attempting to open the passenger window by pressing on a button in the door console, but with no luck.

'It doesn't open, boss. It's stuck.'

Stuck. To be honest I wasn't at all surprised it was stuck. The window frame had probably welded itself onto the glass such was the temperature inside the vehicle. Most of the glass on my side of the cab had totally steamed up in any case.

'You want hospital boss?' the driver asked again.

'No. No. I am fine. I don't want a hospital. I am just hot because there is no oxy...no air in this car.'

Gripping my jacket cuff in my hand, I wiped the condensation clear from the passenger window with the sleeve. I was taking no chances with Real Libel. I needed to see that we were going to where I intended to go. The driver's sudden fixation on hospital was beginning to worry me. Every now and then he glanced over at me as if checking on my condition.

'You look sick boss. You very hot, sweaty. I think you have a fever. My brother, he is a doctor, so I know this.'

'Excuse me. Your brother is a doctor and you think that makes you medically qualified to diagnose me as sick? Really? Don't you think that, perhaps, if your doctor brother was here right now, he might just consider, that because it is hotter than Venus in this car, a simple solution might be to let some air in, something I can't do because all your goddam windows are stuck, and my sickness would be miraculously cured?'

The heat had made me tetchy.

'You getting delirious boss. That is a sign. A sign of fever. Maybe I should take you to the hospital straight away.'

'No. I don't want a bloody hospital. Just get me into town.' I turned and stared from the window and sat as still as I could.

No doubt the cab driver had decided that he did not want to end up with what he considered a sick passenger on board because he put his foot down and I arrived at MacFadden's earlier than expected. Before I went in, I stood outside in an adjacent shop doorway in order to cool down and in the hope that my body might return to its normal temperature before Estelle showed up. It took all of ten minutes before I felt comfortable enough to walk into the bar.

'Hanka Janka' was polishing wine glasses, holding them up to the light to inspect her handiwork and then carefully placing them on a shelf behind her. She smiled at me as I walked in. The bar was half-empty, a typical post New Year Saturday, with the regulars all partied out. By now I was getting used to the anticipation of what in effect was a blind date. The expectation and anticipation was a little easier to deal with but I still felt the butterflies.

Estelle came in right on time. There was no mistaking her. The black hair, dark eyeliner and heavy glasses were very distinct, an exact real life replica of her site portrait. Her lips tinged in a dark ruby colour, with the rest of her makeup, created a striking and dramatic look. She wore a white jumper, jeans and a black coat, drops of rainwater glistening on its shoulders. It crossed my mind that it must be difficult for a woman to choose the right look for a first date. Estelle's was very individual but she seemed to have it right. I noticed she wore no jewellery whatsoever and thought that it was unusual for a woman but I didn't dwell on it. She held out her hand, the nails painted with the same ruby hue as her mouth.

'Matthew. I am Estelle. Pleased to meet you. You look just like I'd imagined.'

I hoped that was a compliment. I didn't ask. I took her smile as a positive reaction. The smile softened her features, which seemed a little austere because of the vampish image she presented. Nevertheless, I actually quite liked the look.

'Nice to meet you Estelle. You look exactly like your picture,' I replied, instantly regretting the comment and wishing I could say something original and unique.

I felt a little nervy but hoped nothing could go wrong on a simple date that involved no more than a drink in a bar. I bought some wine and we sat at a table by the front window. The initial awkwardness of unfamiliarity began to recede as the wine took effect.

Estelle had seemed a little tense at first, understandably, as this was a blind date for her but as she relaxed, she was very easy to talk to. The topic of conversation at that stage was the dating site and what we were looking for. She asked if I had had many dates and about my experiences on the site as she had done in our call. I told her that I'd had no luck on the site and that was why I had left it. I didn't tell her about my many mishaps. It was too soon and I didn't want her to think I was a liability. I raised the bottle offering her more wine. She finished her glass and held it out for a refill. The conversation had focussed a little too much on me and I wanted to find out more about her. As I poured the wine I asked her what she looked for in a man. Her brow furrowed. I wasn't sure if it was because she was surprised that I had asked a meaningful question at last or whether she was giving it her considered thought.

'It's very simple, Matthew,' she said at last, 'what all women want in a man. Honesty, integrity and trust. The rest all comes from that.'

She looked at me intently for a moment, her black eyes unnerving me, the stare exaggerated by the overpowering spectacles.

'Do you have that...Matthew?'

I considered the question. There was only one answer.

'Well I –'

A vivid flash of light illuminated the room, followed immediately by a deafening thunderclap that shook the ceiling above us. For a moment we both sat unmoving, shocked by the sudden power of the storm outside. I opened my mouth to speak first but noticed the strange look in Estelle's eyes as she stared directly at me. If she had a phobia about thunderstorms I wanted to reassure her.

'Are you ok?' I asked.

She stood up.

'I am just going to freshen up. I won't be a moment,' she said, her voice wavering as she walked away towards the lavatories.

If she had a phobia, I was happy to give her time to compose herself.

As I waited for Estelle to return, I sipped my wine and watched the rain running down the outside of the window. It reminded me of Louise Penny and her umbrella. I thought of the last time I was in MacFadden's Bar. How we had sat outside on that cold evening. The hammering click of the rainwater against the glass was saying something to me. A sign that I should contact her. I wanted to see her again and I wanted to open up to her. I had nothing to lose. The rain hammered out its message. I opened my mobile and thumbed in a text.

'*Hi Louise. Hope you are well. I was just thinking that I should get your umbrella back to you. Maybe we could meet for a coffee or a quick drink. It would be nice to chat too. Let me know. Happy New Year. Michael.'* I pressed the send button.

The rain battered the window in waves, blown hard against it by the wind. I picked up my glass and was about to take a sip when I was stopped by the sight of Louise walking towards me. My thought processes came in random patterns. How weird is that? I text her and she walks in. How come she keeps pitching up whenever I go out anywhere? Why is she is not soaking wet when I have her umbrella? Why is she carrying a black dog? And why is she wearing an identical outfit to Estelle?

Where is Estelle?

Louise walked right up to where I was sitting.

'Louise. What are you doing here? I just text–'

I didn't get the sentence finished. She threw the '*black dog*' onto the table. My thoughts, like some overloaded computer programme, suddenly went into a whirl of information assembly, piecing together the bits of data into an unwanted realisation of the facts that were now staring me in the face.

'So, Matthew, you didn't answer my question. Honesty, integrity and trust. Do you have those qualities?'

I stared dumbly at the black wig splayed out on the table. I felt my stomach churn, my hands tense, my face flush and the sweat begin to trickle on my forehead as the grim reality dawned on me. I knew what I wanted to say but the words would not form into a sentence that would have any meaningful effect. Louise continued.

'You just had to be straight with me Michael...Matthew or whoever you are. You've deceived me. As a person. Forget that I am a bloody police officer. You deceived me. And I actually quite liked you. You seemed like a really nice guy. There is no Michael, is there? Just like there is no Estelle. You left me no choice but to investigate you.'

I looked up. She glared at me, her face a mix of anger and questions.

'Investigate me?' was all I could say.

'Yes...go through this charade. Finding you on the dating site. I had my suspicions but I actually didn't want them to be right, Mr Matthew Malarkey.'

'I am so sorry Louise. You don't understand. I got myself in a mess with all the trouble that I was getting into,' I said.

'I am not even worried about all the mayhem you seem to have caused, Michael...Matthew. No, that can be dealt with. What really upsets me is that you have deceived me. That you didn't feel like you could trust me.'

'I was going to tell you –'

She cut me off. 'Going to tell me! Going to tell me? When? You have had plenty of opportunities Matthew. When I first came to your house to find your imaginary lodger. That was a good time. In fact a very good time. It would have kept it simpler too. I saw the bum bag that day. You know that? I did wonder about that.'

'The bum bag?'

'Yes, the bum bag. It was you in that stupid gorilla suit, wasn't it? Wearing a bum bag that coincidently was identical to the one in your house. You even introduced yourself as Matthew that night we stopped you. I couldn't quite figure out what the connection was at first but I believed you when you said Matthew Malarkey was your lodger. You should have been straight with me.'

I noticed a tiny tear in her eye as she said it again. My stomach churned. This was not what I wanted for Louise.

'Look Louise, I was worried, that's all, about the police misunderstanding, about what had happened at that point. That woman said that all her guests had been mugged. And the damage and that. I'd never been in trouble with the police. I just made a mistake. Then the whole thing escalated. I didn't expect to see you again. I mean socially. When I met you that night in MacFadden's I was totally shocked to see you. And I made a bad decision that has backfired on me. I was going to tell you everything. Look, I can prove it. Check your mobile. I sent you a text asking to meet.'

'A text? When? I haven't received a text,' she said.

'I sent it about five minutes ago when you...well, Estelle was in the ladies.'

'You mean you were on a date with another woman and thought you'd text me. I can't believe you men.'

'Hang on Louise. The other woman, Estelle, was you,' I said.

As I finished the sentence she placed both hands flat on the table, palms down, and leaned towards me. I noticed the smear of ruby lipstick across the back of her right hand.

'But you didn't know that Michael...Matthew, did you? You were even deceiving Estelle. You were duping me twice. You think you can just go around playing with women's affections? Bastard.'

'Look, Louise, slow down. Whoa. I didn't know it was you, no. But I like you. And I wanted to contact you. To contact Louise, I mean. I wanted to get it all off my chest. That's why I texted you. I've been thinking about it. It's not my fault that you disguised yourself and pretended to be someone else–'

'Don't go there Michael...Matthew. Don't start twisting things. It's you that's the master of disguise and double dealing.'

'Wait a minute. This is getting out of hand,' I said, trying to hide my inner exasperation. I was acutely aware of what I had done but didn't want an argument to make things worse. 'Let's step back a minute, Louise.'

She took a large gulp of the wine that was still in the glass in front of her, screwed up her eyes at the impact and then drained the glass.

'I want some more,' she said beckoning at Hanka Janka.

Another bottle was duly presented. As Louise's glass was refilled, I started my story.

'Louise. I really, really like you. I–'

'Well you have a bloody funny way of showing it,' she interrupted.

'Louise. Listen. Let me speak for a moment. I like you. I loved the time we sat outside here at Christmas. I loved staying at your house and waking up and seeing you the next day. The smell of your perfume on my jacket. I even like having your umbrella in my house.'

I saw a flicker of sadness in her eyes. She took another sip of wine, this time a smaller one.

'Each time we ran into one another I was pleased to see you. I know I didn't show it. I had a feeling you might even like me too. I thought we had a bit of a connection. You remember when you came here with your brother? That's when I could see something in your eyes. I hoped it was something more than just friendliness. I know I behaved oddly but it was only because I'd gotten myself into a mess with you and I was frightened that if you found out, it would ruin any chance of...well, any chance of something happening between us.'

'Well you've completely screwed up any chance of that now. And anyway, I might have to have you arrested,' she said.

'Arrested? What for?' I was flabbergasted.

Louise placed her wine glass on the table and sat back in the chair.

'Yes, arrested.'

I detected a slight slurring in her voice.

'Arrested because I am part of an investigation into a criminal damage complaint at a stately home which so happens to involve you, doesn't it?'

There was no point in denying it.

'Yes Louise...it does. But I can explain –'

'Oh, you will have to explain, Matthew. But not necessarily to me. You are going to have to hand yourself over to the police.'

She made it sound very dramatic.

'Hand myself over. I'm not a criminal. What do you mean?'

'I mean you are going to have to go to the police station and tell them who you are and make a statement.'

'Well can't I just tell you Louise? Make a statement to you. You are the police.'

'No you can't Michael...bloody hell...Matthew. I am involved now. I know you personally. There would be a conflict of interest. I can't touch it.'

'If you say so Louise...but what's going to happen?'

'I don't know Matthew. It depends what you have done.' She paused for a moment, looking directly into my eyes, waiting for the impact of her remark to hit home.

I sat there in silence not sure quite what I had done, it was all so confused in my head. My lack of a response allowed Louise to continue.

'I knew I'd seen those eyes of yours before Matthew. In that stupid gorilla suit.' She looked away, picking up her glass. 'And one of the muggers at the house in Regents Park where the mugging complaint was made was dressed as a bloody gorilla.'

She seemed to be thinking aloud now rather than talking directly to me. I let her continue.

'There were too many co-incidences, Mich...Matthew. Your name cropped up in connection with those two incidents where two separate witnesses had arranged meetings with you. Both of them women from the dating site that you were on. Then there was the time you bought me a coffee in MacFadden's. You remember, that first time we bumped into each other alone? You paid for the drinks with your debit card. I couldn't make out the name on it exactly but I couldn't help but notice that the surname seemed to begin with an 'M'. Makes sense now. It said Malarkey, didn't it?'

I nodded.

'And then your car was stopped by a patrol car when you were allegedly out of the country. The same one that was on your drive. The data was recorded by the traffic unit. I picked it up in a routine search. It just didn't add up. I then discovered your name cropped up again when an employee reported an alleged mugging at a restaurant in Surrey, not long after I had made the official second visit to your house looking for the elusive Mr Malarkey.'

She reached out, picked up the wine bottle and poured herself a top up. The wine gurgled into her glass as she spoke.

'You remember that Matthew? You told me you thought that your so-called lodger was away again. Every time you said he was abroad on business there seemed to be a sighting of him very much in the country. I was beginning to suspect something was wrong and in fact it did cross my mind to ask you for proper ID.'

She placed the bottle back on the table without offering me any and picked up her glass.

'But I didn't ask you for your ID Matthew. No, stupidly, I wanted to believe that you could not be involved, that you would not be deceiving me. I trusted you. You seemed such a nice a guy and I wanted you to stay that way. So I didn't pursue it. And then when the name Matthew Malarkey came up as having been involved in that mugging incident it confused me even more. The thing is the mugging was reported as having taken place in a restaurant that coincidentally I was in that very same night. You remember...when I was with my brother and I saw you later that evening. And when it came up it threw me. I thought that if it had actually been Michael, in the restaurant at that time I would have seen you and recognised you. So, perhaps it really was Matthew Malarkey and my concerns about Michael were just my imagination. So I let it go—'

'I am so sorry Louise,' I said, not knowing what else I could say.

Guilt was creeping over me, growing more intense as I listened to Louise and saw the emotion in her face. I felt battered. I helped myself to another glass of wine to dull the remorse that was building up alongside my guilt.

'Sorry is all very well now, Matthew, but you deceived me. It's funny, when

I heard about the mugging thing I thought back to when I'd seen you with your cut face and limp and my suspicions arose again. But I kept coming back to the fact that if you had been in the restaurant I would have seen you there. It was only a small place after all. I kept finding ways to deny my fears. The employee's description was sketchy at best, although he said you were with a woman. I did wonder why no official complaint had been followed up and it just lay on the file. And then, as if that wasn't enough, I discovered from computer records that now you are involved in an arson incident in Brighton with yet another woman you were dating.'

'Arson? That's ridiculous. It was an accident Louise,' I protested.

'So you don't deny it then?'

'Well of course I don't deny it. I gave a full statement to the Brighton police. I had nothing to hide. But that was an accident. And as for those other incidents, first of all it was Cecil who damaged the woman's chandelier In Regent's Park, not me and that was a total accident too and–'

Louise put her drink down. 'Cecil? He's never mentioned it.'

'Well of course he hasn't. He doesn't think there is anything to worry about. It was me that was worried. I put two and two together after your trigger happy colleagues stopped me on my way to the cocktail party when I'd heard that Julia...err... that's the lady I was supposed to be meeting...had reported it as a mugging. I panicked. I thought the police would actually assume we were muggers and...well, I don't know. I just thought the whole thing would die a death if I left it.'

'Why were you dressed as a gorilla to go to a cocktail party anyway?' Louise asked, a look of curiosity on her face.

I finished the wine in my glass and poured another. So much for an alcohol free start to the New Year.

'It's a long story Louise.' My deep sigh as I said it perhaps indicated to Louise that I wasn't ready to talk about the details right now.

'So what happened at that stately home,' she asked instead.

That was another long story, I thought, but I owed her some explanation particularly as that was the most serious thing hanging over my head. So, I told her everything. About the date. About how I'd tried to avoid 'Sexyblueeyes.' About hiding in the suit of armour. About not taking responsibility. For good measure I finally threw in the gorilla story too.

By the time I had finished my account Louise's features had softened. It may have been partly due to the wine but more so because she seemed genuinely amused by the stupidity of my actions. But I sensed a slight change. Then the frown and stern eyes returned.

'But Matthew, why did you go to the lengths of calling me and pretending to be yourself, if you see what I mean. You remember...you called me when I left a message with Michael to get your so-called friend to ring me. Why did you not just come clean at that point? Why did you not just trust me?'

'I don't know Louise. I was caught up in my own predicament then. It had started to get too complicated to backtrack and I figured that if I called you up and told you what I knew you...I mean, the police...you would be satisfied.'

The frown on Louise's forehead intensified.

'You even lied to me at Christmas. When we sat outside together and I mentioned your so-called lodger. You could have been honest with me then. It was just the two of us on a personal level. You know something, I liked that evening. I didn't care that we were sitting out in the cold. I was just enjoying the moment together. Enjoying your company. Just the two of us.' She paused for a moment, her eyes moist with emotion. 'You gave me your jacket, Matthew. It was so romantic. And now it has been soured by your deceit.'

The word deceit cut through me, sharp as a blade.

'It wasn't like that Louise. I didn't intend to deceive you. I just didn't want to spoil the moment. I knew that if I said anything then it would just have ruined the whole night. I suppose I stupidly thought it would all go away in the end and the police would just put it down to another unsolved matter.'

'We don't give up that easily, Matthew. You know, I checked the CCTV at Hemmingwell Halls but it wasn't conclusive. Lord Hemmingwell really needs to update his system. He only had one camera for his whole priceless collection, can you believe. And that was pointing at a fire exit. All we had was the back of everyone's head as they left. But we knew you had been there to meet your date from the site as you'd paid with your card. I was curious about the dating connection, which is why I went on the site as Estelle. And it seemed a better option for me than just asking you outright to ID yourself. There was always a chance with the dating site that I was mistaken. I hoped I was anyway. Then I found your profile but you had removed your picture so I couldn't make a positive identification. And that is why I had to arrange this meeting.'

The realisation that Louise was only here on official business suddenly hit me. I liked being with her no matter what the circumstances and I felt a huge disappointment that this was to end now she had concluded her research.

'So, all that stuff on your profile, all that stuff you said to me about looking for love was just your under cover persona Estelle, talking? It was just to trap me.'

She sat upright and lent towards me, her eyes flashing anger.

'Hold on a minute Matthew, don't start getting all hard done by on me now. Trap you? You were the one who had the dual persona remember. You are the cause of all this double-dealing. But as a matter of fact, for what it's worth, and I don't suppose you care too much, what I said and what I put on my profile was genuine. It was me speaking from the heart. I decided that if I was going to do this dating site thing properly I could only do it if I was totally honest and genuine about how I feel about life and love. Which is more than you have been.'

She slammed her glass down hard, propelling several splashes of its contents high into the air and across the table. In a reflex action I sat back abruptly to avoid the liquid spilling over my trousers. My sudden movement caused my chair to tip backwards. I rolled to my left to prevent myself going flat on my back and ended up in a heap on the floor.

Louise stood, calmly picked up the black wig and marched out.

33

On Sunday morning I walked into my local police station and asked to see a police officer. I had thought about it all night, lying awake mulling over my options. There weren't many. Eventually I would be tracked down and have to face up to my responsibilities. And if I ever wanted to build some bridges with Louise it was a no brainer although I couldn't see a way now where there was any chance for me with her. Too much had happened. I'd lost her trust and her professional involvement with the enquiry meant she would have to keep her distance from me in any case. But if I got it sorted, it would be a burden off my back and I would have done the right thing. Maybe at the very least Louise would see that.

'I am the Duty Officer,' responded a man behind the desk who was writing something in a large ledger. I was surprised to see he was a civilian as I had fully expected to see a uniformed police officer.

'How can I help you,' he asked without raising his head but briefly staring over the top of his spectacles.'

'I am giving myself up,' I found myself saying before I had had time to form a sensible sentence.

The man looked up from his writing, looking everywhere except directly at me.

'Giving yourself up? Who are you? Jesse James?'

'No. I am Matthew Malarkey,' I said. His flippant response had thrown me a bit.

'Well Matthew Malarkey, what can I do for you?'

I'd half expected my name to cause a reaction and a subsequent flurry of activity but clearly it had not. I was neither Public Enemy No.1 nor had I hit the '*Most Wanted*' list. The man returned to his writing.

'Well...err...I believe the police wanted to speak to me in connection with an investigation. So, I am here to...well...to speak to them,' I said feeling a little put out that all my worrying to date had been pointless as this particular official did not seem too bothered.

'What investigation is that?' he asked.

'It's to do with an incident at Hemmingwell Halls,' I said, 'Oh, and maybe one other thing...a robbery...well not a robbery, a mugging. Not that I have done any mugging. I mean, someone I know thinks they were mugged and made a complaint and–'

'You sound a little confused sir. Have you been drinking?' He asked.

'Of course I haven't been drinking. It's nine thirty in the morning,' I said feeling a little exasperated at how difficult it was becoming to confess to anything.

'You'd be surprised how many drunks we get in here at that time of the morning Mr Malarkey.'

'Well, that's as maybe but I am not one of them. Now can I see a police officer, please?'

'I am the Duty Officer Sir. I deal with enquiries,' he said, raising his head and looking directly at me for the first time.

'I am not enquiring though. I am giving myself...I mean handing myself...I am here to talk to the police about the incident and the robbery...mugging thing.'

'Oh yes. The mugging. You said someone you know thinks they have been mugged. So why are they not here reporting it themselves?'

'They have reported it. I am here because I was involved in it. Not that it was a mugging. It was a misunderstanding.'

'A misunderstanding? Someone was mugged and misunderstood it?'

'No. No one was mugged –'

'Let me get this straight. You want to report your involvement in a mugging where no one was actually mugged? You do know you can be charged with wasting police time Mr Malarkey.'

It occurred to me that this particular police official should be the one charged - with wasting civilian time.

'Look, may I suggest that perhaps if I give you my full details you could look up the record and then things will become clearer.'

I wasn't convinced that he would take up my suggestion given his apathetic attitude up to that point, but to my surprise he asked me to take a seat and went off to the back office. Ten minutes later he returned with a uniformed officer who was carrying a bulky green document wallet stuffed with papers. He opened a door at the side of the front desk and beckoned me through. Once through he asked me to confirm my name and then led me along a brightly lit corridor to another room. The room contained nothing more than a table and two chairs positioned on either side of it. On one side, there was an adjoining door. I was invited to take a seat and the officer sat down on the other one. He then asked me to explain why I had come into the station. My mind was in overdrive, thoughts flitting through it like random post-it-notes. I began to question why exactly I had come into the police station but I realised I had to go through with it. I told him that I had come voluntarily to the station, as I understood that the police wished to question me concerning a specific incident. I then told him of my connection to the occurrence at Hemmingwell Halls. For good measure, I told him about my connection to the reported incident at Regents Park. As I spoke, the officer referred to papers in the green folder. When I had finished he simply said I was being detained for questioning.

'Detained? Detained for questioning? Why?' I asked.

'Criminal damage, Mr Malarkey,' the police officer replied. 'We have received a formal complaint from Lord Rufus Hemmingwell regarding an incident at his premises at Hemmingwell Halls on the afternoon of Tuesday 18th November. Your account of your connection with this incident supports the information we have on file and therefore I am arresting you on suspicion of the wilful destruction of property belonging to Lord Rufus Hemmingwell at the aforementioned premises.'

Arrested. The word hit me hard. I thought back to my last meeting with Louise. '*I am going to have to have you arrested,*' she had said but I'd thought she was just being dramatic. I hadn't actually expected to be arrested. I felt the sweat form on my brow. The solitary light bulb seemed to glow more brightly. My sight started to blur to such an extent that the police officer almost disappeared from view.

I heard him speak to me again and it snapped me away from the edge of panic.

'You do not have to say anything. But it may harm your defence if you do not mention when questioned something which you later rely on in court. Anything you do say may be given in evidence.'

I said nothing mainly because I was too shocked to speak at the thought of this going to court. My gut reaction was to blurt out that it was all an accident.

The police officer saw the shock register on my face.

'You are entitled to legal representation Mr Malarkey. Do you have a solicitor or would you like to see the duty solicitor,' he said.

I thought of Diana. I recalled what she had said as I was leaving France – '*If you ever need anything just let me know.*' I couldn't call her. It was too embarrassing. And anyway, it had all been an accident. I wouldn't need a solicitor. Once I'd answered a few questions they'd realise that and let me go. After all I had come into the station voluntarily.

'No. I will be fine,' I said.

'Are you sure, Mr Malarkey? Most people take advantage of legal advice. It is free.'

'No, I am fine,' I repeated.

He scribbled some notes on a piece of paper, made a brief internal call and then beckoned to me to follow him. I stood up unsteadily the impact of my situation now weighing on me. The police officer led me along another corridor to yet another room. A sign on the door said 'Custody Suite'. Inside the room another officer appeared to be awaiting my arrival and announced himself as the Custody Officer. After an exchange between the two police officers about my arrest, I was left in his company. During the next hour I began to feel like a proper criminal. I was photographed, fingerprinted and had a swab inserted into my mouth to take a DNA sample. Finally, I was taken to an interview room where I met Detective Constable James Maloney.

DC Maloney looked intimidating. I couldn't determine how tall he was as he was already sitting at a table that had two seats on each side of it. But he had shoulders almost as wide as the table. The seams of his jacket looked as if they were struggling to keep the sleeves connected and the buttons on his white shirt appeared to be under the same duress. A close-cropped haircut, that was more marine than police officer, added to the image. A jug of water and four upturned glasses were positioned on the table. What looked like recording equipment was positioned to DC Maloney's right hand side.

'Mr Malarkey, take a seat,' he said with a hint of a Scottish accent. 'I have a few questions I need to ask you in connection with the incident that you have admitted involvement with at Hemmingwell Halls. For your information I will be recording this interview.' He pressed a button on the machine. 'Now, I understand you have declined legal advice at this stage. Is that correct?'

'It is,' I answered.

'Is there anyone else that you would like to notify about your arrest,' he asked.

I thought of Cecil but then dismissed the idea. 'No,' I said.

'Perhaps, then, you would like to start by telling me, in your own words, what exactly happened.'

Possibly it was the stress of the situation that was affecting my thought processes but I wondered why he had said 'in your own words' since I was the only other person in the room. I could hardly give my account in someone else's words, I thought.

I took a deep breath and tried to focus. During the next fifteen or so minutes I recounted, as best as I could, the events leading up to and at Hemmingwell Halls. When I'd finished I raised the matter of the so-called mugging in Regent's Park.

'I'd like to mention the fact that my name has been associated with an incident in Regents Park as well. There was a complaint about a robbery or a mugging. It's just that I knew the lady who owned the property and –'

'Oh, aye, that. Yes, we have that on the file too. And you are right, your name did crop up in that complaint. But let's get one thing straight Mr Malarkey,' said DC Maloney, 'we are not interested in that fiasco. It turns out nobody was robbed at all. The complainant totally overreacted. Some bloody idiot in a giraffe suit smashed into her lights or something. And there was some other nutter in a bloody monkey suit. Can you believe it? What sort of jokers wander round London dressed like that. Bloody animal activists if you ask me. It's just a domestic insurance job. Waste of police time. What do you know about it anyway?'

A sudden sense of optimism overcame me. One down and just one to go provided I wasn't stitched up for burning Sue's house down in Brighton. It didn't bother me that in DC Maloney's estimation I was a 'nutter' although I made a mental note not to tell Cecil he had referred to him as a 'bloody idiot.'

'Oh, nothing much,' I said, 'as I say, I just knew the lady who owns the house. Yeah, she can over react a little at times. Women, eh?'

DC Maloney turned a page in his file.

'Ok, let's move on then. It seems to me that this little lot is fairly straightforward then. We have a complaint of criminal damage from Lord Hemmingwell and you have admitted responsibility for it. Are you admitting the charge?' He looked up at me for a response.

'No, I am not admitting responsibility for criminal damage. It was an accident. I didn't do anything deliberately,' I said, feeling the recent bout of optimism drain completely away.

'Well, that will be for a court of law to sort out Mr Malarkey. So, according to your account you admit to getting inside one of the exhibits, a suit of armour, which, because of your presence inside it, subsequently fell over setting off a chain reaction that caused several other exhibits, also suits of armour, to fall over too resulting in various degrees of damage to the property. That sounds fairly deliberate?'

'Well...yes, I did get inside one of the exhibits but I didn't intend for it to fall over,' I said.

'So tell me again, why did you get inside the armour?'

'As I said before I was meeting someone at the exhibition. She was from a dating website, and in the end I decided not to go through with it so I was simply avoiding a date.' It sounded stupid as I said it.

'Avoiding a date? Why?' He looked bemused.

'It was a date that I didn't want to be on. I couldn't get out of it so I stupidly hid inside the armour. I thought I could hide there until she had gone.'

DC Maloney pulled a blue handkerchief from his pocket and raised it up to cover his nose and mouth practically obscuring his face. I heard a loud throaty, spluttering sound and a sharp intake of breath, followed by two short coughs as if he was clearing his throat. When he lowered the handkerchief his eyes were watering.

'Excuse me, Mr Malarkey I...I suffer from...from hay fever,' he said.

Hay fever. It was the beginning of January. We were in what appeared to be a basement room and there wasn't a plant in sight.

'I'm sorry. Shall we continue,' he said. 'You say you were avoiding a date. I presume you mean the website woman?'

A bit of an unnecessary question I thought. I hardly meant the fruit.

'Yes. She wasn't what I expected and I didn't have the heart to tell her so I hid –'

The handkerchief went straight to his face again, the same guttural, gasping sound resonating from behind it. When he lowered it for the second time, I noticed that his face had now taken on a crimson hue. He wiped his eyes and reached for one of the glasses. Turning it over, he filled it from the water jug and took a long slurp.

'I am sorry Mr Malarkey. It's bad today...the hay fever. You were saying.'

'Err...yes, I hid inside the suit of armour to avoid her–'

I paused, mid-sentence. DC Maloney's face, in addition to being crimson, had now seemed to tighten, almost as if he was clenching his lower jaw very tightly and was holding his breath. His lips had puckered into a tight point and seemed to be quivering. I noticed that his eyes had started to bulge as well. I carried on.

'And then she called my mobile phone and without thinking I went to grab it which caused the whole lot to topple–'

I thought at first that DC Maloney had experienced a convulsion. In one rapid, reflex movement he grabbed the handkerchief, spun his chair to one side and lurched forward so that his head was practically in his lap. He had almost disappeared completely from my view but the sound of air spurting involuntarily through his nose and mouth followed by an intense bout of snorting and coughing told me that he was still very much in the room. He stayed like that for a full minute. I was completely at a loss what to do. I thought of leaving the room and raising the alarm but it occurred to me that it might look like I had attacked DC Maloney and had run away. I was spared my dilemma when he sat upright and started to sneeze. Except it didn't sound like normal sneezing, more as if he was pretending to sneeze. I dismissed the thought.

'I am so sorry Mr Malarkey. I may be going down with something,' he said.

Looking at his now completely red appearance it looked like the 'something' he was going down with was scarlet fever.

'I think we have enough for now. I will be back shortly.'

He stood up and left the room.

It was at least twenty minutes before he returned, looking more composed, his colour having returned to normal. He handed me what he said was a charge sheet containing details of the offence and informed me that I was being released on bail pending further police enquiries.

34

As soon as I left the police station, I called Louise. Her phone went straight to voice mail. I didn't leave a message. I wanted to speak to her. Back at home I tried again. Same result. I waited ten minutes and tried again. Voicemail again. I called Cecil. At least he answered.

'How are you doing Cecil,' I said in as calm a voice as I could muster.

Cecil, as usual, was straight to the point. 'Geezer, I was beginning to think I had better start advertising for some new mates. Where the fuck you been?'

I went on the defensive. 'Nowhere Cecil. What do you mean?'

'What do I mean? Mate, you know what I'm talking about. I called you several times to go out for New Year and you're not picking up your phone. So, what's going on ?'

There was a note of accusation in his voice.

I sat down in an armchair. I had a feeling this might be a long call.

'There's nothing going on Ces. I just didn't fancy it, that's all.'

'Oh right. I get it mate. You fuck off skiing with the fancy lawyer bird, right, and next thing you know you're dancing to her tune. No pass outs for you to see your buddies. Get yourself a bird in tow and you ain't going out again. I'm telling you mate, there are geezers in prison who can get out easier than some blokes once a bird has got hold of them.'

Cecil seemed to overlook the fact that he was seeing Sheryl but in his mind the same rules didn't apply to him.

'Look, I'm not seeing the lawyer bird...Diana, I mean. I told you. It's not happening Cecil. Anyway, listen, that's not why I called you. I'll tell you all that when I see you, ok?'

'So, what did you call me for?'

'I've been to the police–'

'The Old Bill? What for?'

I explained the whole thing to Cecil including the fact that I'd mentioned the incident in Regents Park, the bit that might concern him.

'Mate, you are a fucking nobhead,' he said, 'Fuck knows why I hang about with you. I told you that fucking hysterical woman would see sense in the end and her chandelier would be insured. Didn't I? I told you to leave well alone. And you had to go to the Old Bill. Now you're gonna unleash untold pain. Nobhead!'

'Cecil. That wasn't why I went. The police wanted to speak to me. And Louise was involved and –'

'I get it mate. You've got a thing for Louise. It's all clear now. Yeah, Sheryl was right. Yeah mate, she said she could tell something was going on there with you, the way you were looking at Louise and all that. But, mate, you didn't have to go walking in to the Old Bill and bend over and start taking it up the –'

'Hang on Cecil,' I interrupted, 'listen, they wanted to speak to me. Right. Sooner or later they would have put two and two together. I mean, for starters they've been round my house. Well, Louise had anyway. She was on the case. I had no choice. And then with the bloody Brighton thing, setting fire to that house and getting stopped in my car it was only a matter of time. I had to get it sorted. Anyway, there's no come back to you, is there?'

'Alright geezer. Keep your hair on. I know that. I ain't worried about that. It's just you making such a fucking palaver over it. You should've just told Louise the whole lot in the first place. She'd have sorted it. I mean if you're gonna know a bird who's a copper, you might as well get something out of it. The Old Bill bend the rules for their buddies, don't you worry about that mate.'

I needed a drink all of a sudden. I couldn't believe what Cecil had just said. All along he had told me to relax about it. No big deal. It would blow over. I didn't have the energy to argue the point with him. It was a typical Cecil situation. Adapt to suit the circumstances. I poured myself a large glass of Merlot and changed the subject.

'So, Cecil, has Sheryl said anything?' I asked.

'About what?'

'Well, about Louise. You know, about what you said...about what Louise thinks about me?'

'You have got the hots for her haven't you mate,' he laughed.

'I think she's nice Cecil. Yeah...I like her. But I've blown it big style now.'

'How d'you mean, geezer?' he asked.

I hesitated. I couldn't face the ridicule so I decided to keep it simple and leave out the bit about 'Estelle' at this stage.

'She knows Ces. She knows that I am not Michael. She knows who I am and that I was involved in the stuff she was looking into.'

'So, what's the mumble now mate?' Cecil asked.

'Well, let's say she was not impressed. I haven't heard from her since. So...

has Sheryl said anything? I mean she must talk to you seeing as how you are shagging her, Cecil. And seeing as how she's Louise's mate. And they are girls. And girls talk. She must have said something?'

'Yeah...she did...she said Louise likes you...yeah, I told you that before, but she thinks there is something odd about you and I reckon she's got a point. You do act like some sort of total twat when you see her.'

I poured some more Merlot and sat back down in the armchair.

'I know that Ces. But it was just the mess I was in. I didn't know how to sort it once it got complicated. You know...all that stupid 'Michael' thing and the fact she's old bill. Don't suppose I can sort it now. She doesn't trust me anymore.'

'Mate, you know what birds are like. You need to be a warrior. A Trojan warrior geezer. Call her up and tell her straight. Tell her you fancy her big style. Lay it on thick. They love all that. And as for all that other crap, just tell her to build a bridge and get over it.'

It wasn't the most helpful solution Cecil had ever come up with and I couldn't see that approach working after the way Louise had walked out on me the last time I'd seen her. The fact that she wasn't taking my calls was ominous.

Monday morning was cold. Too cold to be going back to work after the Christmas break but that really wasn't a great excuse to stay in bed. Outside it was still dark, a typical early January morning. I stood under the glow of a streetlight and stared at the frost on the windows of my car, my breath spiralling into a pale column in front of me as it hit the cold air. I pulled the collar of my overcoat tight against my neck with one hand and began the task of scraping the windscreen with the other. The frost was hard caked, long threads of ice creating sparkling patterns on the glass. The scraper was making little impression as it scratched across the ice. I jumped into the driver's seat and started the engine hoping the heater would soften the frost and waited.

My mobile buzzed. Pulling off a glove, I pressed the key pad, eager to see the message. It was a voicemail.

'Hi Matthew. It's Amanda. Happy New Year. Just wondered if you fancied meeting up soon. Perhaps I could take you out for a meal this time. Maybe even finish it, as well! Let me know.'

Amanda. The nervous passenger. I was irritated at her message. It wasn't her fault but the one message I wanted I wasn't getting. Nothing from Louise at all. As I sat waiting for the frost to clear, exhaust fumes trailing into the cold air, I typed out a text.

'Hi Amanda. Just got your message. Thanks for the invite. Can't really make it at the moment. I'm not eating. I think my fear of food has got worse. Will be in touch.'

Over the next few days, I called Louise's number but each time it went straight to voicemail. I still wanted to speak to her in person especially after the way the last meeting had ended but now I began to realise that continuous calling could start to be a nuisance. It was clear that she did not want anything more to do with me and I would have to accept that. I decided to make one final call and if it went straight to voicemail again I'd leave a message. As I half expected, the answer phone kicked in again and I stuttered out a message.

'Hi Louise...errr...I've been trying to call you...just to explain myself. I realise you don't want to speak to me and I accept that now. I completely understand. I don't suppose I'd want to speak to me either given what I have done...but I...errr...I just felt really bad that we left on bad terms the other night, you know...and I just wanted to tell you that I have now been to see the police to sort everything out. A bit late I suppose...but I realised it had to be done. It looks like I will have to appear in court and –.'

To my annoyance the voicemail cut out.

At work the week dragged by and I was soon into my normal routine. There was still no contact from Louise. I had resigned myself to the fact that I had lost her trust and that the situation was now irretrievable. I decided that I would just focus on getting whatever was in store for me with the police out of the way and move on.

It was just over three weeks later that I received the notification. It was waiting for me when I arrived home from work on the Friday evening. Lord Hemmingwell had filed a civil complaint for damages, the full extent of his grievance listed in court papers. To my horror, he was seeking £35,000 in damages for five individual items in his armour collection. In the space of a few weeks, I had lost any chance of a relationship with Diana, blown any hope of anything at all with Louise, was on the verge of getting a criminal record and now faced a damages case that would cost me an absolute fortune.

I sank into a chair, the court correspondence crumpled in my hand, and contemplated this disheartening new turn of events. It was all coming to a head. Since he now knew my identity following my appearance at the police station, Lord Hemmingwell was after my blood for the damage to his property. The gravity of my predicament began to focus me on the fact that I had done nothing to prepare for any court appearance.

First thing on Friday morning I rang Diana's office.

'Twist, Swivell and Spinn, good morning,' said the efficient female voice on the other end of the telephone.

'Good morning. Could I speak to Diana Twist please,' I asked.

'I'm sorry she is in court this morning. Can I put you through to one of the partners?'

Court. The very word made me nervous.

'No thank you,' I said, 'I would rather speak to Diana Twist. Could I leave a message for her please?' I left my details, my office number and my mobile.

At three in the afternoon I got the call from Diana.

'Matthew. Lovely to hear from you. Have you recovered from your skiing ordeal?'

I got to the point quickly and explained my predicament with the police and the prospect of being sued for damages by Lord Hemmingwell. When I had finished I waited on her verdict. Diana, as usual, sounded calm and cool.

'Well, you are a dark horse, Matthew. You have been a bit of an adventurer. All those broken hearted ladies left in your wake.'

'No, it wasn't like that Diana. It was just a set of stupid mistakes. Bad decisions and now I will have to appear in court. Look, you said I should give you a call if I needed anything. I hate to bother you with this but I just wondered if you could recommend someone that could represent me. A good solicitor, someone—'

'I'll do it.'

I didn't respond.

'I will represent you Matthew,' she said again.

I hadn't expected her response. I had gone to Diana in the hope that with her contacts, she could recommend a firm of solicitors, which would spare me the task of trawling through the internet looking for someone myself. I didn't want to impose upon her or to involve her in the case at all.

'Are you sure,' I asked, 'I wasn't expecting you to take up my cause, Diana.'

'Why ever not Matthew? I am a lawyer. That's what I do.'

'Well, that's great. I appreciate your offer.'

I genuinely felt grateful to her. At least I had someone in my corner that I could trust.

'Excellent. Now, can you come along to my office in London on...let's see... Thursday afternoon, around two? We will need to go through the details and see where we go from there. Oh, and by the way, Matthew, there will be no fee. I don't charge my friends.'

'No fee? I am happy to pay,' I said.

'I wouldn't hear of it Matthew. That's what friends are for.'

As I ended the call I couldn't help but smile at the ironic twist to my dating site experience. I had been looking for love but had found a friend.

35

My meeting with Diana was reassuring. She started by explaining the whole legal process to me. Lord Hemmingwell was seeking damages in a private civil case. The criminal damages case was a different matter. If the police felt they had enough evidence to prosecute, they would take the criminal damage complaint to the Crown Prosecution Service where it would be decided whether to proceed with a case. In the first instance, we would need to deal with the Lord Hemmingwell's private damages claim as he had already filed the complaint at court. There would be a number of processes to go through first, including a raft of court papers, but Diana promised to ease me through them all. I would need to be available to respond to written questions and requests for documents, and several other legal matters that would assist the lawyers with their presentations.

I spent the rest of the afternoon going through every detail with Diana. So many times I had wanted to spend time in her company and now it seemed I had her fully at my disposal for all the wrong reasons. But I was glad she was on my side. Her professionalism and unruffled manner, even when I relayed the most extreme acts of my folly, were encouraging. I resolved to be open about everything and answered all of her questions fully and honestly despite my discomfort at having to reveal all.

At precisely five-thirty I left the offices of Twist Swivell & Spinn feeling a lot more optimistic than when I had arrived and walked across the street into a newsagent. An afternoon of intense discussion had left me with a thirst. I fancied a coke. Nothing stronger, just something refreshing and sweet. Perhaps it was sugar I needed as a comforter. I pulled open the glass-fronted cold cabinet, grabbed a can and made my way to the counter. I should not have been surprised but I was. The co-incidences were happening too often. Standing at the counter clutching a bottle of water was

Louise Penny. I felt the usual wave of unease but this time for a different reason. My misdemeanours had been exposed the last time I had seen her and now I had no alter ego to hide behind. She hadn't seen me. I plucked up the courage to speak.

'Hi Louise. What are you doing here,' I said.

She wheeled around, dropping her police hat in surprise at seeing me. In a spontaneous reaction we both bent to retrieve it, almost clashing heads in the process. I got to it first and handed it to her.

'Mich...Matthew. What are you doing here,' she said, brushing imaginary dust from the top of her hat.

'I asked you first.'

'I've been in court all day in the Strand. I am on my way back to the station to write up a report. I just stopped to get a drink.'

That word again – court.

'Talking of court did you get my message?' I asked.

She looked slightly uneasy.

'Yes, I did. Thank you for letting me know. Obviously I was aware that you had come in to the station.' Her eyes suddenly focussed directly on mine, her gaze intense, yet sad at the same time. 'Look Matthew...you know I couldn't reply. I can't get involved. I–.'

I cut her short not wanting the conversation to go where I suspected she was taking it.

'Louise, listen, why don't we go for a coffee when you've finished work. We could chat there rather than here in this shop?'

'I can't Matthew,' she said, 'that's what I am trying to say. Although I am no longer on the case I can't be associated with you while this is going on. I was part of the investigating team originally but I had to declare that I knew you once I discovered who you were. I can't take the risk. Maybe when it's over.'

She looked away into the distance as if staring at the rows of magazines that lined the shop walls.

'If I'm not in jail,' I said.

She looked back at me again, smiling now.

'I don't think you'll be going to jail, Matthew. You are hardly Public Enemy No.1. You came in voluntarily to the station and told the truth. That is good. You faced up to your responsibilities. They will take that into consideration. By the way, I did get that text you sent when you were on the date with *Estelle*. I did appreciate it, after I'd calmed down.'

A gentle chuckle confirmed that she was indeed calm about it now.

'I realised that you did want to tell me the truth eventually. Anyway, I have to go Michael...I mean Matthew. Bloody hell...it takes some getting used to, a sudden name change.'

The corners of her mouth turned downwards briefly and she shook her head as if trying to rid herself of my former identity.

'As I say, I have to go now. I have a colleague waiting in the car round the corner. You take care. Let me know how it goes. Bye,'

She turned abruptly and walked out into the street. I followed her, watching her purposeful stride, her head held high with not a backward glance. Frustrated, I cracked the ring pull on the coke can and took a swig. The cold, sparkling bubbles had barely gone down when an idea began to take shape in my mind. I slung the can at the newsagent litterbin, unperturbed as it caught the side, bounced off the metal frame and rolled across the pavement, its contents dribbling into the gutter.

'Louise! Louise! Wait,' I shouted after her.

She turned as she heard her name the second time. I ran the few yards that separated us until I was standing in front of her.

'Louise, I know you can't meet me. I understand that. But I would like to see you. I don't want to wait until this case is over. It could be ages yet. I don't even have a date for the court yet and –'

'No, Matthew, I told you I can't see you.' She turned to walk away.

I grabbed her by the arm.

'Louise listen…listen to me. Please. How about I meet with Estelle?'

'Estelle?' She looked astonished.

'Yes, Estelle. No one need know. It would be perfect. And after all the alter ego stuff we...well, I mean I...that I have had, it somehow seems fitting in a strange sort of way, if you see what I mean.'

I had no idea what was going through her mind. I waited for an answer. None came. She tilted her head to one side, staring up at me, eyes wide with curiosity, lips tightly pressed together. Without a word she turned away and began to walk off. A few strides later, she stopped and turned to face me, a smile breaking her earlier stern expression.

'By the way, Matthew…I suggest that you pick that can up before I have you nicked for littering.'

Two nights later I was sitting at home after a quiet Sunday when my landline rang.

'Hello Matthew. It's Estelle.'

'Estelle?' It took me a moment to react. 'Oh, Estelle. Yes...hello. How are you?' I tried to contain the grin on my face.

'I am very well thank you. And you?'

'I'm great. I wasn't expecting to hear from you,' I said, still surprised at the call.

'Well sometimes you have to have a little spontaneity, don't you think Matthew?' The mischief was back in her voice.

'Yes, I agree Loui...err, Estelle. Of course,' I said.

'Ok. Good. Do you know what day it is next Saturday, Matthew?'

'What day it is? Err...Saturday I suppose,' I said, a little confused by the question.

'No, silly. It's Valentine's Day,' she said, placing particular emphasis on the last two words.

I hardly knew what day of the week it was with all the upheaval I had experienced and I hadn't given Valentine's Day a thought. I suppose I should have noticed the shop displays, which would have given me a clue. But I was pre-occupied with other things. My total failure on the dating site, total failure with Diana and complete cock up with Louise had not helped me focus on romance at all, so it was hardly surprising Valentine's Day was not on my radar. Whatever my personal turmoil, I knew that my response had to be right.

'Valentine's Day. Of course it is, Estelle. I was hoping to invite a lady friend out for the evening but she seems to be rejecting me, casting me aside and on such a romantic occasion too.'

'Lady friend?' she said, a note of surprise in her voice.

'Yes. A lady friend. Her name is Louise and she is keeping me at arm's length.'

I heard the laughter on the other end of the phone.

'Ok. Ok Matthew. Now be serious for a moment and you may just find that perhaps your Valentine's Night may not be in vain after all.'

I shut up.

'Look, Cecil has invited Sheryl out to Fad's for the evening. Apparently Carlos is throwing a bit of a Valentine's bash. I talked to Sheryl and she is more than happy for 'Estelle' to join her. So, why don't you call Cecil and arrange to meet him too. That way you will have the best of both worlds.'

I was taken aback but if I could see Louise I didn't mind how we did it. I had not been out for a while and Cecil and I had hardly been in touch in the last few weeks. I was totally out of the loop socially since Christmas and didn't even know that there was a do at MacFadden's.

'It's a deal Lou...Estelle. I'll call Cecil tomorrow.'

'Ok, Matthew. But not a word about 'Estelle' to Cecil. I am taking a risk here so it has to remain secret. Ok?'

'Ok. But what about Sheryl?' I asked.

'Oh she knows everything. We are girls. We talk.'

36

Once again, Carlos had pushed the boat out. Red balloons in the shape of hearts decorated the bar area. The walls were festooned with real roses. On each table, a bowl had been placed in the centre filled with of Love Heart sweets. At the back of the bar, vividly coloured posters promoted a Valentine's night special, something called a Love Bomb cocktail. Hanka and Janka were for some reason dressed as French damsels, in sexy little black skirts, fishnet stockings, red berets and red shoes. They did look good. I guessed it was some sort of *'Paris, the city of romance'*, theme that Carlos was trying to achieve. I was just pleased he hadn't gone the full way and asked them to wear strings of garlic round their necks. Carlos himself was dressed in a tuxedo with a white tie.

I'd called Cecil the night before to find out what he was doing on Saturday. It was then that he had told me that he was going to MacFadden's. What he had actually said was 'I'm on bird duties tomorrow mate. Apparently it's Valentine's Night.' He mentioned that Carlos was doing a theme night and that he was meeting Sheryl. 'She's coming down with a friend so you never know geezer you might get a look in,' he'd added.

I didn't tell him what I already knew.

'Hola, Mateo,' Carlos said at the top of his voice as I approached the bar. 'How are you? Long time no see. Here, have some champagne.' He handed me a glass filled with the bubbly stuff. 'The first one is on the house, for everybody. It is a night for romance.'

'Cheers, Carlos. How are you doing? Any romance in the air for you then?'

He walked round the bar and pulled up a stool. 'Plenty, amigo. Since you introduced me to that little firecracker, Abigail, it's Valentine's Day every day for me,' he said, winking and sipping his champagne.

I'd forgotten about Abigail. The less said the better from my point of view but I wondered if Carlos had discovered her spider phobia yet.

'Is she coming tonight, Carlos,' I asked.

'Of course. I cannae work all night and not see her on Valentine's Night,' he answered.

Cecil's arrival interrupted the conversation.

'Geezer, how you doing?'

Before I could answer Cecil had me in a bear hug, both arms around me clasping me tight to him.

'Long time no see mate.'

It was classic Cecil. Despite his bravado and self-proclaimed 'warrior' persona he was an emotional man who protected his feelings with the image he had created. Only those of us who knew him well, and there weren't many, saw the other side of him.

'I'm good Ces,' I said when he'd let go of me, 'you're looking well.'

'Yeah, I'm all right mate.'

He shook Carlos by the hand. Carlos offered the complimentary glass of Champagne.

'Geezer, it's me you're dealing with. Give us a bottle of your good stuff. I got two birdies coming down here in a minute and I ain't standing here like a mug with a glass of your cheap shit.'

Although he didn't seem to take offence, Carlos still mouthed a protest.

'It's not cheap shit Cecil, it's –'

'Course it's cheap shit Carlos. You wouldn't be giving it away if it wasn't.'

We were on our second glass of champagne when the two girls walked in. Both dressed to kill, Louise in a black all in one dress with matching black open toed shoes and Sheryl in tight white jeans that showed off her figure to its full extent. I caught Louise's eyes for a moment but she quickly averted her gaze. She was totally back in the 'Estelle' character, the black wig, glasses, heavy eye make-up and ruby lipstick all in place. Sheryl greeted Cecil and then began the introductions.

'Cecil, this is my friend Estelle. Estelle, Cecil.'

Estelle kissed Cecil on either cheek. Sheryl turned to me.

'And this is…,' she hesitated for effect, 'Matthew,' and winked at me.

I let the thought pass about what Sheryl may think now that she was aware of my true identity and focussed on Estelle. She greeted me as she had done Cecil, a kiss on either cheek, the scent of her Coco Chanel reminding me of the smell left on my jacket at Christmas. We made our way to a table close to the bar and on the edge of the dance area, and sat down. Cecil was poised with the champagne bottle. Both Sheryl and Estelle declined, opting instead for the Love Bomb cocktail.

'I'll get it,' I offered and went back to the bar.

'Two Love Bombs, Hanka please.'

'I'm Janka,' she replied, a brief flash of irritation clouding her features as she turning away to get the ingredients.

I was about to apologise for my error when felt a tap on my shoulder.

'Hello Matthew, fancy seeing you here.'

Her face registered but I couldn't recall her name. She noticed my hesitancy.

'It's Linda. Remember?'

She stretched her arms out to the side, palms up, her knee slightly bent in a semi curtsy, a gesture of openness that was supposed to aid my recognition.

'Linda...from the dating site. We went for lunch together, oh, ages ago now.'

All of a sudden I did remember. The superstitious one that had caused all the commotion in the restaurant.

'Oh, yes, of course how are you Linda?' I said taking a step back as she picked up her glass.

'I'm fine, Matthew. And you? Are you still on the site? I'd love to have met up with you again but you never got in touch.'

'No...no...err...my dad wasn't too well. Taken to hospital...he was...so I gave up the site.'

I had no idea why I was making excuses to Linda. Perhaps I just didn't like upsetting people.

'Oh dear, what with your mother too. Is she ok now?'

'My mother?' I was frantically trying to recall what I'd said about my mother. 'Yes, she is. It was just...' My eye caught the specials board behind the bar where the dish of the day was chicken casserole. '...chicken pox.'

'Chicken pox? When we were having lunch you said she'd fallen down the stairs. She fell down the stairs and got chicken pox?'

'Yes. I mean...no...she fell down the stairs, yes.... and then...afterwards got chicken pox. Bit unfortunate really.'

'And then your dad was taken to hospital. Did he have chicken pox too?' Linda asked.

'No. He's fine now. He had a virus. Caught it from a...from a....,' Linda stared at me expectantly. I didn't need to say anything really but there was something about her stare that compelled me to come up with something. My sub-conscious must have fixed on her superstitious nature. '...a...black cat.'

'Sorry, Matthew, your dad caught a virus from a black cat?'

'Yes. Well, you know what they say about them being unlucky and all that. Very unlucky in this case. Anyway Linda what brings you here.' I had to change the subject.

'I'm meeting a date from Cupid's Pursuit. Very fitting for Valentine's Night, don't you think? He's a detective I believe. I am quite excited.'

Janka placed two tall glasses of pink liquid and crushed ice on the bar. Each one topped with a strawberry.

'What's in those?' Linda asked.

'Vodka, apple juice and pomegranate,' Janka answered, 'it's a Love Bomb cocktail.'

I picked up the two glasses and was about to head back to the table when Linda turned towards me, placing a hand on my arm.

'Oh, I'll have one of those too then, Matthew,' she said.

I nodded to Janka and paid for three.

'Catch you later, Linda. Good luck…err…with the date. Not that you will need luck. Just a…turn of phrase. No need to worry on that front, eh?'

I got back to the table and Cecil was by himself. The girls had gone to freshen up. He poured the champagne.

'Cheers mate. Good to see you,' he said.

'So what's with the champagne Cecil? No beers tonight?'

'You gotta push the boat out sometimes and impress these birds, geezer. It's like, you know, as you get a bit older you gotta stay in shape, drop a few pounds if you're gonna compete. We're up against younger geezers now.'

Cecil somehow made the dating game sound like a title fight.

'So you serious about Sheryl then?'

He hesitated, sipped his champagne, placed it back on the table and turned to look at me.

'Yeah, mate, between you and me I do like her. She don't give me no grief, she's cool, don't make a mountain out of a fucking molehill like some women. If I go out and party she's not giving me all that where you bin, stuff, you know?'

Cecil's reply was quite revealing. He'd actually taken the trouble to answer my question seriously. Instinctively I knew he felt more for Sheryl than he was letting on.

'So what are you going to do when she goes back to Canada, Ces?' I asked knowing that he would have thought about it.

'Who knows mate. I might just take off there myself. Nothing keeping me here, is there? Anyway, what do you think of her mate Estelle? Bit of alright, eh?'

'She's nice. Good looking girl,' I said casually.

'Yeah she is. But remember, you ain't gonna stand a chance if you start acting like a twat, splurting your drink all over her and groping her tits like you did the copper. Just be cool tonight.'

'I didn't grope Louise, Cecil. I was just cleaning down her top. I–'

I stopped explaining myself. Cecil was shaking his head, a grin splitting his face.

Sheryl and Estelle returned to the table. The champagne and cocktails flowed, the mood chilled and relaxed. Estelle seemed at ease with me. She began to ask questions of Cecil as if she didn't know anything about him and clearly seemed to be enjoying the role-play. For his part Cecil seemed none the wiser. For the first time in weeks, I felt at ease myself.

It was around ten o'clock when I caught sight of him. He was standing leaning on the bar with Linda, tie loosened and dangling at a skew-whiff angle, a whiskey glass in one hand. Detective Constable Maloney. Not only was I surprised to see him but also I was surprised to see he was wearing a kilt. I'd remembered he was Scottish but it seemed an odd thing to wear on a Valentine's date. I turned to Estelle.

'You'll never believe this Louise,' I whispered, 'that big guy at the bar talking to that blonde woman, he's the copper who interviewed me.'

She looked towards the bar in the direction I'd indicated.

'Do you know him?' I asked, 'If it's awkward we can get out of here.'

'No, I've never seen him before. He looks pissed if you ask me. It's cool. He'd never recognise me anyway dressed like this even if we had run into each other before. And, Matthew, don't call me Louise. I am Estelle tonight. Ok?'

I nodded. I couldn't believe the way things kept turning out for me. Of all the places to run into him, a copper who had interviewed me and who was seeing a date I'd been out with. It was weird. He must have been on, or joined the same dating site. I hoped he would have better luck than I did with Linda.

It was another half an hour before I made DC Maloney's acquaintance again on a personal level. The girls were on the dance floor together and I needed the gents. Standing at the urinal I heard the door open behind me. I didn't take any notice. There were just two urinals side by side. It was only when a figure came up and stood next to me at the adjacent urinal that I did what guys do in those circumstances. I took a surreptitious look to my left to see who was next to me. It must be instinct. Self-preservation. It's a vulnerable moment standing at a urinal with your dick in your hand. You need to be aware of your personal space and your opportunity for flight, should you need to get out quick. My covert glance turned, by no voluntary action on my part, into a sudden longer stare. What caused it was the fact that the guy next to me was fumbling under a kilt and before I could look away, he had the front of the kilt up by his waist and had positioned himself for action. The enduring question about a Scotsman and his kilt was suddenly answered for me. No pants. He caught me looking.

'What you looking at?' he said, menacingly.

'Nothing. Nothing sorry. I was –'

'Hey. I know you, don't I?'

I quickly looked down into the urinal.

'Yeah...that's it. You're that guy that likes dressing up.'

I thought that was a bit rich from a guy in a kilt but kept quiet.

'Yeah...I nicked you for something didn't I? Yeah, you're that dating guy I don't forget a face'

His words were slurred and because he wasn't concentrating he started to spray against the wall rather than the urinal. I stepped back quickly, having finished, and walked to the sink to wash my hands.

All I could think of to say was, 'How's your hay fever?'

He turned, looking over one shoulder at me.

'You taking the piss?' he asked rather inappropriately since he had now left a damp patch on the paintwork between the two urinals.

I apologised and made for the exit taking advantage of the fact that he was still in mid stream. He emerged from the gents a couple of minutes later with what appeared to be the remnants of a splash back situation down the right side of his kilt. In such circumstances, I would have been inclined to melt into the darkness of the bar. Instead, he decided it was a good idea to display his lack of dancing skills in the middle of the dance floor whilst waving in Linda's direction to come and join him. Linda was standing by the bar looking decidedly worried and I fully expected her to start throwing the salt around to bring about a change of fortune. Fortunately, there was none at hand.

Anyone observing DC Maloney's moves from the sidelines would have been hard pushed to confirm that it was dancing he was attempting, such was the uncontrolled swaying motion he was exhibiting. And his uncoordinated gyrating was bringing him perilously close to crashing into Sheryl and Estelle. Only their nimble movements prevented it. I looked across at Cecil who was on his feet trying to attract the girls' attention to get them off the dance floor. Having caught sight of his gesturing they both turned to go towards him when it happened. DC Maloney snaked out a hand and grabbed Sheryl's bum. She spun around in surprise. Cecil was across the floor in two strides. His right hand was one Tyson would have been proud of. It caught the big Scotsman flush on the jaw and he went down like Trevor Berbick, his legs having turned to jelly, their support function severed from the brain by the punch.

A commotion duly erupted. A mix of screams and shouts competed with the music. The only movement from DC Maloney that indicated he was still with us was an involuntary roll onto his back. For a moment, Cecil stood over him, like Ali over Liston. I grabbed Cecil by the arm and got between him and the stricken detective.

'You've just decked a copper, Cecil. You got to get out of here before he comes to his senses,' I shouted.

'Copper? He's a fucking mug,' was Cecil's response.

DC Maloney groaned as his senses began to flicker to light again. He shuffled his feet, dragging them towards his body so that his knees were bent and his soles flat on the floor. The unfortunate result of this was that anyone south of him had the perfect view straight up his kilt. With a deft flick of my left foot I kicked at his heels so that his legs fell flat to the floor again. I didn't want him waking up and becoming aware of his lack of decorum on top of the embarrassment at being felled in public.

Carlos was suddenly next to us, Abigail right behind him.

'Get him out the back way, Mateo. Follow me,' he said

I pulled the reluctant Cecil by the arm in the direction Carlos and Abigail were taking, waving at Sheryl and Estelle to follow. We bustled our way through a narrow corridor in single file, almost tripping on one another's heels in our haste. As we made our way towards a green door at the far end of the corridor, Abigail suddenly turned towards me.

'This is so exciting Matt...I mean, Michael. I never, ever thought I'd be involved in your undercover work.'

Cecil's right hook had effectively ended the evening. Sheryl took him home in a taxi. I saw Louise home in a cab too. As we neared the end of the road, she said what I really didn't want to hear.

'Look, Matthew. You know I can't risk being seen with you now. Not even as Estelle. There will be fallout from this. That guy is going to want answers. He's not going to let someone assault him and let them get away with it. It's all getting a bit too close to home now. It won't take long for him to identify Cecil and those he was with tonight. I just can't be associated with you while you are awaiting your day in court.'

The taxi pulled to a halt outside Louise's place, its diesel engine's metallic hum breaking the stillness of the night as the driver waited for Louise to get out.

'It's lucky I had my disguise you know, Matthew. At least I won't be identified. But it was lovely to see you tonight. I'm glad I came.'

She leaned forward, kissed me gently on the lips, and disappeared into her home.

The following morning I drove over to Cecil's. He didn't seem too surprised to see me. His right hand was showing signs of discolouration where it had connected with bone. We sat and talked over a cup of tea. I explained all about DC James Maloney.

'Well he can't do me for assaulting a copper, can he?' Cecil said. 'I didn't know he was Old Bill, did I? I lamped him because he was touching up my bird's arse. Fucking mug.'

'I know that Ces' I said, 'but he's going to be back asking questions. I suggest you keep out of Fad's for a while.'

I stood up and drained my tea. 'Look, I'm going down to see Carlos now, just to see what's going on, see if anything's happened. Ok? I'll call you. Oh, and Ces. If you need a good lawyer, I know one.'

MacFadden's was open for lunchtime business by the time I arrived. Carlos was behind the bar, cradling an espresso. He poured me a filter coffee.

'I'm sorry about all that commotion last night, Carlos. You saw what happened didn't you?'

'Yes, I saw the big guy grabbing Sheryl's bahookie. Mind, I don't blame him. It looked a treat in them wee white jeans. I'd have skelped it myself if I got the chance.'

It wasn't exactly what I wanted to hear but the important thing was Carlos had witnessed what amounted to an assault on Sheryl.

'What else did you see, Carlos?' I asked.

'And then Cecil battered him,' was his response.

'Well, I wouldn't go that far, Carlos. It was just a single punch.'

'That's what I said, Mateo. He battered him. One shot and he took him out.'

I could see Carlos needed a bit of guidance.

'Carlos, listen mate. It's more complicated than you think. You remember I told you that I might be the subject of a police enquiry? Well the bloke that Cecil decked is the copper who is conducting the investigation. The one that interviewed me.'

At first there was no response as Carlos took in the significance of what I had just told him. Picking up his coffee, he rubbed his furrowed brow with one hand and muttered something under his breath, 'Usted está realmente en la mierda ahora, mi amigo.'

'What's that Carlos? What? What did you say?'

'Nothing Mateo. I was just thinking. You are really in the mierda now…in the shit.'

Carlos had succinctly summed up exactly what I was thinking. Whatever language it came out in, he was right. At that point, I was in the shit. Somehow I had to minimise the damage but I wasn't sure how that could be done. If DC Maloney got his teeth into Cecil, it wouldn't be long before he connected him with me and he would be even more determined to pursue me for the criminal damage issue.

I spent the next ten minutes explaining my predicament to Carlos. When I had finished talking he pulled the whiskey bottle off the shelf.

'A drink Matthew, you look like you could do with one.'

'No, no Carlos. I have to keep a clear head. I have to get this sorted.' I pushed my coffee cup towards him and asked for a refill. 'Look Carlos, if the police come asking questions you have to make sure they know that Cecil was only defending the lady. Ok, got it?'

Carlos nodded.

'It's quite important, otherwise they are going to be after Cecil for assault and then it is all going to go pear shaped.'

'And if he realises you are a friend of Cecil's he will think you had him attacked because he is investigating you,' Carlos added.

'Let's not go there Carlos, you make me sound like a hit man. I'm worried enough already without you making it sound worse. It's simple. If the police come make sure they know you saw the big guy grab hold of Sheryl. If you can hold them off it will give me time to think. OK?'

'Leave it to me, Mateo. I won't let anybody down.'

I finished my coffee and stood up to leave.

'By the way, what was Abigail on about last night? About undercover work?' I asked.

Carlos laughed. 'She still thinks you and Cecil are undercover detectives.

You know from that night when you gave her to me. You said you were working undercover as Michael. I let her think it still. That stuff excites her. And when she is excited I get the benefit. Comprendo?'

I didn't have to wait long for events to unfold. On Monday afternoon I got a call from Carlos to say the police had been, in the shape of DC James Maloney. I felt a moment's trepidation as I waited for him to give me the news.

'So what happened, Carlos?' I said.

'He was mad Mateo, but don't worry, I used my charm on a fellow Scot,' Carlos replied.

I wasn't completely sure that DC Maloney was the type to be so easily charmed.

'I am sure you did Carlos but what did he say.'

'He wanted to know who had hit him. He said he was going to press charges for assault on a police officer. I sat him down with a coffee and a few wee drams for the sake of hospitality, you know.'

Coffee and whiskey. All sorted then. Why did I not think to suggest that? My mind was pulsating.

'What are you on, Carlos? So instead of buying us some time you started socialising...with a bloke who is after my nuts ?'

'Calm down Mateo and listen. After you left yesterday, I got to thinking. Sometime you have to take el toro by los cuernos and I–'

'Hang on Carlos. You have to do what?'

'The bull by the horns, Mateo. Go on the offensive, you know...attack. Anyway, listen to me. Mr Maloney asked me if I had seen what happened. I told him I saw it all. But I told him that I had also seen him grab the lassie's wee bahookie and I said that she wanted to report a sexual assault to the police. You should have seen his face. He didn't remember that bit. He'd had a bit too much to drink that night.'

'He didn't remember? Are you sure he wasn't still concussed?' I asked.

'No but he remembered when I told him about it. It all came back pronto. I told him that if he wanted to pursue it I was happy to give a statement to the police about the whole incident but that, if I did, I'd have to tell them everything. I said it was all on CCTV too. I told him the fight was on the camera but so too was him grabbing Sheryl's culito. And if he wanted to take it further he would be...how is it Cecil says...opening a whole world of pain.'

I was stunned at Carlos's audacity.

'But you don't have CCTV, Carlos,' I said, slightly incredulous that he would have stuck his neck out like that.

'No, I know. But you have to read a man. He has pride. He cannot lose face with his men. Maybe having a sexual assault charge brought against you is career threatening but getting decked with one punch is even worse. I gave him a get out. He won't face the shame.'

My incredulity turned to admiration. Whatever way Carlos saw DC Maloney's dilemma the bull had been taken firmly by the 'cuernos' and it sounded like they had been well and truly blunted.

Carlos interrupted my thoughts. 'Oh and one more thing Mateo. While I had Mr Maloney on the ropes I took the liberty of bringing up the investigation he has with you.'

'You did what, Carlos? Are you mental? I am in enough shit already without anyone meddling in that. You'll get done for perverting the course of justice or whatever the bloody hell it is, if you start trying to influence anything.'

'Hey, Mateo, I wouldn't do you a bad turn. I didn't meddle. I just said that the lady he groped was the girlfriend of your best mate. He remembered seeing you in here and I think it's rattled him a bit. He might have behaved like a yobbo but he's smart enough to realise that you know what he did. And now you have something on him. I don't know for sure what he will do but if I was him I'd back off.'

I was gobsmacked. Carlos had totally fixed Cecil's immediate problem and it looked like he had sewn the seed of doubt in DC Maloney's head as far as my criminal investigation went as well. I began to wonder if I should ask him to deal with Lord Hemmingwell's civil action too.

37

I received my court appearance notification at the end of the week. March 17th, at 10am. Relieved to have a date at last, having been through a minefield of paperwork in preparation, I looked forward to getting it over with, whatever the outcome. I called Diana's office. She already knew. I sent a text to Louise but received no reply. It looked like that was the way it had to be and I had a good three and a half weeks to wait before I could hope for any change.

As I arrived at the courthouse in the rain, I felt the nerves begin to increase. It was a large, imposing building. I'd never been in a courthouse before and its sombre aura only served to focus me on the seriousness of my situation. There was an airport-style security scanner to pass through at the entrance. I fumbled in my pockets to find my keys and loose coins and placed them in the tray provided. I was asked to remove my watch too. The whole process was just adding to the tension building up inside me. Once inside I reported to the court usher in the waiting area and took a seat.

The waiting area was long and narrow, rows of seats against one wall, the wall opposite covered in a blizzard of white paper notices. Browsing the notices, I came across my own case on the Court List. *Distinct Judge Lucinda Manningford, Hemmingwell v Malarkey, Court 3*. Every seat was occupied, lots of anxious faces, some with their advisors deep in conversation. The sound of chatter filled the room, each conversation blending into the other so that nothing was clearly discernible.

I stared at my fellow *villains*, wondering what they were all here for. Some were dressed casually as if on a day out shopping, sipping from cans of Red Bull presumably to stimulate their mental capabilities for the rigours of court. Others had made an effort to dress for the occasion, their badly matching ties and shirts clear signs that they were not used to formal events. At the far end of the room, there was a door with a glass window in its centre. A brass plate designated it as a 'Consultation Room.' It was occupied.

People had started to make their way in now in greater numbers. I scanned the faces as they entered in the off chance that I would see Louise. I had hoped she might show up but given her silence of the past few weeks I wasn't optimistic. As the clock on the wall opposite clicked away the minutes, taking me closer to my hour of reckoning, I began to feel my nerves kick in. Standing up to walk around and release the tension developing in my body, I happened to glance through the glass in the Consultation Room door. I got the shock of my life. I knew that face. I knew it only too well. It was etched deeply in my sub-conscious. Sexyblueeyes. Sally. The thirty-eight going on sixty year old in the yellow jacket from the dating site. The very reason I had myself in this mess in the first place. And she was wearing that same jacket. The jacket that I had first seen in her on-line picture, the one that was quite possibly over twenty years old. She sat deep in conversation with a dark haired man in a pin-striped business suit. I assumed he was a solicitor since that was what the consultation room was for. Legal consultation. What was she doing here? Obviously, she had to be connected to my case unless she was the cause of some other poor sap's downfall as well. A witness. That was it. She must be a witness. Witnesses? I had no witnesses. I was on my own. Lord Hemmingwell had witnesses.

I stood alone trying to get a grip on my thoughts and waited for Diana. She came in clutching a folder full of papers under her right arm with a briefcase dangling from the same hand. In the other hand she held an umbrella that she'd clearly just been using. Drops of water were dripping from the folds of the partially shut canopy onto the floor. I watched as she signed in at the usher's desk. Spots of rain peppered the sleeves of a beige raincoat that was open at the front to reveal a dark two-piece business suit. Her shoes were black leather with pointed toes and the usual killer heels. Her make-up impeccably applied. It crossed my mind that if I was a judge I'd just let her win every case, no questions asked. She placed the pen back on the desk and scanned the room. It took her just a moment to pick me out in the crowd, the recognition bringing a warm smile to her face as she approached.

'Good morning Matthew. Foul weather–' She hesitated mid-sentence. 'Are you ok? You look like you have just seen a ghost.'

'No. Worse than that, Diana. I've just seen Sexyblueeyes–'

'I beg your pardon, Matthew. Who has sexy blue eyes?' Diana laughed.

'No. Nobody. From the site. It's Sally. That was her username. The lady I was trying to avoid at Hemmingwell Halls. The one I was supposed to date. I think she's a witness and she can only be here to tell her side of the story, which won't be too helpful for me. I haven't got any witnesses on my side,' I said.

'Relax, Matthew. Yes, she will be a witness. But you don't need any witnesses,' Diana said placing her manicured hand on my shoulder.

'I don't?'

'No. Look. We know you climbed inside one of the armour displays. You are admitting that. It doesn't need a witness to support your side of the story. Once inside you were concealed and any witness who might try to corroborate what you say happened inside the display cannot vouch for you. So you don't need a witness. The lady from the site, Sexy Sally–'

'Sexyblueeyes…Sally,' I interrupted.

'Well whatever she is called,' Diana continued, 'Sally cannot place your whereabouts either since she did not know you were in hiding. So she can only be here to verify that she was intending to meet you, which can only support the fact that you were on the premises, which we know anyway by your own declaration and your card payment for your admission ticket. I will be arguing that any damage that occurred was purely accidental, for reasons that will become apparent. So don't worry about witnesses.'

Diana's presence was reassuring. She looked calm, a woman who had seen it all before, assured and composed in her natural working environment. But I was confused. I was sure she made sense but my head wasn't in the frame of mind to think logically.

At five minutes to ten o'clock we were called to court.

'Hemmingwell versus Malarkey. Court three,' the usher announced.

I took my place on a seat at the front of the room. The wood felt cold and for a brief moment I felt a shiver of isolation. On the facing wall, a giant Royal Coat of Arms had pride of place, its gold lion and silver unicorn guarding the crown and shield. Below, a long desk on a raised platform fronted the main court area, stretching from wall to wall, with three chairs placed at its centre.

A tall, authoritative looking man with a shock of silver hair and heavyset eyebrows walked towards the front benches. His upright gait and brisk purposeful stride lent him a military bearing. I assumed that he was Lord Rufus Hemmingwell. His glare across at me confirmed to me that he was indeed my antagonist. Flanked by two court officials he took his seat.

At precisely ten o'clock Judge Manningford entered, heralded by the call from the court usher to 'all rise.' She walked slowly but confidently towards a seat on the raised bench at the far end of the courtroom. A middle-aged woman with her face set in a stern scowl already, her grey, blonde hair tied back severely. A pair of gold, wire-framed glasses balanced midway down her nose gave her an air of superiority. She looked vaguely familiar in the way that anonymous officials sometimes do, like someone I'd seen in a television courtroom drama. As she took her seat, a sense of trepidation crept over me. My stomach churned as it dawned on me that the situation was now reaching its climax.

There were five of us at the front of the room, the judge, me the defendant, the plaintiff Lord Hemmingwell, seated to my right, and our respective representatives, Diana Twist and Charles Bradleigh-Smythe. Diana knew Bradleigh-Smythe having crossed swords with him in the past. He had his own legal firm, Bradleigh-Smythe and Partners and his services did not come cheap. Tall and thin with a dark hair swept severely back, his most striking feature was a prominent Roman nose which, when he looked down it, something he did a lot, made him appear far more haughty than perhaps he intended to be. Further back in the main body of the court sat Sally 'Sexyblueeyes.' She had stared at me intently as I walked in and I realised that it was actually the first time she had seen me in the flesh.

Court proceedings began with an introduction from both representatives. Charles Bradleigh-Smythe opened with an elaborate presentation of his client's case, emphasising the actions that had caused Lord Hemmingwell inconvenience and financial loss. An opening speech that presented the facts was interspersed with stark reminders of my misdemeanours. In my mind I had not done anything deliberate and was determined to refute that I had '*damaged property belonging to another without lawful excuse*' or that I had '*intended to destroy such property*' or to '*being reckless as to whether any such property would be destroyed or damaged.*' None of that had ever been my intention and I refused to accept it. Diana was prepared to back my stance.

Lord Hemmingwell was called to the witness box. Charles Bradleigh-Smythe eased him through a serious of questions, clearly designed to support the facts of his claim. He had seen nothing of the incident having been away from home on the day. After ten or so minutes, Hemmingwell was handed over to Diana.

'Lord Hemmingwell. How long have you had your armouries collection?'

'It has been in the family for generations, passed down through the ages,' he replied.

'And would you say the collection is of any value,' Diana asked.

'Of course it is of value,' Hemmingwell snorted, 'it's priceless.'

'Priceless?' Diana paused and looked directly at Hemmingwell. 'By that you mean you would be unable to place a value on the collection?'

'With respect Madam you are being facetious. You have already seen the valuations in the court papers,' he replied.

'Indeed I have, and I have also seen the report that shows that the physical damage consists of nothing more than indentation, impact impression and surface scratching. Very resilient items.' She turned towards the courtroom. 'To be expected, I suppose. After all they are suits of armour.'

Hemmingwell looked towards Bradleigh-Smythe as if expecting an objection. None came.

Diana continued. 'Tell me Lord Hemmingwell what kind of security measures do you have in place to protect your valuable collection?' Diana asked.

'The usual stuff. There are security cameras, an alarm system and a rope barrier,' he replied.

'Security cameras? Or is that one security camera that failed to provide any meaningful information. And an alarm system that activates after an incident takes place.'

Hemmingwell looked flustered and made no reply.

Diana continued. 'The security cameras Lord Hemmingwell. How many do you have?'

'One at present. However, we have plans to install others,' he answered.

'Yes, one camera which points towards an emergency exit and gives no meaningful view of your priceless collection at all. Is there a reason for this?' Diana asked.

'It is covering the emergency exit in case intruders enter through that way, but as I say we have plans to upgrade.'

'How many staff were on duty within the exhibition area on the day of the incident, Lord Hemmingwell?' Diana asked.

'One. We usually just have the one staff member on duty within the immediate area of the exhibition.'

'And isn't it correct that this member of staff was at the entrance area checking admission tickets on that day?'

Hemmingwell looked at his lawyer. Charles Bradleigh-Smythe raised his eyebrows and nodded his head indicating that an answer was required.

Hemmingwell cleared his throat and answered, 'Yes.'

'So, in this instance your solitary staff member was not supervising the area and could not have provided guidance, instruction or reprimand had he seen a member of the public interfering with the exhibits.'

Hemmingwell did not respond. His cheeks showed a hint of scarlet rising from behind his ears. Anger or embarrassment, it was not clear.

Diana continued. 'Let us turn to signage, Lord Hemmingwell. Could you explain what signage you have in place at your exhibition?'

'Well, let's see, there are signs directing the public to the exhibition and to the cafeteria and to the souvenir shop. Oh and to the lavatories,' Hemmingwell replied.

'I see,' Diana said, 'signs directing the public to areas in which they can spend their money...or a penny in one case.'

I detected a fleeting smile on the face of the judge at Diana's levity. There was no such reaction from Lord Hemmingwell.

'Are there any signs that indicate how your visitors should behave? For example, signs that might tell them not to touch the exhibits or not to cross the rope barriers?' Diana asked.

Hemmingwell's cheeks flushed some more. 'It is blindingly obvious, young lady, that the public should not touch such priceless exhibits.'

'Thank you for the compliment Lord Hemmingwell but I am afraid you have not answered my question. Are there any signs that–'

'No, there are not. But the type of people who visit my exhibition know that you should not touch such priceless artefacts. They know how to behave. We do not usually get loutish types who have no appreciation of art or history.'

Hemmingwell's dig at me was obvious enough but he felt the need to emphasis it further with a contemptuous look.

Diana ignored the remark and phrased another question. 'Were any of the exhibits secured to the floor in order to stabilise them, Lord Hemmingwell?'

'No, they were not. They were on a raised platform away from the public walkway.'

'So they were freestanding. Freestanding on a plinth approximately four inches higher than the public area, is that correct?'

Hemmingwell nodded, 'Yes, it is but as I say it was not a public area.'

'Your claim for damages, as we have seen in the court papers, includes what amounts to a worthless exhibit Lord Hemmingwell, namely the replica armour. What was the purpose of having–'

Charles Bradleigh-Smythe's clipped tone cut across Diana's sentence.

'Your Honour, I object to my learned friend's dismissal of my client's property as worthless. Whatever the worth of the replica item, a valuation for the full extent of the damaged property has been submitted and clearly it is not worthless as she implies.'

Judge Manningford asked Diana to withdraw her remark.

'Lord Hemmingwell, the imitation suit of armour that was amongst your exhibits, what was its purpose,' Diana asked.

Hemmingwell smiled, clearly feeling a surge of confidence at a question to which he had a response.

'It was a full scale copy of medieval knight's suit of armour in which we intended to install a CCTV camera. Although from an external viewpoint it essentially looked like one of the exhibits it was a modern replica in which electronic surveillance equipment was to be installed. It had only just been delivered four days earlier. The aim was to have supervision of the display at ground level to augment our existing system.'

'Your existing system of one camera?' Diana said.

'We intended to install several replica suits over the coming year,' Hemmingwell replied, 'each equipped with the latest in camera technology.'

'You say it was a copy of a medieval knight's suit of armour, but there was one fundamental difference in that the replica had a door opening that ran from shoulder to waist level. What was the purpose of this opening?'

'It was designed specifically so that engineers could install the camera system and for easy access for maintenance work once the equipment had been installed and concealed?' Hemmingwell replied.

'Easy access, you say.'

'Yes, of course, it had to be.'

'Was it locked or protected in any way?' Diana asked.

'No, not at that stage. There was nothing to protect. No equipment had been installed.'

Hemmingwell looked sure of himself.

'Nothing to protect you say? And as you have already said, there was no signage to tell visitors not to touch the exhibits. Was there anything on the replica exhibit...a label or markings that might indicate that visitors should not touch it?' Diana asked.

Hemmingwell's brow furrowed as he focussed on Diana's repetition of his statement. Again he looked towards Charles Bradleigh-Smythe before answering.

'No. But as I have already said, it was obvious that these were valuable items in a display protected by a rope barrier.'

Diana turned briefly to the open court as if looking for an audience and then turned back to face Judge Lucinda Manningford.

'Except that the replica item had no significant value at all, had a hinged back that was not locked or protected and had no signage telling the public that it should not be tampered with. In fact given its accessibility and its unusual design it could well have been construed as an interactive item, one that would encourage the public's curiosity. In addition, the rope, with its blue design, could well have been considered a decorative addition rather than a barrier. As you say, Lord Hemmingwell, given your lack of security and supervision, it is evident that indeed you thought there was nothing to protect.'

38

Charles Bradleigh-Smythe called his next witness. Sally Cook, better known to me as 'Sexyblueeyes.'

Apprehension took its grip on me as she walked to the witness box. A flurry of questions raced through my mind as I tried to anticipate what it was she had to say. What was she here for? What was her motive? It cannot have been a simple willingness to assist Lord Hemmingwell. It must be a desire for revenge. Revenge for being stood up on a date. She was hardly the woman scorned. It was just a dating site after all. Being stood up and let down must happen a lot. It was the chance you took. Random strangers coming together in high expectation surely meant a high risk of disappointment. Some you win, some you lose, Sally. Get over it.

'Miss Cook can you tell me the circumstances which brought about your visit to Hemmingwell Halls on 18th November last year.' Charles Bradleigh-Smythe was setting the scene for my undoing.

'I had arranged to meet a date at the armour exhibition,' Sally replied

'A date, you say. Who was this date with?'

'Yes a date, with Matthew.'

'Matthew Malarkey?'

'Yes. I didn't know his surname until I was told about the court case.'

'And was Mr Malarkey known to you before this meeting?'

'No, I met him through a dating site, Cupid's Pursuit, and this was to be our first date.'

I shuddered at the expression 'first date' mentally recognising that a second date would never have happened even if the first had not ended in such disaster. Bradleigh-Smythe continued his cross-examination of Sally leading her gently through a serious of questions about the dating site and her visit to Hemmingwell Halls. He then focussed on the incident.

'Could you tell the court, Ms Cook, how your date with Mr Malarkey went on that day.'

'He didn't show up.' She shot an accusing glance at me as she spoke.

'He didn't show up? You mean he stood you up. I believe that is the parlance used when one party to a proposed romantic encounter fails to materialise,' he said, turning his conspicuous nose accusingly in my direction.

'Yes, he did. He stood me up. I had dressed up nicely too and was looking forward to the date. I was very excited about it as he seemed such a nice man and – '

Lucinda Manningford interrupted, 'Can we stick to the facts Ms Cook and dispense with opinion for the sake of a speedy resolution to this matter.'

I had no idea whether Bradleigh-Smythe had prompted Sally in their Consulting Room meeting to elaborate on her view of me but it seemed to be a set up to make me appear like a cad. I also wondered how Sally could conclude that the yellow jacket she'd had for decades would constitute dressed up *nicely*.

With Sexyblueeyes Sally looking suitably admonished, Charles Bradleigh-Smythe led her on to the key issues.

'Ms Cook, can you tell the court what happened next. What did you do when you realised Mr Malarkey was not coming to meet you as arranged?'

'At first I just thought he was late so I decided to telephone him. I called his number and heard it ringing but then it seemed to me that the ringing was coming from inside one of the exhibits. I then realised that he...Mr Malarkey, must be inside one of the suits of armour,' she replied.

'Inside the armour you say. How did you know that?' Bradleigh-Smythe asked.

'I didn't have time to check or think about it too much but as I say, it seemed the ringing was coming from inside one of the exhibits that was right in front of me. I started to leave a message and my voice seemed to echo from the direction of the display. And then the suit of armour moved. The right arm moved first, it swayed to one side and then it completely toppled over. It looked like Mr Malarkey had tried to answer his telephone.'

'And as a result of the exhibit toppling over what happened next?' Bradleigh-Smythe asked.

'It hit the other exhibits alongside it and they all fell over too. I didn't see any more than that as the alarm went off and everybody started rushing to get out. I ran too as I thought that it must have been caused by some sort of explosion, you know, a terrorist incident. But I realise now that Mr Malarkey was trying to get out of the date and deliberately caused the incident as a diversion.'

Sally's last statement was provocative to say the least. I glanced at Diana for reaction but she simply winked back at me and let it go. Charles Bradleigh-Smythe ignored it too, thanked Sally and concluded her evidence.

It was then Diana's turn to question Sexyblueeyes.

'Ms Cook, have you ever seen my client, Matthew Malarkey, in the flesh before today?'

'No, but I had seen his photograph on the website,' Sally replied.

'And do you recognise him from that photograph?'

'Yes, I do.'

'But you say you have never seen him before physically, so I am right to assume that you did not see him at all at Hemmingwell Halls?'

'He didn't turn up,' Sally replied.

'A simple yes or no will do Ms Cook. So you didn't see him at Hemmingwell Halls?'

'No I didn't.'

'So you did not see him getting inside the suit of armour?'

'No I didn't.'

'Tell me about your telephone call to my client.'

'As I said, I called him and tried to leave a message.'

'How did you make that call?'

'On my mobile.'

'I mean, Ms Cook, tell me how you physically made that call. What did you do?'

Sally looked uncertain, and cast a fleeting look in the direction of Charles Bradleigh-Smythe.

'I took the mobile from my bag, and selected Matthew's number...I had him in my contacts as Matthew CP – '

'CP?' Diana queried.

'Cupid's Pursuit. The dating site. I use those initials for all the dating site contacts I keep in my phone.' Sally continued. 'I held the phone to my ear and listened to it ring until it went to voicemail. I then started to leave a message but I was interrupted when the exhibits started to collapse.'

'I see,' Diana said, looking up from her notes, 'so you had your mobile to your ear listening to it ringing yet you claim to have heard ringing inside the armour. Is it not possible that you could have confused where the ringing was coming from?'

'I don't think so. It sounded like I was ringing the armour. I mean –'

'That would have been an unexpected turn of events, would it not, unless you have Sir Lancelot amongst your contacts?' interrupted Diana, her eyes wide in mock astonishment.

A snigger emerged from the back of the court. I turned and glanced over my shoulder catching sight of Cecil, Louise and Carlos sitting at the back of the room. I hadn't seen them come in. My heart jolted in my chest, a mixture of anxiety at my misdemeanours being revealed in court and surprise at seeing Louise. I was glad she had turned up but I suddenly felt very exposed and vulnerable.

'Ms Twist I think you can dispense with the levity and get to your point.

And perhaps you would be good enough to enlighten me as to what that point may be since your client has already stated in the court papers that he was inside the exhibit.' Judge Manningford's frown showed her disapproval.

'Your Honour, I agree that is the case but I am simply trying to show that the witness's perception of what occurred is not reliable and the view, which she expressed earlier, that my client's actions were deliberate, based on that perception, is simply speculation.'

The judge nodded and Diana continued.

'You say that you heard your voice echo from the direction of the display. You were in a cavernous exhibition room and it is highly likely that the echo you experienced was as a result of your location. Indeed, in giving your account of what you heard, you said that your voice *seemed* to echo from the direction of the display, which implies some uncertainty. It is my view that having not seen my client at all during that afternoon you personally cannot be sure that it was him inside the exhibit?'

'But he said he was inside,' Sally responded, confusion spreading across her features.

'Yes, my client has said that that is the case but that was not revealed to you until Lord Hemmingwell decided to pursue this action. You are suggesting in your evidence that you knew he was inside at the time and that his intent at that time was to avoid you by creating a diversion, which resulted in the alleged damage.'

At that point Diana finished her cross-examination.

Charles Bradleigh-Smythe returned to ask Sally a few more questions that appeared to be designed simply to restore Sally's credibility as a witness. He closed his case shortly after reiterating the circumstances and the loss to his client by my actions.

And then it was my turn.

39

I was called to the witness box, asked to take the oath or affirmation and told to give my name and occupation to the court. Judge Manningford seemed to stare intently at me as I spoke which made me ever more nervous. Her gaze was fixed directly on me. Removing her glasses, she asked me a question.

'Have you appeared before me in the past Mr Malarkey?'

'No, Your Honour, I have never been in court before,' I answered.

My whole body was tense, my stomach in turmoil, my fists clenched tightly as I waited for my ordeal.

The judge replaced her glasses shuffled her papers and nodded towards Diana.

'Never mind. Let's proceed?'

Diana began her questions, a gentle serious of enquiries designed to take me through the facts of the incident in much the same way as Lord Hemmingwell's solicitor had done with him. Diana's focus was on what had happened and the outcome rather than why it had occurred. She skirted over the dating scenario and concentrated on my awareness of the layout of the display. She asked about signage and information given to visitors and my perception of whether the display was out of bounds or accessible. It was over in fifteen minutes.

Charles Bradleigh-Smythe began his questions.

'Mr Malarkey, could you tell us in your own words the reason that you were attending Hemmingwell Halls on 18th November last year,' he said

I began my account. There was no easy way to explain it.

'I was on a date. I had arranged to meet a lady and the location was her choice of venue.'

'A date. I see. And what was the name of the lady with whom you had arranged this date, Mr Malarkey?'

'Her name was Sally,' I answered,

'Sally. Sally what?'

'I understand it is Cook, Sally Cook but at that time I didn't know, Sir,' I said, 'I didn't have her surname.'

'You didn't have her surname. Did you, perhaps know her by any other name, Mr Malarkey?'

I felt my cheeks, flush. I looked down the courtroom and fleetingly caught Louise's gaze.

'Yes, I did,' I replied.

'And what might that name have been?' he continued.

'Sexyblueeyes,' I mumbled.

'I'm sorry Mr Malarkey, could you speak up.' He had noticed my discomfort and was taking advantage of having me on the spot.

'Sexyblueeyes,' I repeated much more loudly. I could hear a stifled snigger in the room. I was convinced it had come from Cecil.

'Sexy...blue...eyes.' He said it slowly and deliberately, emphasising each word for maximum impact. 'Was that a pet name you had for Ms Cook, Mr Malarkey?'

'No, it wasn't Sir. We have never actually met. It was a username she had on a dating site.'

'Ah, yes. The dating site. Cupid's Pursuit I believe it was called. How long were you a member of the site Mr Malarkey?'

'About two months, I think in total, Sir,' I replied.

'It was seven weeks precisely according to the record. And why did you join a dating site?'

My embarrassment at my personal life under such scrutiny was growing. I glanced at Diana but she was busy writing notes.

'Well, I joined because...because...I was...was looking for love.'

'Looking for love, you say. And have you been successful in your quest?'

'No Sir, I have not,' I replied

'Did you have many dates in that time, Mr Malarkey?'

'A few, yes Sir,' I said, not sure where his questions were leading.

'A few? In fact it was nine dates for the record. None of which appears to have been successful let alone enabled you to find the elusive love you say you have been looking for. Would it not be right to say that you used the site in a somewhat frivolous manner?'

The next voice I heard was Diana's.

'Your Honour, I wish to object to my learned friend's line of questioning. I fail to see the relevance of my client's dating habits in respect of the case he is here to answer.'

Judge Manningford looked at the solicitor and asked for an explanation.

'Your Honour, with respect, the defendant's dating habits will show that far from looking for love as he claims, he has in fact used the dating site to prey on innocent women and behave in an irresponsible manner which has resulted him being present in this court room today. I am merely trying to establish a pattern of behaviour.'

I couldn't believe it. Somehow he had made me sound like Jack the Ripper. The judge allowed him to continue.

'Let me put it another way, Mr Malarkey. You were not serious about dating at all but used the site on a whim, dating innocent women without regard to their feelings or the fact that they were genuinely looking for a serious relationships. How else would you explain the catalogue of disasters that appears to be part of your dating history, the most recent of which resulted in you burning down the home of one of your dates?'

'Objection,' Diana's voice cut through the courtroom, loud and insistent. 'That question presupposes that my client deliberately carried out the action referred to. In fact, that incident, which is classed as accidental damage, is the subject of an insurance claim and will be dealt with accordingly. With respect Your Honour, I would ask that you ensure my learned friend ceases asking questions of that nature.'

Judge Manningford peered over the top of her wire-framed spectacles. She seemed irritated at Diana's direct request. Choosing her words carefully she responded so that there was no doubt as to who was in charge.

'Rest assured I will be very vigilant about anyone asking improper questions, Ms Twist.'

Charles Bradleigh-Smythe continued.

'My point is that your track record clearly shows you were not serious about dating at all. It is on police record that you turned up at a cocktail party arranged by one of your dates dressed as a gorilla. You would appear to have a penchant for dressing up perhaps to intimidate, shock or alarm your dates. I suggest to you that in fact you sought to utilise the armour display to do exactly that to Ms Cook, in some misguided need to instil concern in her and enhance your masculinity, to overcome some deep rooted anxiety you have with regard to your relationships with women.'

I couldn't believe what I was hearing. He had made me sound like a psycho in addition to Jack the Ripper. It momentarily crossed my mind that the two were synonymous. I made no response.

'Let us turn to the day in question in which you had arranged to meet your date at Hemmingwell Halls. According to Ms Cook, you did not meet with her as you'd arranged. Why was that Mr Malarkey?'

'I...I changed my mind,' I replied, my equilibrium completely thrown.

'You changed your mind? You took the trouble to travel to Hemmingwell Halls, which indicates an intention to meet your date, but then failed to keep the appointment. Your date had also gone to the trouble of turning up for your meeting and was in the building at the appointed time. Could you explain why you did not keep to the arrangement?'

Once again I felt my face flush. 'I...I got cold feet. I couldn't go through with it,' I replied.

'And why was that, Mr Malarkey?'

I hesitated. I was aware of Sally's presence in the courtroom. Before I answered I was inexplicably drawn to glancing across at her. She held my gaze as if awaiting the answer to a long standing mystery.

'I didn't recognise her,' I said unconvincingly.

'Didn't recognise her? Can you explain that, Mr Malarkey so that we are clear as to what you may mean?'

'I mean that she didn't look like the photograph she had used to portray herself on the dating site,' I said.

'She didn't look like her photograph? So in fact you did recognise her then since you were able to make the distinction between the image you had seen on the site and the person you saw in reality.'

'Well, yes, but she...she looked much older.'

'Older. I see. So for that reason you decided to terminate the date. Because she was older than you had expected. Is that right?'

'Yes,' I answered looking down at my hands.

'Bastard.'

I caught a glimpse of Sexyblueeyes on her feet pointing at me as she let go of the expletive, her face contorted in rage. It took me aback. I looked away. Judge Manningford admonished her for her outburst but I detected a sympathetic tone in her voice which was confirmed when she looked disapprovingly at me.

Charles Bradleigh-Smythe paused for a moment, his left arm placed horizontally across his body so that his hand cupped the elbow of his right arm, which in turn pointed up towards his face. The forefinger and thumb of his right hand gripped his chin tilting his head up so that his gaze followed the line of his nose. He stared at me for a moment as if deep in thought. Then he continued.

'So, would you mind telling the court, Mr Malarkey, how, once you had taken the decision not to proceed with the date, you avoided Ms Cook.'

He knew precisely what I had done since it had been necessary to relate the incident in my earlier evidence to Diana but I suspected he was trying to make me look both foolish and irresponsible. I had to answer.

'I hid, Sir. Inside one of the exhibits.'

I heard a titter at the back.

'And how exactly did you hide, Mr Malarkey?'

'I climbed inside the armour,' I answered.

'A bit of an extreme measure to take, don't you think, just to avoid a date with this lady?' He pointed at Sally for the first time.

As if on cue she cast her eyes downward, a pained expression crossing her face. I hoped that her earlier reference to me as a 'bastard' might have negated Charles Bradleigh-Smythe's emphasis on the word 'lady' in the judge's opinion.

'I panicked. I wasn't thinking. I regret my action now, Sir but it was impulsive,' I replied, hoping that in recognising my error I would gain some sympathy.

He ignored it and focussed on the negative.

'Lack of thought. Not thinking about your actions and what impact they may have. In other words irresponsible and reckless behaviour. You say it was impulsive. If I am correct, from the photographs of the display, it would appear that each section was roped off from the public on a raised wood platform. That means that you had to cross over the rope barrier onto the platform. Is that correct Mr Malarkey?'

'Yes it is, Sir,' I replied.

'So in fact your action was not impulsive but somewhat deliberate. It was not an immediate reflex reaction. You had to make the effort to cross the rope barrier and an even greater effort to get inside the exhibit. All of which takes time. I suggest to you, therefore, that there was a degree of forethought in your action. You have admitted to deliberately hiding to avoid your pre-arranged rendezvous with Ms Cook. It was foreseeable that in crossing over onto the display area, you presented a risk to the exhibits and most certainly could have anticipated the consequences of actually getting into one of the display pieces. In your attempt to conceal yourself from Ms Cook, you deliberately interfered with property belonging to Lord Hemmingwell, in a reckless manner, knowing that there was a possibility that the property could be destroyed or damaged.'

'That is not correct Sir,' I replied, 'I have admitted my actions but it was not my intention to cause any damage whatsoever.'

Charles Bradleigh-Smythe closed his notes and asked nothing more.

I walked back to my seat. I felt nothing but doom and gloom. A smile from Louise and a thumbs up from Cecil did nothing to lift my mood. In my mind I had been portrayed as a psycho rapist. My character destroyed. Something I would not live down. What if Louise had been swayed by Charles Bradleigh-Smythe's portrayal of me? A man who preys on unsuspecting women. A man who is so inadequate that he needs to dress up in order to disguise his shortcomings. I was just relieved he hadn't mentioned the nappy incident. I could never have lived it down if it had been revealed to the court that I had dressed as a baby in an overgrown nappy in a dodgy club on one of my dates. Who could cope with that?

And then it dawned on me.

40

The closing speeches from both Diana and Charles Bradleigh-Smythe all but passed me by. My mind was in turmoil. Diana countered all that had been said throughout the hearing with a spirited and well-argued case on my behalf. Bradleigh-Smythe reiterated Hemmingwell's loss and inconvenience and at the same time made sure he emphasised my reckless behaviour both towards Lord Hemmingwell's property and to my dates in general. And then it was time for the delivery of judgement.

Lucinda Manningford took a sip from the glass of water on her desk, shuffled her papers and adjusted her wire-framed glasses. Her verdict was about to be delivered. I felt Diana's hand briefly alight on mine giving me a reassuring pat.

The judge removed her glasses and looked directly at me.

'Matthew Malarkey, you have been brought before the court to answer a claim for damages through the wilful and malicious destruction of private property belonging to the estate of Lord Rufus Hemmingwell. Before I give my judgement have you anything further to say?'

I hesitated, a lump in my throat, nerves gripping me so that my oesophagus contracted and I felt an acute need to cough. I took a deep breath and resisted the urge.

'I intended no harm Your Honour, I did not realise I was doing anything wrong,' I said.

Judge Manningford paused. She sat back in her seat and scanned the courtroom as if making sure that she had an audience before she uttered her next words of wisdom. When she was satisfied she had everyone's attention she leant forward and fixed her gaze directly on me.

'Mr Malarkey, it is my firm belief that a mature man should have more perception of the likely outcome of his actions and therefore should know the difference between what is right and what is wrong.'

My mind buzzed. My mouth dry as I fought to resist the cough urge. It was now or never. A weight lifted from my shoulders. I cleared my throat.

'There is no right or wrong, Your Honour, just impulse. That's my motto,' I said as clearly as I could manage in the circumstances.

I heard the gasp from behind me first. I don't know where it originated from but I knew it was disbelief that I had the audacity to make such a facetious remark to the judge at this critical time.

I kept my gaze fixed on Judge Manningford. Her face had turned redder than the crimson rubber cat suit she had been wearing the night I had met her at the fetish club. Her mouth dropped open, eyes wide in a sudden display of recognition. It had abruptly dawned on 'Loose Lucy' exactly how she knew my face. Her own words, the very words she had spoken with such certainty and playfulness to me that night, had caused her to experience a temporary seizure. Our eyes were locked. I held her gaze. I watched as her face shifted from bright red to ashen grey as the words came back to haunt her. It was a long moment before she recovered from her gaping, open-mouthed astonishment. Her right hand reached forward for a nearby glass of water. Unwittingly she swallowed more than she had intended and began to cough and choke. I watched as the clear liquid began to dribble from her nose. It was her excuse to call for a brief adjournment. I admired the way she did it.

'I need to take some counsel. We will reconvene in an hour.'

The courtroom was suddenly alive with activity. The reverent silence gave way to a general low murmuring. Diana looked surprised. Charles Bradleigh-Smythe looked baffled. I said nothing. I stood up and looked around to see if I could see Louise. The seat she had taken was now empty. We filed out of court for the break.

Cecil was walking towards me.

'How's it going geezer?' he asked.

'No idea Ces. I am just hoping the judge goes easy. Where has Louise gone?' I said

'She's in the ladies, mate. She reckons she can't speak to you until the case is done.'

'Well, I reckon that won't be long. Anyway, thanks for coming. How come you missed the start though?'

'Don't ask geezer. Fucking cab driver. Carlos's bird, that Amanda, gave me a number for a mini cab firm a few weeks ago. Some cowboy outfit called... wait for this. Real Libel Cabs. Reckons he's called Reliable. Reliable my arse. The geezer turns up half an hour late. Says his satnav got him lost. What's that about? A satnav is sposed to get you to where you want to go. Not get you lost. Fucking mug. Give him a right bollocking.'

'Hey, chill Ces. Keep your voice down. At least you made it. I appreciate it. And thanks for bringing Louise too,' I said trying to stop Cecil getting into a rant.

'Well, she rang Sheryl and asked her to ask me if I'd take her. You're in there geezer.'

I felt a wave of excitement about the prospect of seeing Louise. But there was unfinished business first.

Judge Lucinda 'Loose Lucy' Manningford returned to the court precisely one hour later. She looked composed and business like, a complete contrast to her earlier demeanour. I began to worry and wondered if she had taken the opportunity in the break to indulge in one of the poppers she had so readily dispensed at our last encounter. A hush fell over the room and she started to speak. Her conclusion was brief and succinct.

'Mister Matthew Malarkey has appeared before the court today to respond to a claim for damages to property belonging to Lord Rufus Hemmingwell. Whilst admitting to his involvement in the incident that resulted in this civil action, he has asserted that he is not culpable for the extensive damage that occurred as a result of his actions. In determining liability, I have heard submissions from both sides and must evaluate the arguments presented by both. Ms Twist has argued very eloquently on behalf of her client that he could not have foreseen the outcome of the decision he took in entering the replica exhibit that stood amongst the exhibits that day and that the resulting damage was accidental with no intent on the defendant's part. This is supported by the fact that there was no guidance, in the form of signage or direction, given to visitors that would set out clearly the boundaries which the public should not cross. Nor was there any proper supervision that could have prevented an incident of this nature taking place and indeed, if the exhibition had been properly supervised it is probable that this incident would have been prevented. On the other hand it is clear that damage has occurred which resulted in loss to the plaintiff and this has to be redressed. In this respect there is a burden of liability upon the defendant.'

My heart sank as the words echoed through the courtroom. I was about to be landed with £35,000 worth of damages and had no doubt that Lord Hemmingwell's costs would be dumped on me too. I rubbed the palms of my hands across my trousers to dry them and awaited my fate from 'Loose Lucy.'

'In determining the extent of the damages that should be awarded to the plaintiff I take into consideration that there has been a failure on the part of Hemmingwell Halls to take suitable precautions to protect its own property from the prospect of meddling, intrusion or interference which may have put that property at risk. Failure to provide guidance to the public, clear signage, adequate barriers, protection and the securing of the exhibits in a stable manner has been a significant contributing factor to the outcome of the incident that occurred on 18th November last year. It is my understanding from examination of relevant papers that Hemmingwell Halls is adequately insured for this type of accidental damage. Whilst Mr Malarkey, according to his final declaration, suggested he has an impulsive nature, that in itself is not a transgression. It may well have been the cause of his action but it is clear to me that there was no wilful intent on his part to cause damage to the property contained in the exhibition. However, the significant action that the defendant took in entering the replica exhibit can be seen to be the cause of the damage to that item alone. I therefore award damages of £350 to Lord Hemmingwell with £50 additional costs.'

Diana turned suddenly towards me. From her wide-eyed look of surprise, the judgement was better than she had hoped for. Judge Manningford was now gathering her papers. Diana, had her arms outstretched inviting me for a hug. I accepted gratefully. As I breathed in her closeness, I couldn't help but smile. This was the most intimate contact we had managed in all our meetings and now it didn't matter.

'That was better than expected, Matthew. I am so pleased for you,' Diana said, her smile radiant, her eyes showing genuine pleasure.

'It's all down to you, Diana, I am so grateful. Thank you,' I said.

'It's an absolute pleasure to help Matthew. I have no idea what was going on with the judge but three hundred and fifty pounds and just fifty pounds costs is a snip. Most unusual I have to say.'

A wave of concern came over me. 'Is it? Do you think Lord Hemmingwell will appeal then or whatever they do?'

'He could do but if I know Charles Bradleigh-Smythe he will advise him against it, not least of all to protect his image. They are of the same ilk. It won't be seen as tasteful for a peer of the realm to be arguing over money once the judgement has been made.'

'That is reassuring. Well one down, one to go,' I said. Seeing Diana's brief look of puzzlement I added, 'The criminal case. You know...the police thing.'

'Oh that. I wouldn't worry about that. When the police hear the outcome of this case, rest assured they will not pursue it. They will realise there is not a lot to go on and the CPS would be unlikely to feel it's in the public interest anyway.'

I was pleased to hear it and thought back to Carlos's encounter with DC Maloney, additional insurance that it was unlikely to be pursued.

'Right Matthew. I have to go. Keep in touch and congratulations again.' Diana kissed me on both cheeks and was gone.

I looked around to see if I could see Louise. I managed to catch sight of Lord Hemmingwell. He looked apoplectic. A face like thunder, glaring at me as if the outcome was my doing. Maybe it was my doing I thought. Sometimes fate deals you a hand and just sometimes it turns out to be a playable one. Loose Lucy's secret was safe with me. I didn't care what she did in her spare time. She obviously did.

I walked out of the courtroom into the waiting area. Visions of the past few months running through my head. I didn't notice Louise standing by the exit until she spoke.

'Congratulations Matthew.'

She had a broad grin on her face. I had not seen her look so light hearted in a while. There was nothing to say. I walked towards her arms outstretched. She slipped into my embrace easily. I pulled her tightly to me, revelling in the relief of the barrier between us disintegrating as we held one another.

'Thank you Louise. I am so glad it's over,' I whispered.

She pulled back slightly to look at me, her arms still clasping my waist.

'Was it worth it Matthew? Was it worth you going through...or should I say, 'Michael', going through all that hardship looking for love?'

'Of course it was Louise. If you find it then it is worth whatever it takes,' I said.

'Well you know, sometimes we can look too hard. And because we are looking so hard we are missing what is right in front of us,' she said

Louise saw my frown.

'My mum had a friend once, a little old lady...I can't recall her name now. But she used to come out with all these mystic sayings. I remember once, when I was about eighteen and had a crush on this boy, she said this stuff. I didn't get it at the time but I will always remember it. *Is what you seek there already? Only you will find that out if you give yourself time. Look for a connection, not a desire. Love will find you.* Quite romantic when you think about it and so true, don't you think?'

I didn't know what to say. I thought of Mary in the snow that day. The words were still etched in my mind. I pulled Louise close and kissed her. A tug on my arm interrupted us.

'Geezer put the lady down. We got some celebrating to do.'

Cecil's face was beaming at the prospect of a party. Carlos stood grinning in the background.

'Maybe, later Ces. Me and Louise have a bit of celebrating to do ourselves, if you get my drift,' I said.

'Plenty of time for that mate. Let's go get hammered,' Cecil said, nodding towards the door.

I let go of Louise for a moment and turned to look at my best friend.

'That's not happening Cecil.'

GLOSSARY

Slang Expression	Definition
a 'how are ya'	a tip, an amount of money to influence a situation
bahookie	buttocks (Scottish slang)
blag	con, trick
caned	inebriated, drunk
cucaracha	cockroach (Spanish)
culito	a cute butt/bottom (Spanish)
dinnae ken	don't know, don't understand (Scottish slang)
drum	home, house (drum & bass – place) cockney rhyming slang)
foam bath	a laugh (cockney rhyming slang)
geezer	man, bloke, mate, friend
geezered up	to have a boyfriend (for a female)
go medieval	go back to basics, display barbarian tendencies
hammered	inebriated, drunk
hashmadishmalacka	sexual intercourse
mumble	the word, gossip, what's happening
mumble swerve	pulling a fast one, avoiding the issue, going it alone or a dalliance
Old Bill	the police
polis	the police (Scottish)
roll and butter	nutter, (cockney rhyming slang) mad
skelp	slap, smack (Scottish slang)
the dog	telephone (dog & bone-cockney rhyming slang)
troglodyte	a cavewoman (or cave dweller)
tumble	understand
warrior	party lover, hardcore social animal

CREDITS

1. Cupid's Pursuit Cover design by Richard Taylor, bt Graphics, Sutton Poyntz, Dorset.
2. Quotation Page 156 – Kung Fu, TV series created by Ed Spielman for Warner Brothers.
3. Winter Wonderland Composed by Felix Bernard (1897-1944). Lyrics by Richard B. Smith (1901-1935).
4. Rockin' Around the Christmas Tree composed by Johnny Marks.
5. Merry Christmas Everybody composed by Noddy Holder and Jim Lea.

Lightning Source UK Ltd.
Milton Keynes UK
UKOW031930260112

186116UK00002B/7/P